Jen,

Thank you to you and Evan for your tremendous support and enthusiasm through the writing process. Happy BDay!

TCI: RISE

KRETZGE

BOOK 1 OF 5

This is a work of fiction. Names, characters, places, and incidents either are the product of the author's imagination or are used fictitiously. Any resemblance to actual persons, living or dead, events, or locales is entirely coincidental.

Copyright © by Brandon Charette

All rights reserved. No part of this book may be reproduced or used in any manner without written permission of the copyright owner except for the use of quotations in a book review.

First Paperback Edition August 2019

Cover by AlphaVision Studio

Original cover design and all site character art by Pocchito Art

ISBN: 978-1-0726-9431-1

www.kretzge.com

To Cord-John for developing and exploring this vast universe with me, to Jake for letting me be a part of your game in the first place, and those hot recess breaks on the playground where imagination ran wild and without which this series would never exist.

LETTER FROM THE AUTHOR

The book you now hold in your hands is the result of over ten years of careful plotting, world building, and character development.

The concept for the TCI series stems from a live action role-playing game my friends and I would act out on the playground in elementary school. In the decade-plus that followed, I set out on a mission to capture the intensity and imagination of those sweltering recess periods, while at the same time making a massive amount of much-needed changes and adjustments in order to handcraft a story that was as unique, unpredictable, and engaging as possible. It is my hope that this universe and the charming cast of characters that inhabit it will stick with you long after the final pages have been turned.

Strap in for an intense and cinematic journey through the darker side of the cosmos. Thank you for taking the time to step into a galaxy that has become my second home.

GALACTIC INDEX

Each of the ten races that populate the TCI galaxy has been designed from scratch to have a unique appearance, home planet, and culture. Please feel free to refer to this index when an unfamiliar race or planet is mentioned in the text.

DRAEKON

- **Appearance:** The Draekon people have deathly-pale skin, jet-black hair, and dark blue pupils which rest within light blue scleras.
- **Home Planet:** *Oballe* – a snowy, tundra-covered planet where winters last years and the sun shines for only a third of the day.
- **Extra Information:** The Draekons possess a versatile neon purple energy known locally as 'Shaz' which they can spontaneously produce from their hands in the form of everything from flames to slime. The Draekon people have an intense historical rivalry with the Alavites, who they once shared a planet with.

ALAVITE

- **Appearance:** The Alavites have parchment-colored skin, blonde hair, and golden pupils.
- **Home Planet:** *Alavonia* – a planet whose stretches of flat plains and long, winding rivers serve as natural barriers between its many beautiful, sprawling cities.
- **Extra Information:** The Alavites loudly and enthusiastically worship Alavon Acivorai, an ancient and

beloved king of their people who was tragically killed over two millennia ago. Though historically peaceful outside of the occasional conflict with the Draekons, the theocratic Alavites have grown exponentially more blood thirsty and ambitious under the rule of Olivio X, the latest Hand of Alavon.

UDUL

- **Appearance:** The amphibious Udul people are known for their blue and scaly skin, webbed hands and feet, gills, and the small rhino-like horn in the center of their foreheads. They are also completely hairless, sport black pupils, and are the only race capable of breathing and seeing clearly underwater without external aid.
- **Home Planet:** *Cha-leh* – a landless planet covered entirely in a dark-blue sea where the bright dots of the Uduls' underwater glass dome cities light up the ocean by night.
- **Extra Information:** The Udulic navy is the strongest and most feared in the galaxy. Attempting to fight them on the water is a mistake many only get to make once. A strongly patriotic people, they worship their beloved Salt Maiden from beneath the violent waves. The Uduls share ninety-five percent of their DNA with the Dom'Rai, who they have fought three major wars against.

DOM'RAI

- **Appearance:** The Dom'Rai are nearly impossible to mistake with their ashy, maroon skin, blood-red pupils, and the pair of large ram-like horns in the center of their forehead. They

can withstand significantly hotter temperatures than any other race.
- **Home Planet:** *V'otarr* – a planet whose volcanic activity and frequent earthquakes make it among the most unstable in the galaxy. The heat on the surface is so intense that even the Dom'Rai themselves are forced to live within the planet's many large craters, where the temperature is considerably lower.
- **Extra Information:** A historically warlike and tribal people, Dom'Rai are typically (and inaccurately) stereotyped as being intellectually inferior to most other races. They are also thought to have much shorter tempers and be more easily prone to violence. They are the only known race to still actively enslave its own kind.

JOXUN

- **Appearance:** The Joxun people sport an olive complexion, along with dark brown hair and eyes.
- **Home Planet:** *Pariso* – a forested planet once considered the most beautiful and bountiful in the galaxy which now faces a desperate life-or-death struggle against an ever-encroaching desert, which threatens to choke the very life out of it.
- **Extra Information:** Joxuns believe in the inherent intellectual superiority of the female sex and have structured their society around this concept. Their women occupy every position of significant power and influence on the planet while the men are assigned low-paying manual labor roles following their mandatory years of military service, which they take on happily. Sex plays a major role in Joxun culture. This has led their people to become somewhat infamous for their promiscuity, which has perhaps played a

significant role in placing their population at sixteen billion, by far the largest in the galaxy.

AYR

- **Appearance:** Ayrs have a light complexion, dark blonde hair, and light blue pupils.
- **Home Planet:** *Ayr-Groh* – a planet that began as an uninhabitable gas giant, the Ayr capital now houses hundreds of massive cities on its floating metallic platforms.
- **Extra Information:** The Ayr people are stereotyped as being one of the smartest races in the galaxy. When off their homeworld, they rely on a specialized set of goggles known as a virix to be able to see clearly. Wealth inequality is rampant on Ayr-Groh, leading to large, pristine, and skyscraper-filled metropolises such as Ayr-Groh City sitting directly adjacent to run-down zones such as the blue-collar Steel Grotto and the crime-ridden Trax Town.

ZANTAVI

- **Appearance:** The Zantavi are known for their uniquely dark skin tone, curly ghost-white hair, and light pink pupils.
- **Home Planet:** *Saraii* – a planet coated in a suffocating and endless desert that nearly all races aside from its native population do their best to avoid.
- **Extra Information:** Though relatively calm and quiet by day, Saraii boasts a large and extensive network of black markets by night that are among the most lucrative in the galaxy. The planet's illegal drug and sex trades are second only to the neutral, anarchic world of Norann.

QUEXIAN

- **Appearance:** The reclusive Quexians are known for their gray skin, red hair, and light gray pupils.
- **Home Planet:** *Galaros* – an impossibly frigid and mountainous planet with temperatures that can drop hundreds of degrees below freezing. The wily Quexian people live deep below its surface in a large and intricate network of connected tunnel cities.
- **Extra Information:** Quexians are renowned for their natural stealthiness. Many of the most infamous and sought-after assassins and hitmen in galactic history have come from their ranks. Quexians are also the only race to not utilize surnames, believing them to tie an individual too closely to their parents, therefore stripping away their individuality and agency.

ERUB

- **Appearance:** The Erub people's brilliant green eyes are easily their most distinguishing feature. They normally sport tan skin and dark brown hair.
- **Home Planet:** *Erub* – a tropical planet dotted in islands whose beautiful emerald green waters mask a brutal and bloody history.
- **Extra information:** The Erub people are among the most fiercely nationalistic in the galaxy. They have a proven track record of being difficult for a government to control when an unfavorable law is passed or an unpopular (albeit necessary) decision is made. Unfortunately, this has led to a long history

of violent and chaotic instability that has seen more changes in power than any other developed nation in the galaxy.

CARINE

- **Appearance:** The Carine people are perhaps the most extreme outlier of the galactic races, having a wolf-like appearance, sharp claws and teeth, and coats of fur that range from black to brown to white. They can (and normally do) stand on two legs, but drop on all fours to run, which they do far faster than any other race.
- **Home Planet:** *Feralla* - a forest planet overrun by trees the size of skyscrapers. It is within the very trunks of these behemoths that the Carine make their homes.
- **Extra Information:** A historically oppressed and isolated people, the Carine are misunderstood and feared by many due to their unusual and feral appearance. It is for this same reason that they are frequently underestimated in combat, which has led to the brutal deaths of many would-be invaders. The Carine's fight to be recognized as an intelligent, sentient race has spanned many generations.

*For more information and images, please visit **kretzge.com***

PROLOGUE

KADROK KIV
KING'S WATCH, KARVENKULL
OBALLE

A loud boom echoed through the night sky, as though threatening to split it right down the middle. Kadrok watched his frozen breath dissipate before his eyes as a bright flash of yellow light pierced through the thick clouds. He raised a hand to shield his face from the blinding beam which passed over him quickly. It wouldn't be long now.

They are here.

He nodded to no one as he slowly turned his gaze down from the sky and toward the gray mounds of snow that surrounded the foot of the jet-black Karvenkull castle. He took another deep breath as he tightened his grip on the metallic railing, which was now the only thing standing between him and a fifteen-story fall to his death.

Are you ready?

"Can anyone ever be?" Kadrok muttered in response.

I have my doubts about tonight.

"Would you like to propose a better solution?" Kadrok shot back. He hated getting into arguments with this strange voice in his head. The last thing he needed right now was people questioning his sanity.

It is not the plan itself I take issue with, but rather the one seeing it through.

"What is that supposed to m-"

"So, here we are."

He hadn't heard her come out. Thankfully he had been speaking under his breath, and she didn't appear to have heard him. He turned sheepishly. As usual, the intensity of her gaze was such that it demanded to be met.

We don't have time for this right now, Kadrok.

He ignored the voice.

Marielle looked gorgeous, the embroidered blue details in her long black dress caused her to glow just a little bit brighter.

"You really want to have this conversation now?"

She looked at him as though he had just insulted her entire family tree.

"Well Kad, seeing as how they're literally above our heads, this is as good a time as any."

Another thundering boom reverberated through the atmosphere, pulling his focus back to the clouds.

"Look. At. Me!"

He refocused his gaze to his wife's eyes. From their surrounding sea of light blue, her azure pupils narrowed as though she were a hunter stalking its prey. Many considered the Draekon peoples' eyes to be either the most gorgeous or most hideous in the galaxy; there was rarely any nuance there. He had lost himself in Marielle's pools of liquid sapphire countless times.

How charming. Perhaps you two can share a coffin when this is all over.

Kadrok let out an exasperated breath before responding to his wife. "What do you want me to do? We barely made it by when they were by themselves. But now? If I wanted to knowingly send men to their certain death, I'd rather give them the courtesy of executing them myself."

Marielle balled her hands into pale fists at her sides. "We have to go down fighting. Please, Kad. Don't just let them win. Our people deserve better than that."

How I long for that degree of naivety.

He slowly stepped toward Marielle as yet another boom filled his ears.

"Do you understand the size of their forces?" He asked, gesturing toward the sky. "Can you even comprehend it? Three complete fucking armies. We have a quarter of one!" He hadn't meant to raise his voice, but he had been on edge the entire evening.

Marielle was taken aback, the anger in her flashing eyes quickly changing to fear.

Kadrok sighed. "I care about my people; that's why I refuse to let them die aimlessly. I fear I have very few decisions left to make, but you can be damn sure I'll use each one of them wisely."

Well said. Perhaps there is some hope for us yet.

"Of all the words I'd use to describe you, 'wise' is not one of them."

Kadrok ran a hand over his eyes. "This is really about yesterday, isn't it?"

Obviously.

"Of course it is, you idiot" she snapped.

He took another step toward her. "It was the only way there would even be a bit of hope. You know that."

"You had no right. None."

"He has a chance. That's more than either of us can say. If you really love—"

That was a poor choice of words.

She bridged the remaining gap between them quickly. She put her pale face close to his and said in a low menacing voice. "If you so much as attempt to question my bond with him again, I will have you gutted like a fucking fish. I don't care if your entire guard takes turns tearing me limb from limb for it."

He glanced down at Marielle's left hand as she pulled the dark blue ring off her finger and tossed it off to the side forcefully, sending it sailing into the black abyss.

"We have a meeting soon, don't be late." She turned and made an abrupt exit as the black fabric of her dress trailed behind her.

Instinctively, Kadrok extended his right hand and for a few seconds, it began to glow with a bright purple hue before shooting a beam toward the door. He could feel the stained wood along his fingertips as though he were physically touching it. With a quick flick of his wrist, it slammed shut, and the beam retracted into his hand a second later.

That could have gone better.

"You think?" he retorted.

He turned his head back towards the sky and instantly felt his stomach drop as the elaborately designed white-and-gold vessels finally came into full view. Hundreds of them moved through the air in a perfect formation that resembled a swarm of migrating scuttle bugs. The small, speedy ship at the very front of the pack unfurled its massive flag, and it trailed like a cape.

There was a loud, slow knock at the door. If he had been able to control his heart, he would have stopped it right then, he sighed and turned around.

"It's open, Jaerick."

His Master of the Guard bowed slightly as he pushed the door open and stepped into the coldness of the night. His expression was grim.

"A request, your grace."

"From him?"

Who else?

Jaerick nodded solemnly.

Kadrok ran a hand through his hair. If he managed to survive today, he'd more than likely find that the gray strands had finally overtaken the black.

"It is time, my king."

Indeed. It is.

With a deep breath, Kadrok nodded and followed Jaerick indoors. Upon exiting the balcony, he was flanked in every direction by the royal Draekonic guards, who escorted him down to the open-air courtyard.

He turned at the sound of more footsteps and nodded slightly at Marielle, who ignored him entirely, keeping her gaze fixated on the sky instead. He sighed and followed suit.

The vessels' pristine appearances had always struck him as ironic, given their propensity for bringing death and misery wherever they appeared. He had never seen them this close before, and it only now struck him how truly peculiar their rounded triangular shapes were. Each hull was painted in a collection of elaborate writings whose solid gold color sparkled even in the blackness of the night. The words were written in a language Kadrok did not speak yet knew all too well.

'*The Chosen Army. Blessed be Alavon. To Alavon goes the glory. . .*' *The words are many, but their variety leaves much to be desired.*

A small shuttle emerged from the large flagship vessel. Almost immediately, several of the smaller ships broke off from the swarm and surrounded it before touching down on the powdery snow which had accumulated through the night.

This planet is awful. Your people were never meant to live here; no one should.

Their ships now sat on Oballian soil for the first time in history. The shuttle sat closest to the group while its three larger escorting ships parked in a horizontal line behind it. After a few seconds, the doors on these ships opened almost in unison. Soldiers dressed entirely in gold armor flooded out and lined up in rows quickly and efficiently. The Draekon guards raised their black metallic spears but held still.

The shuttle was the last to open its door and extend its walkway. Down the ramp, which was flanked by soldiers, came a man whose face was known to all but the most isolated and ignorant of people—Olivio X, the Hand of Alavon.

An animal wearing a man's skin.

His slender six-foot-five frame stepped down onto the snow. As with almost all Alavites, he easily dwarfed even the tallest of Draekons. His hair was silver, straight, and fell to about the middle of his shoulders. It was painfully obvious that the top of his head was balding rapidly, and his attempts to disguise this were wholly unconvincing. Snowflakes began to fall lightly on his face and collect on his trimmed silver beard. His yellow parchment-like skin was a stark contrast to the dark grays and whites of the snow accumulating around him.

Despite wearing only what seemed to be light, albeit extravagant, robes, the Hand looked not only unconcerned by the bitter cold but also downright comfortable in it. Following closely behind him was another non-armored Alavite whom Kadrok did not recognize; he was dressed in clerical attire and must have been in his early teens at most. He stood silently behind Olivio and appeared visibly nervous. His cheeks were flushed, and his light-yellow pupils darted around the courtyard as though he were in search of nonexistent danger. Unlike the Hand, he began to shiver almost immediately he exited the ship. The poor, curly-haired boy looked miserable. Every Alavite soldier remained on a knee until the final two members of the party exited the vehicle; the Dom'Rai chieftain T'itus Polo and Agrick, the Quexian high overseer.

Kadrok turned his gaze downward to the iconic golden gauntlet on Olivio's left hand, the symbol of his power and status. Its design was peculiar, given that it left the fingers and thumb exposed. The gauntlet would have looked totally out of place against the rest of his elaborate and expensive outfit, were it not made of pure gold with ornate diamond and emerald pieces studded all over it.

Olivio slowly knelt, placing his jeweled hand flat on the ground as he did so. Nobody spoke or moved, as he rose to his feet, Kadrok noticed that the spot where his hand had been planted a mere second earlier was now entirely devoid of any traces of snow or ice. Tiny patches of brown, dead grass saw the stars again for the first time in months.

Kadrok raised his gaze once more to lock eyes with Olivio, who began to address him in Neatspeak, the common galactic tongue.

"A lovely evening, though a bit brisk to be sure. We thank His light for enveloping us all in its loving warmth."

I am sure they do.

As he glanced over at the shivering child, Kadrok wondered whether the poor boy should have perhaps prayed harder.

"Alavon promised us this triumph back when He still walked among us, and I have delivered in His name. *Alavona elobai.*"

Every Alavite soldier repeated the final two words.

"Are you prepared to offer terms of surrender?" He sounded slightly amused as he asked. Kadrok could feel those smug aureate eyes piercing him. He nodded.

The Draekon guards turned their gaze to him. Marielle shot him a look that was a combination of disbelief and anger.

You should have told her.

Kadrok swallowed hard and took a few steps forward. His guards seemed reluctant to let him move, but ultimately, they stayed put, choosing instead to keep the Draekon queen surrounded.

"If the safety of Oballe and its people can be absolutely assured, then yes." Rage and shame plagued his mind, screaming at him to not allow this happen. He silenced them, though it took significant effort.

"I see, approach." Olivio beckoned him forward with his gloved hand.

Kadrok moved with as much pride and dignity as he could muster, and stopped a few feet in front of the Hand, who crossed his arms. A few seconds of tense silence permeated the courtyard. Many of the ships had moved past them at this point, leaving little else to be heard but the occasional sound of the violent wind.

"We lay down our remaining arms tonight. This conquest is over, Olivio."

The Hand raised an eyebrow and shook his head before glancing back at T'itus and Agrick, who began to chuckle.

"Their kind has always been slow on the uptake, haven't they?" Olivio asked the men behind him.

Maintain your composure. Do not give them the satisfaction. Not now.

"My little pale friend, I'm afraid our Lord's vision is far greater in scope than what your mind is capable of comprehending. The fall of the Draekons, while long overdue, is only a small part of the plan. His great conquest has only just begun."

An odd buzzing sound filled Kadrok's ears. He looked up to notice several white camera drones flying around the courtyard. Olivio was filming this, his heart sank.

Nothing kills a peoples' morale faster than seeing their leader in such a vulnerable and pathetic state. The old man is ruthless.

"The Chosen Army will continue to expand and claim territory for our great Lord. It is His will that every last being in the galaxy not only knows His name but also worships it."

Kadrok swallowed. "I assume that doesn't include us."

Olivio nodded. "You do have critical thinking skills after all. I'm impressed."

A drone flew into Kadrok's peripheral vision, he glanced angrily at it before refocusing on Olivio.

"No. I'm afraid your kind still owes a great debt to our people. I attempted to reason with our Lord, I truly did. Unfortunately, He insists that it must be repaid in the same manner in which it was taken; blood."

Frankly, you are a fool for expecting anything less.

Olivio nodded toward the Draekon group. Confused, Kadrok turned to face them.

Whether it was a result of shock or the lack of light, it took several seconds for him to process what he was seeing. Jaerick was on his knees and wheezing as he grabbed at his neck, which was littered with a series of small, nasty looking burn marks. Within seconds, he fell over onto the ground, limp.

How-?

Kadrok turned to look at Marielle. Each finger of her right hand was individually ignited in bright neon purple. She began to move toward him. The Draekon guards exchanged confused glances before they were met by a flurry of white-tipped power arrows to their chests. Marielle smiled innocently as the bodies fell to the ground behind her. Kadrok locked eyes with his wife; he couldn't bring himself to speak.

"You have been responsible for enabling our people on their journey to dishonor the great Alavon for too long." She answered his unspoken question coldly. "I will be taking charge from here on out. *Alavona elobai.*" She knelt gracefully as she spoke the final words.

It appears she never did forgive you.

"Yes. Your great Queen has accepted Alavon's offer. In exchange for aiding the Chosen Army in their capture of the

Draekon citizens, she and her personal guard will be allowed to live out the rest of their days in the castle, undisturbed. Of course, there is complete understanding that no breeding of any kind will be allowed."

Ah, and there it is. She thinks there is a chance.

Too many things ran through Kadrok's head at once. An overwhelming choking sensation overcame him. No air would enter his lungs, let alone exit them. Suddenly he felt nothing, the anger, pain, and shock were gone. He was numb.

Olivio's voice caused a chill to run down his spine. "With all of that said, it seems I have no use for you anymore. It has been a fun time, Kadrok. I wish you luck in your meeting with Alavon, I assume you and the rest of your people will need it."

Kadrok felt his knees hit the ground before his brain could process the pain of the shining blade that had been thrust through his back.

Hold on. I will do what I can for the pain.

He began to gasp for air as he pressed down on the wound, and within seconds, his hands were soaking wet. He heard footsteps, and painfully lifted his head. Olivio's bearded face now filled his vision, so he could no longer see Marielle.

In one swift motion, the Hand placed his gauntlet on Kadrok's forehead. He felt the freezing cold metal against his skin and instinctively attempted to recoil, but the guards held him firmly in place.

No. No! NO!

Kadrok had never heard the voice sound legitimately terrified before.

There was a moment of confusion that quickly faded as the gauntlet began to heat up at an alarmingly rapid rate. Kadrok tried desperately to pull back once more but to no avail. The glove was now burning his skin and sending the fiery sensation through his entire head. Perhaps it was only his imagination, but he could hear what sounded like a distant, female scream. The pain quickly grew from uncomfortable to extreme and then to unbearable. He began to struggle with every remaining fragment of his strength.

Kadrok?

After another second or two, small dark spots appeared in his eyes and continued to grow until they clouded his entire vision, blinding him. The high-pitched wails continued to reverberate through his head. Everyone in the courtyard remained silent as Kadrok's own blood-curdling screams echoed through the courtyard.

Kadrok!

As time began to slow down, he thought about his life, his accomplishments, and his love for Oballe and its people. Marielle's face filled his mind. He opened his eyes as he suddenly felt the pressure and heat of the glove disappear. All traces of Olivio, his cronies, the Alavites, and his traitorous wife had seemingly been wiped from existence. All that was left in the courtyard was a featureless humanoid figure. It shimmered with an intense reddish-blue light that obscured its outline even as Kadrok held up a hand, peering at it between spread fingers. The man approached him slowly and dropped to one knee. They would have been eye to eye, but the figure had none. It reminded him of the generic models that art students used to practice sketching.

It is over now. All of it. You've done well.

Slowly but surely, features began to appear on the blank canvas of a face until its identity became unmistakable. The voice which had lived only in his head for as long as he could remember now emerged from the lips of the man before him.

"You still have a role to play. I will explain everything in time, I promise."

Kadrok shook his head as he stared at a face he knew all too well. "No. That's not possible. It was. . . you?"

The man knelt and put his arm around Kadrok. A sense of warmth took over and this time, it was pleasurable rather than excruciatingly painful.

"It is time for me to go now."

"Where?" Kadrok croaked.

"To fulfill the promise I made to you. Do you remember it?"

Kadrok's eyes widened. "He's still alive?"

The man nodded.

Kadrok shook his head slowly. "I can only hope he fares better than I did. Just get it over with."

The figure nodded and wrapped its other arm around Kadrok. Suddenly, but peacefully, it was over.

* * *

A loud pop rang through the courtyard, and the screams stopped abruptly. Olivio withdrew his now-bloody gauntlet and let the Draekon king's lifeless body fall to the floor. The contents of what had previously been inside his head were scattered around the corpse. After a few seconds, a glowing purple light began to form within the center of his chest. The group watched as the light grew brighter and brighter before it exploded dramatically into a small beam that flew directly upward into the heavens. It seemed to have no end. After what seemed like an eternity, it eventually sputtered and died out, taking with it the remaining light and leaving the body dark and empty. As though on cue, several more beams emerged from the other Draekon corpses across the courtyard. It would seem the guards had taken their oath to follow their liege to the grave.

Olivio crouched over Kadrok's body before looking at his young attender, Daryn Peric, who had begun to vomit violently onto the snow.

"Draekon death lights," Olivio explained once the boy appeared to have finished. "What we are witnessing is Alavon's reclamation of the Draekon soul for eternal damnation."

T'itus took a step toward the body. "I've heard it is a release of all the anger and hatred accumulated throughout their lives."

"That doesn't make any sense. It's clearly some kind of technology that they imbue into themselves. This isn't natural, it can't be." Agrick replied as he squatted and ran a hand under his gray chin.

"I have just explained the process. If either of you distrust Alavon's own Hand, then we need to have a very serious conversation." Olivio replied sternly as he rose to his feet.

"No. Apologies, my Hand." T'itus placed a large, red hand over his heart and dropped to one knee.

"Yes. We misspoke." Agrick agreed but remained upright.

Daryn began to feel lightheaded and wanted nothing more than to get back into the ship.

Olivio sighed as he walked past the two men and toward his young and anxious attender. "You will need to grow stronger, and quickly."

Daryn nodded. He knew the old man was right.

Olivio walked toward the shuttle and motioned to the rest of the group to follow. As they took off, explosions and screams could be heard both near and far, echoing from every direction and accompanied by the harsh whipping of the frigid Oballian winds.

Once they ascended, Daryn could see dense collections of purple spots begin to appear over the cities as they flew by. He wondered how they were supposed to fill the prisons with so many apparent deaths, but he supposed that problem was far above his pay grade. He twitched slightly in his seat as a jolt of anxiety ran through him. The image of the Draekon king's head exploding kept pushing its way into his mind.

He leaned forward and said a quiet prayer for the many who would lose their lives on this night. It was unfortunate, but if Alavon decreed it, it was Olivio's duty to comply with His orders. He turned back to the window and watched as the night sky grew brighter and brighter, illuminated by the beautifully tragic beams that seemed to go on forever through what he sadly speculated must have been the longest night in this planet's history.

ACT I

I

JAKOB KOSS
BARRACKS 17, CAMP IZROK
OBALLE

"In that moment, I was surrounded. Three Akars approached from my left, four from my right, and two from below in the dark depths! It was an impossible situation, surely! But alas, the great Salt Maiden gave me the strength to face the challenge! My spear began to react as though it had a mind of its own, and one by one, through quick reflexes and deft movements, I indeed managed to bring an end to those enormous, slippery beasts!"

The small crowd around Zhaden Karuk stared, wide-eyed, as the Udul finished his tale. Some exchanged glances. Others whispered to each other. The group of prisoners sat in a circle on the floor of the dark, cold barracks building, which was little more than a glorified shack. The only semblances of furniture in the long, narrow room were rows upon rows of poorly constructed wooden cots, which contained no mattresses nor sheets. Even in the dim light, the breaths of the shivering inmates were plainly visible.

"You seem unamused, Jakob! Not that this should be surprising to me. I am not quite sure your face is capable of smiling."

Zhaden's Udulic accent in Neatspeak was still strong, but it had certainly improved dramatically over the years. His manner of speaking was odd and grammatically awkward at times, but he always managed to get his point across.

Jakob took a deep breath and lifted his gaze from the floor to meet that of the six-foot-nine blue-skinned behemoth that was now his oldest remaining friend.

Though their conversations were fairly simple and stilted at times, given Zhaden's rough grasp of Neatspeak, it quickly became apparent how much the big Udul appreciated being acknowledged and how much he loved to talk.

"Is everything alright, my friend?"

Jakob crossed his arms. "Sorry. It's been a long day. Which one was it this time? Did you somehow escape an active volcano on a planet covered entirely in water? Were you sleeping with the Salt Maiden again?"

"*Raegek*! I would never befoul the fair maiden in such a way! Also, I have already explained this to you, my friend. That was a . . . how do call it? A hot hole?" The Udul chuckled slightly as he replied.

"Thermal vent," interjected Zach Koomer from the right side of the circle. He was just one of the thousands of light-skinned, blue-eyed, and dark-blond Ayr people who had flooded into the camps.

"Right then, you let me know when your collection of stories runs out, and I'll look into which ones I find remotely believable." Jakob started to rise to his feet. At five foot seven, he wasn't particularly tall nor imposing, but he had long since gotten used to being on the shorter end of the spectrum here.

Zhaden chuckled. As he did so, the small horn atop his smooth head bobbed slightly. Jakob shifted his gaze toward the Udul's interlocked webbed hands. For a race so intimately connected to the sea, it couldn't have been easy going a decade without even seeing the water.

The rest of the prisoners in the circle began chatting quietly amongst themselves. To Jakob, black had always been a visually striking choice for prison garments, but the color's total inability to blend in with the snow might have had something to do with it. Poor Zhaden didn't remotely fit into his assigned garments and had to have two standard tops stitched together, minus the sleeves, to enable a proper fit.

"Someday, I shall bring you to Cha-leh, and I will prove all this to you before your own eyes, assuming your skin does not char under an actual sun."

Jakob said nothing, choosing instead to simply narrow his eyes at Zhaden, who was clearly fighting the urge to laugh.

"Zhaden, you're going to give him nightmares. The Draekons moved to a snow planet for a reason."

Jakob turned to look back at Koomer, who pulled out a small makeshift radio from his pocket and began fiddling with the knobs on it. His long blond hair fell below his shoulders, framing his dirty, scarred face. As the camp's de-facto genius, Koomer had developed a reputation for turning scrap and other trash from his assigned post into a variety of inventions, a feat that was made even more impressive by the fact that he was missing one of his eyes entirely.

"I wish that were true, actually." Jakob muttered as he interlocked his hands, "beats being kicked out of your old home under threat of death."

Koomer shrugged. "To be fair, you did kill their king."

"'You' is an interesting word choice."

Koomer sighed. "You know what I mean. Your que-"

He cut himself off as his radio began to cackle.

"Gotta take this. Excuse me, gentlemen." Koomer stood up and stepped away from the group as he began responding to the variety of different voices coming from the device in different languages.

"It seems our little Koomer is becoming quite the social butterfly." Zhaden joked. "Please do let us know of any good gossip!" he called out to the Ayr, who shot him a rude hand gesture as he continued to walk away.

Zhaden chuckled as he reached to his right and pressed his fingers along one of the rotting wooden slats composing the floor next to him. The white of his small horn pierced the darkness around him. His blue webbed fingers stopped suddenly as he located the small crease he was looking for. With a single, smooth pull, he lifted the plank up and out of the ground and then set it down gently next to him.

Reaching into the exposed opening, he retrieved the old watch that he and the other prisoners in this barracks used to keep track of time and the corresponding guard schedules. This was yet another of Koomer's creations.

Zhaden closed one eye and pulled the watch close to his face. "Hmm. A bit less time than I did anticipate, friends. We will have to make this one a bit shorter."

He began to place the watch back in the opening.

"Jakob, I assume you will be—?"

He nodded.

Zhaden sighed. "If I ask enough, perhaps one day, you will say no. Perhaps you will say 'I should spend time with my very handsome and exceptionally strong friend Zhaden.' Why are you Draekons so stubborn?"

Jakob shrugged. "Seems like only the stubborn ones are left."

Zhaden sighed again. "You should really join us sometime, my friend. A good song is excellent for the spirit. Back home, they say music pleases the Salt Maiden, who keeps the currents flowing in return."

"I'll keep that in mind. You all enjoy yourselves." Jakob answered, walking away.

"Very well. I shall sing your parts as well, as per usual. It will take me some effort to match your pitch, however. My voice is sadly much too deep for the higher sections."

Jakob rolled his all-blue eyes as he entered the closed-off latrine section of the barracks. He stepped inside and turned to face the open door before opening his left palm. After a second, a bright purple beam extended out of it, and he could feel the rotting wood on his hand, despite being several feet away from it. He swung his hand as though it were physically on the door itself, causing it to swing closed.

New arrivals from foreign races would always give him and other Draekons odd looks whenever they did those sorts of things. Prior to entering the camps, Jakob had not even realized that this purple energy, known locally as Shaz, was unique to his people. Unfortunately, its uses appeared to be limited. His daydreams of firing deadly lasers out of each palm that would slice the Alavites in half still seemed far off, if not impossible.

The voices of the singing prisoners echoed faintly in the distance. Zhaden's was by far the most easily distinguishable of the group. By this point, he had heard "Salty Shores of Aberaca," an Udul classic—or so Jakob had been told—at least thrice per week, and every single time he did, he found himself impressed by the quality of Zhaden's translation of the song into Neatspeak.

Cha-leh is covered entirely in water. I wonder if this shore the Udul enjoys singing so much about is even real.

"Fair point." Jakob responded, answering the voice which had now plagued his thoughts for the past ten years.

Has it been a decade since the invasion already?

Jakob sighed. "It's felt like twice that."

He looked down at his right hand and began to focus in.

Steady. Feel it within you. Don't force it or strain yourself.

He shut his eyes and steadied his breathing as he waited for the familiar sensation. After a few seconds, he felt the jolt shoot up his arm, spreading out across his palm onto each of his fingers. The glow of the bright purple light penetrated his eyelids and he opened them to see that his hand was now completely engulfed in a brilliant, unnatural inferno, lighting up the entirety of the filthy latrine. He turned his head as a small swarm of roaches on the nearby wall scurried away from him.

Perfect. We're making progress. I know it feels slow, but remember it was only a few years ago that you could only light up a single finger.

The voice was right. This was a start, but it was not nearly enough, and the progress that was being made was taking far too long.

Jakob clutched at his stomach as a violent hunger pang ran through it. He turned to scan the room for a few seconds before locking in on his target. He approached a small furry mass in the grime-filled corner of the room. He picked up the cold and stiff scatrat corpse with his left hand before slowly placing it in his right palm. A loud sizzle resonated throughout the small room for a few seconds as he closed the hand into a fist. When he finally opened it, the rodent's entire body emerged soft and hairless.

Again? Really?

The singing outside came to a stop and was soon replaced by idle chatter. Jakob picked the scatrat back up with his left hand and shook his right violently, causing the purple flames on it to extinguish. He sighed as he rested his back against the wall and took a large bite out of the rodent, removing the head from its small body. Jakob's stomach groaned in reluctant pleasure.

At times, I am glad I am incapable of feeling nauseous.

"Have you seen what they feed us?" Jakob replied. "This is a treat in comparison."

Have you considered perhaps putting your abilities to a better use?

"When am I going to learn how to shoot a beam, like Kadrok did?"

The energy expresses itself differently in everyone. For your late king, it was though energy beams. The hand of fate decided you would have fire.

"Like Murderous Marielle."

Indeed.

He was halfway through his second bite when the door of the latrine opened. Jakob turned his head slightly as Zhaden ducked his way into the small, smelly room.

"Jakob, I do indeed believe that you sneaking off to speak to yourself may be concerning our fellow brothers."

He moved across in front of Jakob and sat down cross legged.

Jakob took another bite of his dinner. "They already pushed me in here. Not sure it matters what they think."

"You scare them sometimes, friend, and in more ways than one. This Shaz power is also very unusual, you do understand?"

He slurped up the tail like a noodle. "Not really. We all have it."

The Udul readjusted himself. "They have no way to know that. You must understand that you are the only Draekon most of the men outside have ever seen."

Jakob turned to look at the door. "They call me a demon. On my own planet."

"You must give them time to adjust."

Jakob shook his head. "What time? The next purge could be any day now. I'm not convinced there's even a hundred of us left across all camps."

The slight smile that Zhaden had been wearing for several minutes now evaporated. He swallowed hard and shook his head. "My friend, you must remain positive. We. . . we simply must move faster then. I will not watch them do to you what I have been made to watch them do to so many—"

He stopped suddenly and ran a hand over his mouth. The Udul had always gotten very emotional during and after the ceremonies. It was difficult to blame him, given the horrific nature of what took place.

Not all have mastered the ability to shut themselves off to it as you have. Allow him to feel. It is one of the few things they have not yet taken from him.

Jakob moved slowly over to his large, emotional friend and patted him on the shoulder. Even though the two had spent nearly a decade together, feeling Zhaden's tough, scaly skin was still bizarre for Jakob.

"I'll have Koomer's contacts inform me if they catch sight of any golden guards. We'll have a day or two at most at that point. You know they only come down here for one reason."

Jakob looked down into Zhaden's large pupils.

"If anything happens to me, you move forward with the plan. You continue until your dying breath. Do you understand me?"

Zhaden shook his head slightly. "My friend, that was *our*—"

"Zhaden! This isn't about me or you. It isn't about who gets credit or who executes it. This is bigger than us."

Very well said. There may be hope for you yet, Jakob.

The Udul hesitated, but eventually nodded.

The chatter from the main room stopped abruptly, and a sudden, loud crash made them jump. Yells and screams echoed outside. This meant only one thing: the guards had made their way in. It was too early, and this was clearly something more than just their standard rounds. The guards outside were shouting in Alavic.

A sharp jolt of adrenaline shot through Jakob's entire body. His gaze was quickly drawn down toward his own hands, both of which had become engulfed in the familiar purple flames. Jakob had never managed to ignite one hand without several seconds of intense concentration before, let alone both. He turned and shot a glance at Zhaden, who recoiled slightly.

Interesting. Very interesting.

"Your . . . your eyes—"

Jakob's hands suddenly returned to normal as the door to the latrines slammed open. Six Alavites flooded into the room, surrounding him and Zhaden on every side. Four were standard prison guards dressed in their usual tattered gray armor. The shine on the gold metal that coated the remaining two would have been blinding in better lighting conditions.

Our time has come.

II

CORVUS-JORG (CJ) DROC
YAUN MOUNTAINS, YAUN
ERUB

He lived in an age of impossible flying machines, space travel, and complex interplanetary politics; yet here he was, sharpening his blade on a damn wheel. If nothing else, it worked quite well as a source of stress relief, which was something that could not possibly have been more in demand given recent events. He enjoyed the peaceful repetitiveness of the process and loved nothing more than fading into his thoughts, aided solely by the lovely white noise that the constant grinding created.

"Corvus, get in here."

Only one person alive still called him that.

With a sigh, he slid off his chair and walked over to the next room. This chamber was much darker and had no openings for light to seep through. Makeshift lamps barely illuminated the massive holodesk in the center of the room and those who stood around it. Several cables attached to the device led out of the circular chamber and connected to a small generator, whose whir echoed through the entirety of the base.

Sheressa stood at the center of the table, looking straight down at the screen of the desk. CJ couldn't see what held her attention. Around her stood the other major figures of the resistance movement, including several senators and governors who had been ousted from the various islands on the planet.

"Shaera and Detz think they might have found a passage into the capital through an unfinished sewer system," she said, without looking up to acknowledge him.

She shook her head and ran her fingers along the touchscreen, zooming into the large map of the planet.

"I don't have this mapped out anywhere nor any records of it at all, but at least if we don't, it means they don't either. This could be monumental in getting us back into the city. Go with them to confirm this for me. If you get a chance, head in and see how intact it is and how far in the sewer goes. If the passage seems stable enough, I'll see if I can work it into our invasion plans."

She picked up an e-pen from the table and drew a large circle on the screen. She spent the next few minutes writing notes on the it and deliberating with the two rebels who were standing by her side. CJ just crossed his arms and exhaled, waiting until she finally looked up from the table, making eye contact with him. The contrast between her leaf-green eyes and tan skin left little doubt as to her ethnicity. Her heart-shaped face came from their mother, and CJ occasionally found their resemblance unnerving.

"So, are you just going to stand there or . . .?"

CJ stroked the stubble of his beard. "Yeah, I'll get on it. Where are they now?"

She turned and walked around the table while those who were sitting around it began to talk quietly among themselves. CJ watched her braided dark brown hair, which reached down to her lower back, as he admired its simple, yet elegant design. Even as she stood up straight, the height differential between her and the men around the table was a bit jarring. At only five foot one, she was the shortest of the entire Droc family line, which was a fact that others seemed to place way more importance on than she herself did.

This was the first time he had seen her today, and as usual, she was dressed as though she were in an expensive restaurant instead of a disgustingly humid cave. Today, she had donned a light-blue ankle-length dress held up by a single diagonal strap over her right shoulder. It had several flowery gold patterns embroidered onto it.

From the time she'd broken into her teens, Sheressa had been forced to deal with what had felt like a never-ending barrage of men chasing after her. She tended to deal with them herself, though CJ would occasionally need to intervene in instances where the admirer was overly aggressive or threatening. One 'talk' was usually all it took to never hear from them again.

Sheressa stopped right in front of him, looking him directly in the eyes as she spoke. "You're meeting them down by Niveiro. If this does turn out to be significant, we can consider letting them in."

Even though the mountain caverns were easily the most secure option for them, the location could house only a limited number of rebels.

"Alright. That's not too far. I'll let you know what I think of them, and then you can decide."

He began to turn, but she quickly reached out and grabbed him, reclaiming his attention.

"Hey. Be safe, okay? Stay in contact. I *hate* when you go off the grid on me."

CJ nodded once. "I've got it handled. I'll be back before you know it."

He leaned forward and kissed her lightly on the forehead. Despite the tough and at times callous front she put up, Sheressa truly did love what was now the last of her family line.

"I'm serious, Corvus. I want constant updates. The city outskirts are growing more dangerous by the day."

"I'm not exactly quivering in my boots over the prospect of running into some dirty bandits. Let me go."

She released her grip on him and he turned and exited the room for the hangar, which had been built in the largest of the caves they occupied. As he turned a corner, he ran into the exact man he was hoping to see.

"Watts, get a flyer started for me."

He nodded and stomped his cigarette out before taking off down the hall in a jog.

CJ took a brief detour to get back to his personal quarters. Every turn inside the hangar looked identical, and he had spent what felt like an entire year getting lost within it before finally memorizing the exact route. This wasn't an uncommon problem, and it was perhaps the one major downfall to living here.

He pushed aside the curtains that acted as a door and stepped into his room. He searched around it quickly and moved over to the small opening in the wall he'd fashioned into a closet, where he reached for his old dark green military jacket. He had clumsily cut the sleeves off years ago due to the heat and to his personal preference of having his arms as unencumbered as possible.

As he started for the door, he shot a glance at his weapon rack in the corner of the room. A variety of swords, axes, and many more traditional weapons lay gleaming in the few streams of light that penetrated the room. But as usual, he ignored them in favor of the machete that was already at his hip. It was his oldest and most reliable weapon, and it rarely, if ever, left his side.

He retraced his steps back to the main hallway and, from there, proceeded down to the hangar, where his flyer was already set up. The glass cockpit cover shot up with a whoosh, and Watts climbed out of it. Taking the spot he had just left, CJ strapped himself in and began preparing for takeoff. After a quick systems check, he flashed the headlights on and off three times. A loud roar filled the cavern, reverbing off the walls and vibrating through his bones. After a few seconds, light began to form in a line directly in front of him as the two massive boulders that sealed the entrance of the hangar began to be forced apart by the heavy machinery that had been rigged to move them.

After waiting the full minute, he resumed the takeoff process, squinting as the sun shone directly into his eyes. He gently pushed his joystick forward, setting the wheels in motion. After a brief confirmation of their working condition, he activated the boosters, which quickly caused the entire hangar to zoom by him. As he reached the exit, he pressed the button to switch the wheels to hover mode. Without so much as a stutter, the flyer transitioned from its rolling state and lived up to its name, sending CJ rocketing off eastbound in the direction of one of the many beaches that surrounded the Erub capital city.

The journey was shorter than he had remembered, taking only a little over an hour. Before he knew it, he was stepping onto the hot afternoon sand after leaving his ship in the most well-hidden spot he could find. Niveiro was a complete ghost town. Save for the occasional shady duo completing a drug deal or young couple rolling around in the sand, there was never much life to be found on this smelly, polluted beach. There was no one in his immediate vicinity as CJ looked out over the emerald green waves rhythmically breaking and retreating away from the maroon sand.

And then footsteps came from behind him, and he turned.

They looked pretty much how he had remembered them from their last excursion together. Had it been the liberation of Marau or the strike at Zeeva? It had definitely been one of the two. Detz had grown a beard, and Shaera had shaved his head since then but aside from that, they were completely unchanged.

"Good to see you guys again. Daylight's burning, so we should hit this sewer."

Detz responded first. "Sheressa sent you?"

CJ found this to be an odd question with a fairly obvious answer. "My sister always sends me."

It wouldn't have made much of a difference even if Sheressa had come. She never went anywhere remotely dangerous without protection, and, as her brother, CJ was always her first choice to act as her bodyguard.

The two men exchanged looks and shrugged. They motioned for CJ to follow, and the group began walking into the brush. It wasn't long before they arrived at the very edge of the capital city of Kondi, which rested atop a massive hill. The group was fortunate that the jungle there was so thick, as they'd have otherwise been in plain sight of anyone who happened to be looking out over the edge of the city.

Now, at the base of the hill, the group began making their way around it.

Crack!

The sound of a twig breaking behind CJ sent him into motion. He hadn't even fully processed the sound in his head, but he had already ducked and spun around. In a fluid and continuous motion, he drew his machete from the sheath and struck at the camouflage-wearing figure behind him.

Raiders! They had spawned from the war and tended to congregate around the outskirts of cities, waiting to kill, rape, and rob any passersby. No greater scum existed outside of that constituting the top layer of the filthiest ponds.

His machete caught a good portion of the would-be attacker's side, blood starting to gush profusely from the wound immediately.

The man had painted his face entirely in green, black, and brown, making it difficult to discern any of his facial features. The raider brought his hatchet down quickly and CJ rolled to his left, pulling out his machete from the raider's side.

The injured man grabbed at his wound, groaning, and CJ took the opportunity to glance toward his companions. They were outnumbered three to two themselves, but they were holding their own for the time being.

He took in the situation quickly, and knew he had to put an end to this.

He sped up his attack, hitting the hobbled raider with three quick strikes until the hatchet was forced from his hand. No sooner had it hit the ground than CJ's machete came up and struck him through the chest, the blade protruding from his back.

CJ withdrew his weapon quickly and rushed to the other two rebels as the first raider's body hit the ground with a soft thud.

Coming in with a running start, CJ slid past two of the unaware attackers who had turned their backs to him, inflicting solid slashes on their legs as he did so. Taking advantage of the opportunity, Shaera and Detz put their swords through the grounded criminals, ending their suffering.

CJ jumped up quickly to face the final of the four assailants, now fully focused on him. He was much taller and far more muscular than the rest. Like the others, he was painted completely in camouflage, but the pair of curved horns on his head marked him as a member of the notorious Dom'Rai race.

The two went back and forth, exchanging blows for a few seconds before Shaera and Detz joined in. Despite the three-on-one advantage, the alien being seemed unfazed and quickly disarmed both of CJ's companions, forcing them into a brief and awkward retreat.

Seeing a small opening, CJ slashed at the final raider's chest and finally made contact. The initial shock of the strike caused the man to drop the large bladed staff he had been carrying, but despite the good few inches of penetration into his skin, the behemoth Dom'Rai looked positively unperturbed.

He stopped briefly to look down at the machete that was currently stuck inside of him before delivering a powerful punch to CJ's stomach. He stumbled backward with one hand on the machete. As he moved it came with him, slicing open a small portion of the man's chest in the process.

The two rebels had regained control of their weapons and now stood on either side of the assailant as he groaned angrily. The large raider pounded at his bleeding chest with his mangled hand and began to howl and shout in a language none of them could understand. CJ looked down at his blade and back at the raider.

There was no way this would be over anytime soon. Unless . . .

The raider turned to face Shaera and charged at him, pinning him to the trunk of a nearby tree before beginning to beat him mercilessly with his free hand. After a few seconds, the barrage suddenly stopped, and Shaera was released.

The raider slumped to the ground lifelessly. CJ took a second to catch his breath as he stared at the black handle of the machete, the only part that was visible from the back of the raider's head. It needed to have been a perfect throw, and it had been.

Both men looked at CJ, who walked over to the corpse and struggled to pull his machete free.

"Great. As if the fucking Alavites weren't enough by themselves."

He moved to wipe it down on a nearby tree trunk and looked over at the two men, who seemed to be catching their breath. Shaera looked worse for wear; his forehead was bleeding, and his eyes were beginning to swell.

Once everyone in the group had collected themselves both physically and mentally from the excitement, they continued forward.

"Might want to turn back and get that looked at." CJ suggested as he continued to examine his blade.

"No. I'm fine." Shaera answered quickly.

The remainder of the journey went by uneventfully.

CJ placed his hands on his hips as he examined the opening in the side of the hill. "Guess I'm going in then. Keep watch out here and try to keep your faces intact, alright?"

"Be quick about it," Detz responded roughly.

CJ made his way into the cave opening and into darkness, immediately grabbing a flare from his belt to light. He made his way to the end of a narrow cavern, only to curse under his breath and spin around on his heel when he found that the tunnel leading into the city had collapsed. As he did so, he noticed a reflection of the red light in his hand sweeping across the ground. He leaned in slightly to get a good look at what seemed to be an enormous hole filled to the brim with water as black as the cave itself. For the slightest fraction of a second, he thought he may have seen something move within its depths. He shook his head and rose to his feet with a sigh, extinguishing his flare once he returned to the cave entrance.

Shielding his eyes against the glare of sunlight, he was startled to find himself confronted by four Alavites in gold-plated armor, and an Alavite priest with long, graying hair. Too many by far to take on with his machete.

He glared at his two Erub guides, who clearly weren't prisoners. They at least had sufficient shame to avoid meeting his gaze.

"Corvus-Jorg Droc," the priest said with evident satisfaction. "We've heard a lot about you. I am Pertinax, spiritual advisor to King Reymar Polero."

"I know who you are, Alavite." CJ growled.

A short burst of static came from his hip. "Corvus? Are you planning on checking in sometime this century?"

He yanked the radio from his belt, crushing it to pieces beneath the heel of one boot while the priest looked on in apparent amusement.

"These men," Pertinax continued, indicating Shaera and Detz, "promised me the female Droc. But perhaps you'll work just as well." His mouth twisted into a simpering grin. "Bring your sister to us and things will go much more smoothly for you."

"Do I look like an idiot to you?" CJ sneered.

The priest's smile vanished, and he shook his head. "I don't believe you'll appreciate my response to that question." he said in a strange and child-like singsong rhythm. "Sheressa cares for you, doesn't she? Let's see how she reacts when we toy around with you a bit."

CJ fought to keep his voice steady. "I suppose you're taking me to Mortobal. Polero can't seem to stop rubbing his victory in. You let him know we're taking it back, all of it. He can wear my father's crown all he goddamn wants."

"Oh no," said Pertinax, his grin slowly returning. "We're going somewhere much farther aw-"

"Hey!" shouted Shaera, a scowl on his face. "Are we getting paid, or what?"

The priest regarded him as if he'd entirely forgotten the two men. Shaera met his gaze with angry belligerence. "You said there was a reward."

"Reward?" Pertinax asked in a strangely high pitch. "But of course."

He nodded in the guards' direction. Two of then grabbed each Erub and pushed them to the ground, pinning them. The two traitors began screaming and protesting as they struggled unsuccessfully. The other two guards each pulled out the Erubs' swords from their scabbards and began cutting into the backs of their necks. Their screams grew louder as pools of blood began to form beneath them.

"Their reward is being able to be with Alavon and earn his forgiveness. I would have preferred giving them a few more years among the living, but, as you just saw, they insisted."

Pertinax shrugged casually before turning back to CJ. "Now then, where were we?" he asked, despite clearly knowing the answer 'Ah, yes. Have you ever been off-world?"

CJ said nothing. He wanted to fight. He wanted to take as many of these bastards down with him as he could, even if it meant certain death. But even though he was good, he knew he wasn't good enough to beat heavily armored and highly trained guards when it was four against one. He thought about Sheressa; she was the only thing that kept him from grabbing for his machete. If there was any chance he could get back to her and figure out a way to escape, he'd take it.

"Hmm. I think not. Well, I, for one, do enjoy surprises, so I'll keep this as one. Here's the only hint you'll get: I hope that ridiculous outfit you're wearing is warmer than it looks."

III

DARYN PERIC
MAIN LOBBY, ALAVON'S ALTAR
ALAVONIA

The bright reds, blues, and yellows of the vocay fish painted a perpetually changing image onto the translucent canvas of the massive fountain in the bright and spacious lobby. Daryn had long admired these beautiful creatures and would at times spend his entire shift breaks just staring at them.

Today marked his fifteenth year working as an attender. He wasn't very different from the others in terms of his position, aside from having been handpicked by the most powerful man in the galaxy. To this day, he still didn't have a satisfying answer to his persistent question—*why me?* He was neither incredibly intelligent nor particularly brave. The mission he had taken to Oballe over a decade ago still gave him occasional anxiety attacks and caused him to wake up drenched in sweat.

He sighed, pushed a lock of curly bright blond hair out of his eyes, readjusted his gaze, and began to focus on his reflection in the impeccably clean glass of the tank. Yep. He was still the same scrawny, lanky Alavite he had always been. His skin was looking a bit yellower than usual, which was odd considering he rarely found himself outside for long periods. He arched his head to look up at the stained glass that made up the entirety of the circular ceiling.

"Shocking that I would find you here."

Daryn nearly hit his face against the tank as Olivio approached from behind him and cursed under his breath for allowing it to happen again. He had always been embarrassed by how jumpy he was.

It was one of the rare moments when The Hand wasn't accompanied by at least one gold-clad holy guard. Daryn tried to think of a quick response to the old man's statement, but nothing escaped his lips.

"This is what we call sarcasm, Daryn." Olivio continued walking past, without so much as stopping to look in Daryn's direction. "Come. The ceremony is starting soon. I can't imagine you would want to be late."

Daryn shook his head quickly to refocus before shooting off behind The Hand. Light flooded his eyes as the two proceeded through the Western Hall before entering the elevator, whose walls and doors were composed entirely of glass.

Alavonia was a horribly hot and sufficiently sunny planet to begin with, so sitting in what was essentially a claustrophobia-inducing sauna, even for a short time, was always a terribly sweaty and uncomfortable experience. Why did Alavonian architecture have to rely so heavily on glass?

He breathed in and out, slowly and deeply, before the anxiety could get a foothold on him. He wouldn't be distressed today. He refused to be. It was Yeuma's day. He had never liked being apart from his twin sister for long, as she was all the family he had ever known.

"Do you have any idea what she's going to choose?" Olivio asked, breaking the silence as he looked down at his gauntlet to adjust it.

Not only did he have no idea, but Yeuma had also flat out refused to discuss the ceremony at all. He supposed he would be as surprised by her choice as everyone else.

"Oh . . . uh, no. No, I don't," he answered hesitantly.

Olivio raised his light-gray eyebrow and shot a quick glance at him but said nothing.

As they finally made their way to the top of the shaft, the glass doors split into two before disappearing into the ceiling and floor. A badly needed breeze blasted its way into the elevator. Four of the gold-clad holy guards stood at attention on either side of the open doors. As the duo passed by, the guards followed and quickly surrounded them.

The wind picked up as the group stepped up onto Olivio's launch platform, sending Daryn's golden curls flying in every direction.

He looked to his left to gaze out over the massive, pristine, and organized metropolis as he ascended the ramp into The Hand's shuttle, which was, blissfully, temperature controlled. There was never a quiet moment in this city, which seemed to perpetually be in motion. Daryn settled into his seat across from Olivio, who had pulled out a tablet and was reading something over.

They made the twenty-minute journey in relative silence until about thirty seconds before landing, when the cacophony of the exterior began to penetrate its way inside the ship's walls. By the time the door opened, the sounds of the crowd outside were almost deafening. Daryn and Olivio took their places with the golden guards, who escorted them out of the vessel. Velvet rope barriers outlined the party's path to the monastery's enormous entrance. Olivio waved with his golden hand as they marched along, and his audience responded with even louder cheers. Camera flashes came from seemingly every direction, leaving Daryn with an annoying collection of neon spots in his vision.

He was perfectly happy with his background role as almost an accessory to Olivio. Despite being close by at almost all times, he was mostly ignored by both crowds and the press alike. This was likely for the best, as he honestly wasn't sure that he'd be able to handle the constant spotlight under which his superior seemed to live his entire life. Daryn settled himself into a reserved spot in one of the lavish front pews within the enormous, ornately designed building. Images and sculptures of Alavon Acivorai decorated almost every wall and stained-glass window.

At the back of the stage, climbed up the small stair to take his seat on the ceremonial chair, elevated above both the others on the stage with him and those in the crowd. The absolute silence of the monastery that the two had entered contrasted with the wild screams of adulation coming from outside. The deathly stillness didn't last long, as slowly but surely, the preservers and their accompanying women in training, or WITs, began to fill the massive building, which sat fifty-five hundred. The preservers wore navy blue dresses that covered them from head to toe, as well as large veils that left only their eyes exposed.

Daryn wasn't sure whether Yeuma had ever been happy, not even for even a second during her time in the convent. As the sister of The Hand's attendant, she was guaranteed a spot that many other women, who typically had the lowest paid and most degrading jobs on the planet, would have killed for. Unfortunately for both them and Yeuma, once someone was in, the only way out was death or excommunication, which was invariably punished by death.

After what felt like an eternity of watching the light-blue dresses of the WITs shuffling into the building, he finally spotted her. Her long golden hair reached down to her waist before beginning to fold into curls right at the end. Standing at an even six feet tall, Yeuma's height made her much easier to spot in the sea of blue and blonde.

A holy guard made his way over to the preserver closest to Yeuma, who pointed her out to him. The guard nodded before approaching and offering her his arm. Yeuma shot him a disgusted glare before looking over and making eye contact with Daryn, who had turned around in his pew to look at her. She seemed to sigh before saying something to the guard, who grabbed her arm and began to escort her down the aisle. Daryn noticed several of the other girls shooting harsh glances at his sister as she made her way to the front row, which was normally reserved for high-ranking members of the clergy and their attendants. Olivio had graciously decided to make an exception for Yeuma as a favor.

The golden guard stopped in front of him and remained there until she took her seat. Although the hall was filling rapidly, there was an eerie silence to the room.

Daryn leaned in toward Yeuma and whispered, "You look great. Do you know what you're going to choose?"

She said nothing and continued staring forward as though she hadn't heard him.

He tried again. "Hey. Look, I understand that this wasn't what you would have wanted. But look at the bright side! It's over. You can finally take control and forge your own destiny, you know, so to speak."

Yeuma shot him a side glance without moving her head and then spoke almost under her breath. "Shut up, Daryn."

He would have been stunned if this hadn't been how she'd *always* been. She could never just be happy about anything. Everything had to be a struggle. She lived such a privileged life but was impossible to satisfy. He could have vocalized these thoughts, but he had already done so too many times before, and this wasn't the time nor place for a fight. He just sighed and sank back into the pew.

Thankfully, it wasn't much longer before the ceremony began. Several preservers gave short speeches in front of the crowd, giving the usual rigmarole describing the trials the women faced during their tenure and stating that they were now ready for the outside world. After what felt like an eternity, The Hand finally rose from his chair to address the audience. Given how quiet the room had been just before, the thunderous applause this small action evoked made Daryn jump slightly.

"On this day, these women elevate themselves not only in society's eyes but also, more importantly, in Alavon's. They become preservers in their own right and, upon accepting His blessing, will go out into the world to serve as critical aids to the best men our society has to offer. This will prove to be critical to our ability to expand the influence and reach of Alavon and His chosen people. Now, without further ado, let us begin the ceremony."

He sat back down as the ear-splitting applause picked up again.

If the speeches had been boring, this part of the ceremony was pure torture. Fifteen hundred WITs would now break off row by row and line up at the bottom of The Hand's small staircase, which led up to his makeshift throne. They would approach him one at a time, kneel, swear their allegiance to the faith, and then select their desired role. Upon receiving The Hand's blessing, they would then rise as preservers.

The process took three excruciating hours. Daryn was not sure he had ever been as bored in his life, until he remembered that he had sat through this last year as well. Yeuma's block was among the last to be called up. A golden guard—perhaps the same one from earlier, but it was hard to be sure—came by and motioned for her to stand.

She sighed and rose slowly. After a short stretch, she turned her head to look directly at Daryn for the first time that day. She quickly leaned into him and whispered into his ear prior to being whisked away. "Showtime."

It wasn't until about a minute later that he began wondering what she had meant by her statement. She was going to choose some low-ranking job just to embarrass herself—and, by proxy, him—once again, wasn't she? Or perhaps she would request a job that she knew full well she wasn't allowed to take, just to make one of her "statements." The possibilities ran wild in his mind, and he could feel the familiar tingling sensation in his extremities as his heart began to race. There was nothing he could do but watch and wait as Yeuma slowly but surely made her way to the front of the line until it was finally her turn.

She climbed the steps in such a proper and feminine fashion that he briefly wondered whether he had been tracking the wrong girl. She knelt as she reached Olivio's feet, and he raised his golden hand over her head.

"Yeuma Peric, do you accept the blessing of our great Savior and swear to live your life in service to Him and His message?"

Daryn had been trying to monitor his heart rate, but the thumping was so fast that it was hard to distinguish individual beats.

Yeuma, who had been staring at the floor, lifted her head very slowly to ensure that she was looking Olivio right in the eyes.

"Fuck you."

IV

**ZHADEN KARUK
BARRACKS 17, CAMP IZROK
OBALLE**

Bergon M'og, Izrok's warden, pushed his way through the comparatively diminutive golden guards. Because there were so few of them at the camp, the sight of a Dom'Rai was always somewhat jarring to Zhaden. He had grown so used to being a foot taller than everyone else that meeting someone who could look him in the eye without having to crane his head back had become something of an event. M'og spoke directly to Zhaden in Garyl, the language their two closely related races shared.

"I find you in here of all places. Disgusting."

The warden looked around the room, his face contorted into an expression of utter revulsion. He glanced down at Jakob for half a second before restoring eye contact with his equal in height.

"If you try to fuck this whelp, you'd probably kill him. That is, unless your scaly cock is as tiny as I imagine."

For whatever reason, M'og seemed intent on painting a target on his bald blue head the moment he entered the camp.

"Always a pleasure to see you, M'og."

In contrast to his Neatspeak proficiency, Zhaden was very fluent and comfortable in Garyl; aspects of his speech, such as word choice and phrasing, were comparatively far less awkward.

The Dom'Rai stepped up to him and grabbed Zhaden's face, squeezing his cheeks together with powerful force. "Best keep that smug fucking attitude to yourself. The second these lemon skins leave, I am going to have your head and leave your body for the frost bears. I swear this on V'uulk's name."

Zhaden's words came out distorted through the compression of his mouth. "I believe you meant to say Alavon, friend."

Few people on the planet could deliver a force powerful enough to cause Zhaden's two-hundred-and-sixty-pound frame to stumble backwards, but the brawny warden was one of them. He righted himself quickly, resisting the urge to rub at the stinging pain sparking across the skin of his cheek. The slap had hurt, but at least he was now free.

M'og switched to Neatspeak. Though Zhaden himself was admittedly still getting the hang of the galactic common language, the Dom'Rai's iteration of it had to be among the worst he had ever heard.

"Draekon. You come willing us with. No question. Resist and die, yes?"

Zhaden was unsure whether M'og had intended to end with a question.

The warden finally broke out of the uncomfortable staring contest and directed his gaze down to Zhaden's side, where Jakob stared up silently, challenging him. The Draekon said nothing, sporting the same blank expression that he had seemingly mastered by this point.

M'og made a noise that sounded like a grunt and then stepped over to his right before stooping down to Jakob's comparatively diminutive level. "Saying word? No? Thinking toughness, is you?"

Jakob remained so still that it was hard to tell whether he was even breathing. Zhaden was impressed. M'og began to chuckle slightly and stood back up straight. But suddenly, he jabbed his foot into the Draekon's abdomen before anyone else in the room could react. Jakob doubled over but made no sound. Alarms went off in Zhaden's head, but he fought the urge to help his small friend, now hunched over on his knees.

One of the Alavite prison guards finally spoke up. "You kill him, and you answer to the creepy priest."

M'og turned to face the man. "Pertinax sleep easy. Me prepare him. Only."

He then turned back to Jakob, who had still not taken his eyes off M'og. He was obviously in pain, but his face showed none of it. The Dom'Rai's pride didn't take well to Jakob's refusal to groan or beg as so many others did, and M'og raised a hand to strike him.

Zhaden didn't think about it; his body raced ahead of his mind before the latter could restrain him. He grabbed the warden's wrist and tossed it aside as his large open hand was inches from Jakob's pale face. The Draekon didn't so much as flinch at the prospect of taking a hit that could have easily knocked him unconscious and even left him concussed.

M'og turned his head slowly to look at Zhaden. His eyes widened briefly and then narrowed again. His hard mouth curled into a slight smile. "Draekon do take. I deal Udul with me."

The two gold-clad guards grabbed Jakob and forcibly moved him toward the exit. Before Zhaden could react, he felt the familiar sharp and powerful sting of the electric rod hit the back of his knee and heard its sharp crack echo off the walls. The crippling pain radiated through his entire leg until it collapsed under him, forcing him down to the ground. He clutched at his pained limb and groaned as M'og's deep, booming laughter rang through the room.

The warden looked over Zhaden's head, presumably at the remaining four prison guards.

"Bring out of shit room. I over am take there."

The cool feel of the leather gloves on his skin reminded Zhaden of the sensation of suddenly plunging into a cool body of water after a long, hot day in the glass domes of the Cha-leh cities. He missed this feeling more than anything else, and as the guards grunted audibly in their struggle to take him back to the barracks, he wondered whether he would ever experience it again.

Once they were back out of the latrines, he suddenly felt himself fall as the guards released him. He lifted himself up as much as he could manage and looked around the room. The pain in his leg was some of the worst he had ever experienced. He tightened his grip on it as though this would somehow help. There were, at minimum, seven armed prison guards inside the barracks—at least from what he could see. He had wondered more than a few times whether the guards had been sent to work the camps as a sort of punishment. He couldn't think of any other time that he had seen soldiers who were evidently not trusted to carry lethal weaponry and were subjected to the commands of an individual from what was considered an inferior race in their society.

The rest of the prisoners in their poorly fitted black jumpsuits were left looking like a collection of trash bags that had been thrown carelessly around the floor. The guards kept their gaze on the sitting and kneeling captives, most of whom shot concerned glances at Zhaden. Koomer, who was next to the now-sealed floorboard, winked his good eye at him. He never ceased to be impressed at the feats the Ayr could pull off.

Zhaden sighed. If he was going to die, at the very least, he would be around almost all the people who still meant something to him. All but one.

As M'og joined the rest of the group back near the bunks, he thankfully switched back to the language that he was at least somewhat fluent in. "Ten years, and the moment has finally arrived. I almost don't know what to do with myself. This is going to be the highlight of my year on this fucking ice ball."

He drew the massive, wide-handled knife from his side; for some races, it would easily function as a sword. There were a few audible gasps in the room.

Zhaden stared at the knife as he felt his body tense up. "If you're going to do it, do it. There is no need to make a spectacle of it. I'm ready to join the Maiden."

M'og chuckled slightly. "I did briefly consider ending your miserable existence; this is true. But I was persuaded otherwise."

Two pairs of hands clamped down heavily on him again, holding him in place. He felt a third and then a fourth pair join in as he was suddenly pushed forward and hit his head against the cold floor. He could easily fend off two Alavites, but there must have been five of them compiling their strength at this point. He could do nothing but stare at the blackness of the ground and wonder what was about to happen.

He wasn't kept guessing for very long. The downward pressure on the back of his horn gave him perhaps the most horrifying answer possible. As a gritty, almost nauseating sawing sound filled the room, his heart sank. It took only a few seconds before the most intense pain that he had ever felt in his life overcame him. He forgot about his leg; this blew that out of the water. He forgot about where he was. He forgot everything. Each second surpassed the last as the worst of his life. Through the incapacitating pain, he could hear low-pitched laughter. It was the only thing left that he could focus on in a feeble and pathetic attempt to distract himself from the agony.

He didn't know how long it had been. It felt like a lifetime. The sawing stopped abruptly, and his head suddenly felt several pounds lighter. The guards on his back loosened their grip, but it didn't matter. He was too weak to move. All he could do was struggle to turn his head to the side. His vision was blurry, but he could see the red blob that was M'og examining the bloodied horn that had adorned his head only a few seconds prior. The Dom'Rai tossed it lightly in the air, letting it flip a few times before catching it.

"Not sure what I will do with this yet, but I'll figure something out. I expect your production to double now that you've got less weighing you down."

He switched to Neatspeak to address the guards. "We now go."

One by one, they made their way out of the room and into the cold of the night. The loud, booming thud of the large metal door slamming echoed through the room. Everything was quiet for a few seconds before the sound of a lone pair of racing footsteps grew closer. Someone was yelling. It took him a minute to recognize the voice as Koomer's. As best as he could, Zhaden focused his rapidly darkening vision on the Ayr, who was kneeling over him and seemed to be trying to rip the sleeve off his jumpsuit. As Zhaden's vision began to darken, all he found himself able to focus on was the Koomer's fading voice.

"Shit. He's going to bleed out. I need more fabric. Rick, bring wire from one of the radios! Yuho, cut your sleeves off and give them to me! I'm going to cauterize the wound."

Koomer grabbed Zhaden's face and looked him in the eyes. "Stay with me, big guy!"

V

**TOM EZEKIEL
REMY'S PLEASURE HOUSE, TRAX TOWN
AYR-GROH**

He groaned as he sat up slowly in the large circular bed. The satin sheets that had been so pleasantly cool against his bare skin the night before now stuck to his hot, sweaty body. He peeled them off him as quickly as possible and locked his arms around his knees, taking a moment to look around the suite. It had been the middle of the night when he had arrived, so this was the first time that he was seeing it properly illuminated. The sheer volume of alcohol in his system at the time didn't exactly help. He could remember only bits and pieces of the previous night: glimpses of faces, the dim orange light of the streetlights protruding through the windows, a stray tit here, and an empty bottle there.

It was now silent. The pounding of the loud music and the high-pitched moans from the night before had left without a trace. He turned to glance down at the three female companions at his side as they snored lightly and rhythmically. They were all facing away from him. Various empty bottles of miscellaneous alcohol of varying quality littered the worn chairs and tables at the other end of the room.

Slowly, he pulled himself forward and crawled out of the massive bed, making a silent beeline toward the crumpled pile of his clothes on the floor. There were far better brothels in Ayr-Groh; there was no doubt about that. But none were in a place as charming and familiar as Trax Town, and none had girls anywhere near as filthy.

He stood up straight and stretched as his feet touched the floor. The room had essentially turned into a sauna at this point. It was going to suck to put clothes back on, but perhaps getting it over with quickly would mitigate some of the suffering. He fished through the pile at his feet for his underwear and quickly pulled them up. Next, he shook out his tan pants before sliding them on one leg at a time, leaving him hopping around the room like an idiot. He glanced up quickly as he heard movement from the bed. One of the girls had rolled over into the spot that he had left vacant. The three heads of long dark-blonde hair now shared the bed pretty much evenly. He sighed and sat down slowly to get his socks on, followed by his boots, which were at opposite ends of the room for some reason. To finish, he threw on one of what must have been over fifty plain white T-shirts that he owned and wore almost exclusively.

He reached for his neck and didn't feel the familiar cold sensation of metal that he had been expecting. Where was it? He scanned the desk and dirty chairs in the room. When he couldn't find it immediately, he resorted to tossing items around lightly. He was on the cusp of becoming genuinely frustrated when he noticed a thin black line around the neck of the girl on the far right of the bed. He approached her slowly and rolled her over. The phoenix at the end of the necklace rested comfortably between her bare breasts, rising and falling slightly with each breath she took.

He grasped it gently and began removing it from around her neck. As he was just getting the tread past her ears, her right hand shot up, grabbing his wrist.

"But I like it, Tommy. It's so pretty." She seemed to still be half asleep.

"You're gorgeous enough already, babe. Promise."

Before dropping back to sleep, she made a sad, almost childlike noise, expressing defeat. Tom placed the necklace back around his own neck before moving over to the chair near the entrance, where he grabbed the black leather jacket hanging off the side of it and fished through its pockets, eventually withdrawing a rolled-up wad of cash. He began counting the bills, making sure he got the proper amount. He left what he owed on the desk—plus a significant tip to ensure he retained his status as a "preferred client"—and then took a moment to adjust his short, dirty-blond hair in the mirror that hung on the wall directly over it. He winked a sky-blue eye at himself as he turned toward the balcony door and opened it.

The cool air of the outdoors was a major and very much welcome relief against his damp skin. He walked over to the railing that overlooked the smoggy, slummy ghetto that was his hometown. Tom had always found it interesting that such a place could even exist on a planet so technologically advanced that its cities literally floated in the sky. Though, to be fair, they really had no choice, given that the planet was a gas giant.

He turned around and leaned back against the balcony railing as he finished adjusting his belt. Occasionally, it was difficult to get it on, given the weight of the large daggers in the sheaths on either side of it. Without warning, a loud rumbling exploded in his ears and he whipped around quickly, only to find himself face to face with a flyer hovering just over the edge of the balcony. The word "Police," which was printed on the side in Ayric, didn't exactly make the occupants' intentions subtle. He thought his eardrums might implode as the flyer activated the speakers mounted on its sides.

"Thomas Ezekiel, you are under arrest for multiple counts of grand larceny. Surrender yourself, or we will not hesitate to employ sedative or potentially even lethal force."

He blinked a few times and sighed. "For fuck's sake! Let a man get his goddamn rocks off once in a while. Tell Sprock he can work here if he wants to ride my dick that hard."

"Put your hands behind your head and get on your knees."

Tom raised an eyebrow. "Ooh, now we're getting kinky. I like it. But on a serious note-"

He was forced to quickly drop onto the floor as a large metallic stun bolt flew past him and cackled loudly as it connected with the wall, causing it to fracture.

He turned to look at the bolt then whipped his head back toward the cruiser.

"What the fuck?! Give a guy a warning!" he yelled.

His stomach sank slightly as the sight of a second bolt being loaded caught his eye. He quickly turned and jumped off the balcony, landing on a nearby rooftop, thanking his lucky stars that he was in Trax Town. Most cities didn't have buildings in such ridiculously close proximity to each other. The flyer began blaring its siren as it followed his movements.

He hopped onto a second roof, made of what felt like thin sheet metal, and then a third made of flat concrete. Then, with a whoosh, two more bolts flew past him—one in front and one behind.

Tom turned and smiled cockily at the flyer, but his heart was racing. The vehicle slowed as Tom began to, quite literally, run out of real estate. He skidded to a halt and gazed out over the crumbling city wall, which now acted as the only barrier between him and the seemingly infinite void on the other side.

He looked around quickly. There were no other rooftops within a reachable distance.

"A valiant effort and an impressive athletic demonstration, but it is time for you to come with us," the voice boomed through the speakers on either side of the flyer.

"Alright. You got me. Can I make one last request as a free man, though?" Tom raised his arms slightly. He received no response from the flyer, which slowly drew closer. "Tell Sprock he can kiss his birthday gift from me goodbye. I had a beautiful treadmill ready to be delivered."

There was a brief silence which was immediately proceeded by the clicking of a bolt locking into place.

"Get it? It's a fat joke. Your boss is fat. I don't know how much clearer I can be about this, guys."

Again, silence.

Tom sighed, feigned a military salute, and let himself fall backwards and off the edge of the platform.

The sirens began to fade away rapidly as he fell, replaced by the deafening noise of the wind blowing all around him.

Once he made it through the lower cloud layer, he clicked his feet together, triggering the two boosters hidden in the sole of each of his boots. Small flames shot directly downward, and after a few more seconds of free falling his descent halted, his boots propelling him upward.

He breathed a small sigh of relief. He hadn't had a chance to test them in the last few days, and it would have been *really* embarrassing if he had actually died.

For a few minutes, he panicked, searching frantically around, up, and down the body of the stainless-steel city platform before finally locating what he was looking for. The magnetic landing pads worked like a charm, though seeing his ship parked at such an off angle was bizarre. He had stolen it a few years ago with the intention of abandoning it, but for some reason, he had fallen in love with the piece of shit and had worked toward making it his own. It was designed in the style of a flying bird with short, fat wings aimed at backward-facing forty-five-degree angles. The rest of its body followed a similar pattern—width over length. The black tinted glass of the cockpit caused it to blend in with the rest of the ship and, for nothing other than the cool factor, it was probably Tom's favorite modification of the ones he had made.

He aligned himself with the rear entrance as it slid open, and he flew himself inside before slamming it shut behind him. He cut the power to his boots to avoid igniting the interior of the ship and then fell onto the metallic floor of the vessel. The angle of the ship created enough of a slope to allow him to slowly crawl his way up to his pilot's chair. Once strapped in, he began the process of preparing for space travel.

The engine roared to life, and he disengaged the magnetic landing strips, sending the ship falling backward briefly before adjusting and leveling out. It was a surprisingly huge relief to finally be horizontal and stable again.

As he rose out of the lower cloud layer, he began humming to himself and searching casually through the small glove compartment at his side. When he returned his gaze to the window, the sight of half a dozen space-grade police ships and their accompanying red-and-blue lights awaited him.

He let out a long sigh. "Well, shit."

He quickly jerked the ship upward, barely avoiding an electromagnetic pulse dart.

He flew wildly, performing turns, flips, and other acrobatic feats within seconds of each other to avoid the barrage of projectiles being aimed at his ship to disable it. He spun the ship around quickly, pulling it around to face one of the police flyers head on, holding it until the second when he flew straight up, just in time to miss the dart fired at him from a ship to his rear. Instead, it hit the front of its fellow officer's hull directly. The impacted ship's siren immediately disengaged, and the vessel began to drop out of the sky.

With this new opening, Tom directed himself into the upper atmosphere and put the engine into full gear. He'd need to slingshot as soon as possible. With one hand he nimbly steered the ship, turning every few seconds to avoid the darts flying at him, as he frantically typed coordinates into the small navigation computer with his other hand. He couldn't remember the last four digits— some combination of eight and five—to get to Norann.

A neutral and largely lawless planet would be the perfect place to lay low for a bit. But there was no time to think about it—the remaining vessels still behind him were growing closer, and others would close in on him soon. He quickly typed in eight-five-five-eight and confirmed it. He felt a pulse through the vessel as the wormhole generator fired up and shot out a bright blue light, which flew a few yards in front of the ship and expanded into a portal. He flew through it mere seconds before it closed.

Tom checked behind him to ensure that he had not been followed. With his safety now confirmed, he sighed and sat back for a few seconds before looking into the glove compartment and finally pulling out his virix goggles. He strapped them on, and the interior of the ship suddenly became much clearer. This wasn't particularly important, though, as he probably knew it inside and out—better than he knew his own body. With a sigh, he turned back to the window. Stars were rocketing past at lightning speed. Even at this physics-defying velocity, it would take a few days to get to Norann, and stopping on the way there wasn't possible.

The next seventy hours in the small vessel were among the most boring and miserable he could remember. By the middle of the third day—not that this meant much in space—the ship, which had essentially become a glorified prison cell, began to give the telltale rattle he had been desperately waiting for. After another few minutes, a second wormhole finally appeared in front of the vessel, which rocketed through it without so much as a stutter. The rapid pace of the stars slowed dramatically, and the planet exploded into view, filling the glass of the cockpit almost entirely. He cursed under his breath.

The number had been wrong. This wasn't Norann. This planet was ugly and gray. He didn't have enough fuel for a second attempt, so he resolved to fly in and hope that the locals were friendly and didn't recognize him.

No sooner had he readjusted his course than several other ships exited their slingshot all around him. His first thought was that the police had followed him, but these ships were not from his planet. Tom had never seen anything like these weird, white triangular vessels before. He reached up and activated his radio in an attempt to make contact, but his own ship was suddenly rocked, and its lights went out.

"Oh, come the fuck on!"

He'd spent all that time avoiding darts only to be caught with his pants down only a few days later. He wasn't sure whether he was more embarrassed than pissed. There was nothing to be done now but hope. He waited as one ship approached his and connected its airlocks, the familiar hissing noise of the ship-to-ship bond flooding Tom's small cabin. After a few tense seconds, two men, covered head to toe in golden armor, entered with their swords drawn.

Tom turned his chair around slowly and interlocked his hands.

"Gentlemen. I appreciate you dropping by, but you really should wait for an invitation. It's kinda the polite thing to do."

Neither of them made a sound. They exchanged glances through their helmets and then turned back to him. Before he could even react, the one on the left pulled out a strange needle from his belt and threw it at Tom like a dart, hitting him in the chest with surprising force.

Stun prick. He struggled to remember the last time he had been intimately acquainted with one of these fucking miserable things.

The pain was more than he could bear, and he dropped to the floor and began to spasm. The guards grabbed him and dragged him into their own ship via the airlock connection. He couldn't move his head much, but based on the shiny, pristine white floors, it was clear that these people's sense of design differed considerably from his. Their ship was only slightly bigger than his and became progressively narrower as one approached the cockpit. In the back, where the ship was widest, metal bars had been set up to function as what seemed to be a makeshift brig. He was turned toward it and, within a few seconds, dumped inside of it. The numbness resulting from the stun prick was overpowering. He heard the metal door lock behind him as he struggled to at least get into a sitting position. No one addressed him nor spoke to him for the several minutes it took him to regain feeling in his body.

He scanned the cell; he was no longer a stranger to the incarceration process. He noticed standard metal bars and a Krumler lock. From his vantage point, he couldn't tell which version it was, but he was certain that it would be an easy break if the guards weren't mere feet away. Tom resolved to wait until they landed, at which point he would try to get back to his ship, assuming they hadn't destroyed nor abandoned it.

Tom heard movement to his right and turned to see another prisoner in the cell next to him. He hadn't noticed him when he had first been taken to the ship, but his inability to move or even turn was probably to blame for that. The man was leaning his head against the leftmost bars of his cell and ignoring Tom entirely.

"So, what you in for?" Tom spoke to the man in a voice loud enough for him to hear, yet sufficiently low to not draw attention from the guards.

The man didn't so much as stir. For a second, Tom wondered if he was dead. If there was one thing he knew about people who ignored him on his first attempt, it was that the only reasonable thing to do was to try again, only louder.

"You got a harmonica by any chance?"

The muscular-looking Erub turned his head slowly and shot Tom an annoyed glance with his piercing green eyes.

VI

DARYN PERIC
MONASTERY OF OUR LORD, ALAVONIA CITY
ALAVONIA

He heard her wrong. He must have heard her wrong. He had to have heard her wrong.

A multitude of audible gasps filled the room, followed immediately by an uncomfortable and heavy silence. It hung over the stage, the crowd, and even the planet itself for several palm sweat-inducing seconds.

She wasn't doing this to him. Not to Olivio's face. Not in front of all of these people. She couldn't be that selfish, nor that spiteful. He could do nothing but pray silently that the old man would contain himself and show some ounce of mercy to his stupid and ungrateful sister.

Olivio cleared his throat and finally broke the pained and awkward silence.

"Ms. Peric, it is only out of the respect that I hold for your brother that I will grant you a second opportunity to answer my question. I will assume you misspoke and suffered a brief lapse in judgment."

Daryn couldn't see Yeuma's face. She hadn't moved an inch since she'd last spoken and had seemingly fixated her gaze on Olivio.

"I ask again, Yeuma Peric. Do you accept the blessing of our great Savior and swear to live your life in service to Him and His message?"

Daryn prayed harder than he ever had in his life. He would take never having another request granted again if it meant getting his sister to just say yes.

The back of Yeuma's head finally moved, and Daryn's heart sank deeper into his stomach than he even knew was possible. But before he or anyone else could even begin to try and intervene, Yeuma produced one of the most decidedly unladylike noises Daryn had ever heard from deep within her throat. A second later, a thick glob of spit came firing out with unbelievable accuracy, hitting Olivio directly in the face.

Daryn earnestly believed that he might die right there on the spot. His hand raced out in front of him and latched onto the side of the pew to provide him with some support.

Olivio slowly wiped the saliva from his face with his non-gloved hand and then shook it off to the side to rid himself of the fluids. A second later, at a speed faster than Daryn had ever seen the old man move, he swung his heavy, gloved hand at Yeuma's face, striking her across the right cheek. She groaned loudly and fell to her left, grabbing at her face.

"It seems obvious that your education is still incomplete. Your ungrateful attitude toward the best accommodations Alavon offers His women is, frankly, revolting. You will start again from scratch—this time, from within the confines of a cell. Perhaps that will be more to your liking." Olivio motioned to the two nearest golden guards. "Get her out of my sight. Now."

The men moved quickly and decisively, picking Yeuma up and moving her with ease. As they whisked her off the stage, she struck fruitlessly at the chest of one of the armored guards with her bare fists.

Daryn wasn't sure how long the rest of the ceremony lasted. He didn't pay attention to a single second after that. A preserver approached Olivio and whispered something to him—within seconds, he had abandoned the stage and begun to head directly for the exit without waiting for his attender to follow.

Olivio's shuttle had already taken off by the time Daryn got outside, so he was forced to fly back to the Altar in the smaller and significantly less luxurious guard shuttle. Despite the lack of amenities to which he had become so accustomed, the ride back wasn't overly different from those with Olivio. Daryn sat mostly in silence and stared out the window at the clusters of lights that transformed and painted the Alavonian surface by night. They reminded him of the vocay fish in the Altar's fountain in terms of how they seemed to transform something utterly boring and ordinary into a living piece of art. For a second, an image of the purple lights from that night on Oballe so many years ago rushed into his head, but he shook it off. Thinking about that day caused more anxiety than he was capable of dealing with right now.

* * *

His anxiety returned like a gushing tidal wave the second the shuttle touched down at the Altar's hangar. He made his way out, following the gold-clad soldiers in front of him. Daryn said some half-sincere words of thanks and quickly took off at a jog toward the elevator that would take him to Olivio's quarters. He shut the door behind him and activated the retina scanner, which flashed green after scanning his eye for a second or two. The elevator shifted into motion. Now that the sun had set, it was significantly more comfortable inside. The familiar, periodic electric shock-type feeling shot through him as his heart rate accelerated.

When the doors opened, he stepped out as quickly as he could and made his way to the massive door that led to Olivio's chambers. As always, two golden guards stood outside of it. They moved aside as Daryn approached, allowing him access to inside. He stepped in quickly.

"Oliv—"

But the room was empty. At the back of the room, The Hand's massive bed with gold-threaded sheets sat undisturbed and perfectly made. The white marble floor, which was polished daily, was as shiny and spotless as ever. The case on the nightstand by the bed that held Olivio's gauntlet was still open, revealing the empty socket. The large, one-way, triple-reinforced glass that surrounded the room was covered in the usual white drapes with gold trim. Olivio hadn't been there yet; the window would have been open.

Daryn exited the room, sighed, and jogged over to the only other place where he'd possibly find The Hand at this hour. He arrived at the conference room door, which he opened slowly. He could hear the old man's voice coming from inside. Olivio fell silent and turned to look at Daryn as he stood in the doorway, before motioning him inside. Another electric jolt of anxiety shot through his body as Olivio pointed to a chair at the far end of the extravagant golden conference table. Daryn just nodded and walked over to it.

On the screen at the front of the room was one of the five priests, though Daryn couldn't quite remember which one. They rarely came by the Altar, so he didn't get much of an opportunity to match faces with names. There was something unnerving about this man in particular; whenever Olivio spoke, the priest kept smiling in a way that made Daryn deeply uncomfortable. The priest seemed to be in the middle of a snowstorm in the dark of night. A bright white light coated the yellow-skinned man and the ship in the background.

"Twenty-three? Are you sure?"

Olivio interlaced his hands under his chin and rested his elbows on the table.

"That's what the red brute tells me, my dear Hand. Thirteen from Izrok, and ten from all the others combined."

"No women?"

"Not in the camps. Their bodies were even less resistant to the cold than the men's. Not that it matters, you said it would be a male."

Daryn began to fidget with his hands. He couldn't blame them for not making it; Oballe was not a pleasant place.

Olivio dropped his hand onto the table gently. "It will be. When you find him, you will send him to me. Is that understood, Pertinax?"

For Daryn, this at least solved the brief mystery of which priest this was.

Pertinax nodded profusely in an almost exaggerated manner. "Of course, my dear Hand. We will proceed later in the morning. I will have my findings for you by afternoon."

In the background of the shot, the vessel's ramp lowered.

"Please ensure that you do. Unless you would like to be reassigned to V'otarr, I would suggest placing careful emphasis on your punctuality."

Pertinax began to shake his head wildly as a strange look of fear flashed into his eyes. "That won't be necessary, my Hand. You will have my report before the planet's sun sets."

Olivio leaned back in his chair and crossed his arms. "You are aware that Oballe is dark for three quarters of the day, correct?"

Pertinax chuckled nervously as two golden guards came down the ramp in the background of the shot, each escorting what looked to be a prisoner. One of them looked as though he had tried to dress himself like a forest. Daryn found this to be an atrocious fashion choice, as well as an unbelievably stupid one given that he was surrounded by snow. It was hard to tell from this angle, but his light brown skin tone meant that he was either a Joxun or an Erub. The other foreigner, who seemed to be struggling against his captors still, was dressed in a dark jacket with a white shirt underneath; this attire couldn't have been anywhere near warm enough for that climate. He was speaking rather loudly and could be heard in the background.

"It's been years since I've seen the snow. You guys are so thoughtful! Are we gonna build some fucking igloos? We should make it a competition! Gold buff dudes against me and 'camo boy.' Who says no?"

Daryn caught a glimpse of blond hair just before the man exited the frame, but ultimately, it was unnecessary. The Ayr were the only race who wore those ridiculous orange goggles. From what he had heard, they were essentially blind without them when off their home planet.

"I was told you were only transporting the Rebel Queen's brother. Who is the Ayr?" Olivio raised his right eyebrow as he finished his question.

For a second, Pertinax looked in the direction from which the Ayr had exited. He then turned back to the camera. "We. . . we are unsure at the moment, my great Hand. He was caught on approach to the planet, so the current assumption is that he's some sort of spy. Attempts to question him have been unsuccessful, however, as he has confessed."

"I don't understand. That sounds successful to me."

"He's confessed to literally everything we've accused him of, my Hand. I have trouble believing that this man is a spy, a deserter, an assassin, and a magician."

Olivio shook his head. "I assume you're going to give me a good reason why he's still alive."

"We're concerned that he may actually be someone of relative importance. No one simply passes by this part of the galaxy for no reason. We plan to put him in the Western Block and handle him once the holy ceremony is complete tomorrow."

Olivio nodded. "I will leave the Ayr's fate up to you. It's the Erub I care about."

"Yes. We will handle him as well. It seems he and his sister are very close; from everything I've heard. Shouldn't prove overly difficult to twist her arm."

"Well, I will leave you to it then."

"My Hand, one last thing, if you don't mind. What is the current status on Feralla? I haven't received any updates of our progress from the front."

Olivio remained silent for a few seconds before responding. "The Carine have proven to be a . . . difficult bunch. They have rejected every one of my offers to assimilate with the Chosen army and have been resisting our invasion efforts more successfully than either the Dom'Rai or the Quexians. In the past few weeks, I have been forced to direct more of our military power to the system than I feel comfortable with. Consequently, it is imperative that you return to the Erub home world as soon as possible and secure control of it. It will be a few months before we can break through those thick forests and get any meaningful backup your way. You still have the fleet. Utilize it as you see fit."

Pertinax nodded and began speaking again, now considerably more serious. "I must admit that I am a bit concerned about the lack of a significant military presence on Oballe. The idea of having to rely exclusively on my holy guard makes me slightly uncomfortable."

"Pertinax, we control the only weapons on the planet, as well as the only people healthy and skilled enough to use them. A large military presence is hardly a priority on a planet where the only potential threat to us is constantly dropping dead with no effort on our part whatsoever."

Pertinax said nothing for a few seconds and allowed his unnerving smile to return. "I will speak to you soon, my dear Hand. I look forward to delivering the news we have been awaiting."

"Farewell, Pertinax. May Alavon guide you."

The screen cut to black, and Daryn's anxiety suddenly sputtered back to life as Olivio turned in his chair to face him. The Hand sighed deeply and then stood.

"I apologize for leaving you. I received word in the middle of the ceremony that Pertinax needed to speak with me urgently, so I had to get back here as soon as possible. I trust the journey in the guard shuttle wasn't overly uncomfortable."

Daryn shook his head. "No . . . it was fine."

Olivio motioned for him to stand. "Walk with me. We have much to discuss regarding today's events."

Daryn gulped and rose from his chair. Olivio exited the room, and Daryn followed quickly.

VII

JAKOB KOSS
EASTERN BLOCK, CAMP IZROK
OBALLE

The frigid winds of the Oballian night whipped at his face as the gold-plated guards continued to push him forward in the ankle-high snow. A storm had kicked up and flakes the size of coins were pelting all three of them mercilessly. He could do nothing now but hope with every fiber of his being that his big blue friend would make it through the night.

The time for planning had passed even before it had truly arrived; nothing short of a literal miracle would spare him from his fate with the knife now. With death being pretty much a certainty at this point, it was worth doing something. Anything.

Patience, Jakob.

He continued to stumble clumsily through the snow until the outline of his apparent destination began to materialize in front of him. Another barracks. The black one. He passed it every day on his way to and from his assigned post. He had never seen anyone enter, nor leave it.

One guard held Jakob's hands behind his back while the other unlocked and opened the door. The twenty or so seconds of standing still in the freezing downpour were worse than the entire time he'd spent in motion; at least then the action of walking had provided some warmth. He could feel the icy water accumulating in his jet-black hair, and he shook his head slightly to clear it. With the final turn of a key and the entry of a code into a number pad, the door swung open. He was shoved over the threshold and then roughly thrust inside a pitch-black room. At least there had been flood lights outdoors. Inside, there was no chance of seeing anything at all once the door was shut. For the time being, only a small portion of the wall directly in front of him was illuminated and, even then, only faintly.

The guards suddenly shifted their positions. The one to his left moved away from him, his partner replacing his grip on Jakob's left arm with his own. A second later, Jakob could feel something sharp just barely grazing his back, and the sound of ripping fabric made his heart sink. They were stripping him down. This could mean only one thing.

Hang on. I will do what I can for you.

The cheap, scratchy material that had served as a shirt dropped unceremoniously into the darkness. A second later, his pants came off with the aid of an unnecessarily strong tug. He was now fully naked, and the men pushed him toward the section of the wall that the outside lights managed to illuminate. They motioned for him to place his hands on the wall in two distinct locations above his head.

"Why?"

Unsurprisingly, he received no answer. The familiar loud crack and subsequent low humming behind him caused his muscles to tense up instinctively.

Hold it. Embrace it. Funnel it directly into your soul.

He took a deep breath and closed his eyes as the first blow of the cane struck him across the back of his left leg. Unlike the stun batons, which were primarily aimed at subduing prisoners, the cane had been created with the sole purpose of inflicting as much pure, crippling pain as possible. It took less than a second for the burning sting to erupt, racing up his leg and burning through his nerve endings, agony sparking across his skin. He released all of his breath in a loud, pained gasp. It was hard to tell whether it was the room or his vision beginning to blacken; all he could see was a growing, pervading darkness.

This is your fuel. This is your reason.

Home. It wasn't the happiest nor most stable place, but it was where he had to go to now. It was the only way to endure.

A loud crack echoed through his ears.

He clenched his teeth as hard as he possibly could, but the slightest of whimpers still found its way through. His father gazing out the window, the glass battered by snowflakes. He didn't turn away, or even acknowledge his presence. Perhaps that was best. Even in the freedom of his own fantasy, his mother was nowhere to be seen.

Another crack.

He fell to his knees as his legs gave out.

The small house on the outskirts of the town had never been a particularly warm place in any sense of the word—but there was comfort in its coldness. He floated through the memory into the small room adjacent to the main hall and rose over the stacks of tattered novels and textbooks that surrounded the bundle of old blankets. The thin, sickly child held up a book that was almost larger than he was. His blue eyes scrolled smoothly from left to right and then back again. A small knock came at his window. The child turned to see the toothy grin of the neighbor girl. He smiled and waved at her as her smile faded into a look of genuine fear.

The door behind him slammed open roughly, hitting the wall next to it with incredible force.

He had made a mistake. He had been told so many times that no one was to see him. He was not supposed to exist. He deserved it. The father grabbed the child by the neck and flung him against the wall. The boy knew he would never grow to be that strong. Never. Food, shelter, and any sort of affection were wasted on him. His tiny existence would fade away someday, and no one would ever know, care, nor remember.

Once more, a crack.

As he lay on the floor, the child gazed up at his father's face. The miserable little insect of a Draekon was crying. Why? He should have learned to accept responsibility for his actions by now. He was stupid. He had no business existing in this world or any others. It was no wonder he was handed over to the strange yellow men on that loud, terrifying, and confusing night. The father had given his pathetic son up but was killed anyway. This made sense. Anyone would have been insulted by such a paltry offering.

The child had never been expected to survive inside the gates of Izrok.

Perhaps that is exactly why he did.

* * *

The wooden beams of the ceiling slowly melded into Jakob's view. His eyes had been open for a while, but he had only just now begun to process what he was seeing. Light was filtering in between the wooden planks, but it was still not enough to enable him to see adequately. He slowly rose into a sitting position as the pain in his legs returned. Though it wasn't nearly as bad as it had been during the initial impact, it still sat just below an intolerable level.

He looked around the room slowly; the door was shut, and the guards were gone. Realizing that he was still naked, he began to blindly feel around in the dark. He managed to find the tattered remains of his shirt, but they were useless. He breathed a small sigh of relief as he got a hold of his pants and struggled to get them on. He would take whatever small victories he could at this point. The cuts on the backs of his legs stung intensely as they made contact with the cheap, uncomfortable fabric.

He could hear creaking as footsteps moved around him in the dark. Instinctively, he stuck out a hand and ignited it, flooding the immediate area around it with a bright purple light. A pale face popped into view mere inches away. It made a noise and stumbled backwards, disappearing into the dark. Jakob sat up as straight as he could manage and swung his makeshift torch around the room. There were no bunks in here. In fact, it was completely empty, save for a multitude of pale figures sitting with their backs against the walls. He counted twenty-two of them, including the one who had approached him. Draekons. More than he had seen at one time in a single place in years, and they were all looking at him. Their faces were sunken and shallow, but their eyes opened wide at the sight of the light. Some looked borderline starved.

These men are shells of themselves. I shudder to think of what they have lived through.

The one who had originally approached him finally spoke up. Jakob couldn't remember the last time he'd heard the Draekonic tongue.

"How do you do that?"

Jakob gave no immediate answer.

The stranger swiped his long, unkempt bangs out of his eyes. He looked to be no older than fifteen, but then again, the camps had a way of slowing down the aging process in the most morbid way possible.

"Quiet one? Alright then. Name's Yaunie. Saw you all crumpled up on the floor when we first got shuffled in. What'd you do to get the cane? I'll take any gossip at this point."

"Nothing. I am friends with an Udul; so I assume M'og just enjoys making us both suffer for it."

Jakob ran a hand along his legs. It felt as though the bones within them were slowly breaking in half. He would not walk normally for a few days, at minimum.

"Ah, shit. Forgot about the whole Dom'Rai–Udul rivalry."

"I don't blame you. It's only several thousand years old and extremely well documented."

"Hey, come on now. I didn't exactly have access to history textbooks in Gauk."

Jakob furled his brow in confusion. "Gauk is a female camp."

Yaunie shook his head. "They started running too low on women. Had to start bringing men in to fill the empty spots. We last longer, I guess."

The implications of that are troubling, to say the least.

"The Draekon women?"

Yaunie tightened his lips and shook his head.

"None of them made it past year six or seven. At least not in Gauk. There were only about a hundred left in total when I got captured."

"You lasted six years on the outside?"

"I was sent by my mother to hide away with my uncle in the countryside, but he died before I could make it to him. Spent my days in an underground doomsday bunker. It was pretty cool, actually." He shot Jakob a smile that he didn't reciprocate.

There is something familiar about this young man, but I'm not quite sure what it is.

"Anyways, we lived happily with a community of about twenty people for a good while. We eventually got discovered when one of our members got caught while out hunting and idiotically led the Alavites back to our base."

Jakob shook his head.

"Yep. He didn't make it long once we got to Gauk. Two weeks, I think. Tried to run and got a sword through the chest for his efforts. They did the eye thing on us when we arrived. They're really obsessed with that for some reason."

As interesting as this was, Jakob couldn't continue wasting precious hours listening to this guy's life story. "Do you have any Shaz training? Do you use it?"

Yaunie said nothing for a second, and then he made a strained face as though he were concentrating extremely hard. In his hand, a small, faint purple ball appeared, which he promptly threw at a nearby wall. It splattered against it like a small water balloon, sending streaks of neon-purple goop all over the wall. Some of the other prisoners looked up. Others continued staring down at the floor. None of them had made a single sound this entire time. "Not exactly going to fight off an army with that. Though it actually tastes pretty good."

Jakob narrowed his eyes at him.

Yaunie chuckled uncomfortably. "You'd probably better rest up while you can. We've got a big day today, so it seems. They already tested me in Gauk, and I didn't pass; so, I don't exactly expect a miracle. I wonder if it'll be fun to die."

Jakob looked away from him and toward the other prisoners.

"Don't bother trying to start a conversation with anyone else in here. None of them are very talkative. Trust me; I've tried."

Yes. These poor souls do not even seem to know what planet they are on.

"I assume we'll be meshing with the rest tomorrow for the ceremony."

Yaunie's face dropped as Jakob finished his sentence.

"Oh. You don't know."

Jakob raised an eyebrow.

"This is it. What you're looking at is the full remnants of the Draekon population on Oballe, and, given how lovingly isolated we were forced to be, likely in the entire galaxy as well."

Unfortunately, from what I can detect, the boy is right.

There would be a time to properly evaluate this information and let it sink in, but that time wasn't now. Actually, unless he had missed some major news, this bit of information wasn't completely accurate.

"Well, this isn't *all* of us."

Yaunie inhaled deeply and nodded. "Right. I guess that much is true."

A loud pounding on the door made almost everyone jump. Before Jakob knew it, an enormous and overpowering amount of sunlight flooded into the dark room, forcing him to both squint and recoil. It was difficult to make out what he was looking at. He saw four silhouettes. One, which had a good four inches of height over the rest, was unmistakably M'og. Two appeared to be golden guards, based on how much light was reflecting off them. Whether they were the same ones who had beaten him the night before, he didn't know.

Heavy, metallic-sounding footsteps entered the room, and out of the corner of his eye, Jakob could see the sitting Draekons being roughly pulled up and dragged out by the guards. As his eyes finally adjusted, he was able to make out the last figure, who was barking orders in a voice that was a strangely high-pitched. He didn't have much time to analyze the situation before he was roughly grabbed and pulled toward the door.

* * *

The next half hour seemed to pass by in an instant. The group traveled in relative silence to the same clearing that had been used since this demented practice had started. Every hobbled footstep was even more miserable than the last. The sky was clear today, and the sun was shining, which started to work toward melting the snow. Unfortunately, enough was still left to make the trip yet another cold and wet one. This didn't bother Jakob; his pain was too distracting.

As they got closer, they had to maneuver through the crowd of prisoners in a lane formed by a chain of golden guards. Jakob tried to stop whenever he could to look around for Zhaden, Koomer, or any other member of his barracks crew, but he was roughly shoved from behind each time.

The Draekons were made to line up in the clearing like pieces on a game board. It was jarring for Jakob as he looked to his left and right to see how little of the huge space they actually managed to take up. The opening had been designed to fit hundreds of people, but there were only twenty-three of them.

It took a good ten minutes for the priest to place them in the exact positions that he wanted them to be in: two horizontal lines of eight and one of seven. Jakob ended up in the sixth spot in the third row, with Yaunie taking the final position on his right. Once the priest was satisfied with the setup, he gave the guards a signal, and the Draekons were forcefully pushed down onto their knees. Given his recent trauma, Jakob was unable to put up any sort of resistance and collapsed almost pathetically onto the ground.

The priest turned to address the crowd. The way the man smiled infuriated Jakob for some reason.

I cannot stand this spineless cretin.

"Good morning, inmates! Today, we fulfill the promise our people made to the Great Alavon Acivorai before his tragic and horrifying death at the hands of the wicked Draekon Queen. I don't need to explain how this goes at this point, I assume."

He stopped, as though expecting applause. The only thing to be heard was the sound of the wind.

"Very well. Unlike the rest of you, my life plans do not involve this decrepit planet; so, let us begin so as to get this over with as soon as possible. A new day dawns tomorrow. I look forward to welcoming you all to it."

And, with that, it began—the moment Jakob had been dreading for ten years. He had imagined this scenario countless times, to the point where he could visualize every single fleeting second—usually with minor variations in details, such as the weather. As the first kneeling Draekon faced inspection, it occurred to Jakob just how anticlimactic and disappointing the reality would actually be compared to the dramatic image that he had created in his mind.

A rejection. The priest moved on to the next. Jakob found it morbidly ironic that today of all days was one of the sunniest, warmest, and clearest that the camp had seen in months. With such a tragic, inhumane, and undeniably evil event unfolding, how could the sun just look on and continue to beam down its warmth so complicitly? Where were the clouds? Where was the rain to show solidarity with the tragedy that was about to occur?

It seems there truly are no gods. Or perhaps they all died long ago.

Jakob continued to stare straight ahead for what felt like only a few minutes but must have been significantly longer. The priest had now begun to inspect his row. In his various visualizations of this moment, Jakob had wondered whether he would be nervous, angry, or even scared. As the robed Alavite proceeded with his seventeenth and eighteenth consecutive rejection, Jakob realized that the answer was none of the above. He felt an encompassing, drastically inappropriate sense of calm and understanding. Nineteenth rejection. Nearly time. He decided to take one last glance at the crowd, and then he saw him. Zhaden. He was being aided by Koomer and another inmate from the barracks. They both stood almost entirely straight under each of his arms and seemed to be attempting to prop him up. Jakob had been searching for the horn and the blue skin. The former was now gone, replaced by a massive, dark-purple wound that seemed to have been cauterized fairly poorly.

Twenty, rejection.

A fire of rage erupted from deep within Jakob, slaughtering the calmness he had been cultivating up to this point. He clenched his fists with a painful amount of force.

Twenty-one, rejection.

I am with you, Jakob. Always.

The priest walked in front of him in his pristine white-and-gold sandals and stared him down as his long silver hair whipped in the wind. Jakob met and silently challenged his gaze, just as he had with M'og. The Alavite stopped for a few seconds longer than he had done when inspecting the others. A faint ringing filled Jakob's ears as the priest took a step forward and put a hand onto his forehead. The Alavite gazed into his eyes back and forth and then back again for several more seconds.

"No." He pushed Jakob's head back roughly and began to turn toward Yaunie.

No?

Just as it had the night before, Jakob's body reacted on its own. In spite of the crippling pain and severity of such an action, he rose to his feet. He did so without so much as a single thought. Audible murmurs came from the crowd, which had suddenly woken up. From what he could see in his peripheral vision, it seemed as though several of the kneeling Draekons were turning to look at him as well. He glanced down at his arms, which suddenly felt strange. Bright purple flames now ran from the tip of his fingers to around his elbow on each arm.

"Ooh, I do so love when they decide to play hero. It is so ador-"

The priest stopped suddenly and dramatically, as he finished turning to face Jakob. An unmistakable look of not only fear, but also pure terror flashed across the old man's face.

There it is: the rat behind the smirk.

Jakob could hear the footsteps of a guard approaching from behind, and he braced himself to feel the sting of the electric rod. But it never came. The priest shot out a hand, halting the guard before slowly stepping back over to Jakob. The crowd had gone silent again. The weight of hundreds of stares now rested on the rebellious Draekon's shoulders. His arms suddenly felt cold. He briefly glanced down to see they had returned to normal.

"Do you think I fear those cute little party tricks of yours?" The shaky tone of the priest's voice betrayed the confidence that he had attempted to portray with his words.

Jakob said nothing, and simply continued to stare the old man down.

Pertinax cleared his throat. "Take this one. We're going to the Western Block. Now."

Jakob felt the familiar sensation of two metal hands tightening around his arms. He finally broke his gaze for half a second to look at Yaunie, who was staring up at him wide-eyed.

Interesting. Have you ever known a purge to be cut short?

M'og, who had been standing off to the side, spoke loudly enough for the entire audience to hear. No microphone was necessary for him. "One left. No take, or yes?"

The priest stopped and turned to face the lone remaining Draekon. "Just . . . bring him too. I'll check him there. Let's go. Now."

It seems you have saved two lives today, at least for the time being.

The guard behind Yaunie lifted him violently and began to push him to join Jakob. The small group moved briskly out of the clearing.

The priest, who was following closely behind, turned back quickly to the guards standing over the kneeling Draekons. "Go ahead. Quickly."

Jakob let out a long and drawn-out breath as he heard the familiar medley of blades being drawn from their sheaths, followed closely by the all-too-familiar sound that defied description. The small thuds of bodies falling to the dirt floor served as the period to the horrifying sentence that the day's experience had been. As the pools of blood formed around the bodies, Jakob could do nothing but hope that their next lives would be better ones.

The Western Block was on the other side of the camp, giving Jakob plenty of time to process what had just occurred. It took a few minutes, but the familiar hissing whoosh did eventually come. He didn't care whether he got punished or not. He turned to look and caught a glimpse of the beautiful purple spires rocketing into the sky. Twenty-one of them. It wasn't nearly as beautiful a sight during the day, but perhaps this was for the best. The more of a visual spectacle they were, the easier it was to forget their dark and twisted roots. His head was forcibly pushed forward before he could see the lights die out. He turned to look at Yaunie, who, surprisingly, had yet to say a word.

The group continued moving in silence for a few more minutes. It was refreshing to finally get a break from the priest's babbling.

Jakob looked down at his legs. He only now noticed that they no longer pained him in any significant way. It took at least a week for most people to recover from a cane strike. For some reason, Jakob could manage a full recovery in under a day. It was perhaps one of the reasons he had not been selected for the ceremony in the previous decade.

You are not like the rest of them; you should know that by now.

Two golden guards were at the ready and held the door of the prison open for the group as they entered. The two-story building wasn't exceptionally huge, and it didn't need to be. Only about one or two hundred prisoners were kept here at a time, according to Koomer.

Much like at the black barracks the night before, Jakob was tossed into a cell. As he was about to turn around, he felt a sharp stabbing sensation on the right side of his neck and immediately fell to the floor. He was unable to control his motions as his body spasmed painfully. All he could do was continue to stare in the direction in which his head happened to be facing, directly into Yaunie's cell. There might as well have been a mirror on that wall, as his fellow Draekon was jerking and twitching on the floor as well.

As he finally managed to rise into a seated position, Jakob could slowly make out what sounded like fourteen different conversations going on at once. The voice of the priest also echoed from somewhere outside the cell: "Get me The Hand. What? Well leave a message for him, then. Yes. Urgent. Category five."

Jakob turned his gaze to look directly through the bars of his cell door. Evidently, he and Yaunie were being watched this entire time, though not by the priest nor his guards. Three men in consecutive cells—an Ayr, an Erub, and a Zantavi—were staring at him. Jakob wasn't sure how long it had been since he had seen an Ayr who had been allowed to keep his virix goggles in the camps. Maybe things worked differently in the Western Block. Only the Zantavi was wearing the actual prison garments. The other two must have been new. The Ayr spoke first in a surprisingly upbeat and confident tone.

"These fuckers really like their stun pricks, huh? You guys look like shit."

That may well prove to be the understatement of the year.

VIII

CORVUS-JORG (CJ) DROC
WESTERN BLOCK, CAMP IZROK
OBALLE

He rolled his eyes.

CJ had known Tom for a grand total of about six hours, and he was already thoroughly annoyed every time the Ayr opened his mouth.

"Can you just . . . not? Just once? Can you please just shut up?"

Tom crossed his arms and made a strange noise that sounded like a gasp. "I'm just trying to get a conversation rolling. If we're going to be here for a while, I'd at least like to make some friends."

CJ raised an eyebrow. "You really think prison is the right place to do that?"

"Oh, my bad. I forgot that us dirty common folk are too far below you to even warrant interacting with."

"That's not . . . ugh." CJ was already deeply regretting sharing anything about his past with him.

"I'll have you know that some of the realest and most genuine people in the galaxy are on the wrong side of a cell."

"Exactly how many times have you found yourself in prison, again?"

"I didn't realize you wanted my full life story. I'll give you the exclusive interview, but it'll cost ya."

CJ exhaled and knocked his head lightly against the bars. The sooner he could get farther than a few feet away from this jackass, the better.

The Draekon in the cell in front of them continued staring ahead in a curiously analytical fashion, as though he were taking everything in before preparing his response. The other one was lying face down in the cell next to him and looked to have not yet recovered from the stun prick. He was unsure what exactly the guards had done to them before they had been brought here, and he wasn't overly eager to find out.

The awkward stare-down continued for a few seconds until CJ cleared his throat. "I'm CJ, and—"

"Come on! That's no fun. Tell him your full name. We're all friends here."

He rolled his eyes slowly and shot a side glance at Tom, who had eagerly pressed himself up to the bars between their two cells.

"Technically, my full name is Corvus Jo—"

A loud, poorly restrained chuckle came from his right. "Fucking Corvus . . . Your parents hated you, dude."

Tom had given him a similar reaction in the Alavite vessel. In both instances, he had a solid wall of steel to thank for keeping his face intact. Once again, CJ turned fully to the mouthy Ayr, whose face twisted into a small, arrogant smirk. The silver phoenix at the end of his necklace swung back and forth gently. He continued speaking to the Draekon but kept his eyes on Tom.

"This is Tom. I don't know his last name, and I don't care to."

"Ezekiel. You could have asked. If we're going to be friends, we should know these things, Corvie." Tom leaned to his right, up against the front bars of his cell.

"You know what-"

"Jakob." The Draekon's voice sounded strained.

CJ nodded and refocused his attention away from Tom.

"I saw much more than I would have expected from a traditional prison when we were walked in. What is this place?"

The Draekon stared at him as though he were looking into his very soul. There was a strange sadness to his eyes, but also an unmistakable anger. He said nothing.

The conversation, which seemed destined to die in awkward silence, was suddenly brought back to life by the man in the cell to the left.

"Don't expect either of them to be too talkative. They've had a pretty rough day, if I heard the guards right."

The Zantavi had already been here when he and Tom had arrived, but he hadn't spoken a single word until now. It had been the first time that CJ had seen one of their kind in person. The man's light-pink pupils, nestled in white irises, contrasted sharply with the ebony-colored skin that wrapped his body. His curly dreadlocked hair, whiter than the sand on any beach on Erub, would probably have been about shoulder length were it not tied back. He was in exceptionally good shape for someone who was presumably locked in a cell for the majority of the day.

"You understand Alavic?"

The Zantavi shrugged and walked up closer to the bars to get a better look at Jakob before responding. "You meet a lot of people when you're part of a royal family. You learn how to speak their language—both literally and figuratively."

"You the Zantavi king I hear so much about?" Tom's voice came from CJ's right.

The man moved over slightly in his cell to look past CJ and get a better view of Tom.

"No. I am his son, though."

CJ's eyes widened.

"Robert Josso. . . Your name has been all over the international news! You were reported kidnapped years ago. Have you been here the whole time?"

"Most of it."

CJ was expecting a longer answer, but he didn't get it. "I suppose the Alavites like their princes, then. We're more alike than you know, Robert."

"Most people just call me Josso. It's what I tend to prefer." It was hard to tell in the dim light, but it seemed that the prince had shot CJ the slightest of winks.

Tom sounded as though he were about to interject with yet another of his unsolicited comments, but he stopped himself abruptly as heavy metallic footsteps approached from down the hall. Jakob, meanwhile, stayed perfectly still, his face giving away no indication of fear or distress.

Aside from knowing that they existed, CJ wasn't sure he had ever had a significant thought about Draekons before. Yet, he somehow found himself unable to look away from Jakob's pale and sunken face.

Two golden guards flanked Pertinax as he approached from the left. The guards went to work unlocking the cell next to Jakob's, where the other Draekon still lay motionless. While they fiddled with the lock, the priest took a few steps over toward CJ's cell.

"I'll be right back with you as soon as I get my agenda taken care of for today. We have a lot of fun times in store, I assure you. I would have preferred to have your sister here, but I'm sure I'll learn enough about her through you."

There was that smile again. CJ said nothing and looked away from Pertinax as the old man spun slowly to face his more immediate concerns.

Within the cell adjacent to Jakob's, one of the guards had lifted and turned the other Draekon around. The poor guy looked to be barely conscious. Evidently, some people had more resistance to the effects of the prick than others.

To CJ's surprise, the Draekon actually rose to his feet slowly as they entered.

Pertinax pulled a small box from within his robes. He began to chant in Alavic as he opened it, holding his right hand up with his fingers spaced apart. What looked to be several pieces of metal hovered out of the box slowly and attached themselves to his fingers. After about a minute, the shards had formed what seemed to be a makeshift glove.

CJ let out a slight gasp as he noticed the Draekon's once-blue eyes had become entirely neon purple. His pupils were nowhere to be seen, at least not from this distance. Pertinax seemed a bit alarmed by this as well, as he took a sudden half-step backward and turned to the guard on the left, as if unsure of how he should proceed. Jakob opened his mouth, but the voice that escaped it was too deep and booming to be his own.

"Look at me, you cockroach."

Pertinax's head shot back in the Draekon's direction. The priest hesitated for a second, apparently caught off guard by Jakob's boldness, before stepping back towards him slowly. It was hard to see what was happening from his angle, as Pertinax's back was blocking Jakob entirely from CJ's view. The priest looked down at the metal fragments on his hand. Jakob's strange, almost demonic voice spoke up again, this time in a language entirely foreign to CJ.

"Vidi foaci coama ful! Coama ful!"

Pertinax moved quickly and erratically. His hand raced downward, presumably onto Jakob's face. Almost instantly, the entire hallway was flooded in a blinding purple light, the intensity of which continued to grow until CJ was forced to avert his eyes and turn around.

"FUCK!"

Tom whipped off his virix and covered his eyes with his hands.

Even with his eyes protected, CJ's vision was totally overwhelmed. Screams and groans from other nearby prisoners rang through his ears.

Pertinax began to chant, though his voice was shaky. "*Shaevero balavili. Carmona foati. Deblara coumi Alavon. Deblara coumi viri vi . . .*"

He kept repeating this over and over, sounding increasingly frustrated. Suddenly, the same odd deep voice from earlier filled CJ's ears again. It had boomed loudly the first time, but its volume now rose to such an unnaturally high level that it seemed to shake the very foundation of the prison.

"*Calgara montavi moro Sai! Da fa verat. Sira monvolara sai!*"

A high-pitched scream more primal and horrifying than any CJ had ever heard erupted from the cell that was now to his rear. It went on for several agonizing seconds before going out with a loud and sickening pop.

Then it was over. The screaming was gone. The darkness behind his eyelids took over once more as the light vanished. CJ slowly opened his eyes and whipped around.

Pertinax and both golden guards lay crumpled on the floor of the cell. The priest's head was missing entirely from his shoulders, and the variety of the blood spatter around the corpse gave a definitive, albeit horrifying, answer as to what had happened. Jakob stood alone in the cell . . . or, at least, CJ assumed that it was him. The Draekon's arms and upper chest had become entirely consumed in what looked to be bright purple flames, which had sculpted themselves into blade-like formations near his hands and forearms.

Jakob looked straight at him and spoke in a voice that sounded like a hybrid of his own and the one that had rung through the room a few minutes ago. "Can you fight?"

CJ was still trying to comprehend what he had just seen and was currently looking at. All he could do was nod. Too many thoughts and questions were running through his mind; yet he couldn't get his brain to focus on any of them. Jakob stepped out of the cell and swung his left arm at the lock on CJ's cell door, destroying it almost effortlessly.

A voice came from his right. "So, I guess I'll go ahead and speak for all of us: what the fuck just happened?"

Tom had such an elegant way with words sometimes.

Jakob stepped over to him. A purple imprint of each of his last few footsteps followed him closely, leaving a small trail behind him.

The Draekon looked directly at Tom as he stood in front of his cell. "You said you get along well with prisoners, even violent ones?"

Tom nodded. "Oh yeah. These are my kinds of people."

"Good. Help them all out. We're taking this place."

"Yeah . . . uh, yeah. I can do that. I need my daggers, though. Not looking to get my ass beaten down without a fair fight. I don't have a problem with an unfair one, but only if I'm the one with the upper hand."

Josso pulled up to the front bars of his cell. "Confiscated weapons and materials are in the basement. They stay there for a few days before the guards take them to the main collection building at the camp. There's also a small armory down there. We can use it to arm some of these guys. I can lead the way."

Jakob nodded, sliced Tom's lock, and then quickly freed Josso as well. Both newly liberated men took off down the hall toward the basement. The entire block was in an uproar, with every prisoner pleading for his freedom, screaming, or yelling some form of obscenity.

CJ turned to face Jakob. This was his chance. "What . . . what are you? What's the plan? What . . . just what?" The series of questions had been much more coherent in his head.

The dark blue pupil that had been only barely visible before was now nowhere to be found in Jakob's new purple eyes. It was hard to tell whether the Draekon was looking directly at him or not. The drastic change in his voice was jarring, but CJ figured there would be a better time to discuss this.

"We can't waste this opportunity. The bulk of Olivio's army should be in the Feralla system dealing with the Carine; that gives us a few weeks at minimum."

Jakob began to move, but CJ placed a hand on his lower chest, stopping him. The heat coming off the Draekon's arms was so intense that he was forced to withdraw his hand quickly. Jakob turned and looked at him. His decidedly neutral expression gave little away.

"I'm going to level with you, Jakob. I can't die here. I'm needed back at home. My sister needs me. My own people need me. I promised her I'd make it back outside of a body bag, and I don't have . . . whatever the hell this is." He gestured at Jakob's arms.

The Draekon stared through him. "I can't promise you that you won't die today if you fight, but I can guarantee you will never leave this planet if you try to run."

There was an awkward silence between them.

CJ would have felt angry at the loosely veiled threat, but ultimately, he understood. He would demand the same if the roles were reversed. If he did die, he'd go knowing that Sheressa would hunt Jakob down until her dying day, demonic sword arms be damned. He nodded once to show his understanding.

Jakob turned toward the cell that the other Draekon was in. He was now not only conscious, but also on his feet and holding what appeared to be a bright purple ball in each hand, which he quickly threw at his cell door; they hit two bars and splattered against the rest. A loud sizzling sound emanated from the glowing purple goop, and a few seconds later, the bars melted and fell apart. At this point, CJ had simply resigned himself to accept whatever was happening. Clearly, nothing was going to make sense today.

The second Draekon held up his left hand to his face and inspected it.

He said something to Jakob in Draekonic, Draekonian, or whatever their language was called. Jakob seemed to cut him off, but it was hard to tell without knowing the language. He began pointing—or rather, aiming the tip of his arm-sword—at the wall at the back of his cell.

The other Draekon nodded and created a new ball to replace the one that he had already thrown. With full force, he launched this one at the back of the now-empty cell. Jakob walked over to the goop as it was still dripping down the wall. He then gave the wall a strong kick, knocking almost the entire affected portion out of the back of the building and filling the cell with light.

Without another word, he took off running, and the other Draekon followed. The loudest alarm that CJ had ever heard went off almost as soon as the second Draekon stepped out, causing CJ to jump.

He covered his ears as he started for the stairwell that led to the basement, running past what felt like a thousand pleading faces and hands. He sighed just slightly as he made it to the stairwell that led to the lower level of the prison. For a second, he considered abandoning everything and running for it, consequences be damned, but something stopped him. He turned and looked back at the inmates in the cells. This could have easily been Erub; hell, the Alavites were already on the damn planet. If the roles had been reversed and Sheressa had been locked in a place like this . . .

A strange surge of anger and determination swelled within him. He took the first step onto the stairwell, followed by the many that came after as his stomach began to yearn for Alavite blood.

IX

DARYN PERIC
THE EYE, ALAVONIA CITY
ALAVONIA

Two golden guards flanked him as he proceeded through the impeccably clean and organized prison. Daryn would never have imagined himself walking through a place like this—one filled to the brim with dangerous and unhinged criminals. The walls and floors were sculpted entirely out of bright, reflective steel, allowing him to see the white reflection of his robes whenever he glanced down.

The small rooms that served as cells in this prison were eerily similar to those that Daryn had seen at a pet shelter a few years ago when he'd accompanied Olivio to its grand opening. It left those within the cells fully exposed at all times in an almost voyeuristic way. The Holy Alavonian Correctional Facility's nickname—"The Eye"—could not possibly have been more appropriate.

As Daryn crossed the threshold into the women's section of The Eye, he found himself shielding his eyes quite frequently. Something about having a perpetual unobstructed view of the women, who could potentially be in compromising positions, made him extremely uncomfortable.

A strong, metal-clad arm clamped his shoulder lightly. As he had been shielding his eyes this entire time, he hadn't noticed that he had almost walked right by his sister's cell. He thanked the guard who held him as the other entered the security code into the door, which took a surprisingly long time to unlock.

Yeuma sat at the edge of her bed in the brightly lit room. Her hair, which had been so long and beautiful at the ceremony a few days ago, had been buzzed to a length even shorter than his own. It was a jarring and somewhat depressing sight. He walked over to her and sat down on an uncomfortable and cold metal chair about a foot away from the bed.

"Are you here because you want to be here, or because he sent you?"

She crossed her arms and leaned back against the metal wall. The orange hue of the prison jumpsuit was rather unflattering on Alavite skin.

"I wanted to. I could have chosen not to come, and honestly, I shouldn't have. What were you thinking? Do you know what kind of damage you've done to me and my position?"

Her amber eyes widened, and a look of disgust came over her face as she shook her head slightly, never breaking eye contact. "Daryn, the man hit me across the face with that metal glove! He assaulted me, your sister, on stage in front of thousands of people. What warped version of reality do you live in for you to say I'm the bad guy here? Like, are you fucking kidding me?"

Here she went again—always trying to pull the family card to excuse being the way she was. An odd, low rumbling began to echo through the cell.

"You can't keep doing this to me. You knew exactly what you were doing on that stage. Not that it was evidently very well thought out. I just don't understand you or your thought process sometimes."

She rolled her eyes. "I love you, Daryn; I honestly do. But all this time at that old man's side has made you forget who your real family is. Do you see this?" She leaned towards him and grabbed at his robe. "This is not who you are. Your purpose in life is more than just to kiss Olivio's glove. It has to be."

The rumbling grew louder. Daryn found himself struggling to focus on his sister's words.

"I'm not going to spend the rest of my life slaving away just to gain approval from old men in dresses. That's just not who I am, and you damn well know that."

He nodded solemnly. He did know. He always had. Even if she hadn't caused a scene at the ceremony, she would have almost inevitably done something equivalent to whichever man she worked under.

"I guess I should have seen it coming when you started throwing tiny fists at the preserver when you were first taken to the convent."

She smiled. It took Daryn some effort to avoid smiling back.

"Old bitch hit me with a ruler more times than I can remember. Didn't beat the fight out of me, though." She chuckled.

He nodded. "No. No, she didn't. But that fight is going to put you on the street . . . and that's if you're lucky."

Her smile evaporated. "Daryn, I would rather live five more years digging my food out of dumpsters than live for fifty the way women do here. I'm glad kissing up to Olivio for all these years worked out for you, but things didn't exactly go to my liking."

Daryn shook his head and gestured at the entire room. "Well, clearly."

She chuckled, which caught him by surprise. He didn't understand what was so funny.

"If you really have such a warped perception of me now that you think I did everything I did without a plan . . . well, there's a lot more catching up to do than I thought."

"Wha—" Daryn started to say but was interrupted by a loud clack from above their heads. He shot his head toward the origin of the sound, which seemed to be the back wall of the cell.

He looked back down at his sister, who was grinning ear to ear.

"Making friends on the outside while you're in the convent isn't easy, but it also isn't impossible."

The low rumbling that had been annoying Daryn this entire time suddenly and violently erupted into a loud, blaring roar. The two golden guards standing outside jumped at the sound and turned to look at him through the glass.

He whipped his head back toward Yeuma and began to say something, but he was interrupted by a loud creaking noise coming from the wall. Daryn could hear the guards starting the unlocking process, but it would still take time. He had no idea what was happening.

"What is that?!" He yelled over the noise.

Yeuma continued to smile smugly, and with a quick nod of her head, she directed him to look back at the wall. The horrific screech had now transitioned into a full high-pitched wail. Daryn thought his eyes were playing games with him at first, but as he continued to stare, it became clear what was happening. The wall was bending into a concave shape.

Daryn began to turn his head back to his sister, when a loud crack made him jump to his feet. A rush of cool night air swept across his face; the wall he had just been staring at had been ripped right out of the back of the prison. He heard what sounded like a rope snapping and, several seconds later, a loud faraway crash several stories below. The building's alarms began blasting at full volume, and the lights in the cell and hallway began to flash. He stepped cautiously toward the opening and looked out into the night sky. Three large neon-green lights sat directly in his line of sight and grew larger and larger.

The golden guards, who would have been mere seconds away from opening the door, suddenly began banging on it heavily. Something was wrong with the lock.

The green lights grew increasingly closer until they were practically blinding, melding with the bright white light of the cell as the approaching ship's rear bridge opened and its ramp extended. A silhouette that seemed to be in the shape of a woman stood at its base, but it was impossible to make out any significant details.

Suddenly, Daryn felt hands cupping his face. He turned to Yeuma, who was staring into his eyes intently. "Daryn, listen to me. This is our chance. We have to leave. There are better places out there; there must be. As your sister, I'm asking you for once in your life to just please trust me."

Daryn couldn't think. He reached his hand up to his cheek, touching hers. He turned to look through the glass. Some of the prison's own security had taken over for the golden guards. They'd be in any second. He turned back to his sister.

"Yeuma, I . . ."

A female voice called out from the ship in Neatspeak. "We need to go NOW!"

Yeuma's eyes looked as desperate and sad as he'd ever seen them.

Daryn shook his head and withdrew. "I . . . I can't."

Yeuma sighed. "I guess my childhood wasn't the only thing that Olivio took from me."

She hugged him tightly, before turning for the ramp. It began to withdraw almost as soon as she stepped on it, forcing her to run up the length of it. As she reached the entrance of the ship, she turned to lock eyes with him for a few seconds before the door slammed shut, and the vessel began to move. Only two police flyers had arrived at the scene, but whoever was piloting the ship that Yeuma was on seemed to have little issue shaking them off. Daryn felt hands around his shoulders as he watched the green lights grow smaller and smaller in the distance. Soon, he couldn't tell them apart from stars that littered the night sky.

* * *

Daryn stared out the window of his shuttle as it headed back to the Altar. For a few seconds, he considered what would have happened if he had accepted his sister's offer. He wondered where she was headed, who had rescued her, and whether he would ever see her again. Through all of these thoughts, one that he would never share with anyone kept crawling back into his head: he was glad that she had escaped and would be able to live the rest of her life, however long that may be, somewhere other than in a cell.

It almost felt as though his life was traveling at triple speed. Before he knew it, he was in Olivio's chambers, sitting across from him in a luxurious white leather chair near a large open window that the old man liked to gaze out of during the evenings.

Olivio tapped his gauntlet on the windowsill, producing a small clanging sound each time. His eyes were facing the stars. "Did she mention where she was headed?"

Daryn shook his head.

"Daryn, do not lie to me." Olivio turned his head to look him straight on.

"She didn't say."

Olivio nodded. "Very well. We shall see what we can do to get her back. I'll do my best to do that for you."

Daryn almost spoke up. He wanted to say no—to leave her and let her be happy. He wanted to scream at Olivio to allow her the chance at the potentially fulfilling life that this place could never give her.

But he couldn't do it. He nodded slowly.

"I apologize for not accompanying you, but I find myself rarely having personal time anymore. Even my responsibilities are now overlapping. Pertinax tried to contact me during a meeting today, and I still haven't even been able to get a hold of him. In any case, The Fist should be wrapping up his mission and returning soon. Once he is back, I will—"

He was interrupted by the opening of the room's large golden door. An elderly preserver walked in. Daryn had seen her a few times around the Altar, but he was unsure of what her actual job was. She bowed as much as her frail body would allow.

"My Hand, I have urgent news for you."

Olivio stood slowly from his chair.

"I specifically requested that I remain undisturbed for the rest of the evening. Why have you entered my quarters uninvited at this hour?"

"Urgent message from the Izrok's warden on Oballe. Our brother Pertinax is dead."

Daryn wasn't sure he'd ever seen the expression Olivio currently bore on his face before. His mouth began to move as though to say something, but the elderly preserver beat him to it.

"From what I hear, however, that is the absolute least of our problems."

X

ZHADEN KARUK
EASTERN BLOCK, CAMP IZROK
OBALLE

The Udul's mind wandered as he struck the red-hot steel repeatedly. Zhaden hated this monotonous work, and he had been terrible at it early on, with little improvement over the years. Despite his lack of experience, his unrivaled size and strength made him an ideal smith. He shook his head, and as he did so, the incredible pain stemming from his forehead took its place back in the front of his mind.

He ran a hand over it. M'og had apparently sliced through an artery when he'd done his clumsy amputation job, and Zhaden would have bled out in under an hour if his wound hadn't cauterized. He'd forever be in debt to Koomer and the rest of the barracks' residents for saving his life. And here he was, working, not twelve hours later. There were no sick days there—even in extreme cases such as this one.

He looked over at Koomer, who was at his station located only a few yards away. The one-eyed Ayr was doing what he always did: sorting through small piles of miscellaneous scrap metal. Today, though, perhaps understandably, he seemed particularly uninterested.

Zhaden loosened his grip on the tong-like tool, which he had never bothered to learn the name of, as he withdrew his cooled-down sword from the filthy water in the bucket next to him. As he swung his arm to place it with the other finished swords, it slipped free and slid across the floor, stopping just next to Koomer's feet.

It was an extremely short walk, but he tried to think of what he would say during the two or so seconds he could convincingly drop down to pick the sword up. A dozen different potential questions ran through his mind as he took the few steps over.

As Zhaden arrived within inches of the Ayr, he bent over, reached for the sword, and opened his mouth, still unsure what exactly would come out of it. As it turned out, it didn't matter.

The eardrum-splitting sound of the camp alarm made many of those in the building jump. Koomer turned to him with a wide and questioning eye. Within seconds, the guards on duty began yelling and rounding up the workers into lines for transportation back to the barracks. Zhaden ended up behind Koomer in one of the four improvised lines. He heard the familiar violent crackling sounds as the guards beat one or two stragglers with the electric rods.

The shutter-style doors to the rickety makeshift work building lifted, letting the sight of natural light and melting snow penetrate the cramped space. They began their march.

Zhaden's eyes remained on the guard who was leading his line, looking for any indication of what was going on. The sounds of other guards speaking in Alavic could be heard from the radio on the guard's hip.

The guard leading Zhaden's line quickly grabbed the radio, stopping the march as he did so. He looked to his left as he spoke and, very suddenly, stopped both moving and speaking. The radio fell out of his hand and landed with a soft plop on the powdery snow.

Almost every prisoner in the line turned to see what had inspired such a reaction. They had been marching past one of the multiple large, rocky hills that lay within the borders of Izrok. This one, unlike the others, had electric fences on either side of it, marking it as the border between the eastern and western regions of the camp.

Standing at its relatively low peak and gazing silently out over the lined-up prisoners were two pale figures. Each had varying body parts that were engulfed in a vibrant neon purple.

Zhaden smiled broadly, recognizing the color.

Several guards who were leading other lines had stopped at this point and were staring up as well. No one spoke for a short time, seemingly unable to believe their eyes. Had Zhaden not already seen smaller examples of the Shaz abilities from Jakob before, he might have been in the exact same position.

A few of the guards finally began to approach the hill slowly, drawing their electric rods as they did so. They outnumbered the Draekons twelve to two. Jakob turned his head slightly from one to another as they moved, as though taking the time to get a good look at each. As they reached the very base of the mound, a second, much more erratic and disorganized sound reachedCed Zhaden's ears. No one else seemed to notice it yet, which made sense, as Uduls had fairly sensitive hearing. As proximity of its source grew, so did its volume and, with it, its familiarity.

The guards, now about a quarter of the way toward the Draekons, suddenly stopped dead in their tracks. Neither Jakob nor his companion moved. Zhaden looked down and smiled at Koomer, who raised the brow over his good eye. The Udul then began to laugh as the realization of what was happening struck him.

He whispered to himself under his breath in his native tongue, "Well done, Jakob. Very well done."

The Draekons stood completely still as a horde of what must have been hundreds of prisoners, most of whom bore some form of weapon, ran past them and down the side of the hill, charging directly at the guards. The black-clad mass moved like a terrifying wave down the slope. Several of their members stumbled in their excitement, falling over their own feet, even.

As the guard who had been leading his line attempted to run past him, Zhaden stuck his hand out and grabbed him by the neck before pushing him strongly off his feet and onto the ground. In the process, Zhaden took the guard's electric rod, which he then jabbed into the Alavite's chest.

There was no turning back now. Following Zhaden's lead, almost every prisoner in the lines swarmed the now severely outnumbered Alavites. He heard footsteps from behind him and turned to see a crowd of what seemed to be well over a hundred guards sprinting their way. Unlike their now fallen brethren, these were properly armed and showed no signs of fear.

The small, makeshift inmate army rushed past Zhaden and the other poorly armed prisoners. Fueled by incredibly fulfilling adrenaline, he began to run as fast as he could behind the mob, leaving most of the other prisoners, including Koomer, behind him. The sounds of screams, metal against metal, and obscenities in varying languages rang through the late-afternoon air. He came up behind a guard and swung his rod at the back of his head with great force, incapacitating him. As the man fell to the ground screaming, Zhaden quickly dropped the rod in favor of the battle-axe that the guard had been carrying, before driving it down hard into the center of his chest.

It had been over a decade since Zhaden had last held a real weapon, and he couldn't think of a better feeling he had experienced since. Though clearly designed to be used with two Alavite hands, he could hold it perfectly well in a single clenched fist. He moved through the crowd, weaving his way through multiple one-on-one battles.

As he continued through the disorganized mess of the fight, he stumbled into an Erub who appeared very poorly dressed for the Oballe climate. The man was fighting three guards at once. Shockingly, he seemed completely comfortable doing so.

The Erub swung his machete at one guard's lower leg, and as that Alavite fell to his knees, he turned back just in time to deflect a blow from the guard behind him.

As the third tried to rush him from the side, the man jumped and threw a powerful kick at his chest, sending him reeling. It was an impressive spectacle, and Zhaden almost felt the urge to sit back and watch before remembering where he was.

The first guard had now gotten back onto his feet behind the Erub and was out of his view. He took a second to pick his sword up from the ground, and he began to move in an angry and determined sprint. Zhaden didn't miss a beat and shot quickly toward the Alavite. Even with his slight limp, Zhaden's longer, larger legs helped him gain significant ground.

A mere second or two before the guard could drive his sword through the Erub's exposed back, Zhaden plowed into him from the side, leading with his shoulder. The guard bounced away violently at the surprise impact and fell to his knees in pain, losing his weapon in the process.

He reached for his sword desperately as Zhaden brought down the axe. The Alavite readjusted his body and attempted to block the blow, but it was no use. The force of Zhaden's swing was too powerful, and the blade snapped with a loud crack, allowing him to finish the job quickly with a blow to the Alavite's head.

Zhaden turned and looked all around him quickly. In battle, staying still for too long was the surest way to get killed. Two other guards, with swords drawn, were running in his direction. He backed up a few steps, bumping into something behind him, which caused him to look back quickly in alarm.

He was now eye to eye with the Erub. As both men realized that the one at his back was a friend rather than a foe, they refocused on the threats in front of them.

"Thanks for that!" The Erub yelled intermittently between strikes over the cacophony of the battle.

"I serve with pleasure, friend!"

Zhaden knocked one guard back and deflected the blow of the other.

"I'm CJ by the way!"

The fact that this man was comfortable giving introductions mid-battle spoke highly of his confidence in how things were going. Zhaden smirked slightly as he forced an approaching guard back with a deflection.

"I am pleased to meet you on this most noble of battlefields, CJ the Erub. I am Zhaden Karuk of Cha-leh!"

Zhaden felt CJ move away from him. He couldn't tell what was happening without looking, but the sound of a screaming guard answered any questions fairly quickly. He felt the man return a second later. Another of the guards from Zhaden's line rushed at him.

With a swing of the axe, Zhaden knocked the sword out of the guard's hand by pure force, and then, in a single, fluid movement, brought it back around to his neck, effortlessly separating the Alavite's head from his body.

"I like your grit!" CJ responded before suddenly breaking off again. Zhaden was about to turn to look behind him when three guards, who had taken down their opponents, began to charge toward him in unison. Zhaden tightened his fingers around the axe and took a deep breath.

Just as the tips of their swords were mere inches from his blue skin, a bright purple light flooded his vision. It took him a second or two to realize that the lights were coming from the arms of a man who stood in front of him. Jakob moved faster and more gracefully than any fighter Zhaden had ever seen.

He moved through the guards as though he were dancing, using his arms as searing-hot blades. He had come from Zhaden's right, and he drove one arm clean through the midsection of the first guard, who toppled over like a tower of blocks. The second took an arm through the chest. The third guard, aware of what was happening, refocused solely on Jakob and attempted to strike him while his one arm was still lodged inside the second guard.

The Alavite swung down hard, forcing Jakob to put his free arm up to block the blow. As the sword contacted the Shaz energy, it broke apart in a flurry of purple sparks. Before the man had time to readjust, Jakob withdrew his arm and used both to slice an X in the last guard's neck, sending his head flying into the mass of fighting bodies.

Jakob turned to look at Zhaden. His eyes were bright purple and lacked a discernible pupil, just as they had the other night for those few fleeting seconds. Zhaden began to say something, but Jakob took off into the crowd to continue fighting before any words could escape his lips.

Zhaden turned around to try to see how CJ was faring and was immediately tackled violently into the snow. The world was a series of rapid and intermittent flashes of white as he struggled to turn onto his back and face his attacker.

All he managed to mentally process before the barrage of fists began to fall one after another was the sight of his own horn dangling from a large, red, and veiny neck.

XI

TOM EZEKIEL
WESTERN BLOCK, CAMP IZROK
OBALLE

After five consecutive days of being cramped in small spaces, Tom couldn't help but marvel at how amazing it felt to run again. He kept his eyes on the bouncing bundle of snow-white hair sprouting from the back of Josso's head as the two of them moved quickly through the snow. Light crunching sounds accompanied each of their steps. If he had seen his new Zantavi acquaintance from this angle before getting a look at his face, Tom would have assumed that the man was ancient.

"Mind telling me where the fuck we're going?"

Josso glanced back over his shoulder quickly before shouting his response. "I don't like not knowing what's going on. I intend to find out if we're about to be free men or dead ones."

Tom couldn't help but smirk. "Fuck yeah. I love me an old-school prison riot."

Josso slowed his pace suddenly, eventually coming to a halt. Tom followed suit.

"You . . . you have no idea what this place is, do you?"

"It seems pretty straightforward. You've got shady-looking people in jumpsuits behind iron bars paired with some torture thrown in here and there for good measure. It's nothing new to me. Hate to burst your bubble, my man, but I'm more familiar with the system than most."

Josso sighed and looked away from him. "I think you'll find this galaxy always finds ways to surprise you." With that, he took off again.

Tom sighed and continued following him. The two didn't share another word until they reached the base of what seemed to be some sort of rocky hill. Large fences set up on either side of it eliminated the option of going around it. It had an incline to it, making it look like something of a steep natural ramp. Without breaking stride, Josso began to scale it.

"Oh, you've got to be fucking kidding me." Tom muttered.

Evidently, Josso wasn't. The unmistakable sounds of battle rang through Tom's ears as he slogged his way behind the Zantavi prince. The sound of his heartbeat pulsed through his head, and his breathing grew increasingly labored. He looked up at Josso, who seemed to be moving along effortlessly. The muscles along his back seemed to be threatening to break out of his prison jumpsuit.

After a few painful minutes, and several seconds after Josso, Tom reached the peak. He bent over with his hands on his knees to catch his breath. The Zantavi prince stood with his arms crossed as they both looked out over the center of the camp, where all hell had apparently broken loose.

The first thing Tom noticed was that the large, dark mass of fighting bodies seemed to be split into two groups. One, farther north of where they stood, was made up of what seemed to be equal parts prisoner and guard. The second group, which was much closer to the foot of the hill, was composed primarily of prisoners, most of whom seemed to be either unarmed or equipped with only some sort of stun rod.

The guards in this group were vastly outnumbered but were racking up kills much faster than their more northern counterparts. Wherever it wasn't already covered by a body, the snow had become either pink or red with blood, of which there was no shortage. Tom activated the spectator on his virix, which gave him an estimated body count of five hundred and thirty-six corpses.

Josso ran his hand over his dark chin. "Izrok holds about two thousand. That must be just about the entire population of the camp down there."

Tom felt for his right dagger.

"Let's not let this party go on without us, eh?" He turned and smiled at Josso, who simply raised an eyebrow in response.

"You do realize you can just go find your ship and get out of here. Leaving this all behind is a completely viable option."

Tom shook his head. "I haven't had a good fight in fucking forever, and in my line of work, I can't afford to get rusty."

"What line of work would that be?"

Tom forced a slight cough. "Are you coming or not?"

Josso crossed his arms. "I hate to break it to you, but I'm not allowed to spill blood in my religion."

"Are you shitting me? You're fucking jacked!"

Josso merely shrugged his broad shoulders.

Tom sighed and looked straight up at the sky. "Alright then. Do me a favor and let me know how cool I look from up here."

Before the Zantavi could respond, Tom grabbed a long piece of rotting wood that was sitting half-buried in the snow next to him and tossed it onto the slope of the hill. With a nod at his dark-skinned accomplice, he jumped onto it and began to slide down the hillside. It went much faster than he had anticipated, and at one point, he only narrowly avoided wiping out entirely. As he reached the bottom of the hill, he clicked the button on his belt, sending both daggers shooting up out of their sheaths. He reached up and grabbed them out of midair as he set foot on flat ground.

He loved the blades, which were black from handle to point, and had held onto them since he had first learned to fight on the streets of Trax Town. They certainly had some mileage on them at this point, but he maintained them faithfully. The edge of each blade's back side was coated in sharp ridges that looked like waves when viewed from the side.

Tom picked his pace up as he approached the first, and clearly less battle-oriented crowd of prisoners. A few feet away from him stood a fellow Ayr, who looked uncoordinated and indecisive. He was armed with only a stun rod and was doing nothing but blocking the advances of a guard who seemed to have locked in on him.

The Alavite suddenly took three consecutive swings, the third of which knocked the rod out of the Ayr's hands. He was in the midst of coming down hard with a vertical killing blow when Tom's dagger shot through the side of his neck, interrupting his swing and sending blood spraying like a fountain into the frigid air. The guard instinctively reached to cover the massive cut, but it was too late.

He collapsed a second later, forming a red pool on the ground around him.

"Fuck yes. Still got it," Tom muttered under his breath as he made his way over to the guard. He had been aiming for the head, but he would take a neck shot as a consolation prize.

He straddled the corpse as he pulled the dagger free. As he did so, the Ayr spoke up from behind him in their shared native tongue, "Thanks. Fighting is not exactly my specialty."

Tom wiped the dagger on a clear patch of snow to clean the blood from it. There were still multiple people between him and the nearest guard, so he supposed he could chat quickly. He turned to face his fellow countryman.

The man's empty eye socket drew Tom's gaze immediately. He had to make a conscious effort not to stare.

"Where's your virix?"

The man shook his head. "Haven't had one in years."

Tom turned to look over the battle. The guards were pushing their way in his direction. He grunted and reached behind his head, unstrapping his goggles. He whipped them off quickly and held them out to the one-eyed man.

"Are you insane? You're fighting! You need it!"

"I can fight fine without one, and you've got one fucking eye. Put it on and get the fuck out of here. If you can't see, you're going to get killed."

The man hesitated for a second but nodded and took it. He began strapping it on. "Wait. Does this have an integrated radio?"

"Yeah. An Octo VII."

The man's eyes widened, and he immediately took off running without another word.

Everything farther than just past Tom's reach was incomprehensibly blurry now. He grabbed the handle of each knife and held the blades facing downward.

* * *

He wasn't sure how long he fought for or how much blood he had drawn, as everything seemed to blend together at a certain point. The sky was a canvas painted in orange and pink as the sun began to dip below the horizon. Night wouldn't make things any easier.

Once he ensured that the unskilled group was mostly guard-free, he ran across the considerable gap to join the other. The corpses were beginning to form small hills, creating obstacles on the battlefield. There wasn't much time to plan right now, so Tom resolved to simply throw himself into the first fight he could. It took him only a few seconds to locate his objective: two fighters locked together and fully enveloped in battle. Was it unfair to attack a man who wasn't even facing in his direction? Probably. But that was hardly his concern.

He had a clean shot at the guard's exposed back. He was now only feet away but had to skid to a quick stop when the gray blob was suddenly enveloped in a bright purple light. An animal-like shriek escaped the Alavite's lungs as he collapsed onto the ground. Tom turned to his right to see the small, pale-faced outline of a Draekon—the one who had been in the cell next to Jakob's.

The Draekon smiled at Tom, "I saw you fight over there. You're dirty."

"Well—"

"I like that."

Tom was a bit taken aback at that oddly flirtatious comment.

"Relax. I don't mean it *that* way."

"It works for me. I'm not exactly a huge fan of rules or procedures."

"We may get along just yet. Name's Yaunie."

Tom nodded, even though he realized that the Draekon wasn't looking at him. "So, you throw purple goop, huh? That's your thing?"

Yaunie shrugged. "I guess so."

Tom heard footsteps coming from behind him. He quickly turned and threw a dagger, which hit the rushing guard in the chest. Half a second later, the guard was enveloped in purple goop and began to scream as he fell to his knees.

Tom turned back to Yaunie. "You really had to steal my kill, eh?"

Yaunie chuckled and disappeared back into the crowd without another word. Tom turned back around and pulled his knife free before his attention was captivated by the sound of heavy, powerful punches to his left. On the ground, about ten yards away, a red blob and blue blob had seemingly abandoned their weapons and were now rolling in the snow and throwing fists at each other.

Each one would spend a few seconds on top before the other would take over. They were yelling obscenities at each other. He began to run over, having locked in on his next target, but the red blob suddenly stood up and began to flee toward what Tom could only faintly make out was a building. The blue blob followed a moment later. He seemed to have a slight limp.

Tom had only just begun tailing them when a blade suddenly appeared out of the corner of his vision.

He ducked instinctively but suffered a cut right above his eye where the sword grazed him. He grabbed his wound with one hand and stabbed the attacker's leg with the other. As the screaming Alavite dropped to grab at his wound, Tom rose quickly and jabbed the length of his dagger through the guard's skull. He wiped his face with his hand as the guard plopped onto the ground. When Tom examined his hand, it was almost entirely red.

"Shit."

But he couldn't stop. Not yet. He moved over to the building that he had seen the large figures enter. As he ran, he passed what he thought might have been CJ's camouflage outfit, but he wasn't sure.

He stepped inside the tall, yet compact building, the composition reminding him of the large cargo crates that had occasionally been used as makeshift housing in Trax Town. He could hear low grunting echoing throughout the metallic chamber; they seemed to be coming from upstairs. Tom slowly approached the metallic steps that had been welded to the side of the crate slowly.

He removed his hand from his cut and grabbed his second dagger as he reached the seventh floor, resolving to let his face bleed if it was going to bleed.

He slowed to a crawl now. The lights inside had gone out completely, thereby helping him stay out of sight despite his relative proximity to the two men who must have been nearly seven feet tall and three hundred pounds each.

The room was completely empty and seemed to have been abandoned for quite some time. Two large and uneven square holes were cut into the side of the crate, presumably to serve as windows. Something about the dimness helped Tom's vision to clear up a bit more, allowing a few more details of the Dom'Rai and Udul, who was missing his horn, to come into focus. They spoke in Garyl again.

"I should have started my cut much lower. I will not repeat that mistake again," the Dom'rai growled.

"You are a small and bitter man, M'og." The Udul responded calmly.

The Dom'Rai roared and threw a strong punch, but the Udul dodged it, causing a healthy dent to form in the wall behind him.

"Making sure animals know their place doesn't make me evil. Your brother is an honorable man, and he was right about you."

The Udul charged at the Dom'Rai, pinning him against the side of the building. He got a good shot or two in before the Dom'Rai kneed him in the groin, causing him to drop back. The large red man readied himself to kick the keeled-over Udul in the face.

Now.

Tom jumped up, causing the confused Dom'Rai to look over. In half a second, he had flung his dagger, hitting the Dom'Rai square in the head. Tom was in the midst of patting himself on the back for his accuracy when the Dom'Rai began to laugh. He turned and kicked the Udul, who fell to the floor. The blade in the red man's head seemed to be of little concern to him, even as blood trickled down his face like a fountain. This was a problem, because he had now set his sights on Tom.

Before he could even attempt to run down the stairs, the Dom'Rai cleared the small gap between them and grabbed him by the neck, lifting him off his feet. Tom grabbed at his throat and attempted to pry the dinnerplate-sized hand off him but to no avail. He could feel himself choking. His vision began to spot as the Dom'Rai walked him over to the makeshift windows.

"Try platform make before fall do you Ayr smart. Thank you for gift knife. Now can kill yes Udul," he said in what had to be the poorest Neatspeak that Tom had ever heard.

Before he knew what was happening, he was thrust forward with great force and began to fall. He did his best to right himself before clicking his boots together, but they merely sputtered, failing to ignite. He fell down another two storeys.

Tom closed his eyes with force, summoning all the hope he still had.

He clicked his feet once more. The booster at the bottom of each boot sputtered again and then quickly ignited, stopping Tom's fall when he had less than a foot to go before hitting the ground. He breathed a sigh of relief and began making his way to the window from which he had just been forcefully ejected. There was also no way in hell that he was leaving his knife behind.

He had to move quickly. He hadn't had a chance to refuel the boots since the last time, and they were low enough as it was. They began to sputter when he was around the level of the fifth floor.

"Come on. . ." he muttered to himself.

He began to feel them dying out and reached out for the edge of the seventh story window frame to his left as the flames in his feet sputtered out. The Udul was now pressed against the window to Tom's right and was being pushed out of it. The big blue man looked to his left and briefly made eye contact with Tom before returning his gaze to the Dom'Rai, who had apparently not noticed him yet.

He had pulled Tom's dagger out of his head and was holding it up to his opponent's neck. The blood from his head was dripping onto the Udul's chest. The horn on the necklace dangled just above him as well.

"I will make sure that every prisoner who raised arms today suffers until they beg for death. You . . . you are a different situation. I will have your head and place it next to the flag of our glorious army for all to see."

The Udul began to speak but was cut off by a loud rumbling that cut through the sounds of the battle and ripped through the sky. Tom knew that sound anywhere—ship engines.

He turned his head as best as he could to see as he continued to hold on for dear life. To his utter delight, the vessels he was now looking at weren't the same type as the one he had been arrested in. These were brown, rounded, and had green engines.

Tom turned back at the fighting giants. The Dom'Rai's mouth had fallen agape as he looked up. The Udul took advantage of the distraction and delivered a powerful punch to his assailant's face.

As the Dom'Rai recoiled, the Udul grabbed at the horn around the red man's neck and yanked it free before thrusting the sharp end of the horn up under his chin. He did this over and over until the Dom'Rai fell to his knees and grabbed at his neck as what looked to be gallons of blood spilled out onto the dirty, metallic floor.

The Dom'Rai made a valiant attempt to rise to his feet but was met once more by the shockingly sharp tip of the horn. This time, the Udul simply thrust it with incredible force directly into the red giant's forehead. The horn began to fracture as he continued to push it until only a tiny portion of it remained exposed.

The Dom'Rai attempted to speak, but he was entirely incoherent. He shot a look of utter disgust and hatred at the Udul as he fell over, going limp immediately. Without missing a beat, the victor ran over to the window and helped Tom up and into the building.

"You should indeed be more careful, my friend. This was hardly a fight you could have won," the large man said in Neatspeak as he handed Tom back his dagger.

"Yeah. I'll leave the big guys to you then from now on. What should I call you?"

"I am Zhaden Karuk"

Tom nodded. "Tom Ezekiel."

The Udul smiled. "It is a pleasure to meet you, but we truly have no time to chat. We must ensure the battle is won, and we must find Jakob."

"You know him?"

"More than most others, but it would seem not quite enough." Zhaden looked quietly out the window for a few seconds before speaking again. "We should also discover the identity of our visitors."

"Yeah. Who the fuck are they?"

"I confess that I do not know. But those are neither Alavite, Dom'Rai, nor Quexian ships. That would seem to mean it can only be good news for us."

The two stepped over the dead body of the Dom'Rai as they headed down the stairs.

"You don't want the horn?"

Zhaden chuckled. "M'og seemed to desire it quite badly. If that is the case, he can keep it."

Tom liked this guy already.

XII

DARYN PERIC
UPPER CHAMBERS, ALTAR OF ALAVON
ALAVONIA

If he had ever seen Olivio move this quickly before, he certainly couldn't remember it. Daryn found himself needing to increase his pace to a slight jog to avoid being left behind by his surprisingly nimble attendee. The silver hair that surrounded the top of The Hand's bald head bounced slightly as he moved rapidly through the Altar's reflective white hallways. The old man manually pried open the automatic door to the conference room and quickly stepped inside. Daryn shuffled in right after. The Hand quickly headed over to his table, sat in his large gold-trimmed chair, and typed a code on the keypad that was attached to the former.

A steady whirring came from the ceiling as four extra monitors slowly dropped down. Within a minute, four screens lit up, with the face of an elderly robed man filling each of them. Daryn couldn't remember the last time he had seen them all together at the same time. Arturo, Nicholas, Alejandro, and Mateo all bowed as each one synced into the teleconference. None of them said a word.

"Pertinax is dead. Izrok is currently in an open uprising, and the bulk of the chosen army is still entrenched on Feralla dealing with the Carine."

Each screen was labeled with the name of priest on it; so it was easy to tell who was who. Nicholas spoke up first. "How could this have happened? They are starved and weak! You said so yourself."

Olivio waited a second or two before responding. "It seems that the moment we have long awaited has finally arrived."

The priests' faces erupted in a strange combination of excitement and fear.

"Are you certain of this?" Mateo asked, running a hand under his chin.

Olivio smiled slightly. "It seems our dearly departed Pertinax accomplished his mission after all. But we have other matters to attend to before we can proceed with our plan."

The priests nodded, and Nicholas cleared his throat. "Shall we send orders to set the reserve Erub army in motion toward Oballe, my Hand?"

To everyone's surprise, Olivio shook his head. "If we send the army to Oballe, the Erub girl will recapture the planet in one night with her rebel army. We will lose two systems in one go. I won't have that."

The priests began to show varying levels of confusion.

Arturo spoke. "My Hand, if we are not to send the Erub forces, and the bulk of the army is much too far away to be of any aid, how are we to secure the camps?"

The Hand, once again, stunned everyone. "We will not. Izrok will fall, and the other camps will follow." No one spoke for a few seconds. Olivio continued, "Let the criminals have their victory. They have no reliable sources of food, water, or weapons. No radio on the planet is powerful enough to reach any civilized nation. With no ships to evacuate them, the prisoners' basic instincts will take over at some point. They will tear each other apart and die in darkness."

Some of the priests began to nod slightly. Alejandro, however, looked unconvinced. "My Hand, if there is to be chaos and violence, should we not be concerned about *his* safety?"

Olivio chuckled slightly. "If he is truly our man, he can easily outlast them all. When we return to what remains of that wretched frozen hellscape, he will be there, waiting."

The priests all nodded.

Alejandro ran a hand through his waist-length beard before speaking up again. "Are we to assume that no system powers will come to rescue or aid them?"

Olivio ran his golden gauntlet over the table, creating a soft scraping sound. "The camps have been poorly defended for over half a decade. If outsiders had wanted to invade, they would have done so a long time ago. None are willing to accept the consequences such an action would bring upon their planet and people for the sake of a few hundred criminals."

The priests remained quiet, seemingly taking everything in.

"How soon can we expect The Fist to return?" asked Mateo, breaking the silence.

Olivio exhaled with a bit of extra force as he leaned back in his chair. "Soon."

"May I ask how—?"

"You may not."

The priest looked slightly annoyed but nodded anyway.

There was an awkward silence for a few seconds before Olivio continued. "While I have all of you here, I would like to take this opportunity to fill our empty role as quickly as possible. I believe there to be no better candidate than the young man sitting next to me, unless any of you would like to nominate your own attenders."

None of them spoke.

Daryn's mind went blank for a second as he wondered if he had just heard that right.

"I know you are all busy, so I'd like to set up another call tomorrow to formally begin the process. I will keep Daryn here for a few weeks as I train him for the role. Then, he will take over Pertinax's post on Erub in support of King Polero."

The priests nodded and began to clap.

Daryn could feel his face going red. Attenders usually had to wait decades before getting called up. Many died or were dismissed from their posts before being given the chance. Yet, here, at twenty-one, Daryn was set to become the youngest priest in Alavite history.

The Hand turned in his chair to face Daryn and joined in the clapping. "Daryn, since you won't be my attender for much longer, please go fetch us some sparkling wine from my quarters so we may celebrate."

Daryn nodded quickly and left the room. He felt as though he were floating as he moved down the hallway. This had been a dream of his since he'd been five, and even then, he was always much older when he got the news in his fantasies.

He could hear triumphant music blasting through his head as he turned the corner toward Olivio's bedroom door. The golden guards out front hesitated for a few seconds and shuffled aside awkwardly to let him in. The sound in his head came to a screeching halt at the sight of two unconscious and naked Alavites on the floor. He was midway through turning around when a cold metallic hand grabbed him from behind and another covered his mouth.

He struggled to no avail as a third impostor shut the door behind the three of them. The one holding onto him began making his way toward the balcony. Daryn was dragged roughly through the doorway and into the cool of the night. He heard the hum of a flyer's engine before he saw it. It was hovering just slightly away from the railing that overlooked the city, which was lit up extravagantly in the night. All the lights on the flyer and on the balcony had been turned off, making it hard to see exactly what was happening and who was responsible for this. He looked down and noticed that two more guards were splayed out across the ground out there, though these were still wearing their armor.

Daryn's plans to make a run for it as soon as possible fell to the wayside as a damp cloth was suddenly placed over his nose and mouth, causing him to become overwhelmed by an undeniable urge to sleep.

He was dumped onto the floor of the flyer by two pairs of hands. With no ability to move on his own, he was stuck looking at whatever happened to be in front of him. As his eyelids grew unbearably heavy, he managed to process a few final fleeting images that felt more like a slideshow than real life. Most of these snapshots were of faces, all of which were totally foreign to him, save for that of his sister.

XIII

YAUNIE
EASTERN BLOCK, CAMP IZROK
OBALLE

He had been standing off to the side overlooking the battle when he had first seen the tan vessels and the green streaks of their boosters cutting across the sky. The quick crunching of footsteps in the snow came from behind him. He readied another of his Shaz orbs in his right hand and turned to see the Ayr whom he had met earlier—Tom, was it?—accompanied by a large and, bizarrely, hornless Udul.

"Please tell me those are your friends. We could use some more of this purple magic shit."

Yaunie lowered his hand as turned to look back at the ships. "No one would be more pleasantly surprised than me."

"I do indeed recognize those green trails. Unfortunately, I cannot seem to recall from where," the Udul added.

The ships turned straight down and began to approach the camp. In the darkness of the night, they resembled shooting stars.

"Well . . . I mean, I had a good life. How 'bout you guys?"

No one answered Tom's question. The noise of the engines became increasingly loud as they grew closer. They pulled up and leveled out to give themselves enough time to halt their descent before hitting the ground, leaving them hovering at around the height of a flyer.

As they moved closer still to the surface, giant doors on either of their sides lifted, revealing what looked to be several dozen men dressed from head to toe in brown-and-white armor. Each of them drew their power bows and began letting loose onto the crowd below. The sight of hundreds upon hundreds of arrows and the yellow streaks left in their wake was impressive, to say the least. Yaunie followed the arrows with his eyes as best he could as they rained down onto the horde, but it was almost impossible to tell who was being hit.

Understandably, the crowd began to panic and disperse quickly. Other ships began splitting up to follow them. As the large group thinned, a lone figure broke off from the group of runners and turned toward the three of them. Yaunie prepared to attack but lowered his hands and the orbs within them as the Erub's face came into view.

Tom's voice came from behind. "Nice to see you in one piece, Corvie."

The Erub was panting and sounded out of breath after what must have been over two hours of fighting at this point. Small drops of blood slowly fell onto the snow from his black-and-green machete. They spread out slightly as they contacted the white, powdery ground.

"Don't call me that." He took a deep breath. "I think these guys are after the guards, not the prisoners."

"I do believe this is the case, CJ. We should indeed try to investigate the identities of our mysterious saviors." The Udul had an unusual way of speaking, but Yaunie agreed with his point.

The Erub looked up suddenly at Tom and raised an eyebrow. "What happened to your virix?"

"What's with the twenty questions?" the Ayr shot back.

"That was literally one question."

Yaunie interrupted. "Guys. Let's try to stay focused, eh? I'd like to figure out who these guys are and make sure they aren't here to kill us as well."

They didn't need to wait long for answers. One of the ships began to slowly descend and activate its landing gear over the now-abandoned center of the camp.

The group was blinded for a second or two as the ship's spotlights were activated and then directed at him.

The side doors of the vessel opened, and around thirty armored men stepped out of it. They lined themselves up with their power bows, their glow covering the men in a dim yellow light. They reminded Yaunie of the bright-blue variants that the old Draekon army had once used. One of the soldiers, who had a series of white lines on the area of his upper left breast, walked briskly over to the group and removed his helmet as he approached. The man's skin almost blended into the darkness of the night. If not for his white hair, it would have been hard to tell that he was even there.

"We search for the prince. Do you know him?" The man asked in a thick Zantavic accent.

Yaunie was about to ask what the man was talking about when the Erub responded. "Josso? Yes. He—"

"Where is he? You take us to him. Now."

Tom cut in. "He's been hanging out on the hill. Apparently, his blood is too fine for him to get into a tussle like the rest of us." The soldier didn't so much as give a hint of a smile. Tom cleared his throat. "Uh, yeah. He should be over here. Come on."

He took off running. The soldier seemed hesitant at first but called a few of his men over to him, and they followed. The rest of the group seemed to come to a silent agreement that they should go along as well, unless they planned to stand in the cold staring down power bows for the rest of the night.

Tom began muttering curses under his breath as he began to scale the side of the snowy hill. The rest of them followed. After reaching the top, the Ayr looked around and ran a hand through his dirty-blond hair.

"Uh, so . . . he was here earlier. I promise. Then again, my vision is shit right now, so if anyone else sees him, feel free to speak up. Please."

The Zantavi soldiers pulled their blades halfway out of their sheaths in a threatening manner, and Tom instinctively reached for the daggers at his side.

"Whoa, let's just take it e—"

"*Ascarabet. Molono uyoui bociai.*"

The soldiers knelt as the Zantavi approached, but he ushered them back to their feet. They began to speak in their language while the rest of the group stood around somewhat awkwardly. The wind was much stronger up here, and Yaunie found himself shivering after only about a minute.

The prince turned back to them. "The army is going to liberate the other camps on the planet and lock down Izrok. Once the situation is deemed to be under control, there will be at least one shuttle bound for each major home world for those who choose to go. Once there, local governments can handle the rest."

It was difficult for Yaunie to comprehend how the nightmare he had been living for the past ten years could be undone in the span of a few sentences. It didn't seem possible. Something was going to go wrong. It had to.

"I do admire your decisive nature, my dark friend," said the Udul. Yaunie cringed slightly at the last part of the comment, but the prince just smiled. "My father already had the entire thing planned out. I'm just the messenger. After this is all over, I'd like to visit Cha-leh at some point to fish."

The Udul laughed.

"There is no better fisherman than Zhaden Karuk. I will teach you my ways. If my rod fails, I dive in after them! I have yet to find a fish I cannot outswim!"

"Why is it that I always arrive just in time to hear the most ridiculous parts of your stories?"

Everyone turned to face the other side of the hill as the bright purple figure emerged. The Zantavi soldiers drew their weapons and moved in front of Josso in a defensive stance.

"Do not approach! We will strike!" the leader yelled as Jakob began shaking the excess snow from his pants nonchalantly.

The prince yelled something in his language, and the men hesitantly lowered their weapons. He pointed at Jakob as he spoke, apparently filling them in on the events of the day.

Jakob took advantage of the first bit of silence he heard.

"Why are you here?"

The leading soldier's eyes continued to scan Jakob up and down as he answered. "We keep unit on nearby moon for past few months. Secret. One of yours contact today. We had tried for long time to hear from prince. Wanted to strike but scared for prince safety."

Yaunie didn't realize how good the prince's Neatspeak was until it was put on display against that of his soldiers.

"Wait. Who contacted you?" Jakob tilted his head a bit.

The soldier shrugged. "Did not get name. Used virix radio."

Tom made a noise that sounded like a chuckle, and Yaunie turned to him. Zhaden and Jakob suddenly looked at each other.

"Koomer?" the much larger man asked.

"Is that even a question?" Jakob confirmed.

Josso explained to Jakob the plan that he had relayed to the group a few minutes earlier. He nodded in approval before turning to the non-Zantavis on the hill.

"Zhaden, get to the radio tower. If Koomer got the signal off, he probably did it from there. He's not a fighter, so he's likely hiding out there for the time being. Make sure he's okay, and then join up with the group. Tom, you go with him. Zhaden's not at one hundred percent and might need the backup. I saw you out there, and if that's how you fight while half blind, I feel comfortable trusting him with you. He's going to need the help."

"Not from what I fucking saw."

Zhaden looked questioningly at Tom but spoke before he could get another word in. "It is quite alright. Tom the Ayr shows an impressive will to fight even against those who would easily overpower him. He has already assisted me in the battle." He looked at Tom with a smile as he finished speaking.

"I appreciate that, dude. But I really didn't do shit. Might have given him a headache, if that. Was probably a stupid thing to do, honestly." Tom muttered the last sentence.

"I have no idea what you're referring to, but that already sounds like an understatement," CJ chimed in.

"You know wha—" Tom began to shoot back.

"Enough." Jakob raised his voice right to the edge of a shout. The entire hilltop went quiet. "Tom, I saw a black Ayr cruiser in the hangar's impound lot. I assume it's yours. When the two of you find Koomer, use it to meet with me at Karvenkull."

"The fuck is that?"

"The castle. It's all black. You can't miss it."

"Oh, gotcha."

"Go."

Zhaden and Tom began carefully making their way down the side of the hill, and Jakob turned to CJ.

"You go with the Zantavi men and quell the panic in the camps. Let them know they're safe and that the foreigners aren't the enemy. You have a presence that I've picked up from seeing you in that horde of bodies. You seem to be comfortable leading."

The Erub crossed his arms. "In this makeshift army and the one I lead at home; most men aren't well trained or disciplined fighters. If I hesitate or stay behind, men will die. That's not going to happen. I was hesitant to fight at first, but when I committed, I committed. I don't give fifty or seventy-five percent, and certainly not against fucking Alavites."

For a brief and bizarre moment, it looked as though Jakob's pale lips curled into a smile, but it dissipated so quickly that Yaunie wondered whether it had just been his imagination.

"When you finish rounding up the prisoners, get into the Zantavi shuttles and then head to the castle gates. Given the current disorganization and chaos, they may be difficult to convince, but tell them if they want to have the opportunity to go home, they will be there."

CJ's eyebrows raised slightly. Yaunie was impressed at how comfortable he looked despite the cold, especially given that his arms were almost entirely exposed.

"Why do you need them at the castle?"

As he spoke, Jakob pointed one of his odd Shaz arms at the area that had been enveloped in combat and bloodshed over the past several hours. "We're a disorganized mess. Everything that went on today will mean nothing if we can't get ourselves in order and build up quickly. The second Olivio gets the Carine to surrender, they'll be on the way here. The Chosen Army will eat us alive in our current state. Yaunie and I have seen what they can do at full strength, and we're nowhere close to where we need to be. Go. Now."

CJ hesitated a second but nodded and took off down the slope. Josso and all but one of his soldiers followed closely.

Jakob looked at Yaunie now. "You're with me. We're going inside and doing what we have to do."

He knew what was going to happen in there. There was no doubt. But was he ready? Time seemed to pass in a blur as he ran the scenario over and over in his head. He and Jakob took off running, accompanied by the remaining Zantavi guard, who led them back into the ship that had landed in the clearing earlier. The journey took about twenty minutes, and Jakob seemed to be directing the pilot the entire way. Yaunie's heart sank as the tall, ebony spires of Karvenkull came into view. It was time. It had to be done.

The ship landed quickly and opened its side door, letting the two Draekons out into the snow. They exchanged a look as they took their first steps outside campgrounds in years before rushing toward the massive front door, which Jakob kicked open. They stepped into the lobby, which provided welcome relief from the cold outside.

All the lights were out. The massive staircase leading up to the throne room stood before them, with two large hallways off to either side. Jakob began to turn left.

"No." Yaunie called out.

Jakob turned to him.

"Follow me."

He led the way up the steps and through the empty throne room. Their steps echoed as they ran through it. Yaunie grunted as he pushed open the large black door in the back-left wall of the room, revealing a spiral staircase that led to the upper chambers of the castle. Yaunie took the lead. Jakob moved behind him slowly, tapping his arm on the rail intermittently, creating small purple sparks with each contact. Upon reaching the top, they took a right and moved down the long hallway, which ended at a much more elaborate black door with the Draekon insignia engraved into it.

Jakob looked back at Yaunie as if to ask whether he was ready. When the latter nodded, Jakob kicked the door, which swung open and slammed against the back wall. Both of them moved into the king's quarters, which were significantly colder than the rest of the castle. The lights looked as though they were formed by candles. It had always been much too dark in there for Yaunie's liking. Standing at the other end of the room, facing away from the two intruders as she looked out the window, was an all-too-familiar woman with graying black hair.

Murderous Marielle, as she had become known, spoke without turning. "They finally lost the camps. I never thought I'd see the day. I don't expect you to spare me, but, if I may, I'd like to explain—"

She turned around suddenly and stopped speaking. At first, Yaunie thought she was reacting to Jakob's shocking appearance, but tears suddenly began to form in her eyes. She was not looking at Jakob at all. After all this time, she still recognized him. "Oh . . . How? It . . . it wasn't my decision. You have to know that."

He wasn't ready for this. He didn't want to do this now.

"It was. You betrayed Kadrok and helped them round us up. Everyone saw it. You sent us to die so you could live a few more years in a slightly more upscale cell." The pure vitriol in Jakob's words was almost palpable.

"That's not what she's talking about," Yaunie interjected.

Jakob turned to him and raised an eyebrow.

"No. It isn't," she affirmed.

Marielle approached Yaunie slowly and flung her arms around him, hugging him tightly as she began to sob. "Yozak, I'm so sorry. I tried to find you. I tried."

Yaunie looked to Jakob, whose eyes widened as the reality of the situation set in.

"I did what I had to do. I promise. Olivio was going to kill both of us. It was the only chance I had." She was sobbing. Tears began to find their way to Yaunie's eyes as well.

"I love you so much, and I will do anything for you. I will join you in rebuilding. I'll take on the lowest of roles in the new society. I'll go to prison if you promise to visit me. All I want and all I ever wanted was to be with you again."

Yozak Kiv slowly wrapped his arms around his mother, who was now several inches shorter than he was, in sharp contrast to the last time he had seen her.

"The Lost Prince," Jakob muttered from behind them.

"The Zantavi are freeing the rest of the camps as we speak." Yozak's voice was lower than he had intended.

Marielle pulled back to look him in the eyes. She touched his face and ran her fingers up and down his cheek. "Tell me. How many of us are left? A part of me dies inside when I see those lights. I was sure at some point that one of them was you."

Yozak swallowed hard as he tried to think of a way to phrase the bad news, but Jakob handled it for him. "What's left *is* us. In this room . . . where we stand."

She looked as though she didn't understand. "No . . . That . . . but we had . . ."

"They're all gone, Mother. Lost to either the cold, hunger, or an Alavite's blade."

She pulled into his chest and continued sobbing. "I never meant for that. I didn't know they'd handle things the way they did. All I wanted was a chance to see you again." She dug her fingers into his back.

Yozak turned to look at Jakob, who was scanning the room, before he turned back to his mother. "It . . . it doesn't matter. We will rise again, Mother. I am Kadrok's son. You will never be able to be in the public eye again. I'm sure you understand that. But we can keep you hidden somewhere."

She smiled and seemed to nod slightly. "Yozak, I love you. I've loved you every day. It wasn't until years later that I understood your father's actions, and by then, it was too late. I hated him for over a decade before that invasion, and I allowed that anger and resentment to cloud my thoughts."

His throat began to burn, and his blue eyes began to fog. He pulled his mother close and spoke to her as hot tears ran down his cheek. "Why, mother? What did he do?"

She shook her head. "I will never speak of it. He did not lay a finger on me, this much I promise you. He was a good man in that respect. But he manipulated me into finishing something I had never wanted to start. I still see those eyes in my-" She moved her head to the side to look past her son, presumably at Jakob. "Wait. I. . .I know you. . ." Her eyes suddenly widened as a look of pure terror flashed across her face. "That's not possible. . . No! NO!"

Yaunie was about to turn around when he felt the sharp sting followed immediately by incredibly unbearable heat running through his chest. A split second after it arrived, it was gone, replaced by more pain than he had ever known; yet, he found himself unable to pull air into his lungs to scream. He looked down to see a large, bright purple wound right through not only his chest but also his mother's. Her mouth twisted into a frown as the life left her dark blue eyes. She fell limp, and with the strength sapped from his body, he was forced to drop her onto the floor. The world began to spin and grow dark. He felt intoxicated and turned around slowly and unsteadily to face Jakob, who stared him down with an expression that conveyed neither guilt nor remorse.

Yozak fell to his knees. The room turned gray, and everything seemed to freeze. A faceless, featureless purple man stepped out of Jakob and stood over him. Yozak gasped, pulling enough air into his failing lungs to utter a single word at the traitor as the strange figure before him wrapped him in a hug and everything melted into warmth and peace.

"Why?"

XIV

ZHADEN KARUK
EASTERN BLOCK OUTSKIRTS, CAMP IZROK OBALLE

"So, are we going to talk about Jakob or . . .?"

Tom had apparently decided to keep a conversation going; not that Zhaden, of all people, minded this. Some would say talking was his specialty.

The two of them had gained considerable ground as they'd headed on foot toward the radio tower, but it would still be a while before they arrived there. The lack of meaningful light sources outside the main living areas of the camp meant that Zhaden was forced to rely on his sensitive hearing to pick up what faint radio signals he could while traveling in its general direction. Tom did have a small flashlight built into one of his gloves for some reason, but it was almost useless, as its bright white light coated only a few feet in front of them.

"I do not think such a topic is pertinent at this time. The clock is ticking, so to speak. We will have more than ample opportunity at a later time."

"You're no fun, you know that?"

"Ah . . . If you come to know me better, perhaps you will change your mind! Zhaden Karuk is the lifeblood of any party."

"Sure you are, bud."

The Ayr was beginning to pant slightly.

"You cannot be getting tired already, surely?"

"How about you mind your own business, eh? We don't all have two hundred and fifty fucking pounds of muscle to work with."

Zhaden chuckled. "I am actually two hundred and forty, though I was around forty pounds heavier when I first arrived. The diet we were provided was . . . lacking, to say the least. You can still see Jakob's ribs even under all the Shaz."

"The what?"

"The purple energy around him. It is quite hard to miss. I have seen him use it before, but never quite like this."

"You a poet now?"

Zhaden shot a confused look at Tom.

"Just. . . never mind. Do you think we should be worried about him?"

Zhaden shrugged. "I do not know. Only the Draekon people can ever understand the power. I am as much of an outsider as yourself."

Tom was evidently satisfied with that answer, as he remained quiet for several minutes before groaning loudly.

"If I never see snow again in my fucking life, it'll be too soon." He was now lifting his boots to about knee height as he continued to trudge forward. Zhaden thought it best to try to keep the grumpy Ayr's mind occupied.

"What of the injury over your eye? It appeared to be quite painful earlier."

Zhaden looked back over his shoulder as Tom ran his finger over the cut. It had stopped bleeding but had left a large imprint that looked like a second eyebrow atop his right one. He had seen enough injuries like it in his time to know that it would almost certainly scar over.

"Yeah. I actually totally forgot about it with how insane this entire day has been."

"If we forget our injuries, dear Tom, we forget our mistakes. If we forget our mistakes, we live life on a treadmill, only ever breaking when we fall off."

"I don't do metaphors, bud."

"Very well, then tell me: what is your home like? I have never traveled to your people's system, I'm afraid to say."

"Oh, you know . . . Ayr-Groh is a . . . ugh . . . fucking utopia. We've got awesome buildings, expensive-ass resorts, and lots of rich and snobby types everywhere. It fucking sucks."

"I am confused. What do you mean?"

"So much of Ayr society is about showing off how much better you are than other people. It's just rich assholes everywhere tossing their shit buckets down onto the rest of us. I'm honestly glad my parents didn't want me. I'd have turned into a monster like the rest of them."

Zhaden stopped abruptly and signaled Tom to do so as well. He thought he heard something moving in the dark, but the sound stopped. He looked around for a few seconds before deciding to continue forward. "Apologies. I thought I heard something. Where did you come from, then?"

"Trax Town. Not exactly the place you take someone to and still expect them to like you afterwards. I spent my early days in an orphanage until they kicked my ass out."

"That is outrageous. How could they send you off by yourself at such a young age? That would never be allowed in Cha-leh!"

Tom chuckled. "This may be hard for you to believe, but I wasn't exactly the best-behaved child. There may or may not have been some stolen toys and mysterious fires here and there. But, you know, that's who I am. I'm a piece of shit, and I accept that."

Zhaden shook his head and looked over his shoulder at Tom.

"I may have known you for only a short time, but even I can tell that you are far, far more than that. A true criminal would have killed M'og and I both, robbed us, and taken off. Should the future that Jakob and I have planned come to fruition, there would absolutely be a role for you to play—one far more significant and meaningful than petty theft."

"Grand larceny, actually. I moved up from petty theft a fe—"

He was tackled to the ground by something that had rushed at him in the dark.

Zhaden ran as quickly as he could through the snow and over to the light, which had suddenly moved several feet to the left and was now flying wildly in every direction. Tom grunted and cursed as Zhaden made his way over to him.

He reached down and grabbed hard, expecting to feel the leather of an Alavite guard's armor. When his webbed hands touched fur, he realized that he was in for a whole different ordeal.

He improvised quickly and decisively, wrapping an arm around the animal's neck and putting it into a chokehold before purposely dropping his weight backwards, forcing the beast off Tom. As Zhaden hit the ground, the mysterious predator slipped from his grasp and turned. It then attempted to pin him down.

Unlike Tom, Zhaden had the strength to hold its powerful clawed paws back. For a brief moment, they were face to face, and the beast's foul breath flooded his nostrils. Somehow, through the adrenaline and tunnel vision, Zhaden was able to recognize it. He had seen these beasts in films back on Cha-leh. Their names varied based on region and culture, but they were known as "bears" in Neatspeak.

He had nearly pushed the animal back enough for him to be able to stand up, when it suddenly became heavier. Zhaden looked up questioningly, only to see Tom's face appear on top of the bear's. He was repeatedly stabbing it in the neck with his knife and yelling between strikes as he did so.

"Fuck! Off! You! Furry! Fucking! Bitch!"

The beast writhed in pain and swung a powerful arm backwards, knocking Tom off and sending him tumbling into the snow. Zhaden took advantage of the distraction and pushed all of weight forward onto the bear, pinning it against the ground. The beast struggled and attempted to bite him a few more times.

Zhaden's strength was giving out rapidly, and his arms began to tremble. He looked the beast in its sky-blue eyes as a black blade came down directly into the center of its skull with force. A second later, the bear's body went limp. Zhaden rolled off to the side and plopped down into a seated position, breathing heavily.

"Fucking hell. . ." Tom muttered as he also struggled to catch his breath.

Through the sound of his racing heartbeat, Zhaden could hear more footsteps in the snow. These were fainter, though. Tom seemed to pick up on them as well and reached to withdraw his dagger from the dead bear's skull.

Stepping into the light slowly and timidly was another bear, but this one was far smaller and looked to be, at most, a few days old. It ignored Tom and Zhaden completely, walked over to the carcass between them, and began pawing at it while producing high-pitched wails.

"Well, that's fucking great." Tom muttered as he rose to his feet and holstered his blades.

"It will die without its mother. I viewed quite enough nature documentaries back home to know this much. Their fate is grim, especially during frost peaks." Zhaden spoke softly and calmly, so as to not scare the cub.

"Isn't your planet totally covered in water?"

"Yes. We actually have an aquatic variation of it known as *fea'volah*."

Tom looked down at the cub and back at Zhaden. "Should we kill it?"

"No." Zhaden shot an angry glance back at the Ayr, who shrugged.

Going down onto his hands and knees, he crawled over to the cub, which stopped paying attention to the corpse to look at him. After a few tense seconds, it began slowly walking over. It sniffed him once it was about an inch away.

"We need to get moving, man."

"Shh."

The cub took two whole laps around Zhaden before climbing up clumsily onto his back and wrapping its paws around his neck. Zhaden stood up slowly. "It seems I am large enough for this one to consider me friendly, and I believe it understands its situation."

"You're going to adopt a fucking bear?"

"I will not let it die, Tom. We killed its sole source of food and protection."

Tom ran a hand through his hair and exhaled. "Alright. Don't come crying to me when it decides blue is an appetizing color."

With that, the two continued their journey. The cub was remarkably silent and occasionally licked Zhaden's neck.

"You got a special lady back home?"

Zhaden smiled at the question and turned slightly back to Tom. "I have not seen my lover for a decade. I can only hope that I have not been forgotten. What of yourself?"

"I don't really do relationships, honestly."

"Quite unfortunate. There is no greater joy than walking through life with a partner."

"If you can find someone willing to put up with me, I'd be all ears. I have a hard enough time dealing with me myself. I have money for my . . . uh . . . other needs."

Zhaden shook his head. "Prostitutes fill only a small portion of the hole that the heart longs to repair."

"Thanks, Mom."

Zhaden looked back quickly to glare at Tom, who shot back a sheepish smile. His blue eyes were the most visible part of his face in this amount of light.

"They do say imitation is the sincerest form of flattery. I am glad to see you were so impacted by the death blow I delivered to M'og that you would copy it almost exactly."

"Oh, shut the fuck up. I should have let your fish ass get mauled."

Zhaden chuckled.

* * *

They lapsed into silence as they reached the area where the tower should be located. Zhaden could hear the radio frequencies quite clearly when he focused in, and they were stronger than ever before. He was about to ask Tom to help him search the area when a blinding amount of bright yellow light sent them both recoiling slightly and shielding their faces. After a few seconds, the tower came into focus as Zhaden finally managed to keep his eyes open. All of its lights had suddenly been switched on at the same time. At the very top of the tower and leaning over the railing was Koomer, who waved to them as they approached. He was wearing some sort of odd, orange goggles.

Koomer called down. "You guys alright? It's good to see you again. Wasn't totally sure I would."

"Yes, my friend. Do come down! The camps are being secured by the Zantavi army. We are to meet with Jakob at the castle!"

Koomer's face suddenly dropped at the mention of Jakob's name, and he looked frighteningly somber. "I . . . I think you should come up here first. There . . . there's something you need to see . . . both of you."

His tone was alarmingly serious. Zhaden and Tom exchanged looks before trotting up the staircase.

Koomer greeted them as they reached the top. "Sorry about nearly blinding you. I wanted to make sure I could stay as hidden as possible. As soon as I recognized you two on the night vision security cameras, I flipped the switch. Oh, and here." He whipped the goggles off his head and handed them to Tom. "I was able to sync them into the system and reach the Zantavi. I'm glad they got here as quickly as they did. The ones I've been keeping in contact with from the other camps say Rey Josso has been desperate to secure the safety of his son. At first, I thought it would take days, but it turns out that they had set up a base on a nearby moon to keep a close eye on the situation. We got lucky. The second they knew he was no longer in danger of being executed immediately, they set their plans in motion."

"You are indeed a hero, Koomer." Zhaden patted the one-eyed Ayr on the shoulder as he spoke.

"I'm really no . . . Is that a bear?"

The two took a moment to fill him in on the events that had recently transpired.

"Hmm. That explains the torn-up Alavite bodies I saw on the way down here. Which reminds me . . . Come here."

Once more, his voice and expression dropped suddenly. He walked over to the tower's control panel and pressed several buttons, which activated spotlights that were aimed outside the gates of the camp. He said nothing and looked down, apparently unwilling to see whatever it was for a second time. Zhaden and Tom approached the window slowly and looked out.

After only a few seconds, Tom turned away and sat slowly on the floor, facing away from the window. He began muttering to himself. "What . . . What in the fucking . . .?"

Zhaden couldn't blame Tom for his reaction; it took several seconds for his own brain to truly understand what he was seeing. He grabbed onto the wall of the tower for support out of fear that he might faint.

No one spoke for several seconds, until Zhaden finally broke the silence. "We need to go to Jakob. Now."

Zhaden chose not to address it. Nothing needed to be said. The scene spoke more eloquently about itself than any words that could be put together to describe it. The two Ayrs seemed to understand this and nodded, and the trio made their way down the steps, moving briskly back to the campgrounds.

* * *

The trip was mostly quiet, which was likely due to what they had all witnessed. The only significant sound was the high-pitched whine of the cub, which Zhaden attempted to soothe by petting it. This worked, but only for short bursts at a time.

The noise level rose significantly as they stepped back into the lights of the main area of the block. A large crowd of prisoners were standing around, seemingly in wait. In front of them, CJ, Josso, and the Zantavi soldiers were talking. Zhaden used his size to create a lane for the group to move toward them.

"Perfect timing. We're about to start loading up the ships. Cute pet." Josso smiled at the sight of the cub.

CJ, who was in a conversation with one of the soldiers, seemed to be distracted by the sight of the animal, and raised an eyebrow higher than Zhaden thought possible. The Erub broke off his conversation and went over to him. But he ignored Zhaden almost entirely and reached up to pet the bear.

"Frost bears. One of the few species native to Oballe. Never seen one in person. It's holding you in a familiar grip, so it trusts you. You'll have to give me the story later."

Zhaden nodded. "What of the other camps?"

"The occupying forces mostly surrendered or fled. As we speak, Josso's men are hunting down those who ran. Rounding up the prisoners was much easier there, since they were all organized into their barracks. They'll be taken to the castle directly, so I hear."

"Wait. There's no one in the cities? The towns? Nothing?" Tom asked incredulously.

"Have you looked at this planet? No one would live here as anything but a last resort. The Draekons only settled here in the first place because no one else would have them." CJ was still petting the bear as he spoke.

"What? Why?"

"Draekons and Alavites have a very complicated and unfriendly history. It's a longer story than that, but we don't have the time right now."

"Well, that fucking blows."

"That's putting it mildly." CJ finally turned away from the bear as he finished speaking.

"How do you know about that shit?" Tom had to speak up a bit to project his voice over the sound of the crowd.

"I had some pretty rigorous education, and that included galactic history. It was boring as all hell, but I learned it. Unlike Josso here, I actually took some time to learn how to fight too."

"I don't refuse to fight because I don't want to, but because I can't. Strict regulations of the Church of the Grains. Only military members, which I am not, are exempt." The Zantavi seemed more exasperated than mad, like he'd already explained himself several times over.

Zhaden turned to look over the prisoners' faces. Many of them looked tired, underfed, or otherwise unhealthy, but there was also an undeniable spark of true, genuine hope in their eyes. He couldn't remember the last time he'd seen this within these gates in anyone but Jakob.

Josso used the loudspeaker on one of the ships to address the crowd. "Based on the groupings we discussed before, make your way into your designated—"

A loud, low whooshing noise swept over the entire crowd, which immediately became engulfed in blinding purple light. Most shielded their eyes as Josso, Tom, CJ, Koomer, and Zhaden turned around to face the source.

Zhaden tried his best to keep his eyes open, but it was almost impossible. His retinas burned with every fraction of a second they were exposed to the enormous purple spire. Like everyone else at the camp, he was no stranger to these lights by any means, but something was different about this one. It was far brighter and wider than any he had ever seen. It took a few seconds of intermittent staring for him to realize that what he was looking at was not a single purple spire; rather, two of them were spiraling around each other endlessly on their journey into the heavens.

Aside from a few slight murmurs and intermittent gasps, no one in the crowd spoke a single word for the entire time that it took the beams to slowly ascend into the clouds. Zhaden could not remember having ever seen one last more than ten seconds, and this one far exceeded that length of time. Finally, after about the two-minute mark, the lights vanished, allowing the darkness of the night to engulf the campground once more.

A strange combination of despair and anxiety began to overcome Zhaden.

"Let us go, Josso. Now."

The Zantavi nodded.

"Everyone to your shuttles."

The prisoners moved in a surprisingly calm and organized manner, and within a few minutes, the campground was just as barren as it had been when they had looked at it from the hill.

Zhaden swung the door of his ship open and went inside quickly. Josso, Tom, CJ, and Koomer followed.

"So . . . anyone want to tell me what the fuck that was?"

CJ shifted forward in his seat and gazed around at the others. "For once, I second Tom's question."

No one answered.

XV

**JAKOB KOSS
KING'S QUARTERS, KARVENKULL
OBALLE**

His vision returned slowly as the blinding lights evaporated.

The room that had been erupting in an all-too-familiar neon-purple glow only a few seconds before was now just as quiet as it had ever been. The crumpled bodies of the two Kivs lay silently on the floor before him.

I suppose Olivio's genocidal crusade was ultimately unnecessary. It would seem you are perfectly capable of ending the Draekons on your own.

"I don't answer to you."

You are alone now; you do understand that?

"I need to be. It needs to be me. You said that yourself."

The voice sighed. *You did not need to kill them.*

Jakob stared down at the lifeless blue eyes of the corpses. "I don't have the time to wait through a bureaucratic process. Planets give their leaders ultimate power in times of war and chaos for a reason. Even if it took only a day to convince the two of them to listen to me, that is a full day where Olivio has the advantage over us. Everything from here on out depends on having a single, uncontested leader who can lay the foundation my people so desperately need."

What people?

"You know how I grew up. Zhaden, Koomer, and my other brothers in chains are closer to me than any Draekon ever was. I'll die in agony before I let any of them suffer the way my kind did. Do you think a man related so someone as spineless as Kadrok Kiv would say the same?"

The mysterious voice was quiet for a few seconds.

They deserve better than to be left here to rot. Touch them.

Jakob was hesitant but complied. He reached out and pressed the tip of his Shaz-consumed arm to both Marielle's and Yozak's foreheads. A bright light engulfed the exact points of contact, eventually spreading out through their entire bodies. The glow began to dim before disappearing entirely, taking all traces of the corpses along with it.

Now then, where do we begin?

"We've spent the last decade with our faces buried in the dirt and snow. I'm done with that. We're not crawling on the ground anymore. Now, we rise."

This was the first time since his "reawakening" that he had a few minutes to himself to analyze things. He moved over to a large mirror that was hanging in the corner of the office. The light that radiated from his eyes and arms reflected slightly off the mirror. The violet glow seemed to accentuate the paleness of his bare chest. He looked down at his sharp and glowing arms. "Is this permanent?"

Not any more or less than simply igniting your hand once was.

He could still feel the pain that Pertinax's glove had sent exploding through his skull. He had truly thought that he was about to die.

"At what point will you tell me who or what you are?"

Not now, but the time will come. I promise you.

Jakob sighed and moved from the mirror toward the open window where Marielle had been standing when he and Yozak had first entered the room. It looked out over an empty, dreary-looking courtyard. He wondered what had been so captivating about this view.

I must ask: are you ready to rule?

"That's not a question worth asking, because the answer doesn't matter. I have to, and I will. I'm the only one who can."

Power is a dangerous and curious thing. You may find it to your liking, or you may find yourself wishing you had let the lost prince take his proper place.

There was silence for a few seconds. The cool night air blasted his face. It must have been far below freezing, but the warm Shaz energy made the breeze feel light. It was good to finally take a breath in a day that had been so consumed by blood and adrenaline.

Prepare yourself. This won't be pleasant.

"I just said that I have been preparing."

*Tha*t *is not what I meant.*

Jakob fell to the floor as his knees gave out completely. He was suddenly overcome by a total and utter sense of weakness that was exponentially worse than any stun prick. He was unable to even prop himself up with his arms, which had suddenly returned to normal. The world began to spin around him. He gagged and wheezed as his world threatened to fade to black over and over again.

But he refused.

He used every inch of his strength to get back onto his knees. He reached over to the desk and struggled to get to his feet. Every fiber of his being wanted him to fall to the floor and become lost in the peace of unconsciousness. But he would not. This was not how it would end. No.

Hold on, Jakob. A single individual holding this much raw Shaz energy is almost historically unheard of. It is a rough and jarring adjustment for your body to go through.

He flung himself over from the desk to the railing in the back-left corner of the room, barely managing to grab it as his legs gave out. It took another minute-long struggle for him to get his feet back under him before he could finally begin making his way up the steps, albeit slowly. This would give him roof access—or, at least, so he hoped. If not, his body would be falling down these steps, because he certainly wasn't going to walk back.

It felt like an eternity, but he finally made it to the door and was blasted with frigid wind as he forced it open. With the Shaz energy gone from his arms, he was now unable to warm his shirtless body. He began to shiver harshly, and he fell to the floor as his legs gave out, though he kept his head as high as he could manage.

The King's Watch, as the tower was known, was Karvenkull's highest point. Nothing they had built throughout the course of their history there had ever come close to matching its height. The small balcony was, perhaps unsurprisingly, composed of the exact same black stone as the rest of the castle. A reinforced railing sat at the precipice of the platform, and Jakob crawled over to it slowly, wincing in pain. He took a deep breath and used what remained of his sapped strength to reach out, grip the bars firmly, and pull himself to his feet. He tightened his hold on the railing as his legs wobbled beneath him.

A loud groan escaped his lips as what looked to be at least forty pairs of neon-green lights approached him as the sound of ship engines began to fill his eardrums. He gazed out at them silently as another blast of wind engulfed his exposed body. Something about the sight of the lights revived his spirit. He threw his head back and not only took on the cold but embraced it. His short jet-black locks whipped wildly in the night air.

All the ships but one slowed down and began to hover just a bit away from the castle's dark walls before slowly lowering themselves one by one. Their doors flung open as they landed, and the prisoners began to frantically climb out and scurry onto the wide, elevated walls of the palace. These filled quickly, and the remaining prisoners aboard the later ships had to be dropped at the base of the castle. What had to be thousands of faces of a multitude of races began to look up at him. A lone vessel broke from the swarm of shuttles and continued upward toward him. Jakob followed it with his eyes as it moved closer and eventually hovered just off the edge of the balcony. Its massive side door opened, revealing a collection of far more familiar faces than those below. Zhaden, Tom, CJ, Josso, and Koomer all hopped out and joined him on the platform. The Udul, who seemed to have some sort of animal on his back, immediately reached out to him and wrapped him in an extremely tight embrace.

"Jakob! Thank the Maiden! Are you alright, my friend?"

"I'll live."

"The lights..." There was a palpable mixture of sadness and relief in Zhaden's eyes.

Jakob shook his head. "Marielle killed him and then herself."

Zhaden looked down and nodded. "You need to get back inside, Jakob. You're going to start suffering from hypothermia without proper attire."

A plethora of shouts began to come from the wall below.

"What did you want us here for again? I need to get home." CJ asked as he crossed his arms.

"And while we're asking questions, where the fuck did all the purple shit go?" Tom added as he jammed his hands into the pockets of his leather jacket.

Tell them to give you space.

"Back up for a second."

The group exchanged confused looks but obliged. There wasn't much space to be had on the small balcony, but everyone pressed themselves as close to the edges as possible.

The noise from the prisoners on the walls below had come to a grinding and sudden halt. Jakob looked down at himself to see several tiny purple beams circling his body. They moved rhythmically and slowly, unlike the death lights to which he had become so accustomed. He couldn't help but admire the grace and beauty of the lights as they floated in and around him. The small particles began to speed up as more and more started to appear and join what quickly became a frenzied swarm.

He looked up as he noticed that they were coming from the sky. They traveled together intelligently like a flock of tiny migrating birds. Each one couldn't have been more than an inch long and a quarter of an inch wide; yet, in numbers like these, they began to form a solid barrier around him from all sides. It wasn't long before his vision became obscured entirely. His mind began to race as he realized that he was also being lifted ever so gently off the ground. He rose around a foot or so before hovering in this exact position.

The beams created a buzzing noise every time they passed his ear. With so many of them flying around now, it was impossible to hear anything, which meant that he was now effectively deaf as well as blind. He lifted his head to the sky as an incredible, inexplicable feeling of power coursed through his veins from the tips of his toes to the top of his head, and then again, and then a third time. He didn't know how long he had been up there. It could have been a few seconds or several hours. The experience was as indescribable as it was strange.

Protect them, Jakob. You are all that's left now.

He fell slowly back to the black stone and touched a hand to the ground. Suddenly, every single one of what must have been millions of light beams stopped all movement and shot themselves inside of him from every conceivable direction. He couldn't feel them at all but could see several out the corners of his vision. He felt his life and energy return to him stronger than ever before as more and more of the beams melded with him. He rose to his feet slowly and approached the railing to look out over the crowd. A deathly silence permeated the black castle and the area around it.

He focused his mind the same way he had on countless nights in the barracks when he had worked on igniting a single finger, and later his entire hand. However, something was different now.

He raised his arms slowly. The confused murmurs of the crowd became audible. He could feel far more energy and power coursing through his veins, aching to be released. He closed his eyes, breathed in slowly, and concentrated.

Rise, Jakob Koss.

His eyes flew open as his body began to move on its own. His right hand closed into a fist and moved to his chest while his left arm extended itself fully out to his side. This Draekon gesture of respect and reverence was normally performed in the presence of kings, priests, or other respected members of society, not a crowd of downtrodden prisoners. His arms ignited slowly and dramatically, starting from the tips of his fingers and eventually spreading to his upper chest. The Shaz was brighter now than before—or at least it felt like it, as it spread across the entirety of his chest.

He had been so focused on evaluating himself that he initially didn't notice the cheers coming from down below. This wasn't the type of praise that one gave to a stage actor or musician at the end of a particularly impressive performance. No. This was deeper. This wasn't an applause of politics nor appreciation. This was one of spiritual and religious significance. This was a resuscitation of thousands of souls who had long since surrendered themselves to death and misery and were now waking up and crying out for their savior.

And just like that, the plan's first of a seemingly unending series of borderline-impossible hurdles had been overcome.

The responsibility of a king can be overwhelming enough, but it pales in comparison to that of a god. Be wary of what you let others expect of you and, more importantly, what you expect of yourself.

Jakob was taken slightly aback as he realized that there were multiple individuals in the crowd who were copying his gesture. They began in small clusters, and once they started to spread, they never stopped.

Hope spreads like wildfire amongst those deprived of it. If you are not careful, you will soon have millions falling to their knees at your feet, pleading for things you can't possibly provide.

Jakob spoke in a voice that was barely above a whisper as he stared back out over the prisoners, well over three quarters of whom were now copying the gesture.

"Good. I'll take them all."

For once, the voice in his head was speechless.

XVI

ROBERT JOSSO
KING'S WATCH, KARVENKULL
OBALLE

Things had a way of remaining stagnant within the shifting sands of Saraii. Josso had grown up as a prince on the desert planet he had once, naively, thought was the only one in the galaxy. In his twenty-six years of life, he had never seen an uprising, an exchange of power, nor a dramatic fall from grace. It took traveling halfway across the galaxy to a planet that could not possibly be more unlike his own for him to witness what the birth of a true king looked like. It was equal parts fascinating and unnerving.

Without saying a word, Jakob opened his flaming arms as though he were about to accept someone's embrace. Within seconds, a large beam erupted from his chest and shot several feet in front of him and into the night sky. The crowd, which seemed to alternate perpetually between raucous and silent, suddenly became the latter once again. The beam stopped abruptly and spread out in a sort of strange fog, which began to solidify into the form of a featureless purple being.

"What in the fucking . . .?" Tom muttered almost under his breath.

Jakob's lips began to move, but the words boomed unnaturally from the figure in front of him, which now hung over a dozen stories in the air. It would have been impossible for any normal being to project his voice down to the prisoners from this height without an external aid, but it had long become clear that this wasn't and would not be a normal situation.

"My fellow prisoners, the fiercest enemy we face is not in Alavon's Altar, but in our own capitals. Every single one of your leaders knows you're here. Don't let anyone tell you otherwise. They know what has been happening to you every day, and they have done nothing. That, in my book, is a declaration of war."

The prisoners began shouting angrily in agreement. Some, who were presumably still in a state of shock, simply kept staring in silence.

"Now, we could head back and raise chaos in the streets, create political uprising, and accomplish nothing but weaken our homes for the Chosen Army in the process. Or we could rebuild, reconstruct, and redesign ourselves from the ground up."

Josso turned to look out over the crowd. Almost every person below seemed absolutely captivated by the brilliant display before them.

"I want there to be no confusion: your leaders who abandoned you are your enemy, and what does one do with an enemy with whom he seeks to make peace? They sign a treaty, and that is exactly what we are going to do."

Confused murmurs began to run through the crowd.

"Olivio sits on his golden chair and calls us infidels. For years, my people resented and feared that term, as did many of you. But the old man was right; that's exactly what we are. We have always kept our eyes forward while they were busy looking up. We told tall tales in freezing barracks while they sang songs of worship in their luxury churches. Most importantly, we chose to stand while they kneeled. Let us make sure our boots meet their faces the next time they do."

An extremely enthusiastic cheer rang through the crowd. Josso could feel his heart rate increasing.

"Fellow heathens, black sheep, and scum of the earth: I present to you the Treaty of Cosmic Infidels, or TCI, —our vision for a stronger and more unified society where the Draekon, Joxun, Zantavi, Ayr, Udul, and Erub people can join together as one. I know my days of being preyed upon are over. Are yours?!"

Josso shook his head as another ear-splitting cheer rang through the crowd. Jakob was absolutely killing it. The prisoners were eating out of the palm of his hand. He had them, and, based on the slight smirk on the Draekon's face, he knew it.

Josso looked around at the others. Tom was moving his head frantically, as though trying to come to grips with what was happening. CJ had narrowed his eyes and crossed his arms, seemingly just wanting to get this whole ordeal over with. Zhaden and the other Ayr were a completely different story. Both looked on at Jakob as though he were their child performing in a school play. The beaming pride and joy etched on their faces were unmistakable.

"These men behind me . . . every single one was instrumental in everything that took place today. All proved themselves to be as capable as they are reliable. As a result, I will be sending each of them to deliver the treaty to their system leaders and entrusting them with doing whatever is necessary to get them signed. In doing so, they will bring us one step closer to what I would hope is our shared goal."

There was another eruption of cheers.

"Of course, there are those of you who will want to go home and who want all of this to just be over so as to begin the recovery process. To you, I say this—look around. This is my home. Look at the Draekons next to you. There aren't any. It happened to us. It can happen to you."

A gust of frigid wind blasted across the group, causing Josso's teeth to chatter involuntarily. Jakob pushed forward with his speech, seemingly unaffected.

"As the sole remaining living Draekon, I take on the responsibility of overseeing Oballe's future. My name is Jakob Koss. I don't have to be *your* leader. But on this frozen wasteland, I am king."

As quickly as it had come, the spectral figure disappeared back into Jakob's chest. The Draekon shook his head a few times before turning around slowly as the crowd below grew louder.

"Jakob . . ." Zhaden began, but he stopped himself short as he realized that the self-proclaimed king was looking up above all of them. Josso and the rest of them turned their heads. The iconic gold-and-white flag of the Chosen Army flapped slowly and hauntingly in the dark night sky about another story or two above their current position. It was easily among the largest that any of them had ever seen, and it would have been able to wrap a small ship entirely within it.

No one attempted to stop Jakob as he made for the wall near the door and stuck both arms into it.

"I would think about this first."

Jakob ignored CJ's comment completely as he began to slowly make his ascent up the side of the spire.

Massive cheers and fanfare erupted as those below began to realize what he was doing. After around two or three minutes, he reached the very top of the spire where the flag continued to flap. Jakob stretched his arm out toward the fabric and pressed the flaming Shaz tip against it. Within a few seconds, the spot he was touching erupted into a neon-purple flame, which quickly spread across the entire length of the flag. The cheers grew louder than ever before and briefly seemed to shake the very foundation of the castle.

Jakob leaned back slightly to look over the prisoners. His facial expression gave nothing away. He certainly wasn't the most charismatic leader that Josso had ever seen, to say the least, but it was hard to say that he didn't inspire people.

"JAKOB KOSS! JAKOB KOSS! JAKOB KOSS!"

The chant caused Josso to turn around and move to the railings. His heart sank slightly as row after row of prisoners dropped to one knee and laid their weapons down before them. He had expected the Draekon to proclaim himself king, but there should have been a struggle. There was supposed to be a fight, a disagreement, or, at worst, mere indifference as the prisoners went home and back to their lives. They weren't supposed to bow to him, nor indulge his fantasy.

He turned back around to find that Jakob had made his way halfway down the top of Karvenkull's tower. Ashes from the massive burning flag began to fall lightly around the Josso and the others as it dissipated into the blackness of the night. By the time Jakob made his way back onto the balcony, the prisoners' shouts and cheers reached deafening levels. He motioned for the crowd to be quiet, and this was heeded, if only slightly. Finally, he turned to face the others on the balcony.

"I need to know if we're all in this. I need commitment from everyone."

CJ began to speak up, but Jakob cut him off. "Yes, except for you. You've done more than you needed to."

CJ nodded, evidently content with not having to repeat himself.

Zhaden chuckled.

"Is that even a question, my friend? Until the end and thereafter!" The Udul's smile and enthusiasm was contagious.

He grabbed both sides of Jakob's face and leaned down to press his forehead to his. Josso could see CJ and the second Ayr exchange confused glances. He had seen this before on a diplomatic mission to Cha-leh. It was a gesture to symbolize a level of trust and respect that was usually reserved for close family. The idea was to touch horn to horn, although this would have been a bit difficult given that neither man had one.

"If you have mastered control of these new Shaz abilities, then we are off to a great start." Again, during a freezing night on an abandoned and forgotten planet, Zhaden's smile beamed brightly.

He took a step back. Jakob nodded. "I think I have, and I agree." He turned to the one-eyed Ayr, who gave a small smile before giving his own response. "I've stuck with the two of you for this long. I'll follow you until it kills me."

They exchanged a nod.

It appeared that it was Josso's turn now, as Jakob's glowing purple gaze latched onto his.

"I have terms I'd like you to present to your father. As with CJ, I can't exactly ask too much of you, but if you'd like to come back and join in the most important fight the galaxy has ever seen, then, we'd be honored to have you on our side, Prince of the Sands." Despite the monotone nature of his voice and the relative lack of expression upon his face, there was a bizarrely charismatic element to Jakob's demeanor.

Josso sighed, figuring there was really no way out of this at this point. He could only hope this wouldn't cost him his life nor his position.

"I'll ensure he receives it. As for the latter, I'll see what I can work out," he replied with a smile, thinking it wiser to remain noncommittal.

"Oh, I see how it is, Jakob. Leaving me for last, huh? Do I detect some racial favoritism?"

"Tom, you do realize we're the same—"

"Shut up, Koom."

The one-eyed man sighed and shook his head.

"Right . . . Tom. What about you?" Jakob asked with the slightest hint of exasperation as he turned slowly to face the talkative Ayr.

Tom smiled cockily. "Look, I'm glad you chose me to be your treaty guy, but this isn't really my thing."

Jakob raised an eyebrow. "What part of it isn't your thing, Tom?"

"You know . . . negotiation . . . diplomacy . . . all that boring, old-people shit."

"I can find someone else if you don't think you're up to this. The fact of the matter is that you seem to find a way to get things done, Tom, and that's ninety percent of what that 'old-people shit' is all about." Jakob's purple eyes seemed to flash for a half second as he spoke.

"Don't take this the wrong way or anything, but you barely know me. Why are you trusting me with this? If you knew me better, you wouldn't even consider it."

Jakob looked him up and down. "You're here standing in front of me right now. That tells me that you didn't run and escape when you could have. You're covered in blood and have a cut over your eye; that tells me that, on top of refusing to flee, you also actively fought for me when you had no real reason to. When I saw you on the field, you didn't have a virix on, and now you do; that tells me that you probably gave it to someone you felt needed it more, which shows me that in your soul, there is concern for the well-being of others. I don't have to know you as long as I've known Zhaden to trust you. If you can play the type of role I think you can in the growth and development of TCI, then I don't care about your past."

Tom swallowed hard. He seemed speechless.

"Meet with Sprock. I don't want you to hide your talents but rather to use them. You're a talker and a charmer. Bring both of those to the table."

"Well . . . slight problem on that front. Sprock and I are pretty well acquainted. I'm kinda on his shit list, actually."

Jakob sighed. "You'll be arriving with all the prisoners, and I'll have word sent out ahead about the key role you played in freeing them. With how heavily democratic Ayr-Groh is, you should be perfectly fine once public opinion swings heavily in your favor, and it will. In any case, I'm sending Koomer along with you. He'll keep you company on the journey over. The man has stayed alive here with one eye and no virix; I think he's fine-tuned his negotiation skills by this point."

"Sounds good to me. I'd like to get my own virix first, though," Koomer chimed in.

"Don't worry, my guy. I've got you covered. Let's get this done. 'Tommy and the One-Eye.' I like the sound of that."

Based on Koomer's reaction, it would seem he did not agree.

Jakob rolled his eyes slightly and turned as the shuttle appeared just over the edge of the balcony once more.

"Alright, people! Let's get a move on!" Josso called out as he motioned the group onto the shuttle.

The thought of Jakob's flaming arms flashed through Josso's brain. There was no telling if or how it would react with the metal of the shuttle.

"Jakob, could you—?" he began to ask as he turned back to face the Draekon.

"Yes?" Jakob responded without a single trace of Shaz energy emanating from his body. He was the same scrawny and unassuming Draekon he had been back in the cell.

"Shit. Is that it? It's gone?" Tom sounded genuinely concerned.

"Until I want it to be." Jakob answered as he climbed into the shuttle.

That was an unnerving statement for Josso to hear, but he shrugged it off.

"It's time, Zhaden. You still know it?" Jakob asked as they all settled into their seats.

The Udul smiled and nodded. "Only death would have taken the words from me."

The shuttle landed gently, and the first thing that Josso noticed was how alarmingly quiet it was. When he had been on the roof, the chatter and chants of the crowd had been deafening. Now, there was nothing. The doors swung open, revealing the now silent crowd of black-clad prisoners, most of whom were only now seeing the new king up close for the first time. The starved and poorly clothed masses had split into two to give Jakob and the others a lane to the castle. The new Draekon king walked forward as light snowflakes began to fall. Some prisoners fell to their knees, while others simply stared at him in his much more unimpressive form.

Jakob hesitated for a second as he reached the front door of the castle. His hands moved slowly toward the dark double doors. He took a deep breath.

"Everyone in."

The second the final syllable left Jakob's mouth, he pushed the doors open with a level of intensity that genuinely caught Josso and, based on the gasps, a few others by surprise. Jakob disappeared inside quickly with Zhaden shadowing him. The crowd of prisoners which had been so loud and exuberant not too long ago was now mostly silent, with a few assorted cheers and claps. It would seem they were just as tired as Josso was himself. The Zantavi soldiers worked to organize the prisoners and keep them from dispersing too far into the castle as Josso trailed behind Jakob and Zhaden out of curiosity. His pursuit ended at the doorway of what he soon discovered was a massive and very cozy-looking library.

"Let's get this done." The look of determination in Jakob's eyes was as strong as ever.

The two of them went to work almost instantly writing on what legal grade mascavi paper they could find. They worked in unison on the first one before breaking off to make handwritten copies. Josso leaned on the doorway arch and watched them work largely in silence for a bit before eventually getting bored and rejoining the Zantavi captains in the large throne room. Hours passed as he aided the soldiers in organizing the prisoners, many of whom had sought out whatever space they could find to stretch out and sleep, for extraction. He was in the midst of finalizing the last group's evacuation route when Zhaden and Jakob reemerged, each carrying multiple mascavi papers in their hands. The two spoke to each other near the throne as the crowd continued to shrink. It was nearly afternoon by the time they were down to the final three vessels, and the remaining men made their way outside.

CJ was helping to load up the lone vessel that was bound for Erub. A Zantavi captain was putting supplies into it as well. Because only one person was bound for the tropical planet, it made no sense to load him into the other ships. CJ would be traveling with him aboard the royal shuttle, which would stop at Erub before continuing back to his own home planet Saraii, well, at least in theory.

Tom and Koomer were sitting on crates outside of an all-black Ayr cruiser that Josso had seen in the scrap lot on the outskirts of Izrok. Tom had taken off his boots, and Koomer was now scrutinizing them closely for some reason.

"We almost ready?"

Josso turned to face CJ. "Yeah. Give me one second."

He walked over to the Cha-leh-bound shuttle, which Jakob and Zhaden had decided they would both travel aboard.

"I cannot wait for you to finally see my home, Jakob." Zhaden said, clapping his hand to the Draekon's shoulder.

"I'm happy for you. You must miss the water." Jakob gave him the slightest hint of a smile. It was a surprisingly distressing sight.

Zhaden seemed to choke up for a second before shaking his head. "Here, my friend. Do not forget these." He handed Jakob the other five copies of the treaty. Jakob thanked him, and the Udul made his way into the shuttle.

"We're about ready to head off!" Josso called out, causing Jakob to face him.

"My father has sent orders for a small fraction of the army to stay behind until you return to make sure nothing drastic happens here. I have already spoken to him, and he has committed to bringing our people into the fold and signing the treaty when I hand it to him."

Josso extended a hand to Jakob. "It's been an honor, and I look forward to working with you in the future."

Jakob took his hand and shook it firmly. He handed him a copy of the treaty before either one of them could forget. "Have a safe journey, Josso."

The prince nodded and took a step back as he quickly looked the treaty over.

CJ walked up from behind and got Jakob's attention. "I felt I should thank you for getting me out of the prison and . . . well, everything else. I'm not dead, so my sister won't be coming for your head. The ability to sleep soundly at night should be a reward in itself."

Jakob nodded. "No thanks needed. I was going through with this whether you were here or not. I look forward to our continued partnership. Speaking of which, I'd like to propose an offer to you."

CJ's eyes perked up, though seemingly more out of concern than excitement.

"I would like to offer you an opportunity to join the treaty. I know you have no authority as it stands, but I'm very confident in my ability to bring the Ayr, Udul, and Joxun into the fold. The Zantavi have already given a verbal agreement. If you can convince the rebel queen to agree to join Erub to the cause, I will send the TCI army to your planet as soon as it's ready and help you take it."

Jakob extended a copy of the treaty to him.

CJ looked down at it for a few seconds and ran a hand across the sandpaper scruff on his face. "I'm sorry, but no. As much as I appreciate everything, Erub has always been and will always be an independent sovereign nation. The entire reason we're at war is because the man who killed my father betrayed that and tried to push toward a union with the Alavites. I'm confident that we're close to winning the war ourselves, especially with Pertinax gone."

Jakob stared at him for a few seconds before nodding and withdrawing the sheet. "Then may we see each other again soon."

He extended an empty hand to him.

"We'll see." CJ took Jakob's hand and shook it before turning and heading for the ship.

Josso sighed and began to head for the shuttle as well. He could hear Jakob off to his left as he addressed the Ayrs.

"I hear Sprock is finicky. You two may have your hands full."

He held out the paper that he had just offered to CJ.

"I can deal with that fat sack of shit. We're well acquainted," said Tom as he fiddled with his virix.

"And I suppose I'll try to make sure he doesn't blow this whole negotiation up." Koomer stared his new partner down before taking the treaty from Jakob.

"Alright. I've had about enough of this place for now. No offense, Jakob. Let's get going, KoomKoom. The other shuttles have a pretty decent lead on us, and I don't want to be late to the party."

Tom slipped the virix back onto his head, opened the door, and walked up the ramp. Koomer followed closely behind. The two kept talking once they were inside. It sounded as though the one-eyed Ayr was asking a variety of questions about the ship, which he seemed very interested in for some reason. Soon, its engines kicked into life. The landing gear was pulled up and the ship shot off into the sky like an arrow. Unlike the Zantavi pilots, Tom performed a variety of twists and flips on his way up and out, evidently for no other reason than to show off.

Jakob watched until the ship disappeared into the atmosphere before he turned back to face Zhaden, who was waiting on the ramp of the last remaining vessel. He sighed and made his way over to him, eventually disappearing up the ramp.

Josso settled into his bedroom quarters as he felt his own shuttle begin to rise. It would take about a week to get to Erub, and he sure as hell was not going to pass the time alone. He pressed a button on the side of the wall. "CJ, come in here please." The tired, dirty-looking Erub emerged in his doorway a few seconds later. "Feel free to hang around here. Neither of us are going to benefit from letting boredom drive us insane."

"Yeah, I guess that's f—"

CJ suddenly went silent, and his eyes widened. It took Josso a second to realize that the Erub was reacting to something outside the glass behind him. Josso turned around as CJ quickly stepped over to him.

The captain's voice cackled over the ship's speakers. "Sir . . . we have identified—"

Josso pressed the button.

"Yes . . . I see it, Captain."

"I . . . How . . ."

CJ's words were sparse, but perhaps this was exactly as it should have been. The scene before him defied description. He had heard rumors and, of course, knew what had happened at the camp. But he had never seen it—not like this.

Josso pressed the button again.

"Captain, get us into orbit. Now."

ACT II

XVII

DARYN PERIC
DESERT HIDEOUT, SEA OF SAND
SARAII

As someone who was perpetually anxious, there had been many times throughout his life that Daryn had imagined being kidnapped. In each instance, it had always been a terrifying and shadowy figure who'd locked him away, never to return. His imagination tended to run rampant, but even then, he could never have imagined that his true abductor would be his own flesh and blood.

He gripped the rusted bars of the small cell, which was barely wide enough for him to lie down in. Had it been a week? Two, maybe? It was hard to remember. He had spent much of the time within the brig of a Zantavic ship and had only recently been transferred to this new and significantly smaller setup. Yeuma had come down multiple times to try to talk to him, but he had adamantly refused to give her the satisfaction and had not spoken a word to her or anyone else on the ship.

He had woken up wearing rags that had reminded him of the dirty sacks that the custodians of the Altar would collect garbage in. In lieu of gloves or shoes, his hands and feet had been covered in white tape. A piece of old rope tied around his waist served as what turned out to be a vital belt, as the pants he wore were a size or two too large for him. Why they had done this to him and what had become of his expensive, hand-sewn white robes, he did not know.

He wiped yet another accumulation of sweat off his forehead. Even on the hottest days of the solar season on Alavonia, he had never experienced heat quite like this. The light-brown walls and ceiling of the cave that acted as the group's shelter weren't the most pleasing to the eye, to say the least. He looked to his left and toward its large opening, which acted as the only source of light in there during the day. Scattered boxes, desks, generators, and other equipment lay strewn haphazardly along the entire length of the makeshift base. He was alone, as he had been for several hours every day since they had landed and set up camp there. What exactly his sister and her fellow kidnappers did during the day wasn't entirely clear.

He had just stepped back from the bars and slowly dropped into a seated position on the cool, soft sand that lined the floor of this place, when footsteps began to echo off the cave walls. He leaned forward and looked to his left. For a second or two, shadows ran up the wall, making the person look thirty feet tall before quickly compressing to reveal a much more accurate silhouette. With the sun shining brightly from behind them, it was hard to tell who it was. Daryn failed to recognize Yeuma until she was almost directly in front of him.

The attire she donned for this climate could not have been more different from the beautiful blue dress he had seen her in back at the monastery what felt like half a lifetime ago. Dark-brown boots came up to her lower shin, meeting tight light-brown pants that would certainly have never been allowed at the convent. A black belt with a large silver buckle in the shape of a skull accentuated her midsection. A dirty white button-down shirt that seemed to have been designed for a man covered her chest. Over her shoulder, she carried her dark-brown bomber jacket, which usually completed her outfit. She tossed it onto a nearby crate to the side as she straddled the stool and sat down in front of Daryn's cage. She spit disgustingly on the ground before looking him in the eyes.

"So, let's try this again, because I'm going to keep coming back until you talk to me. You and I both know the Eye is bugged from top to bottom. I wasn't exactly about to tell you the entire plan for Olivio to hear."

He glared at her. Sweat was forming in beads on her forehead as well.

"I'm sorry for lying to you. I'm also sorry that you seriously thought I'd leave you behind and let that old sack of shit continue to manipulate you. When we discussed the plans in the first place, I told them the only way I'd sign off was if we extracted you too."

"Abducted."

And there they were—the first words that had escaped his lips in over a week and a half. The sound of his own voice was off to him, and he cleared his throat.

Yeuma gave no meaningful reaction and simply moved on as though they had just been speaking only a few hours ago.

"Call it what you want, Daryn. I can't believe you chose him over me."

"It wasn't easy. That man is basically a father to me."

"And he milks that for all it's worth. You're unbelievably naive."

"I was about to get a promotion. I was going to be—"

"The youngest priest in history. Exactly what you always wanted to be."

He stared blankly at her. "How did you know that?"

Yeuma crossed her arms and rolled her eyes. "I had Oslo bug the conference room and Olivio's quarters months ago. Those Quexians are damn ghosts, honestly. Olivio only found and disabled the mics last week while we were in slingshot. Nothing made me happier than hearing that old cunt rant and rave at everyone who would listen. He didn't take very well to your sudden disappearance." She leaned forward and lowered her voice slightly.

"Do you know what I've found out over the last week? Aside from a few scattered and mostly abandoned moon bases, the Chosen Army's numbers on Erub are the lowest in the entire galaxy. It's the battle of titles down there: the Rebel Queen, for whom support grows by the day against the Traitor King, whose military backing has continued to diminish. Everyone and their mother know how that's going to end, Daryn, and Olivio is no fool. Apparently, the queen's brother is as good of a fighter as the planet offers. If you had ended up on Erub, your head would have been mounted on the gates of their palace within a month, maybe less."

Daryn shook his head and pressed back against the bars at the rear of the cell. "Who do you possibly know on Erub?"

Yeuma smiled. "You didn't think there were only four of us, did you?"

Daryn said nothing. Yeuma ran a hand through her boy-length hair and sighed. "He wasn't sending you there for a tropical vacation to pair with your promotion, you thick-skulled twat. He was sending you there to die. Why do you think that was Pertinax's post for all these years? Do you really think Olivio just forgave him for the Carine incident?"

Daryn had forgotten about that. Pertinax's brutal massacre of the chieftain's wife behind Olivio's back had been intended to accelerate the surrender of the wolf-like people. Instead, their resolve had only grown.

Daryn turned his head away from his sister. "He would send the army for me if I was in trouble. He cares about me."

Yeuma ran a sweaty hand down the length of her face and exhaled dramatically. "If he cared about you, he would have kept you as his attender, and not 'promoted' you into the line of fire."

Daryn stood up and walked over to the bars. "Why is he so upset at me being kidnapped then? Wouldn't he just be happy that someone had taken care of me for him? Or why not just have me 'accidentally' killed on Alavonia? I don't believe you."

"You have more in-depth knowledge of him than pretty much anyone . . . knowledge that would be very useful to his enemies. On Erub, he could rest easy knowing you'd only ever speak to allies until you took a sword or arrow to the heart. We think there's something more to it than that, but we're not exactly sure what."

Daryn honestly had no idea what that would be. Most of the extent of his private knowledge of Olivio consisted of his favorite foods, clothing preferences, and things of that nature. From an intelligence perspective, he had only been exposed to things that most officers in the Chosen Army knew. He, too, was unsure why Olivio would be so distressed at his abduction.

"Let's say you're right. Why would he want me dead? He must have people he hates far more than me. It doesn't make any sense."

"We don't think he hates you. We think you scare him."

"What? That's insane. He's the most powerful man in the galaxy!"

Yeuma shook her head. "We don't know why. We were trying to figure it out when our bugs were discovered and shut down. But it's clear that you pose a threat to him in some way, which makes you both extremely valuable and dangerous to keep around."

Daryn opened his mouth to respond when more footsteps approached from the left. The remaining three members of 'The Others,' as they called themselves, made their way down the small slope into the cool, dark interior of the cave, escaping the smoldering heat of the exterior. They stripped off their protective sun gear and tossed it in their respective corners before joining Yeuma. Daryn hadn't spoken to any of them but had heard their names enough times at this point to be able to easily identify each one.

Oslo, the Quexian with stone-colored skin and fiery red hair, was as stealthy as they came. He had apparently made his way in and out of the Altar multiple times in the past few months without being seen, heard, or caught on camera. Da'garo, the demonic-looking Dom'Rai, had apparently been imprisoned in his home world for refusing to bow to Alavon and had spent his days as a slave mining prior to escaping. He was incredibly strong, was evidently a ferocious fighter, and had been the one who had single-handedly taken out all Olivio's golden guards. He had the darkest red skin of any Dom'Rai Daryn had ever seen, and unlike most of his race, his horns bent backward rather than to the sides.

The last of the three, Namira, was perhaps the most unusual, in that she wasn't from an occupied planet at all; rather, she was a Zantavi. In his time in the cell, it had become clear to him that she was the de facto leader of this group. She had alluded several times to having chosen the location for their base, which made sense, given that it was situated in the Zantavi home world. The combination of her dark skin, light-pink pupils, and waist-length white hair, curled into multiple intricate dreadlocks, made her one of the most bizarre sights that Daryn had ever seen. But perhaps this was due primarily to his lack of exposure to her kind.

They were all dressed in color schemes similar to Yeuma's. Daryn assumed that this had been done purposefully to enable them to blend in with the impossibly large amounts of sand that surrounded the cave. When they had first arrived, he'd been certain that he would have sunken into it with every step, and it had seemed to extend outward in every direction as far as Daryn could see.

"He finally speak up?" Namira asked without taking her eyes off Daryn.

"Yeah. He's not very happy, though."

"Like I said, I can get him to talk if we really need him to. Chemically speaking."

Oslo motioned to an open beaten-up briefcase in the corner of the room; it looked to have several syringes in it.

"You stick one of those in my brother, and I'll put my foot so far up your ass that I'll be able to tell what you had for breakfast when I pull it out."

Oslo was silent for a moment. "Very well, then."

"We managed to get some more water from the well. We're going to try to contact the town tomorrow, but we decided that Namira should go alone at first, for obvious reasons." Da'garo's deep voice was several octaves lower than that of anyone around him.

The sun had almost completely set, and Oslo had begun walking around the cave to turn on the makeshift lights within it.

Namira was presumably about to respond to Da'garo's comment, when Daryn spoke up. "Who are the Others? What do you do?"

All four of them widened their eyes at Daryn. Namira chuckled before answering.

"He speaks after all. Well, we're primarily composed of societal misfits and outcasts. The majority of our five thousand or so members are exiles from planets dominated by Olivio's army who would be killed if they were to return home. A few, like me, come from free systems . . . at least for the time being. I'm here because the man who ran the sex-trafficking ring I was put into as a child now occupies one of the highest positions in Zantavi society. When I finally snapped and strangled my umpteen-hundredth client, he sent out a message to all his paid-off officers to find me and have me killed. I was fourteen then. He found himself in the good graces of Rey Josso and continues in his position to this day. I don't know if he remembers me, but I don't intend to find out."

Daryn didn't know what to say. It was the most sobering story he had heard in a while. "I'm sorry."

"Don't be. I don't mind talking about it. This life suits me. It connects me with those who have been cast aside or abandoned by their societies. It's the happiest I've ever been."

"How did you connect with my sister?"

Yeuma smiled and looked up at Namira as the Zantavi spoke. "I contacted Yeuma a few years back on a covert recruiting run through Alavonia. She was the only one who responded to my radio message, but it was too difficult to break her out at the time. The convent's walls, being much older than the prison's, were several layers thicker. She was also never in a room by herself at any given moment, which complicated things. Point is, she's here now, and so are you. I do have to say that you are the first member I can think of that we've had to bring with us against their will."

"I'm not one of you."

"You can say that as much as you like. You are now."

Several smashes followed by a sudden, harsh whooshing sound seemed to engulf the entire cave. All heads turned to the entrance, the path to which was now completely engulfed in flames. In the pitch black of the night, four silhouettes stood at the entrance. A bottle flew into view and crashed to the ground, exacerbating the flames. Two more bottles followed.

"SHIT!" Namira shouted.

Oslo immediately began scrambling to the sides of the cave and attempting to step around the areas that were covered in flames and toward the attackers. Namira quickly followed behind the Quexian. Da'garo grabbed nearby blankets and tried to put out whatever flames he could. When the rags themselves caught fire, he threw them off to the side and ran to join the others.

Yeuma and Daryn exchanged terrified glances as the flames continued to approach. Whatever was in those bottles was causing the wave of fire to move faster than any inferno Daryn had ever seen. Yeuma ran to the right of the cage and began knocking items over desperately, presumably in search of the key for the cage. The flood of flames continued to trickle toward them and had almost reached the metallic floor of the cell.

"Fuck. Fuck. FUCK!" Yeuma abandoned her search and ran to her section of the cave, which was positioned relatively close to Daryn's cell and had not yet caught on fire. She grabbed a scythe off her bare-bones cot and scrambled back over to the cage. The weapon was certainly unusual looking. Rather than being long and straight with a curved blade protruding from its side and going all the way to its top, this variation was significantly shorter, and it was curved. Its blade was also nearly as long as the entire length of its handle. On the first day that they had arrived, she had returned with it during her shift outside the cave and had apparently fallen in love with it. The sounds of loud grunts and steel hitting steel taking place at the mouth of the cave echoed through the walls.

"Back up!" Yeuma yelled with a level of intensity Daryn had rarely seen from her.

He obeyed as she swung the blade with all her might, and a sharp clang proclaimed its impact with the lock. The flames were now beginning to spill inside the cell. Daryn pushed himself as far to the right as he could as Yeuma reached in and flung the cell door open. As she extended her arm to grab him, she was suddenly tackled from the side.

One of the invaders, a Zantavi soldier, pinned her to the ground as the flames continued to approach. Instinct and adrenaline took over. Daryn made a quick move to exit the cell and jumped onto the back of his sister's assailant. He scratched and threw uncoordinated punches at the man's head.

He was shaken off relatively quickly, but the distraction gave Yeuma an opening to kick the man in the chest. Daryn backed slowly into a corner as the sharp clanging of metal on metal echoed through the cave. The two shadowy figures went back and forth, their strikes landing in line with every other pounding beat of his heart. Yeuma rolled away as the flames came within inches of her ankle. The blade of her scythe emerged through the Zantavi's chest before he could react. Daryn watched in horror as the man collapsed forward onto a puddle of blood.

His stomach was flopping over as he was pulled forward forcefully. Yeuma led him up the small area to the far right of the cave, which was still clear of flames. They hugged the wall as the heat grew increasingly unbearable. Daryn looked back briefly at the Zantavi soldier, but he had been swallowed by the fire.

Daryn and Yeuma gasped as they stepped out of the burning cave interior and into the cool air of the night. It was as great a relief as he had ever experienced. He had yet to experience lying with a woman, but there was no possible way it could top this feeling. He fell to his knees and buried his hands in the cold sand. The flames stopped a few feet inside the mouth of the cave, but he could feel the heat on his back even from here.

The rest of the Others stood bloodied and panting around four bodies. All of the intruders were dressed in white-and-brown armor and carried packs of what looked to be a dozen more bottles filled with black liquid.

"Those are official Zantavi colors. They're soldiers. He sent them. We need to relocate," Namira instructed between pants.

"What exactly made you come to that conclusion?" Da'garo asked as he motioned to the burning cave.

Oslo grabbed one of the bottles out of its pack and examined it. "Kaluma. The Arsonist's Bride. One bottle can burn a small house down to its foundation."

Da'garo shouted something in Garyl, aggressively kicking up sand. "All of our things are gone. What are we going to do now?"

"I'd like to know why no one tried to get my brother out."

Everyone looked at Yeuma.

"We didn't know it would move that fast. We thought we could take care of them and make it back in time. I'm sorry." Namira sounded sincere.

"I'd like to hope that it won't happen again." Yeuma took little care to conceal the hint of anger in her voice.

Namira turned to Da'garo. "Like I said: we're going to have to relocate. Again. If the middle of the desert on Saraii isn't safe, nowhere will be."

They all exchanged looks and then directed their attention to the burning cave before Namira continued speaking. "But there is good news. I was going to bring this up later in the evening or tomorrow. However, given the circumstances, I guess there's no time like the present."

Everyone, including Daryn, now looked at her intently.

"King Josso leaves most local duties to the man whose name I will not speak, but he handles everything outside the system personally. The king himself has no real interest in us either way."

Da'garo interrupted her. "We can't go anywhere else. No other planet has as much quiet and rural land as Saraii. Our other options are practically nonexistent. Cha-leh is too difficult and impractical because of the water, not to mention the fact that as a Dom'Rai, I'd be arrested the second I'm seen. Erub is too dangerous, thanks to the civil war, and in my experience, its people are far too nationalistic and racist to even consider going near the planet. Pariso has a serious shortage of habitable land as it is. We would have nowhere to hide where we could also survive. Norann is a possibility, but Olivio has spies everywhere on it."

Da'garo crossed his blood-red arms as he finished speaking and looked down at Namira, who simply smiled. The light from the flame-soaked cave framed her face beautifully as if extracting it from the darkness of the night.

"If you would have let me finish, I could have saved you an ample amount of breath. There is a place I believe will have us in an open and official capacity . . . one where we can continue our operations against Olivio in the most structured, viable, and significant way we ever have."

Yeuma nodded slowly as though urging Namira to continue.

"The Draekon home world of Oballe became a popular destination for The Hand to send captured members of our organization to, along with a host of miscellaneous political prisoners. I received a transmission earlier today from a few of the inmates who took control of one of the prisons. They've managed to launch a successful uprising with the aid of a Draekon who, in their words, 'defied death.' The reports are unconfirmed, but it sounds as though he might well be the last one left alive."

Daryn felt his entire soul sink into his stomach.

"It's not ideal. We're heading into a very risky and unstable situation. But we do know what's waiting for us everywhere else, including here, and it's not good. I'll take the unknown."

The crew nodded. Namira's face suddenly became very serious. "The men who contacted us have likely been underfed and sleep deprived. They have been reporting some extremely outlandish things about this supposed last Draekon, who they call 'Neon King'. However, on the off chance that there is even an ounce of truth to what they are saying, we need to get there. Immediately."

XVIII

**CORVUS-JORG (CJ) DROC
ROYAL QUARTERS, ROYAL ZANTAVI SHUTTLE
DEEP SPACE**

"You must be excited to see your sister again," Josso commented, causing CJ to look up at him and set the hand-held sharpening tool he had been using on the nearby desk.

He sheathed his machete before turning toward Josso, who had closed the book he was reading. "Yeah. I am. Still going to be carrying this weight on my shoulders until the war is over, though. Sheressa will make sure of that."

CJ had originally set himself up to sleep across a few of the benches in the general passenger area of the ship, but Josso insisted that he join him in the much more cozy side chamber, which held two small but surprisingly comfortable beds situated directly across from one another. The beds were clamped onto the wall for support and were covered in the softest sheets that CJ had ever felt. It seemed that the prince's previous claims that Zantavi weavers were the best in the galaxy were not completely unfounded.

Josso tossed his book to the side. "How many hours have we known each other now for? I have yet to ask you what you're even fighting over." The prince smiled slightly as he spoke.

CJ exhaled and crossed his arms. He hated having to go over this yet again, but, in all fairness, Josso had been nothing but good to him thus far.

"My sister and I lived in Mortobal, the Erub palace, for our entire lives. When my father, the king, began to make some. . . questionable decisions, Raymond Polero, the governor of the capital city, began openly accusing him of losing his mind. He was consumed with this idea that the traditional Erub culture was too violent and barbaric, and began to secretly plot against my father, going as far as to reach out to Olivio, who, of course, jumped at the chance to get his disgusting hands on another planet."

Josso ran a hand across his chin but said nothing.

CJ continued. "They came. All of them. Polero, coward as he is, ended up taking the throne by killing my father during what was supposed to be a peaceful negotiation. Shortly thereafter, the Alavite army burst through the castle gates, forcing all of us to run for our lives. I wanted to grab a ship and leave via the hangar, but Sheressa convinced me to follow her through the maintenance hatches. Turns out the Alavites had already been waiting near the ships, where they killed everyone who passed by. That was just one of the many times she's saved my life."

"Well then, I can see where your peoples' bloody reputation stems from."

CJ shook his head. "We aren't exactly proud of it. At least I'm not."

The Zantavi prince raised his eyebrows and leaned back against the wall. "I thought you were the one out there on the battlefield leading the men in this rebellion."

CJ nodded. "The gods, whoever and wherever they may be, apparently decided it would be very funny to make my greatest talent something I also hate doing."

"I saw you hacking and slashing back at Izrok. You didn't exactly strike me as miserable."

"If you're being chased by a deadly predator, you don't just sit down and take a nap because you'd rather be doing something else. When the situation calls for it, I step up. I always have. Sheressa maps out our battles, and I lead them. Once we do win and place Polero's head on a pike, Sheressa will go to our moon, Shiken-pah, where she will be crowned in front of the same ancient cave as every Erub king and queen in the history of our people."

"What's so special about this cave?"

CJ hesitated for a second. "I honestly don't know. Only those being crowned and Mortobal's Grand Shaman get to step inside, which they do immediately after the ceremony. Details of the interior are rarely shared, but it's rumored to be beautiful. Sheressa will be finding out soon enough, I suppose."

"Well, if you do manage to win and survive what's left of the war, please let me know. I'd love to attend the ceremony."

"Attendance to the coronation itself is normally restricted to a relatively small group but given your role in keeping me alive and bringing me home, I somehow doubt my sister would mind."

Josso smiled. "That sounds lovely, I'll see what I can do."

He turned to look back out the window before speaking up again. "What are your thoughts on Koss?"

CJ shrugged. "He's certainly. . . stoic. I was surprised he could muster the charisma to deliver that speech, though I imagine people will be impressed by him no matter what he does, thanks to . . . well, you know."

"I meant about his ideas. His vision." Josso produced his copy of the treaty and tossed it before him on his bed without turning away from the window.

CJ looked down at it before answering. "He's a dreamer for sure, but also very naive. I just don't see any way of it working out for him, if I'm honest. Convincing a single system to surrender their autonomy is hard enough, let alone five of them. He came to me with an offer for Erub, and I turned it down. I don't see why anyone else would do any different."

"I understand your perspective and honestly share your opinion. I wouldn't sign this were it up to me, but my father will not be swayed. He has made it clear that this is happening regardless of how anyone back home feels about it. How the public will react remains to be seen."

The two men remained silent for a few seconds. It was always borderline alarming to CJ just how quiet space travel could be. It always felt odd and unnatural to him, and he had never been particularly fond of it.

"How did you end up on Oballe?" CJ asked partly to kill the silence and partly out of genuine curiosity.

Josso finally turned to look back at him. "I was captured while off-world. I began heading out on longer and longer stints as my father made it increasingly clear that I wasn't wanted at the palace. Evidently, a known drug lord and human trafficker is a preferable option to me as his second in command."

"That's a bizarre choice."

"He wasn't the first. A man named Jorvah . . ." Josso trailed off, and his entire demeanor changed. He began to gaze out the window once more.

"Jorvah . . .?"

"Jorvah Jarem. He was the first choice. He died before he could take on any responsibilities."

"How?"

When Josso turned back to face CJ, a bizarre and frightening look of anger had engulfed him. "Violently."

While that was technically an answer to the question, it hadn't been what CJ was looking for.

"The Alavites found me while I was out hunting on a moon not far from home. I was brought to Oballe from there to serve as a bargaining chip against my father."

"Hunting? I thought you couldn't kill."

"That only applies to sentient beings. Animals are, quite literally, fair game."

CJ nodded politely. He couldn't imagine not being able to defend himself based solely on an abstract concept.

"We're more alike than different, you know. I look forward to seeing you again and under better circumstances." Josso began to stand and stretch as he spoke.

CJ chuckled before answering. "Well, it'd be hard for them to be worse."

Josso nodded in agreement.

The watch on the Zantavi's wrist began to glow green and flash rapidly. He looked down at it and seemed to read something on its screen. His look of confusion was followed quickly by one of frustration. "Pilot needs me up front for something. Stay here."

CJ could sense by his tone that something was wrong. "You sure everything's alright?"

Josso exited the small room and sealed the door behind him without answering. Once again, CJ looked out of the chamber's only window and watched as the mass of stars moved by with blinding speed and then stopped suddenly. He quickly turned his head toward the door. He found this odd. Pilots rarely stopped mid-slingshot unless there was some sort of catastrophic failure. Unless . . .

The ship rocked suddenly, sending him tumbling to the ground. The lights aboard flickered violently before going dark. They'd been hit with a bolt.

He got up and felt for the door, but with the power off, it was sealed shut. He tried the handle multiple times, but to no avail. He gave up and looked out of the small window that was embedded in the door. From there, he could see a few small lights coming from the ship-to-ship airlock on the opposite side of the shuttle as it slid open.

A few seconds later, several gold-clad Alavite guards, identical to the ones whom he had seen on Oballe, stepped into the Zantavi shuttle. He ducked as one turned to look in his direction. The beam from the small flashlight on his helmet blasted through the glass and filled the top of the small room for a few seconds before the light disappeared. Clearly, he'd looked away.

If a ship followed the exact same path in slingshot, it could theoretically get close enough to shoot out an incapacitating bolt. But the precision required for this was borderline ridiculous. CJ had only ever heard of one instance of it happening before, and it had been between two teams of scientists who had established a precise route that both ships had followed carefully.

Questions ran through his head as he heard several banging noises behind him. He slowly rose back up to the window to get a look at what was happening. The pilot and the other four Zantavi guards aboard the ship lay dead on the floor. Josso locked eyes with him as he was escorted away. His face was expressionless, and almost reminded CJ of Jakob.

The guards hardly even looked in CJ's direction as they made their way through the airlock with Josso in tow. It sealed shut behind them, and for several tense minutes, CJ was left alone in pitch blackness.

It took about an hour for the effects of the bolt to wear off and for power to return to the ship, which was now stationary. Thankfully, the shuttle's emergency life support systems had a six-hour supply of oxygen. The lights flickered back to life, and the door that CJ had been leaning against swung open, almost causing him to fall backward out of it. He approached the front of the shuttle slowly. All the Zantavi bodies had been brutalized and now lay motionless on the floor. He moved up to the controls and sat down. For a second, he considered going after Josso, but he realized that there was no way he'd ever get close enough to help him in any meaningful way—at least not alone. Besides, his own people needed him, and he couldn't afford to go off on yet another side mission.

He took a deep breath, reached over to the computer, and reconfirmed Erub's coordinates before punching the launch button. Luckily, most of the actual piloting work mattered during takeoff and landing only, and he resolved to cross that bridge when he got to it. CJ spent the next several hours collecting the bodies and doing his best to cover them up with what materials he could find, including the sheets off the beds.

He was half-asleep when the ship's vibration jolted him awake. Before he knew it, the emerald green waters of Erub exploded against the cockpit window, filling it entirely. He could have stayed up there forever, just marveling at the beauty of this amazing planet that he was proud to call home, but he had work to do. He took over the manual controls and clumsily began aiming for the Yaun region. He kept one hand on the joystick as he used the other to dial into a frequency on the radio. It took a few tries, but he finally made a connection. The ship began to heat up as it entered the atmosphere.

"Yaun base? Does anyone read me?"

"C . . . CJ?"

"Watts, I need you to open the hangar for me. Questions later."

"Y-yeah. Of course!"

CJ's entire window flooded with red as he broke through the atmosphere. He activated the hover functionality as he passed through and leveled himself out. It took him a few minutes to figure out the sensitivity of the joystick, the shuttle turning and shifting wildly until he got it under control. As he grew in comfort and confidence navigating the ship, he slowed his descent to the mountain hideout.

He slowed his speed to a crawl as the hangar doors took their sweet time to roll open, before entering slowly and steadily. Flyers were parked haphazardly all over the place; it seemed they had rushed to move them to create space for the considerably larger shuttle. Once CJ was sure that he was in far enough to allow the door to be closed, he halted and took a second to look around for the landing gear. He accidentally activated the alarm, loudspeaker, and multiple door locks before finding the proper switch, causing the ship to touch down and shut off its engines.

He activated the ramp before getting up from his seat, and he could hear it rolling out on the opposite side of the shuttle's main entrance. CJ was hit with clouds of steam as the ship depressurized. Finally, the door slid open with a soft noise that reminded him of the sound of rotating gears.

He stood at the top of the ramp and looked down. Standing just a few feet away from the end of the ramp were Watts, several of the rebellion officials, and Sheressa, who was wearing a white-and-green dress. She held her hands together and stared directly at him while maintaining an unreadable facial expression. CJ walked slowly to the bottom of the ramp before finally making contact with Erub soil once again. No one spoke.

His sister took a step toward him. One of her hands moved over her face quickly, and she began to sob as she ran to embrace him. She cried into his shoulder as she held him with more strength than CJ knew she had. The smell of his sister's flowery perfume invaded his nostrils, and he felt his throat get hot as tears filled his eyes. No one spoke a word. It was as if it they were the only two people there.

After a few seconds, she stopped suddenly and stepped back from the hug. She looked him in the eyes and began throwing punches at his chest, which had a surprising level of force behind them. CJ found himself needing to take a step or two backward while bracing himself.

"WHY? WHY? FUCKING WHY?" She hit him once to coincide with each syllable.

"Shaera and Detz turned me over. I had no choice."

"I want them dead. Immediately."

"The priest already handled it for you."

Sheressa sighed. "Why didn't you contact me? Or at least tell me what was going on, like I specifically asked?!"

"I had to destroy the radio. I didn't want them to be able to talk to you and possibly force you to give something up. The future of our planet is more important than any one person."

She relaxed a bit and wiped a tear from her eye. "I heard you got sent to the Draekon world. What was that like?"

CJ stared down at the ground briefly as the horrible sight he had witnessed back in the ship with Josso flooded into his mind. "I have a lot to fill you in on. Come on."

He turned back quickly to face a few of the rebels who were standing around. "We have bodies in the shuttle that will need taking care of."

"Bodies?" The concern in her voice was blatant.

"I'll explain as we go."

He shook several hands as the two made their way back to Sheressa's quarters. Along the way, and for a long time after they arrived, he spent time telling her about everything that had happened: the camps, Jakob, Josso, Tom, and the rest. By the time he had finished, several hours had gone by. Sheressa sat at the foot of her bed staring up at him. She offered him a spot next to her, but he didn't feel like getting off his feet. Not yet.

"If this Jakob character really does manage to pull the Uduls, Joxun, Zantavi, and Ayr together, Polero wouldn't stand a chance against them."

CJ ground his teeth slightly.

"No. I don't need Jakob. We don't need Jakob. You're the Rebel Queen. Your name has spread through the galaxy already as it is. I know firsthand. What would it do to that name if people knew we needed another army to come save us?"

"It would tell people that we value our home and people over our own pride, Corvus. That's what it would tell them. I'm glad you brought that up, by the way. I do not appreciate you turning down this offer without consulting with me first. Make sure you don't forget your place."

"You weren't seriously going to consider signing, were you?"

His sister's emerald gaze was piercing as she stared him down.

"Probably not. But that's irrelevant. You seriously overstepped your boundaries. There will be severe consequences if anything like that happens again. Are we clear?"

CJ bit his lip and nodded before sighing deeply and moving over to the window. "We can beat Polero without signing ourselves away in perpetuity. We're a great nation. We don't need to surrender to anyone else's will—certainly not to the will of some foreigner whose motives I'm not even entirely convinced of. We can do this. Without Pertinax, Polero is exposed. We should move forward with my plan. There's never been a better time." He looked back at her as he finished speaking.

She raised an eyebrow slightly. "The shipyard, you mean? You still want to go through with that?"

He nodded. "Yes. I can slip in quietly an—"

"Are you out of your fucking mind? You think I'm going to let you go anywhere alone again? After this? No. You're taking Watts and a team of the best men we have."

CJ exhaled deeply. He knew his plan was better, but he wasn't going to fight her on this. She was fully entitled to feel this way. "Okay. I'll lead the men. We'll go tonight."

"You will go tomorrow night. You are still wearing the clothes you left with, and you probably haven't eaten nor slept well in a while. You aren't leaving here until at least tomorrow and possibly even the day after, depending on how I feel. The crew is under orders to stop you if you try."

"Fine. I'm taking the clawdadons when I go, though."

Sheressa placed her right leg over her left and interlaced her fingers. "Fine."

CJ nodded and began heading for the door.

"Where are you going?" She tracked him with her pupils.

CJ stopped and faced her. "Comms room. The Zantavi king is going to be wondering what happened to his son . . . and this." He pulled out Josso's folded copy of the treaty from his pocket.

XIX

ZHADEN KARUK
ZANTAVI SHUTTLE, OLERA SEA
CHA-LEH

Jakob moved rapidly up and down the length of the shuttle, darting his azure eyes in every direction as the blinding sun beamed through its various windows. With all the enthusiastic singing that had taken place over the past week, Zhaden would have been surprised if the poor Draekon hadn't been driven halfway to madness by now. A series of loud pops broke the seal between the interior of the vessel and the crisp, salty air outside it. The overwhelming and unmistakable smell of the sea flooded in almost immediately.

Zhaden walked over to the closest unoccupied window and gazed out for a bit. The movement of the large waves gave texture to the deep dark blue of the water, which ran uninterrupted across the entire surface of the planet. The black shadow of the shuttle raced gracefully across the blue tapestry.

"We have visual. On approach," the voice of the Zantavi pilot came over the ship's onboard speakers.

Zhaden took a deep breath and slowly walked over to the back of the ship, where its main entrance and exit were located. He dropped to one knee, which was still sore and aching from the hit that it had taken from the electric rod. He ran a hand over it briefly before reaching up to touch his forehead. The hard scab over where his horn had once resided had finally stopped bothering him. He shook his head and returned his hand to its original position.

He heard rattling metal and shot a glance at the cub, who had turned over in its sleep within its cage. It had taken Zhaden and the crew quite some time to find something the bear would eat, as it seemed uninterested in most proteins and vegetables. When its eyes widened and its face lit up at the sight of a Zantavic trout, Zhaden knew that he had found the answer. Fish was a large part of Udul cuisine and was his favorite meal, but he had no issue giving portions of his rations to his new furry friend for the duration of the voyage.

He looked back at the door as tears began to fill his eyes. He had known for a week now that this was going to happen, but something about the event unfolding right before him left him helplessly overwhelmed with emotion. He fell into silence, his emotions going haywire as he waited for them to land.

The ship stopped, and he could feel it begin to turn slowly. A pale hand appeared on his right shoulder, and he looked up to see the new Draekon king standing over him and staring straight ahead. He looked much better now that he had managed to put on some halfway decent clothes, even if they were slightly large, given that they had been designed to fit a Zantavi. A sudden crack followed by the turning of gears rang through the ship, stemming from the door. A small vertical line of light began to appear as the two large pieces of steel moved aside slowly. As they pushed further and further apart, the entirety of the beautiful sea came into view, and a large gust of salty air blasted the two men.

A massive, stainless steel naval vessel was the only thing that broke the monotony and continuity of the dark water. Dots of varying shades of blue lined the vessel's upper deck. Most of the men standing on it were wearing dark gray naval uniforms. Roaring cheers and applause broke out aboard the cruiser once the doors parted completely.

Zhaden placed a hand over his mouth as he felt his throat burn and his eyes sting. He was home. Finally. The tears that he had been holding back trickled down his blue cheeks helplessly. He heard rapid footsteps coming from behind him and turned to watch as several of the Uduls on board the shuttle ran and dove off the edge, heading straight down into the sea. The sounds of their bodies hitting the water in what must have been the first time in years brought a smile to his face, and he chuckled through his tears. As the shuttle lowered itself further, he could see the former inmates being helped aboard the cruiser and being welcomed with hugs and tearful embraces.

The shuttle moved slowly toward the deck of the ship as it began to extend its ramp. Several crew members secured it in place as it contacted the metallic floor.

"Ready?" Jakob questioned.

Zhaden nodded quickly at Jakob before rising slowly to his feet and making his way down the ramp. He could hear the Draekon's footsteps following closely behind him as applause began to ring out. As his foot contacted the cool metal of the deck, seven figures emerged from the crowd. He would have recognized them even without their attire. He knew all their faces, except for one, which was new. His heart skipped a beat as he realized who had been replaced.

The newest member of the oligarchy known as 'The Pillars' stepped forward, and the crowd quieted completely as he spoke. "Zhaden Karuk. I speak for us as one and for the people of Cha-leh when I say this: Welcome home." He bowed, and Zhaden returned the gesture. "There is no way to undo what has been done. We know that. We do not expect to be given your forgiveness but hope that in time we may earn it. You are as true a son of the seas as any and deserved a far better fate than you received. The tales of your actions at the horrific Oballe camps have reached our ears and captivated our hearts. You are a hero to us and our people forevermore."

A short burst of cheers and applause broke out. The former inmates were significantly more enthusiastic in their praise.

"I appreciate the gesture, but it would not have been possible without a man who is no longer a friend to me, but a brother: Jakob Koss."

Zhaden turned and motioned to Jakob, who looked confused. He forgot that the Draekon did not speak Garyl. He moved over to Zhaden and stood to his right.

"Ah, yes. The Neon King we have heard so much about. We are preparing our royal suite in the capital building for you. We would like to hear much more about what took place in your home world," the Pillar said to Jakob in Neatspeak.

"It would be my pleasure. But, unfortunately, I am needed elsewhere. As soon as the shuttle is unpacked, I will be heading off. I am sure we'll have more than enough time to talk in the coming months."

Jakob had spoken in his usual tone, which Zhaden briefly feared would be interpreted as him being uninterested or bored. The Pillar looked slightly confused at the second half of the comment, but he brushed past it.

"Very well. We'll have the crew get to work on refueling your shuttle for you."

Jakob bowed again. "Thank you."

Zhaden turned back to the group. The long, ornate gold necklaces that the Pillars wore glimmered in the sunlight.

The same Pillar spoke again, this time returning his attention to him. "We cannot give you the last ten years of your life back, but we hope this will act as a start."

The group moved aside, revealing an Udul who had been standing behind them. Zhaden's eyes widened, and his mind went blank.

Kamro Ravull stepped forward slowly and looked at Zhaden with that same damn smile that always sat above his handsome, chiseled jaw. The dark blue freckles on his cheeks compressed as he grinned. He had clearly been crying.

The dark blue veins in his muscular arms protruded slightly as he approached, holding a bright silver medal in his hands. It was as if nothing had ever happened. Zhaden ran to him, and the two embraced before locking into the strongest and most desperate kiss he could ever remember being a part of.

Applause rang through the air. Both cried intensely and unabashedly. Kamro ran a hand over Zhaden's scab. "Who did this?"

Zhaden chuckled. "Do not fret. He will never see another day."

Kamro shook his head and smiled. "I love you. I'm so sorry I didn't-"

Zhaden grabbed his face and looked him square in his beautiful eyes. "No. There was nothing you could have done. Do not bear that burden. Never. Do you understand me?"

Kamro swallowed hard and nodded. The two hugged again before separating.

Kamro took the medal and put it over Zhaden's head. "You may be a hero to these people, but don't let it go to your big head, okay?"

Zhaden chuckled but was too choked up to respond. He turned to look back at Jakob, who shot him what seemed to be a slight smile.

"Give me a second."

Zhaden turned and walked back over to the Draekon.

"Jakob—"

"I think you had more than enough time to talk to me over the years. Go. Just don't forget about this." Jakob handed the copy of the treaty to Zhaden, who took it and nodded.

"I'm off to see the Queen of the Seven Springs."

"Tread carefully there, friend. I have heard rumors that she castrates men she finds disagreeable."

"It's a good thing I'm extremely charismatic and charming then," Jakob replied as monotonously as possible.

"I am quite serious Jakob. I am not sure the plan you last relayed to me will be enough."

Jakob took a deep breath. "I agree. I'm considering using your suggestion. It may be the only way to ensure she stays with us for the long run."

Zhaden smiled. "Do not sound so miserable! It is a great idea. Zhaden Karuk himself came up it!"

The Draekon rolled his eyes as Zhaden wrapped him in a strong hug and lifted him slightly into the air.

"Take care of yourself and get this done." Jakob replied as he patted the Udul's back. Zhaden lowered him slowly back to the ground and ruffled his hair.

They exchanged a nod, and, with that, Jakob turned and walked back toward the shuttle's ramp, which withdrew a second or two later. Within a few minutes, the shuttle, now sealed, repressurized, and refueled, took off once again. Zhaden turned and walked back to the Pillars as the shuttle moved up through the graying clouds and out of sight.

"Do you want to see him?"

The question caught Zhaden off guard. He remained silent for a few seconds and exchanged a glance with Kamro before looking back at the Pillars' new chairman. "Where is he?"

"Locked up in The Trench, where he should be. I would advise against—"

"Take me to him."

The Udul looked back at the other Pillars before turning back to Zhaden. He nodded and bowed slightly as the ship's alarm began to ring out.

The gray-clad Uduls began running in seemingly every direction, but with a level of purpose and determination that Zhaden hadn't seen in years. They tied ropes, pulled levers, sealed doors, and escorted the guests, including the Pillars, into the interior of the cruiser.

One jogged up to Zhaden and Kamro. "Will you two need to be escorted inside?"

The two of them exchanged a look. "I'll head in. I'm not sure Zhaden has ever refused to ride deck. I can't imagine you'll be breaking that tradition now."

Zhaden laughed. "You know me well. Here, take this, and keep it dry for me."

"What is it?"

"I'll explain later. I promise."

He handed the treaty to Kamro, who turned and followed the crew member inside with the rest of the Pillars and the bulk of the on-board families.

Once they vanished from sight, Zhaden moved up to the bow of the ship and looked out into the endless depths of the ocean. He motioned a crew member over to him. The man was carrying the bear cub's cage, and Zhaden instructed him to leave it inside with the others.

The overwhelming smell of salt would take some time to readjust to, but he loved it more than any other. He placed both hands on the railing and looked to his left and right. Several crew members began strapping themselves in, preparing for the ride.

Looking down, he saw his own foot straps. As he bent over to begin tightening them, another crew member approached, presumably to help him, but he waved him off. If he was still a true Udul, he would do it alone, and he did. He had to grab the railing with a bit more strength than he would have once to avoid falling over as the ship was set in motion, but that was to be expected. It picked up speed incredibly quickly, and within a few seconds, the frigid wind was blasting Zhaden's entire body. He laughed loudly as it continued to batter him. Nothing could sully his mood today. Nothing.

Once they had maxed out their speed, another announcement came over the ship's speakers: "Prepare for submersion."

Zhaden braced himself and tightened his grip on the railing in front of him. After a few seconds, the bow of the ship began to dip into the sea, but this did little to stop its blistering pace. Lower and lower it dropped until water began to flood the deck and coat Zhaden's feet. He took a deep breath and closed his eyes. An instant later, he felt the satisfying rush of the ocean water plowing into him as he and the rest of the crew on the bow went under completely.

He lost himself for a minute or two as he savored the joyous sensation of being submerged completely, his gills stirring into action as he took his first breath underwater in a decade. He opened his eyes and looked back. The ship was now entirely beneath the surface. He turned to the front in time to see a massive striped fish quickly zigzag its way past him.

The way in which water quieted the world had always fascinated him. On the surface, there was a cacophony of noises: moving feet, alarms, and yelling, just to name a few. But down here, there was nothing but relaxing and persistent white noise. The water always seemed to remove the stresses of life and, quite literally, drown them out of existence.

He spent the next several minutes just taking everything in. A flood of captivating golden light became visible as the ship crossed a small mountain on the ocean floor. After another minute or two of travel, the enormous transparent dome that housed the city of Olera came into full view.

He looked through its glass walls as the ship slithered by silently. He recognized some buildings, but others were new. For the most part, the city looked the same as when he'd last seen it, which was good. At least he wouldn't feel like a total foreigner in his own home.

The large glass door of the dock opened slowly, and the ship pulled into it at a crawl before coming to a full stop. A dull vibration ran through the flooded room once the door shut. Zhaden looked up in time to watch the water level drop quickly and drastically. Once the room had been emptied, he and the other on-deck crew members unstrapped themselves, while those who were inside opened the hatches and escorted the guests out. The process took about twenty minutes, but before he knew it, he and Kamro were being escorted into the city by the Pillars and their guards.

The neon lights of the bright advertisements on the sides of buildings, the rumbling of flyer engines, and, most of all, the sound of his own tongue being spoken everywhere around him made it clear that he was home. This was the place that he had left, and this was the city he knew. He would have taken the time to truly enjoy it, but the knowledge of where he was going dampened his enjoyment a bit.

The group moved into a small but luxurious shuttle. Once inside it, they sat in relative silence for about half an hour before arriving at and stepping into the almost imposingly dull and unassuming gray building. Kamro waited behind with the remaining Pillars as Zhaden and the Pillars' chairman stepped into an elevator and rode it up a few stories.

"You must excuse me, Mr. Karuk. With all the madness of today, I've neglected to properly introduce myself." He extended a webbed hand. "Garrond Zharr is the name."

Zhaden shook it firmly. "Not a problem. I can hardly blame you, Chairman."

They exchanged a slight nod as the doors opened in front of them. One great thing about being back home was that things like elevators, ceilings, and especially doorways were now properly sized for him, which meant no more ducking nor having to worry about banging his head. After a few minutes of walking in silence through a few more rows lined with cells on either side, Garrond finally came to a stop and motioned to his left. Zhaden nodded at him as the chairman made a swift exit down the hall to give him some privacy.

Zhaden sighed and turned to look at the bars of the cell in front of him. Like those in every cell in The Trench, they were horizontal, flat, and translucent. He placed both hands on the bar that was at about the height of his face and finally lifted his gaze so that he could look inside the cell. Within it, sitting against the back wall and staring up at the ceiling was a man whose face it hurt Zhaden's very soul to look at.

"You didn't die." He looked down and established eye contact as he finished speaking.

"I didn't die." Zhaden confirmed.

"Ten years living in close quarters with sweaty men... Must have been an incredible experience for you."

Zhaden looked down and swallowed hard before looking back at him. "Why?"

He chuckled. "Is that a serious question?" The prisoner then stood slowly, walked over to him, and placed his hands on the bar just below the one on which Zhaden's own rested. His eyes burned with scorn and disgust as he stared up at him. "Karuk is a name that has survived three wars against the Dom'Rai, the algae pandemic, and six mega-storms. It has been printed on the badges of esteemed generals, doctors, artists, and multiple Pillars throughout history. Think about that, Zhaden: an unending chain stretching back a millennium or more before finally reaching the two of us. I shudder to imagine what Father and Mother would think of our bloodline coming to an end because you decided it was more fun to stick your cock in other men's—"

"Enough, Marok!" Zhaden slammed his hands down on the bar, the banging noise reverberating down the hall. This, combined with the dramatic rise in the volume of his voice caused a few other prisoners in nearby cells to move up to their bars to see what was going on.

Marok Karuk took a step back from the bars and crossed his arms.

"The fact that such an idea would even cross your mind, especially given my condition, is unforgivable."

Zhaden tightened his grip on the bar. "You took ten years away from me over that?"

"If your own life was more important to you than every single person who has ever been a part of this family line, then I couldn't care less what happened to you. You are selfish and shortsighted."

"You didn't even have the courage to face me before having me shipped off. Do you feel even the slightest remorse?"

"Do you still like fucking men?"

Zhaden's only response was an angry glare. Marok approached the bars slowly and leaned as close to his brother as he could before speaking in a whisper. "You'll always be an animal. I should have gone after your so-called lover as well. Question: which one of you is the girl?"

Zhaden reached a hand through a gap between the bars and pulled Marok forcefully against them, creating another loud clang.

Marok groaned as Zhaden released the man who was his brother in blood only.

"Evidently, your brutish nature didn't change either. Good to know. Perhaps it's for the best that you won't reproduce. With you as a role model, your kids would be dead or in prison before hitting puberty."

Zhaden had to summon every ounce of his self-control to avoid assaulting Marok a second time. He took a deep breath and allowed the anger to pass through him before responding. "The fact that you were ever allowed to be a Pillar rattles my trust in every level of our government."

The two glared at each other in silence for a few seconds.

"I was one of the best to ever do it. Feel free to look at our unemployment percentage and GDP with me at the helm. And be sure to let people know who they can blame when we begin slipping again. Why did you have to break out? Everything would have been so much easier if you'd just died."

The words pierced directly into Zhaden's soul. His throat began to feel hot.

"Enjoy whatever is left of your life, Zhaden. Your judgment day will come. *Alavona elobai.*"

Zhaden's heart fell into his stomach. Things made more sense now. The creature behind the bars was beyond any chance of redemption. He began to step away. "I will always love you despite what you are, Marok. I have nothing more to say to you. There's a fair chance you will be facing execution for this. I will make sure I have a good view."

Marok's eyes widened, and his grip on the bars tightened as Zhaden began to walk away.

"No! I will not be executed! Not publicly!"

Zhaden continued to move down the hall, giving no indication of having heard him.

"They can't do that to me! Come back here! Zhaden!"

He turned the corner.

"Zhaden! ZHADEN!"

He kept walking until even the faintest echoes of Marok's voice faded away.

He found Garrond waiting near the elevator.

"If you are willing to testify against him, I can almost guarantee you that he will face execution. Would you like me to start laying the groundwork?"

Zhaden shook his head as he fought to keep tears from forming in his eyes.

"No. Keep him here until his condition takes him and his skin blackens to match the color of his heart."

**TOM EZEKIEL
DOWNTOWN, TRAX TOWN
AYR-GROH**

The clouds surrounding the outside of the cockpit exploded into a bright yellow glow as Tom switched on the ship's LED headlights. Tom reached into a small compartment near the command console and pulled out the yellow mascavi paper that Jakob had given to him.

"Why did we break off from the rest of the shuttles?"

Koomer swiveled toward Tom in his chair. The makeshift half-virix that they had put together for him out of some old spare pairs over the past few days made him look like an old-timey naval pirate. The reflective orange goggles covered his good eye, and the attached elastic straps held them in place.

"We're not going to the capital, Koomster."

His companion raised the eyebrow over his exposed bad eye. "What?"

"I mean . . . we will go. Just not now. It's going to be a clusterfuck for a bit while all the prisoners are unloaded and saying hi to their families and whatnot. I'm gonna let them have their moment. Sprock knows we're coming and believe me when I say he'll wait for us."

Koomer didn't look any more pleased by the answer. "And we're going where then exactly?"

"Home sweet home. Something tells me that regardless of what happens, I won't be back for quite a while. I need to grab my shit."

Koomer sighed and leaned back in his seat. "I thought you said you were living on the run. How has your house not been raided by now?"

Tom chuckled. "I called it my home. Never said it was a house."

The scattered yellow and orange lights of Trax Town appeared as the vessel passed below the clouds. It was the dead of night, but Tom imagined that there would be no shortage of people who would be wide awake regardless. Flyers moved around every which way below them, and several poorly maintained street lanterns flickered, threatening to be engulfed by the darkness. He slowed his speed as he drew increasingly closer to the metallic ground.

"I've never been to Trax Town. I grew up in the Steel Grotto. My mother always told me I'd be robbed, killed, and possibly violated if I came here."

"Your mom was a smart woman."

A period of uncomfortable silence followed as the ship touched down on the abandoned, run-down parking lot that Tom had converted into his personal launchpad. He cleared his throat. "So, tell me . . . Do you see in 2D? Like, does everything look like a cartoon to you?"

Out of his peripheral vision, he could see Koomer turn to look at him. His one-eyed companion's expression seemed to be a mixture of confusion and disbelief.

"So, I'll take that as a . . . no? Yes? No. Definitely no. Unless it's obviously a yes. No?"

Koomer shook his head as he stood up from his chair and made for the exit.

"Okay but like . . . I kinda want to know. Didn't really get a definitive answer there."

No response that time either.

Tom sighed, grabbed his leather jacket from the back of his chair, and slipped it on as he followed his companion. The two removed their virixes as they stepped into the cool, yet smoggy night air. Were it not for the single flyer alarm echoing through the air, it would likely have been completely silent.

"Why is this place so . . . different?" Koomer asked, evidently trying to change subjects as Tom led him through an alleyway.

"You mean shitty?"

Even in the dimness of the night, he could see Koomer's cheeks flush red.

"Nah, don't worry. Everyone here accepts the craptastic nature of this place. In all seriousness, though, I'm not sure. It's been this way for as long as I've been alive. The story floating around is that the first Grand Skylord gave this land to his son, Trax, who was renowned for being a drunk who loved gambling and women more than being a respectable leader. As punishment, the town was purposely underfunded and under-policed. Instead of changing his ways, Trax doubled down, using the lawlessness of the region to turn it into his own massive playground. He apparently only got to enjoy it for a few years before he was poisoned by local gangs."

"Oh, man. I remember hearing about that, actually. I thought that one of his whores cut his throat in his sleep."

Tom shrugged without turning around. "Either way, what an absolute legend."

Koomer shook his head.

They walked down two more alleys before Tom stopped and faced what looked to be a solid wall. One brick in the wall was only ever so slightly out of place. When he pushed it, a loud click rang through what seemed like the entire structure at once before a small door-sized potion of it slid backward and then to the left. A sewer grate sat in the tiny space that was revealed. Tom leaned down and pushed it open before pressing a button on the wall next to it. A strange metallic grinding sound began to come from the exposed hold. After about thirty seconds, he climbed in slowly and began to make his way down the now fully extended ladder. He could hear Koomer's footsteps trailing behind him, followed by the brick wall sliding back into place, killing the small amount of light that had been present.

His foot hit solid ground before he expected it to, though it seemed like it always did. He felt his way over to the left wall as Koomer's footsteps followed his own.

"Are you going to hit the —?"

The bright white neon lights along the ceiling flared to life, and Koomer shielded his eye. Tom laughed.

It wasn't a luxurious place, but it was his. The small room was only about the size of the tiniest of studio apartments, and the layout did little to work against that. A bathroom, kitchen, living room, bedroom, and workstation were all crammed into the small space that he called home.

Tom walked over to his safe, located in the back-left corner of the room near his bed. He knelt as he began to unlock the safe. Hearing Koomer moving around, he shot a glance behind him. He saw his companion leaning over the three wooden tables covered in lamps which served as his workstation. Koomer had picked up an older version of Tom's boost boot and was looking over it with interest.

Tom shook his head and went back to working on the safe. It took about thirty seconds, but he finally lined up the code correctly and swung it open.

"Holy . . ."

Tom jumped up at the sound of Koomer's voice, taking his exclamation as a sign of trouble. He looked back to see the one-eyed man's mouth hanging slightly open as he faced him.

"Shit, dude! You scared me."

Tom knelt back down and got to work placing the stacks of bills into a bag next to the safe. He could hear Koomer approaching him slowly.

"How . . . how long have you been at this?"

"Ten-ish years, I want to say."

Tom picked up his speed, but it was still going to take a while, and he hadn't even gotten to the gold bars yet.

"How much is that?"

"Well, isn't that a rude question?" He looked back at Koomer, who appeared unamused at his comment. "Haven't counted it up in a while, but a few months ago, I was at three hundred or so."

"Thousand?"

"What am I . . . some kind of amateur? Million, obviously."

"Why would you keep going then? You could retire and move anywhere."

"As you can see, I don't exactly have anyone to come home to. Besides, it's pretty much all I'm good at."

Koomer motioned to the workstations. "No, it's not. Look at this. This is impressive stuff."

Tom shook his head. "I'm an Ayr. That's like congratulating an Udul because he can swim."

"If everyone could build and invent like you and I do, no one could touch us as a race. We tend to be smarter and better at inventing, sure. But that doesn't make us all geniuses, and it certainly doesn't mean we can all invent self-propelling boots with a portable fuel supply integrated into them. How did you manage that, anyway?"

Tom had continued packing while Koomer was speaking. Now, he was nearly done. "Took some pheris containers and compressed them as much as I could without them exploding. Work after that was mainly finding a way to ignite them on command."

Koomer placed the shoe down and walked over to another table as Tom finished packing his bag. It was heavy, but not impossibly so. He slung it over his shoulder and turned to see the one-eyed man inspecting a black battle hammer. He pressed a button in its handle, causing it to extend to its full length.

"I thought you were a knife guy." he said with a slight chuckle, running his hand over the weapon.

An enormous sense of dread came over Tom as he stared at it.

"I am. Put that down."

Koomer raised an eyebrow and pressed the button again, causing the weapon to contract back down to its much more manageable size. He placed it back on the table as Tom motioned toward his makeshift closet.

"Go in there and take whatever you need. Get the fuck out of those rags. You're not a prisoner anymore, and we're about the same size anyway."

"Tom—"

"No, seriously. It's going to be a bad look for us if you go to the capital like that. Sprock doesn't like me as it is. We need to dress to impress and all that bullshit."

"And you think having two people who look like you will do that?"

"Fair point. But I'll take my chances."

Koomer sighed and walked over to the wardrobe, whose doors had been torn off. He pulled open the squeaky drawers and grabbed a black shirt, tan pants, and white high-top shoes. He reached for a black jacket that was hanging in the closet.

"Mmmm . . . not that one."

He turned to Tom, who smiled and shrugged. "Sorry. Lost my virginity in that jacket."

"Could have done without knowing that. On second thought, I'm just going to go with the shirt."

"Suit yourself."

Tom spent the next few minutes collecting clothes and whichever prototypes he felt were worth bringing. He was looking over a modified glove when he heard a familiar whirring and hissing, and he looked up as alarms rang in his head. On the other side of the room, Koomer hit the small black button on the wall, causing a glass capsule to descend slowly from the ceiling. Tom sprinted over to him as it touched the floor, where it settled itself slowly. The water inside the tank stirred slightly, but he still appeared to be asleep. His blonde hair moved slowly and gracefully in the liquid, and the respirator over his mouth and nose remained perfectly in place. Tom let out a loud sigh of relief.

"What—?" Koomer began to ask.

Tom moved in and quickly pressed the button again. The mechanical supports around the capsule began lifting it back up into the ceiling.

"Don't." He glared at Koomer through his virix for a few seconds before moving back to his workstation. Tom could hear the nosy man following behind him.

"Tom. Why was that—?"

"I really don't want to talk about it, Koom."

"That was you. Or . . . your twin? Why are you keeping your twin in a medical tube?"

Tom put his hands on the table. "He's not my twin."

"So, would you care to explain why he looks exactly li—?"

"He's my clone."

Koomer's eyes widened, and he stared at Tom for several seconds. "How do you have a clone?"

Tom sighed. "It's a long story, Koom, and we don't have time to get into it now. Point is, he *cannot* wake up. It can't happen. Period."

"Bu—"

"Can't. You have no idea what it took for me to get his ass back in there."

Koomer bit his tongue and shook his head. "Fine. But you just became exponentially more interesting to me."

Tom wrapped up grabbing what he needed, locked the place up, and, with Koomer's help, moved the bags back up the ladder and into the ship. Within minutes, they were back in the air and en route to the capital.

"If you don't come back, won't he die?"

"He's got enough nutrients left to last a year. I'll be back before then, or I'll have someone I trust take care of it."

"Why are you keeping him ali—?"

"Seriously . . . enough."

Koomer seemed to finally get the message, and he sat back in his chair.

The dull, distant sounds of chatter could be heard from that height and within the confines of the ship, meaning that the capital must have been erupting in sound and life, in sharp contrast to the quiet Trax Town streets. Tom flew low, and both Ayrs marveled at the sights. Try as they might, neither one of them could find a single significant spot of any major road that wasn't occupied. The people of this planet, who had just seen close to a thousand of its sons and daughters return, had come out in massive numbers.

"You've been asking questions all night long and I think it's about time I get one in. How'd you lose the eye?"

Koomer ran a hand over his empty socket. "Like you, I grew up pretty poor. Started working under the table at a factory when I was around nine or ten. A man that I worked with on my station had a mental breakdown one day. He stabbed multiple people and forced my head down onto a drill I was fixing, which I took right through the eye. My boss kicked me out and my parents had me shipped off planet to escape the child exploitation charges they'd be facing. I was forced to handle the entire process of dealing with the wound myself."

Tom drummed his fingers on the dashboard as he desperately fished in his brain for an appropriate response. "And I thought my childhood was fucked up."

Koomer chuckled. "I had a long time to get over it."

"You going to pay a visit to dear old mom and dad?"

"No. They were pathetic, exploitative, abusive junkies. By now, they've more than likely died of an overdose or a deal gone wrong. One thing I learned at the camps was to respect and cherish my life, which means not wasting any more of it thinking about them."

Tom sighed. "You're a better man than me, Koomster."

They let the music from outdoors fill the silence of the ship for the next few minutes. With the barrage of auditory stimuli, Tom almost missed the cackling of the radio. He nearly dropped it as he fumbled to pick it up.

"Hello. This is Tom speaking."

The man on the other end of the line sighed. "Hello, Ezekiel. I was told you would be meeting me at Sky Tower. You are not here."

"Are you sure? Can you check again?"

"I'm glad you find this amusing. Do you ever take anything seriously? Is that even in your DNA?"

"Of course, Melvy. I thought we were friends. Friends joke around, don't they?"

"I am not, nor will I ever be your friend, Ezekiel. You are a felon, and if it were up to me you would be rotting in a cell."

Tom shook his head. "Now, now Melvy. We've had this little lovers' quarrel before, and I always end up getting out of whatever you try to stick me in. I'm beginning to think this might be a sex thing, and just so we're clear, I'm not into that. Now then, I think it's better if we sit down together again and have one of our lovely chats that we both enjoy so much. I've got something to run by you."

"'Lovely' is the last word I'd use. The luckiest thing that ever happened to you was the abolition of the death penalty. That said, I am very grateful to the new Draekon king for returning our people to us. It is only out of this respect and gratitude that I even considered meeting with you. My men will greet you on my landing platform. I'll be expecting you."

"Sounds good. Love you!"

The radio cackled loudly, and Tom put it back down.

"I think he likes you."

Tom smiled at Koomer. "How could anybody not? Anyway, you got it?"

Koomer held the yellow paper up. Tom nodded and looked back out of the cockpit window. The large, three-hundred-story Sky Tower was the most enormous building he had ever seen back when he was a boy, and this still rung true. He hovered slowly, moving upward as a small square of light opened on the top floor and a large, flat landing strip extended outward. From this distance, the Ayr soldiers who rushed out to line both sides of the strip looked microscopic.

As the ship grew closer and closer to the platform, Tom turned back to Koomer. "Word to the wise. As difficult as it may be, it's probably best we avoid fat jokes."

XXI

THE FIST
ROYAL ALAVITE SHUTTLE, PINOLL FOREST
FERALLA

The chrome accents on his gauntlets, chest piece, and reinforced boots glimmered, reflecting the small amount of light coming through the window of the shuttle as it approached the meeting point. The shuttle rocked slightly as it continued to lower its altitude.

The Fist looked at himself in the mirror on the wall of his designated chambers in the shuttle. Its black coat of paint isolated it from the white-and-gold swarm of the other Alavite vessels in much the same way that his dark armor differentiated him from regular soldiers and golden guards. There could be many of them, but there could only ever be one Fist, just as there was only ever a single Hand.

Colors aside, the Alavite insignia that had been engraved into the center of his chest piece gave little doubt as to who he worked for. He ran a hand over it, touching metal to metal. The ship halted suddenly and began to rotate. They had arrived.

He stood up and grabbed the helmet from the nearby display as he made for the door. He pressed the small buttons on each of its sides as he slipped it over his head in a single fluid motion just as he had done hundreds of times before.

Once the helmet was firmly in place, he pressed the buttons again, causing the straps on the back and sides to tighten. Technically, it was more of an armored mask, as it covered the entirety of his face and neck but left the top and most of the back of his head exposed. He had specifically requested this to allow his long hair to fall freely. A large, tinted, chrome-bordered glass triangle on the front of the helmet acted as his visor. Four small triangular openings over his mouth ensured that he could breathe and speak without an issue.

He exited his chambers and headed toward the main section of the ship. The ever-silent golden guards were already standing and waiting. They bowed slightly as he walked past them. The group waited in silence as the ship depressurized and the door slowly slid open. The ramp had already been extended and attached to a platform.

Olivio stood almost exactly where metal met wood. The Fist exchanged a nod with the man whom he was sworn to his death to protect before walking down the ramp briskly, his boots clanking with every step. He took a brief look around once he was on solid ground.

Olivio smiled at him and motioned for him to follow. "It's good to see you again. You look well. I was afraid you'd lose muscle."

"And I was afraid you'd die of old age."

The Hand chuckled slightly as the two began to walk side by side.

On this planet, the skyscraper-sized trees seemed to go on forever, and they began to look like blackened spires as the sun started to set. A few lights began to flicker on from several of the small holes that had been dotted into them, turning the forest of ancient and lifeless bark into a surprisingly beautiful collection of wooden skyscrapers. He looked up over Olivio and the small crowd of golden guards with him. The tree they were standing outside of was darker and appeared much more cracked and weathered than its nearby counterparts. The landing platform was about ten stories up from the forest floor; yet it was still nowhere near the top of the tree, which was easily wider than most buildings on Alavonia.

"I hope your accommodations weren't too, shall we say, uncomfortable. I'm sure you understand why I couldn't arrange for special treatment."

"Yeah. I get it."

Olivio now lowered his voice slightly. "I hear the Zantavi army has escorted the prisoners off Oballe. I also can't help but notice there is no Draekon prisoner with you."

"There was nothing I could do, especially without my armor or weapons. Even if I had them, any attempt at striking at Koss would have seen me swarmed by hundreds of men, all of whom have sworn loyalty to him."

Olivio sighed and shook his head. "This has placed a very frustrating wrench in my plans; you do understand that?"

"I apologize, my Hand. If I had been given some backup-"

"You know that wasn't possible. I would have expected that the best fighter in the galaxy could have handled untrained and disorganized prisoners."

The Fist tensed up slightly as a slight anger coursed through him. "It doesn't matter. There is no possible way he will be able to rally the kind of support he'll need to form his union. He will be kicked out and sent back to Oballe with his army of undisciplined prisoners. Then we can put an end to what we started."

"What you failed to finish." Olivio corrected.

The Fist gave no response.

"With the stories I have been hearing, I would caution against underestimating our pale little friend. It seems as though he is far more capable and determined than I initially predicted."

The Fist nodded as the two of them approached the massive doorway to the temple, and he turned to meet Olivio's gaze.

"The Forest Chieftain has arranged to meet to discuss the terms of surrender. You will be accompanying me inside. I'm hoping you aren't rusty."

"Don't think that's possible for me."

"Good. That's the answer I was hoping for."

The Fist took a quick look around. "Where is Daryn?"

Olivio's mouth tightened. "We will discuss him later."

Two golden guards opened the doors through which they entered. Olivio turned to the guard on his right as he arrived at the threshold. "Give it to me."

The guard he was eyeing removed the weapon from a steel case that was sitting next to him, and he handed it to Olivio. A smile came to The Fist's lips as he saw it, and The Hand held it out to him.

"Here you are. The team restored it while you were away after your last . . . accident. Seeing as it has been years since I've seen you use any other weapon, I wanted to make sure you had it at your disposal."

The Fist grimaced slightly. He would have preferred not to be reminded of his last outing. He reached for the black metallic staff and weighed it in his hands for a second. Along its top left side was a large, curved blade. In contrast to most similar weapons, the curve faced the staff rather than outward, leaving a crescent-shaped blade exposed. Just as with his suit, the staff had been custom made.

"The Fist goes with me. The rest of you stay at the door."

The guards' body language made it clear that they were unhappy with what Olivio's instruction, but, as always, they remained silent and allowed the two men to proceed.

The enormous wooden doors creaked shut behind them as they stepped into the temple. Every part of the large, circular room had been sculpted and carved out of the tree itself. The Fist took some time to look around at the intricate decorations that surrounded the space. In the middle of the room was a table surrounded by large wooden chairs.

"Color me impressed. Haven't seen anything like this before."

Olivio glanced up at what he was looking at. "Yes. The Carine have a spiritual attachment to these trees. Convincing them that we are willing and able to respect their traditions will prove essential to securing a quick surrender. We need one now more than ever." He shot a glance back at The Fist, who swallowed and nodded.

Within a minute or two, the Carine party arrived. There were five men, one of whom was very luxuriously dressed. He was most likely the chieftain. They were certainly an oddity of a race, even in a galaxy with the likes of the Dom'Rai and Uduls in it. They looked like large dogs who had decided one day to stand upright. Their coats and furs varied from black to light gray, their ears either stood up or flopped to their sides, and their teeth protruded slightly from their mouths. Anyone could be forgiven for considering them more fit to be in a zoo than an office.

The most well-dressed Carine sat in the chair opposite Olivio, and his guards stood behind him.

The conversation went on for what felt like a lifetime. Despite his upbringing, The Fist had never cared for politics more than he needed to pretend to. The chieftain presented his terms on a long sheet of paper, which Olivio took several minutes to read. They went back and forth on changes and exceptions.

"I feel this deal is now agreeable by both sides. We will not stand to see our sacred forests destroyed or more of our citizens' lives lost. We will not fight in your army, but we will provide supplies and pool our technology, weapons, and intelligence. In return, we ask that you give us the same level of autonomy that the Dom'Rai and Quexians have received."

Olivio remained silent for a second and interlaced his fingers. "The Quexians and Dom'Rai earned the right to be ruled by their own with less oversight by demonstrating unrelenting and unwavering loyalty to our Lord. Your people worship tree gods. This will have to change. Your temples will remain intact and operational, but they will need to start spreading Alavon's word. Until such time, we will have our missionary division working here with military backing."

The Carine leader sighed. "If it ensures that no more lives will be lost and that our future will be secured, I will do what I can. But I cannot promise you that the people will cooperate."

"That is not something any leader can promise. We will not hold it against you."

He sighed again and extended his furry paw–hand hybrid across the table.

Olivio reached for it with his gloved hand.

Movement. A blade.

The Fist pulled Olivio backward forcefully, nearly sending the old man tipping over in his chair as one of the Carine guards roared and sent his blade through the back of his own leader's head. The chieftain's eyes glazed over as the bloody tip of the sword protruded from the middle of his face. He spoke incoherently for a second or two before falling onto the table.

The Fist twirled his staff in his hand calmly as the guards began to close in around him. "Stay behind me."

A pounding came from the door to his back. He darted his head back quickly to see that the door had been barred shut by a steel beam.

Two Carine men rushed from either side of the room. For a second, everything slowed down. The Fist was back in the hot sands training with the other children. They were weak and slow. He smiled despite the situation. He was outnumbered four to one, but he already knew that he would win.

He blocked and deflected one of the attacks with the blade of the staff and the other with the base. He then ducked under a second strike from the rightmost guard and quickly responded by whipping the staff around and striking his neck with the blade. The Carine's head came off with a pop and little resistance.

The second guard moved in on Olivio as the other two also closed in on him. The Fist ran over to the last guard and flipped the staff over so as to strike at the Carine's left calf, forcing him to the ground. As the dog-man grabbed at his leg, The Fist pressed two buttons on either side of the rod. A sharp, metallic sound pierced the room as a small, pointed blade emerged from the bottom of the staff and locked into place. Time slowed for a mere second or two before The Fist brought it down forcefully onto the back of the Carine's neck. The man-beast whimpered as it pierced his furry skin.

He withdrew his blade as the final two Carines rushed Olivio, who was now parallel to him. He moved as fast as he could and barely got there in time to block both swords with the side of his staff, the force of which made him take a step backward. With a powerful thrust, he threw both swords off him and quickly brought the main blade of the staff around and then across their midsections, slicing them open. They panicked and howled for a few seconds as their multitudinous pink and maroon organs began to dangle out of them. He sighed and brought the blade across again, this time slicing their necks. Both bodies hit the floor, and the room fell silent, save for the pounding on the door.

He looked back at Olivio. "You alright?"

The Hand straightened his elegant robe, which had become stained with small spatters of blood. "Yes. I assumed they had become a more civilized people, but I suppose their animal nature will always win in the end." Using his ungloved hand, he wiped sweat from his brow.

The Fist grabbed Olivio by the shoulder and began to move him as he kept scanning the room through the dark visor of his mask, only for a loud boom to echo through the room from the other side of the door. He pushed Olivio's head down and crouched as splinters from what used to be the massive double doors of the temple now covered the two men. He looked up a second later as the golden guards rushed in with their handheld rams.

"We're moving."

The times when Olivio took orders rather than giving them were very rare, but the old man simply nodded and followed where he was led.

Four of the golden guards surrounded and escorted them while two others entered to survey the room. The Fist turned his head as he heard footsteps approaching from where the Carine party had originally entered. Several more of their soldiers were running into the room on all fours. Their weapons, sheathed on their backs, bounced up and down slightly with each stride. They came to a halt and rose on their hind legs as they reached the table.

The one in the front of the pack groaned and violently threw a chair aside. He spoke loudly, and his deep voice boomed off the curved wooden walls. "'Alavon the Merciful', they say. I would rather worship demons." Although he spoke calmly, the anger in his voice was palpable.

The Fist shook his head and kept moving. There was no time to explain, nor risk this being a trap. More golden guards moved in and drew their weapons as the wolf–men advanced, forming a barrier between the two of them and the advancing Carines. The Fist and Olivio went out onto the landing platform and into a waiting shuttle as swords began to clash behind them. The ramp of the shuttle closed as they made it through the doors, and the pilot launched the ship almost instantly.

"We need to slingshot. Now." The Fist shouted.

"We'll need to exit the atmosphere first." the Alavite pilot shot back.

Both The Fist and Olivio nearly fell over backward as the ship rocked suddenly. Their forward movement had been completely stopped. The engines now whined to no avail.

He shot a confused glance at Olivio, whose eyes narrowed.

"We are hooked in. It is a new tactic they have been employing. Their flyers will surround us any minute."

The Fist exhaled and reached for a small metal container that was attached to the wall. He withdrew the small pieces of metal from inside and quickly clamped them on to his boots. Within fifteen seconds, he was climbing up to the emergency hatch that was located in a maintenance section of the ship. He dragged himself up on top of the hull of the shuttle as the hatch closed behind him.

The wind blasted him and nearly threw him off before the magnetic rods on his feet locked onto the surface of the ship. It took him a second or two to find the culprit: two large, metallic claw-like devices on either of the shuttle's rear. He moved slowly and steadily toward them, making sure to take careful and deliberate steps on the uneven hull. These magnetic clamps were effective, but not infallible. He was forced to crouch as a particularly strong gust of wind blasted across the top of the ship. As he rose again, what must have been at least seven different Carine flyers entered his line of sigh. They were only a bit behind the tree temple, and they were closing the gap quickly.

He redirected his sights to the hooks and quickened his pace as he cursed under his breath. In the haste to get up there, he had left his staff back inside the vessel. He threw himself on the first claw and examined it desperately. There was text in the Carine language written all over it, but try as he might, he couldn't understand a word of it. One particular phrase, placed next to what looked like a small lever, drew his attention. He pulled it, causing the cable that was attached to the back of the claw to be released. The shuttle swerved wildly to the right as it gained more slack, forcing him to briefly grab onto the claw for dear life.

It took a second or two for the ship to readjust itself and level out, and he looked back up into the sky. The flyers were nearly there, already close enough that he could see the glow emanating from the power bows of the men inside. He grunted and moved clumsily to the second hook, where he repeated the same process that he had carried out with the first. He was in the midst of planning his escape when his hand slipped from the lever. He blinked and tried to pull it again. It wouldn't budge. His mind raced as the sounds of the approaching engines grew louder. He took a deep breath and reached for his right foot, pulling one of the sharp metal clamps off it. He deactivated its magnetism and placed it underneath the lever, using it as a makeshift crowbar. The engines grew louder still as he struggled once and then twice; on the third try, the lever finally gave way. He grabbed onto the claw quickly as the newly freed ship shot off with a surprising amount of speed and force, sending the clamp flying from his hand and into the dark abyss. After several seconds, the ship finally leveled out a bit, and he was able to alternate between hopping on his still-magnetic foot and dragging himself as he raced back to the hatch.

They were moving, but the flyers were closing in. He heard a familiar whiz as a bright pink-tipped arrow hit the hull, missing his head by only a few inches. More arrows began to follow as he continued his struggle forward. The sky began to blend into a dark navy blue as the clanking of the arrows began to become less frequent. He took what would likely be his final breath as he worked to open the hatch.

He was halfway inside when his grip on the ladder slipped, sending him tumbling inside the hatch, which then sealed above him with a loud hiss. He groaned as he rose into a sitting position and removed his helmet, tossing it to the side. A few seconds later, the door to the small chamber opened, and almost instantly, he felt two sets of hands helping him up.

He shook his head as he focused on Olivio, who was standing in front of him. The Alavite guards on either side of him relaxed their grip as he became steadier on his feet.

The Hand crossed his arms as he spoke. "You might very well be the only one of your people in history to have ever saved multiple Alavite lives in a single day. I'm quite impressed."

"I'm not much like the rest of them. You know that." He was still catching his breath.

"Yes, I suppose I do." Using his head, Olivio motioned for the guards to leave. "I was tired of waiting on these glorified dogs in the first place. Without a unified leader, they will be plunged into chaos. While it would probably be best to let them rip each other apart in whatever civil war may be brewing, we simply don't have any more time to spare. I've summoned the flame brigade. I anticipate that they will surrender within a few days. Once that happens, we bring out the collars."

The Fist nodded.

"We will have some time before we arrive at our next destination. Please meet me in my chambers soon. We have much more to discuss about both Daryn and this so-called Neon King. How are you feeling?"

"I'll live."

"Good. I'll be sending you out again shortly on another task for me. I'll provide you with the details later."

The Fist continued to catch his breath as Olivio turned and began to walk out of the room. Just before going through the doorway, he turned around once more. "Try not to keep me waiting, Robert."

Josso nodded before removing his helmet.

XXII

MARIJAH JHAEL
PALACE STEPS, JEWEL OF THE SPRING
PARISO

The olive-skinned man kneeled before her and laid his left palm on the hot concrete. Large beads of sweat formed on the top of his head, created by the unison of dozens of smaller ones. He drew his blade with his right hand and stabbed the ground forcefully, causing small chips of stone to fly into the air. He shook visibly as he looked up with desperation in his eyes.

Marijah sighed as she signaled to her servants to increase the speed of her fans. This was yet another example of the worst part of being a single queen: the seemingly unending chain of marriage proposals. Compounding this misery was the reality that she was going to need to choose a partner soon, before the Ladies of the Spring convened once more.

"I'm sorry, but no."

She didn't particularly care for men in general. They were stupid, brutish, and foul-smelling. It had been unbelievable to her when she'd first learned that they could hold any meaningful positions of power in other societies. Here, at the very least, they knew their place and kept to it successfully. Her husband-to-be would need to shatter all her expectations for her to even consider him. This trembling fool at her feet was not even close to accomplishing this. He began to plead for her to reconsider but was escorted away almost immediately by the guards.

The palace, which was known as the Jewel due to both its jagged edges and the reflective nature of its mostly glass composition, towered over the surrounding city. At night, the powerful lights within its walls turned it into a bright and iconic monument to the queen's commitment to lighting the path for her subjects. At least, that was what her mother had told her.

A small girl, who could have been no older than ten, stepped up to the small red square at the foot of the makeshift throne. Marijah leaned forward and motioned for her to speak.

"My queen, the sands have pushed their way through half of the farm that my father and I share. We can no longer grow enough crops to sustain ourselves, and we fear that the approaching desert will take our lives along with what remains of our money. We ask Your Highness for her aid in this difficult time." She bowed politely as she finished speaking.

Marijah ran a ring-adorned hand across her olive cheek. The rapid desertification of the planet had become a topic of growing concern over the past few decades. She felt as though she had heard from more and more of its victims with every passing forum.

"Where are you from, my dear?"

"Calauro."

It was six hours from the palace by flyer.

"And where is your father?"

"He could not come. He needed to stay with the crops we have left."

"I assume you do not have a license yet. How did you get here?"

"I walked, my queen."

Marijah moved a lock of curly brown hair out of her face. Someone in the crowd gasped audibly.

"I . . . I will have my guards take your information, and we will see what we can do for you."

The girl nodded solemnly and walked over to the nearest guard, who escorted her aside with a hand on her back. It felt awful to be so helpless while simultaneously being looked up to by sixteen billion people. It was a lot to handle for a woman who was still a half decade from turning thirty. But she had to be the face of strength. One major issue that the record-breaking Joxun population had brought with them was an incredible demand for housing and space, which led to large-scale and unregulated deforestation. This had started long before Marijah's mother had even brought her into the world. As the decades passed, more and more of the once rich and bountiful rainforest planet had turned into deadly and suffocating dust.

The harsh truth of the situation was that she had nothing to give. They had tried a variety of government-led initiatives, but nothing had worked consistently in the long term. The sands, which brought death with them, continued to approach, and unlike the Zantavi on Saraii, the Joxun people were neither physically nor culturally able to adapt to living in such an environment.

She looked over the crowd once more. There looked to be at least fifty more people waiting to come up for their turns. As the queen's eyes darted around, she noticed one man who was wearing what looked to be tattered black rags. He shot her an uncomfortably blank stare, which he maintained adamantly. He was thinner than most of the peasants, and yet he stood straight and looked calm. She was about to tell the guards to call on him when she spotted another in the crowd . . . and then another. Each looked thinner and more underfed than the last. She looked back and noticed that they were slowly flooding in through the back gates. She shifted to her left and saw even more coming in from the entrance that was in that direction. Apparently, the guards had noticed something was awry and had placed their hands on their weapons.

The murmurs of the crowd grew louder but all the black-clad Joxuns remained silent, keeping their sights on the queen. As she was about to open her mouth to speak, the strange intruders separated in a bizarrely organized fashion, forcing the crowd back with them. They created an open lane in the center of the palace, leading from the front gate directly to her feet.

Her eyes darted to either side and then toward the back gate, where yet another large group of black-clad Joxun were shuffling in.

"Should we seal the gates, my queen?"

The voice of the guard to her left startled her a bit, but she held up a hand as she spotted something that immediately caught her attention. The figure at the front of this next group of emaciated Joxuns was not one of hers. The short, pale, black-haired man looked up at her. His completely blue eyes would have blended in seamlessly with the sky. A Draekon. She couldn't remember the last time, if ever, that she had seen one in person.

As he walked through the gates of the castle and up to the red square, the black-clad Joxuns to his left and right began to kneel. Those who had been accompanying him from behind did so as well, effectively blocking the main entrance to the palace in the process. Marijah stood from her seat and looked over the intruders defiantly. She was determined to challenge this pitiful attempt at intimidation as strongly as possible. The guards at her sides drew their swords and stood in front of her.

To her surprise, the Draekon stopped moving upon reaching the red square at her feet and calmly sat down on it cross-legged. The emaciated-looking crew that had accompanied him rose to their feet once more and turned to face her. There it was again—that look of emptiness. It varied in only the tiniest of details from face to face.

"I will give you five minutes to explain yourselves before I have my men escort you all out of here. I have too much on my plate right now to devote time to dealing with this."

She steadied her eyes on the sitting Draekon. He was dressed in brown-and-white robes that were of a considerably better quality than those of the men around him.

"You seem awfully comfortable for someone who is one wrong move away from rotting in a prison cell. Stand up and explain yourself. Now."

"My name is Jakob Koss, and I won't be standing."

She blinked twice rapidly. "Excuse me? I can arrange to have you forcibly brought to your feet, if you'd prefer."

"I mean no disrespect to you, Queen of the Seven Springs. It's just been quite a walk to get here, and there was far more sand to trudge through than I was expecting."

She sat down slowly and dug her nails into the arm of her seat. He was playing games early. This would be interesting.

"May I ask *you* a question?"

She straightened up and shot a quick glance at the guard to her right before turning back to Jakob and nodding.

"Do you recognize any of the men in black behind me?"

She looked them over as best she could, but she couldn't recall having seen any of them before in her life. "I do not. Why does—?"

"How much do you know about Oballe?"

She cocked her head to the side slightly. It was impossible to tell where he was going with this. "It's the Draekon home world and the place where you should currently be."

Murmurs began to spread through the general crowd, but Jakob's men remained still and silent.

The Draekon narrowed his eyes at her and slowly rose to his feet. The guards drew their weapons once more and took a step forward.

"You really don't know. How can you not know?"

"What in the searing blazes are you talking about? How did you get here?"

"How long have you been in power?"

"Since my mother passed five years ago. I would like to know where this line of questioning is going."

Jakob turned and motioned for one of the Joxun behind him to join him up front. The man shuffled over to him slowly and stripped off the section of his robe that covered his torso. Gasps ran through the crowd. Marijah's hand involuntarily raced to her mouth. She had thought that they looked thin, but this was something beyond that. Anywhere skin could compress itself into his body, it did. His ribs were outlined as though covered with plastic wrap. A small area on the left side of his chest was spasming. Her stomach flopped slightly as she realized that it was his heart.

"These are my people and yours, and over the years, the Alavites have subjected them to things you could not possibly imagine. All this time they spent hoping and praying for a savior, and you didn't even realize they existed. How? I want you to tell me how that's possible."

Her throat felt as though it was stuffed with thick, dry cloth.

Jakob ran a hand through his jet-black hair and exhaled forcefully.

Marijah straightened up in her seat. "Forgive me for not necessarily taking you at your fairly enormous word here. How can I be sure that this isn't some sort of trick or elaborate plot against me?"

Jakob said nothing and simply looked to the man on his right, who turned around to face the back exit of the palace courtyard. Marijah was about to speak up again and ask what was supposed to be happening, when she spotted it. On the back of his neck, slightly below where his hairline ended, were the numbers 4312 tattooed in an elaborate curved font. She looked up at the rest of Jakob's crowd, who had all turned and removed their upper robes as well: 4232, 4101, 4432, 4253, 3954 . . . the codes went on and on.

Her words lodged in her throat once more. She looked back at Jakob as he stripped off the upper section of his robe and tossed it aside casually. Despite being smaller, he was far less thin than the others and, in fact, sported a shockingly muscular chest and back. His upper shoulders were lined with what appeared to be light burn marks, but they didn't seem to bother him in the least. She shook her head slightly as she shot her eyes up to the back of his neck—0317.

Jakob turned back around. She felt a strange jolt-like sensation run through her as they locked eyes again.

"We have a lot to discuss, Marijah. I would like to do so in private."

"That is 'Queen' to you."

He said nothing but nodded.

At just a hint of her rage, Joxun men would tremble at her feet, but this Draekon simply stared right through her, and even had the audacity to shoot her the tiniest hint of a smirk. It was equal parts enraging and . . . something else she couldn't quite put her finger on.

"I understand that, but I am a king as well. These men bowed to me for a reason."

She dug her hands into the edges of her seat for a few seconds before exhaling deeply. "I sympathize with your cause, Jakob. But please don't push your luck by attempting to taunt me. You're lucky I don't have you all hanged for treason, prisoners of war or not."

"Well, that would definitely delay our negotiation process."

She sighed. "We shall meet in the evening. Your men can set up camp on the palace grounds. We will postpone the rest of this forum for the time being. Thank you, everyone."

There were some audible boos from those who had been in the crowd from earlier in the day. She would have preferred not to have ignored them, but this required her immediate attention. If these claims turned out to be true and were released publicly, she would be seen as weak and incompetent. It would be disastrous to her relationship with the Ladies of the Spring.

Two guards moved up to Jakob and began escorting him up the palace steps. The man who had been standing next to him joined the rest of the prisoners as they dispersed around the courtyard. The same odd warm feeling shot through her body as the Draekon's stunning blue eyes pierced her own. There was unmistakable pain in those pupils, but it was masked by an undeniable aura of determination.

XXIII

TOM EZEKIEL
SKYLORD'S PENTHOUSE, SKY TOWER
AYR-GROH

Tom placed one boot on the desk in front of him and brought the other over to rest on top of it. The small collection of knickknacks on the dark, glossy wooden surface rattled slightly as each foot settled into place. He leaned back in his chair, interlaced his fingers behind his head, and looked over to his right at Koomer. His half-blind buddy was sitting up straight and looked tense. He shot a glance in Tom's direction as if to question his significantly more casual approach to the upcoming encounter.

It had begun to rain outside, and droplets were collecting on the enormous one-way glass walls of the massive luxury suite. As was the case with most homes designed by Ayrs, Sprock's luxurious suite was totally open. The living room, kitchen, bedroom, dining room, and office all melded into the same space with no walls to interrupt them. The fact that most buildings on other planets were stuffed with so many unnecessary barriers had always struck Tom as bizarre. It seemed like such a waste of space.

"We should probably try to make a good impression, Tom."

As he spoke, Koomer's eyes shot to Tom's feet, which still rested on the desk.

Tom sighed. "He and I are way, way past that point. But I'll humor you, I guess." He groaned slightly as he reluctantly sat up straight.

Almost as if on cue, the doors to the apartment swung open, and the High Skylord waddled in slowly. No one said a word for the several seconds that it took him to make it to his seat. He took a brief moment to settle himself in, and then he exhaled dramatically. "Hello, Ezekiel."

"Always a pleasure to see you, Melvy."

"Please don't make this more painful for me than it already is."

Tom shrugged.

Koomer leaned in and extended a hand to the Skylord. "Pleasure to meet you, sir. Zach Koomer."

Sprock eyed Koomer suspiciously and ignored his attempted handshake. "How'd you lose the eye?"

Koomer said nothing and withdrew his hand.

Tom chuckled silently to himself as Sprock continued as if nothing had happened.

"I'd apologize for the delay, but I honestly could not care less about inconveniencing either of you. For the past two hours, I've been on the radio and video calls with the survivors and their families. Many now claim that they no longer serve me and have instead pledged themselves to this Jakob Koss. I assume you're here to explain the unbelievable gall these people have developed."

"It ain't really a difficult explanation. He freed them, sent them home to their families, and gave them hope they hadn't had in years. Hard to blame them for losing loyalty to a guy who sat on his fat ass while they starved and died."

Sprock stared at Tom in silence for a few seconds. "I'd explain how dangerous and stupid it would be to invade one of Olivio's territories from a political perspective, but I feel it would be too much for you to process. I neither want, nor need, the Chosen Army's fleet to show up at my doorstep. A few thousand lives aren't as important as the billions here. I won't apologize for that."

"First of all, ouch. Secondly, I think you have your answer."

Sprock ran a hand under his second chin. "If they no longer feel like they are my subjects, perhaps they should feel the consequences of that. Maybe a swift deportation and stripping of their citizenship are in order."

Koomer finally spoke up. "Sir, with all due respect, further antagonizing these people will only serve to demolish your popularity. They are prisoners of war and are regarded as heroes. You will have immense riots on your hands if you—"

"Yes, I know. Do you think I'm some sort of idiot? I was simply thinking out loud. I will allow them some time to become reintegrated into society before I determine a less severe punishment for their treason."

Tom chuckled. "They aren't staying, Melvy. They're going back to Oballe to fight for Jakob."

"They're weakened and largely untrained. If this is what the Draekon considers an army, he won't last very long."

Sprock stood slowly from his desk, walked over to the window to his right, and gazed out into the void of darkness and rain. "The prisoners have had some interesting things to say about Koss. Some are calling him 'the Neon King.' It appears others believe he's some sort of god. I thought we had advanced enough as a civilization to do away with such concepts."

"It's true what they say. All of it. What Jakob has done and what he is defy explanation. One of my plans is to study what has happened to him and try to form some sort of scientific explanation for it."

Sprock's blue eyes scanned Koomer for any signs of dishonesty. The white hair that surrounded his bald head looked even thinner than the last time Tom had seen it, and his rugged face was littered with scars. Tom had always thought that the man must have looked far more at home in a police uniform than in the ornate light-blue-and-bronze robes that he was expected to wear nowadays.

"I suppose we can discuss Jakob later. That is not my priority right now."

Koomer nodded and produced the piece of mascavi paper from his pocket. "This is the Treaty of Cos—"

"I know what that is, boy."

Koomer's mouth tightened.

"Look, as much as I hate to say this—and believe me when I say that—Koss has something significant here. This is exactly what the galaxy needs right now if we're going to have any chance against those damn lunatic zealots."

Tom blinked a few times. Was it really going to be this easy?

"So . . . you're gonna sign?" Tom thought his jaw might drop.

Sprock gave a chuckle that seemed to come from deep in his exercise ball-sized gut. "No. First and foremost, as you know . . . actually, who am I kidding? You probably don't know. Any sort of major international or diplomatic move has to be subject to a public referendum."

"So, you'll set up a vote?"

He looked at Koomer and smiled. "I might. But I need something from you first."

Tom leaned forward in his chair. This was getting interesting—and quickly.

"I'm up for reelection next year, and I think it's in our best combined interest if I remain in power. I can't guarantee that my successor won't try to back out."

Tom nodded, though he wasn't sure where this was going.

"So, it turns out that my main opposition, Henry Torvin, has come into possession of some . . . shall we say, indecent photographs of me from a lonely night a few years ago. He plans to release them come peak election season, which would almost certainly cause my poll numbers to plummet."

Tom couldn't believe what he was about to be asked.

"I need you to acquire those for me. With that obstacle out of the picture, I can more than likely keep my lead in the polls, meaning that you'll have an ally for the next six years. You have more than enough on your résumé to prove that you're up to the task."

Tom laughed. He couldn't help it.

"I could also just send you back to Koss empty-handed."

He shook his head. "Nah, man. I'll do it. It's just . . . I can't believe you of all people are asking me to rob someone."

"Quiet down!" Sprock looked at the door and then back at Tom before lowering his voice drastically. "It's not robbery; it's a preventive measure. I'm attacking blackmail at its core."

"Call it what you want, bucko. I still gotta steal it all the same."

Sprock sighed and leaned back in his chair, which seemed to squeal in pain as he did so.

"So, will you do it?"

"Uh, yeah. Just give me the address."

"I need it done tonight."

"Tonight?" Koomer looked stunned.

"You got it." Tom stood from the chair and stretched.

"What?" Koomer stood up and looked at him wide-eyed.

Tom ignored him, grabbed a pen and paper off the desk, and scribbled down a series of numbers on it before sliding it into Sprock's meaty palm.

"Send the coordinates to my ship. That's the mailing number. Please don't use it to send me ads for dick-enlargement pills. I don't need them."

Sprock seemed to ignore the last comment. "I have a blueprint of his estate and the location of the safe they're in. You'll need to either take or destroy his computer as well."

"Melvy, I've never been prouder of you. Hug?" Tom opened his arms.

"Touch me, and you lose the arms."

"We're such a power couple, you and I."

"Get out of my home."

"It's a pleasure to do business with you, Skylard."

"What did you call me?"

"Skylord. Why?" Tom's face was the picture of innocence.

Sprock mumbled something and made a hand motion to dismiss the two men. Koomer followed Tom as the guards escorted them back to the ship and returned their weapons.

By the time the door of Tom's ship closed behind them, he could tell that he was about to be barraged with questions. He sighed as he kicked the engines into gear. Koomer strapped himself into his seat.

"So, we're just doing this then? We're going to pull off a robbery of some guy's house on a whim?"

Tom was busy checking the multiple screens on the ship's cockpit dashboard. "Yep. Pretty much."

Koomer ran a hand over his face. "Okay then."

"Koom, I robbed a small bank once because I was horny and didn't have money for whores. I made it back twenty minutes before they closed. We've got this."

Koomer sighed as the ship turned and blasted off into the rainy evening. After a few minutes, a message with the coordinates came in, signed with the initials M.S.

"Okay. What's the plan then?"

"Don't have one."

"You don't have a plan?"

"Look, Koomster, If I don't even know what I'm doing in advance, no one can plan ahead to stop me. Just stay close to me and do what I tell you to."

Koomer seemed ready to ask another question before apparently giving up and nodding reluctantly.

They spent the next fifteen minutes in silence before landing on an abandoned rooftop about a block away from their target destination. Tom grabbed a small bag from his hidden compartment before joining Koomer at the bottom of the ramp, which then retracted behind them. He looked up at the sky as the rain droplets covered his face. It had been artificially introduced via massive water factories and had always felt "off" to Tom, compared to planets where rain occurred naturally. He tossed the bag to Koomer without looking at him.

"Grab the boots. They're older but still mostly stable. We wear pretty much the same size. Put 'em on."

Koomer nodded and did as he was told.

"Alright. Let's go."

Tom ran to the edge of the rooftop and leaped off, activating his shoes in midair and using the propulsion to reach the next rooftop. He turned to Koomer and cupped his hands around his mouth. "Slam 'em together!"

The one-eyed man nodded and copied Tom's action, albeit somewhat more clumsily. They repeated this three more times before finally reaching the correct rooftop. Tom had Koomer toss him the bag again. He pulled out a small black tablet and placed it on the floor of the rooftop. With the droplets accumulating on the screen, it was a bit hard to see, but a thermal image of the room below came into focus. Empty. In the corner sat a large cube, which had to be the safe.

He motioned Koomer over to the door where he stood, and he had him watch his back as he picked the lock. Once inside, they moved slowly and quietly. Voices could be heard coming from downstairs. Koomer held up three fingers to Tom, who nodded. They entered the room with the safe, and Tom cursed under his breath. The three green lights on it meant it was one of the new top-of-the-line models, which had to be locked and unlocked remotely via a computer. He looked around the room, but there was no computer to be found.

Tom scratched his chin and pulled out the tablet again before placing it on the ground. Its screen revealed a kitchen below them; the image had three red-and-orange blobs on it. There they were. He picked up the tablet, crept slowly out of the room, headed over to the other end of the hallway, and placed the device down on the floor again.

It appeared to be a server room of some kind, based on the heat emanating from the large computer cases.

Tom grabbed a few small metal balls from the bag and leaned into Koomer's ear. "You familiar with Etor 8 systems?"

Koomer looked at him as if he had just asked him the stupidest question he had ever heard. "Does Sprock break every scale he stands on?"

Tom's eyes widened. "Koom! I've never been prouder of you! Get down there and disable the lock on the safe. You'll know when to move."

"What—?"

Before he could say anything else, Tom jumped over the railing and landed with a thud on the floor beneath.

"What the fuck?" came a voice from the next room.

Tom crept into the kitchen through a side door as footsteps made their way into the foyer.

"Search around!" He heard the familiar sound of swords being unsheathed.

Tom smiled to himself as he found a bar in the corner of the room and a cowbell on the counter. He took a few seconds to get set up before shaking the bell with full force, its loud and obnoxious ring echoing throughout the house. The men ran into the kitchen a second later, only to find him pouring alcohol into a fourth shot glass.

"Evening, gents. Ready for some shots?" He threw his head back and swallowed the entire glass of Ayric whiskey in a single gulp.

"Who the fuck are you?" said the first man as he approached with his sword drawn. The other two came around the side of the island in the center of the kitchen, sealing off Tom's only route of escape. They were all dressed in navy blue uniforms with insignia over their left breasts. Hired guards.

"That's a pretty rude way to treat a guest. Torvin sent me."

Tom saw a brief glimpse of Koomer as he moved past the doorway, presumably into the room next door. He quickly redirected his eyes to the first guard.

"He didn't tell us to expect anyone. What's your name?"

"My name is actually not important. I'm here to give these to you."

Tom pulled out the small metallic balls that he had grabbed from the bag earlier.

The men eyed them curiously. "The fuck is that?" one of them questioned.

"These are Zantavic steel . . . the most valuable metal on the planet and in the galaxy. He wanted to give you guys an extra reward for your hard work. Each of these is worth thousands. Seriously . . . take 'em."

He offered one to the guard on his left, who took it hesitantly and then held it up to the light as he looked it over. He offered the remaining two to the other men, who followed suit.

"Why didn't he tell us about this?"

"Kind of a shitty way to handle a surprise now, isn't it?" Tom leaned back against the wall of the kitchen. The tips of the swords were still inches away from him.

The man frowned and enclosed the ball in his hand before suddenly starting to laugh. The other two followed his lead, and Tom joined in as well. They lowered their weapons and downed their shots.

Suddenly, the house alarm sounded for only a second before turning back off. The men turned to the doorway quickly before facing Tom again and pulling their swords back up.

"Well . . . it's been fun, gentlemen. But I'll leave you to clean yourselves up. Cheers."

The first guard raised an eyebrow as Tom pulled out a small detonator and pressed it, causing the balls in each man's hand to burst and squirt sticky black ink in every direction, leaving them blinded.

Tom jumped over the island and ran for the stairs as a female robotic voice came from the house speakers: "SECURITY DISENGAGED. SECURITY DISENGAGED. SECURITY DISENGAGED."

He was surprised to find Koomer at the top of the stairs with three manila folders already in hand.

"Koom! We need to destroy the computers before we—"

The one-eyed man smiled.

The robotic voice grew disturbingly deeper and slower.

"SECUUURITYYYY DISSSENNNNNGAGEEEDD. SEECUUUUUUUUURITYYYYYYY DISENGAGEEEEEEEEED. SEEEECUUUUUUUUITY DISSSENNNNN . . ." It trailed off before going completely silent. The sound of loud sparking came from below.

"You son of a bitch." Tom grinned heartily at Koomer, shaking his head in amusement.

Koomer shrugged. The ink-coated guards were not happy as they made their way back into the foyer. One locked eyes with Tom and scrambled for the stairs.

Tom looked back at Koomer. "Time to go."

They rushed back to the roof and jetted off to the next rooftop. The sounds of the guards yelling from behind them grew fainter as they got closer to the ship.

Koomer threw the envelopes down on Sprock's desk as they made their way back into his office. He looked each man in the eye.

"Good work. You handled the computer?"

Koomer crossed his arms as he spoke. "Full reformat with a side of catastrophic hardware failure thrown in."

Sprock nodded before turning to Tom. "The envelope is still sealed. I'm stunned."

Tom's criminal protégée had caused him to be so enveloped in pride that he had forgotten all about wanting to know what naughty adventures Sprock had been getting into. It occurred to him that some things were probably better left unseen.

"I'm a professional. What can I say?"

"Mhm." Sprock rose out of his seat. "Well, about an hour ago, I sent out a national statement detailing the properties of the treaty and expressing my support for it. We have been collecting votes since then. I'm still skeptical about this whole thing, but I cannot and will not allow Ayr-Groh to fall the way Oballe did. There is no telling when Olivio will get bored and decide to add to his trophy collection of planets. We can only hope that the populace feels the same way. I am the most powerful man on this planet, but I cannot overrule our constitution. If they say no, we will have to find another way."

"There is no other way. Without forming an alliance of some kind, Olivio will roll over us." Koomer sounded oddly serious.

Sprock turned to look at him. "I know."

Tom decided to kill the awkward pessimism in the room. "I feel so flattered. You knew I was going to pull it off."

"You slipped out of my grasp more than enough times for me to know how you operate."

Tom winked at him. Sprock ignored it.

"By starting the referendum early, I could ensure that the results are available in as little time as possible. Now, then . . . I have yet to look at them. Are you ready?"

Tom and Koomer exchanged a look, and then they both nodded. Sprock pressed a button on his desk, causing a screen to drop down from the ceiling. On it was a graph with a blue bar and a red one, and both stood at zero.

"Blue represents 'Yes,' and red represents 'No.' Let us see what the people have decided."

Sprock pressed a button, and the bars began to grow. Red held the lead for only a second or two before blue began what could only be described as a continuous, violent, and dominant demolition of its competitor. By the time the last of the six hundred million votes had been tallied, the red bar was barely visible next to the skyscraper that the blue one had become.

Koomer nodded and banged lightly on the desk in celebration. Sprock turned from the graph to face them and exhaled.

"Well, then. Now it's your turn to tell me: what is our next step?" For once, Sprock's tone was neither sarcastic nor condescending. He was asking a real question and seemed to expect a legitimate answer.

Koomer stared down at the treaty before speaking. "Prepare your travel party and cancel your plans for the next two weeks or so."

Sprock raised a white eyebrow. "Can I not just sign it here? Where exactly do you expect me to go?"

Tom's lips curled into the biggest shit-eating grin of his life as Koomer looked back at him with a small smirk of his own.

XXIV

DARYN PERIC
THE TREASURED CIRCLE, SCARAB STONE
SARAII

Daryn's hand raced to his right eye as yet another grain of sand assaulted it.

He maneuvered his yellow fingers through the opening in the fabric of his black headscarf and rubbed it, although the action did little to relieve his discomfort. The dark and unassuming outfits that he and the rest of the group had donned would help keep as many wandering eyes as possible off them. With the death of the Zantavi soldiers who had raided the cave a few nights ago, keeping a low profile had become more important than ever before. Given the sheer impossibility of disguising his race and the attention it would bring, Da'garo had volunteered to stay with the ship while the rest of the crew made the hour-long trek to the marketplace of the nearby town of Scarab's Stone to buy fuel. They had spent the last few nights hunkering down within the ship from which Daryn had initially been kidnapped. Thankfully, the ship had been hidden in a separate cavern that was located about a mile from the now scorched and uninhabitable hideout.

Although the nomadic Others had a solid and reliable backup shelter in the green metallic hull of Namira's ship, it quickly became clear why they hadn't simply remained there in the first place. Without fuel to run the climate control system, the lifeless metallic shell shifted between acting as an oven during the day and a deep freezer at night.

The marketplace, which was apparently known by locals as the Treasured Circle, was arranged in the style of a cul-de-sac, with several stores set up in a wide circular formation and a large clearing in the center. The constant movement of feet by the hundreds of people in the space caused a cloud of dust to form and hang ominously over the area. The lines for the one-story cinder-block buildings that acted as stores stretched out into the center of the clearing to different degrees. The Zantavic shouts and chatter coming from every direction left Daryn suffering something of a stimulus overload.

Aside from the deathly conditions, things had gone mostly smoothly up until this point. All that was left to do was stand in line for the fuel containers.

Namira stood in front with Oslo behind her and Yeuma and Daryn taking up the rear. They'd need at least four large barrels, and as such, they had brought Oslo's handcart with them from the ship to aid in their transportation. They spent about an hour in the enormous line in silence, thinking it better to avoid the suspicion of utilizing Neatspeak. For obvious reasons, Namira, the only Zantavi in the group, was chosen to handle the transaction.

As they neared the front of the line, with only two people before her, a booming sound cut through the air. Before Daryn had enough time to guess its source, three large trucks ran through the defensive fences around the market and rolled into the clearing, forcing a large chunk of would-be customers to dive out of the way. He tensed up and could feel his heart beginning to accelerate as the familiar electric tingle of anxiety exploded through his chest. He and the rest of the group followed the example of the locals and backed up slowly while keeping their eyes on the now motionless trucks, whose engines continued to hum smoothly.

"Stay calm. Could be anything," Namira whispered to Yeuma, and presumably to Daryn as well. As the extra layer of dust kicked up by the vehicles began to settle, they finally killed their engines. The doors to their sides were flung open in perfect sync, and several men dressed in varying shades of brown camouflage stepped out of them. Each of them was armed with some form of dark blade, and a few also sported compressed power bows on their backs.

"Military."

Though Daryn appreciated Namira's clarification, he could have worked that out for himself.

Evidently, soldiers weren't all that these vehicles were carrying. The crowd let out an audible gasp as an elderly Zantavi man tumbled out of the passenger-side door of the front-most truck. He hit the ground with a thud and was briefly enveloped in a cloud of dust. He coughed violently as he struggled into a sitting position.

Directly following him, in a very calm and composed manner, was a very well-dressed Zantavi. He wore elegant dark-brown robes and an almost obnoxiously large pair of reflective sunglasses. For a second, they redirected the glare of the sun into Daryn's eyes as the man looked in his general direction. The strange man slammed the passenger door shut behind the elderly Zantavi before reaching down and grabbing him by the neck, forcing the old man to sit up straight. With the dust settling, Daryn was able to get a better view of the victim. The only hair on his entire ebony head came in the form of a paper-white beard that ran across his chin. It was a bit difficult for Daryn to tell from this distance, but his eyes appeared to reflect more exhaustion than fear.

The man with the sunglasses spoke loudly in the Zantavic language. Daryn kept shooting glances to Namira to see whether her face would give him any indication of what was being said.

After a minute or two of listening to the man's speech, she leaned in slightly toward the rest of the group. "It's him. He says he knows I'm here, and he says the old man will die if I don't show myself."

Oslo turned his head slightly toward Namira before whispering back. "Nam, I like old people as much as the next person, but we can't give ourselves up over some random—"

"He's my grandfather."

Oslo didn't say another word. He simply turned his head back to its original position.

Namira took a deep breath and began making her way forward. Yeuma made a move to stop her, but little could be done without causing a scene. Daryn locked eyes with his sister. He couldn't see most of her face, but she certainly didn't seem enthusiastic about what was going to happen. He turned the other way to look at Oslo, but the shifty Quexian had disappeared.

Namira stepped into the street and removed her headscarf before tossing it into the wind. The man in sunglasses turned to her, and a large smile that made Daryn very uncomfortable ran across his lips as he suddenly switched to Neatspeak.

"Ah. There she is."

He shoved the old man's face into the ground, releasing him in the process.

"Why have we switched languages?" Namira called out.

"I wouldn't want your friends to miss any of this, sweetie."

A chill ran up Daryn's spine. He began to grind his teeth as anxiety set in.

"As much as I have wanted to find you and bring you back home to where you belong, I have a different objective in my mind's eye today."

Namira drew her curved blade from the hidden sheath behind her.

"Oh. We're getting feisty already. Save that for the bedroom, dearie. You know how I like blood on my bed sheets."

She seemed to tense up at that.

"As I was saying, while having you back will be quite the prize for me, I do actually have an entirely different primary goal today. My sources tell me you've been traveling with two Alavites who are commanding a very hefty price tag at the moment. I want them, and I know they're with you."

Namira responded calmly, with no trace of alarm nor indecisiveness in her voice. "Your spies are mistaken; I know no Alavites."

Daryn felt strong hands behind him a second before he was shoved forward roughly through the crowd. He looked to his left to see Yeuma getting the same treatment. She had left her scythe back on the ship for obvious reasons, but she was using every bit of fight within her against the Zantavi soldier who was pushing her. She bit down on his hand and managed to wrest herself free briefly before running right into another man's grasp. They were moved next to Namira, who had been stripped of her blade and forced to her knees.

The Zantavi in sunglasses walked over to them, and the entire marketplace fell into deathly silence.

"A strong day for the Zantavi people indeed. We get two of these genocidal cunts off our planet *and* make some good money off of it. On top of that, I get you back in my bed. Try as they might—and, believe me, they did—no one has come close to the raw energy you fucked me with. Sure, you're older than I'm used to now, but I'll make an exception for you."

Namira had to have been in her early twenties at most. Daryn suddenly felt sick to his stomach.

The man approached Namira and ran a hand under her chin. She recoiled, and Daryn could see the beginnings of tears forming in her eyes.

"Fuck you."

"Exactly. I'm glad we're on the same page now."

Daryn turned his head in an effort to find Oslo in the crowd, but it was impossible. There were just too many people, and the Quexian was dressed far too inconspicuously.

The man ripped off Daryn's and then Yeuma's headscarves, and the crowd around them erupted into boos and angry shouts.

"That's right, fair people of Scarab's Stone . . . the very same people who murdered and imprisoned our brothers have been living among you. Of course, we can't also forget their kidnapping of our glorious prince, can we?"

Chants began to run through the crowd.

"What are they saying?" Yeuma whispered to Namira.

"Kill them."

The man in sunglasses motioned to the crowd to quiet down. "As much as I would like to, we can't risk those maniacs coming down on us . . . not until His Majesty meets formally with the Neon King."

The three of them exchanged looks. Evidently, they weren't the only ones tracking him down.

The man moved over and stood in front of Yeuma. He crouched down to meet her eye to eye.

"Hmm. Maybe we can delay your extradition a bit. I like short-haired girls. Do you play nice with others?" He looked over at Namira and winked as he spoke the last sentence.

Daryn shot up onto his feet as rage enveloped him. He spoke loudly and with a level of confidence that surprised even him. "If you touch her, I will make sure Olivio knows, and he does not take kindly to me being wronged."

Yeuma glanced up at him with a look he hadn't seen on her face in a long time.

The man sighed and stood back up. "No one can take a joke anymore, apparently. I won't lay a finger on her." He briefly touched her forehead with the tip of his index finger. "Okay, I lied. But I won't do it again."

"Good. You lose the finger if you do!" Yeuma shot back.

Daryn glared at the man as he walked over to him and pulled a needle from his pocket. A stun prick. The Alavonian police had thousands of them. He moved his arm as though to jab it into Daryn's neck but stopped an inch short. Daryn stared the man straight in the eyes as the tip of the needle hung mere millimeters from his yellow skin. His breathing rate was accelerating, and the already ludicrous amount of sweat on his face was incrcasing. Despite all of this, he remained perfectly still.

The man smiled, withdrew the needle, and instead delivered a kick to Daryn's legs, forcing him back onto his knees.

"Just kidding. Having you passed out is boring, and I think you'll have a lot of interesting things to share."

The man tossed the needle forcefully over his shoulder, and a second later, it landed on the rear bumper of the truck he had arrived in and stuck there. Upon initial contact, it cackled and sparked for a second or two.

"It's magnetic. Pretty cool, eh?"

Daryn said nothing.

"Alright. You are all officially boring as fuck." He turned to the soldiers. "Get them all into the trucks . . . and kill the old man."

"What!?" Namira shrieked.

The man in sunglasses looked back at her with a half-smile and shrugged before turning around and snapping his fingers. The guards began to move in, when one, two, and then innumerable loud shrieks of pain pierced the air.

Daryn whipped his head around to the sources of the sounds just in time to see the Zantavi soldiers being impaled, decapitated, and otherwise butchered by men whose heavy gold armor reflected the sun's rays to a blinding extent. The man in sunglasses looked absolutely panicked as he swung his head left and right in search of an escape route, but the golden guards had formed a solid circle around the market and were closing in.

The man scrambled back over to Daryn and grabbed him roughly by the shoulders. "You called them?! Why would you call them?! I was going to send you back! I spoke to The Hand! You ungrateful piece o—"

A sharp blade pierced the back of his head and exited his nose, completely obliterating it in the process. His sunglasses slid off his face, revealing pure-white pupils as his eyes rolled back into his head. His grip loosened, and he fell to the ground lifelessly, revealing the masked, black-armored man behind him; he was impossible to mistake.

"You okay?"

The Fist extended a hand out to him.

Daryn nodded as he was helped back onto his feet.

"Give me a few minutes and we'll get you home."

With that, The Fist joined the golden guards in their fight. The familiar whizzing of power bow arrows filled the air. The crowd had largely dispersed and had begun running for their lives. Daryn looked back at the fuel stand to see Oslo stacking as many canisters on his handcart as he could.

He felt a tug on his shoulder.

"Let's get the fuck out of here!" Yeuma ran in front of him and climbed into the truck in which the now-dead Zantavi man had arrived, and Namira was helping her grandfather up off the ground.

Daryn turned around to see Oslo running the handcart over to the truck, and he went over to help him. The fighting was dying down, so they needed to speed up and get out of there. Namira and Yeuma helped the old man into the vehicle before climbing in themselves. With no time to open the back of the vehicle, Oslo attached the handcart to its side magnetically. Without a second thought, Daryn climbed in, cramming in next to Namira and Oslo, and Yeuma put the pedal to the metal. She pushed the truck directly forward, forcing the Zantavi locals in front of it to dive out of the way. The vehicle broke through the gates of the market with relative ease, clearing the way for miles and miles of desert.

"Who the hell was that?" Namira asked with her arms wrapped around her coughing grandfather.

Daryn turned to face her. "The golden guards. They're the royal Alavite—"

"Not them! Everyone knows them. The guy in the black."

Yeuma answered this time, glancing at them occasionally through the rear-view mirror as she spoke. "Alavon's Fist . . . personal bodyguard and errand boy to The Hand. He's one of the best and most ruthless fighters in the galaxy. If he wasn't too busy gargling Olivio's nuts, I'd put his mouth to better use."

"Yeuma!" Daryn glared at his sister through the mirror.

She smiled and shrugged. "I like men who kill and kill a lot. But he's a bit too much of a bitch for my taste, as yummy as he may be."

"Have you even seen his face?" Namira asked from the back seat.

"Don't have to. I know all I need to know."

"I thought you liked women," Oslo interjected.

"Why does everyone think that?" Yeuma shook her head.

"I really think we should focus on getting into the ship and getting out of here before delving further into Yeuma's sexual preferences." Namira sounded genuinely annoyed.

Everyone nodded in agreement.

The next half hour went by in consistent, albeit tense, silence, with Namira speaking only occasionally to her grandfather in Zantavic. Daryn was unsure why he had climbed into the truck instead of simply waiting for The Fist to take him back to Alavonia. That was home . . . or, at least, it was supposed to be. He didn't even hesitate when the time came to make the choice, and it bothered him more than he wanted it to.

The truck rolled into the cavern that held their ship. When it came to a halt, Da'garo emerged quickly from the dark-green vessel with his sword in hand before he recognized them.

Yeuma jumped out of the driver's seat with a start. "Let's fucking go! Get the ship loaded. We need to leave NOW!"

She and Oslo began detaching and then unloading the handcart with the fuel, and Da'garo began pulling it up the ramp of the ship. Namira got to work, helping her grandfather to embark as well. Daryn was halfway up the ramp when Yeuma called down to him, asking him to check whether they had missed a barrel in the back of the truck. He turned around and approached the rear of the vehicle, when a hand grabbed and pulled him fully behind it and out of view of the main ship. The Fist motioned for Daryn to be quiet before he released him.

The black-clad super soldier then spoke quietly. "Are you hurt? Are they torturing you?"

"No."

"Good. I'm taking you back to Olivio."

"How did you get here so fast?"

"I rode on top when I saw that they were taking you. But that's beside the point, Daryn. I need you to get your sister out of here."

"What's going to happen to her?"

"Did the sun fry your brain? She's going to be re-educated."

Daryn felt around the bumper of the truck with his left hand. "So, back to prison then?"

"Yes. Obviously. How long have you been gone again?"

Where was it? He couldn't turn to look.

"How has Olivio been doing without me?"

"What? He's fine. He can fill you in himself. Can we just get out of here? Call your sister. My men will be here soon, and we can get out of here."

There it was.

Daryn turned to face the ship and inhaled, as though he were preparing to yell, before quickly turning and jabbing the stun prick into the side of The Fist's exposed head. He began to spasm violently before falling to the ground.

Daryn stood over The Fist's paralyzed body.

"Daryn?" Yeuma's voice came from the ship.

"Yeah, I got it. I'll be right there!" he called back before turning to look back at The Fist.

"You're not taking her. Not today."

The Fist appeared to be about to say something, but his head rolled to the side, and he seemingly fell unconscious before the words could escape his lips.

Daryn looked up as he heard other trucks approaching. He grabbed the surprisingly heavy barrel out of the back of the truck and sprinted up the ramp with it. Apart from Yeuma, they were all already in their seats.

Namira turned to look at Daryn as he entered. "Good. We were taking off without you if you didn't show. Da'garo, how's the fuel?"

"We're in the green, Nam. We'll add the last barrel later!"

Namira nodded and activated the engines, which sputtered and died. "Shit! Come on!"

She tried again—same result. Daryn looked out the window. The trucks were rolling in, and golden guards were running out of them. Some rushed over to The Fist's unconscious body.

"For fuck's sake! Let's go, Namira!" Yeuma yelled from across the vessel.

Namira attempted once again to start up the engines, breathing a sigh of relief as they finally roared to life. They lifted off the ground just as the golden guards reached the hull, and they hovered over them before heading toward the exit. As soon as the entire length of the ship was under open sky, Namira blasted away at a steep angle, almost causing half the crew to fall out of their chairs.

Daryn watched through the rear window as the opening of the cave grew increasingly smaller. Before he knew it, he was staring at the beige planet in its entirety.

XXV

MARIJAH JHAEL
QUEEN'S QUARTERS, JEWEL OF THE SPRING
PARISO

Marijah tapped her long leaf-green fingernails rhythmically on the iron railing, taking extra care to avoid the large and annoying ornamental spikes as she gazed out over the reflection of the sun setting on the waters of the oasis. She hadn't stopped thinking about what had happened on the steps of The Jewel earlier that day. How could she?

"My queen?"

She turned her head quickly and then spun around to face the young handmaiden fully.

"It is almost time. Shall we get you dressed?"

Marijah nodded at the girl, who could not have been more than sixteen, and followed her into the chambers and over to the dressing room. This one was new. Handmaidens usually alternated their shifts between the queen and the various Ladies of the Spring, so seeing a new face wasn't entirely unusual.

She sat down as the girl went to work almost mechanically on her hair and makeup.

"You do good work. I may have to ask the ladies to let me keep you around for longer. What's your name?"

The girl smiled slightly. "Kalara."

They exchanged polite small talk while Marijah stripped down and then started putting on the dark-green jumpsuit that she had picked out for that evening. Its wide legs, fitted bodice, and loose sleeves that gathered at the cuff of her slender wrists left no doubt as to which nation had handcrafted it. Most upper class Joxun women essentially lived in this style of outfit, so Marijah took extra steps to ensure her different looks stood out from the crowd. These included requesting less fabric over her shoulders and neck, as well as the addition of a diamond-shaped cutout over her cleavage to allow her girls to breathe a bit.

"I saw the Draekon come in earlier. Is he the one you're dining with?"

"Yes. He's a persistent one. This should be interesting."

"He's quite good-looking, isn't he?"

Marijah turned slightly to look Kalara in the eyes. "That's an awfully inappropriate comment. He's technically a prisoner."

"I apologize, my queen."

The rest of the dressing process went by in relative silence. Kalara was working on lacing up Marijah's second high-heeled sandal when there was a knock at the door. It creaked open slightly after a second or two.

"The Draekon is asking after you, my queen. He insists that he is ready to eat."

Marijah bit her lip slightly. "Get him from his chambers and tell him that the next demand he makes in my home will be the last."

"Yes, my queen."

The door shut softly. She hadn't even seen the guard's face.

Once her second shoe was on snugly, she walked briskly over to her wall mirror. After taking a few seconds to ensure that she looked as fierce as she intended, she walked over to the door and knocked twice. Four heavily armed guards met her on the other side, ready to escort her.

She walked with a confidence that bordered on arrogance as she made her way toward the table in the dining hall. The lights had been dimmed, and candles had been lit. A roasted pig was already waiting in the center of the table, and bowls of legendary Pariso oranges had been arranged around it. A handmaiden pulled out the chair at the head of the table, and Marijah nodded at her before sitting gracefully in her seat. She waited in silence for a minute before the echoes of footsteps approached from down the hall.

A second or two later, Jakob came into view, flanked on either side by Joxun guards who were gently but sternly ushering him forward. He looked up and down the table. His slightly sunken face revealed no discernible expression, which she found mildly frustrating. She loved nothing more than seeing the blatant fear on men's faces whenever they were brought to her. Perhaps it would take a bit more work to get him to that point.

She extended a hand toward the empty chair that was directly across from her. "Take a seat."

Rather than doing as he was told, he began to slowly walk toward her while reaching for something in his robe. The guards moved in quickly to restrain him, but she held up a hand to stop them. It couldn't have been a weapon, as it would have been found when he'd been patted down upon entering The Jewel. Her intrigue only grew as he produced a piece of yellow mascavi paper. She could see the drops of sweat forming on her guards' faces as Jakob reached over and handed the paper to her slowly. He turned around and walked back over to his seat before settling down into it.

"Raise the lights."

The handmaiden by the table nodded, ran toward the knob on the wall, and turned it. The words on the paper emerged almost instantly.

Several minutes went by before Marijah finally finished looking it over and then put it down. He still hadn't eaten and was just staring at her with his fingers interlocked and resting on the table.

"For your sake, I sincerely hope this is a joke."

As she slid the paper away from her, he followed it with his eyes. He then blinked a few times before leaning forward in his chair. To her surprise, he began to calmly pile food onto his plate.

Perhaps he hadn't fully understood her; after all, men tended to a bit slower when it came to processing information.

"Jakob, my answer is no. I don't see how you can thin—"

"The oranges here are the finest in the galaxy, as everyone knows. Also, I can hear you perfectly fine. You don't need to speak that slowly."

She tilted her head slightly as she began trying to figure out what the Draekon's little game was.

"I hope they're not too ingrained in your culture. Between the desert and the Alavites, I don't see them being around for much longer."

She took a breath and forced a slight smile. "What happened to your planet, while certainly tragic, is not my concern. Your contract—"

"Treaty."

"You interrupt me again, and I'll put you in the middle of this table. We can save the pig for tomorrow."

Jakob said nothing, but his expression remained unchanged. Her threat wasn't serious, but even then, she couldn't imagine anyone else on the planet not being terrified by it. If he felt any sort of fear or was intimidated in any way, he wasn't showing it.

"As I was saying, your contract would have me sacrifice the autonomy of my army and a fair amount of my resources and provisions. I'm not sure you understand how ludicrous that is."

"You seem to be under the impression that I, Jakob Koss, am asking you for some kind of personal favor. What I'm looking for here is nothing more and nothing less than the bare minimum that you can and should do."

She narrowed her eyes and dropped her voice slightly. "Why would I owe you anything? Oballe and the Draekons are not my responsibility."

Jakob put his fork down gently. "Hundreds and maybe even thousands of your men died slaving away on my home planet. Thousands more are outside these walls on the brink of collapse. You are the queen of the Joxun people, and unless the crown symbolizes something completely different on this planet, this means you're in charge of them. My people weren't your concern, that much is true. They weren't anyone's, and that's why I'm all that's left."

Marijah's eyes widened. There was no way that she had just heard him correctly.

"If you don't act, you'll find yourself in smaller and smaller company as time goes on, until one day, your home imprisons you, leaving you with nothing to see but mountain after mountain of sand in every direction you look. That's if the Alavites don't decide to make you their next target. I doubt a glass castle will prove to be too difficult to demolish."

"Do you seriously mean to tell me you're the last living Draekon?"

She hadn't paid attention to anything that he'd said after that.

"Marijah, I grew up poor, have no political experience, and spent the last ten years on the brink of death at a labor camp. If anyone else were left, I wouldn't be the one sitting here with you right now."

She wanted to scold him for his informality, but she found herself frozen in the wake of the information he had just provided. She took a breath and gazed down at her plate, which was still empty.

"How exactly does melding my soldiers into this makeshift union help the Joxun people?"

"The TCI armed forces will pool the militaries, resources, and technologies of each of its members, and these will be used to defend every allied planet and its inhabitants. Signing this assures you that what happened to my people and my home will never happen to yours."

She raised her eyes from her plate and locked onto Jakob's deep-blue orbs. "I'm sorry, Jakob. It's too large of a commitment to make. It would destroy any historical precedent that we have, and I have enough pressing needs as it is."

"Oh, I'm well aware."

He gently placed his utensils down next to the plate. "The planet is dying. That's not exactly a secret, and it's becoming increasingly difficult to hide. The fact that you're currently sporting a population of fifteen billion—"

"Sixteen."

"Right. Sixteen billion people. You need space, and losing livable land is just about the worst-case scenario. That's why you were sending the prisoners to other systems in the first place, and this is how the men outside were captured."

"That was my mother. I had no power at the time and, besides, we had no way of knowing where they had been sent off to."

"Maybe you should have at least made an effort."

She shot to her feet, causing her chair to nearly topple over behind her. "I am not about to sit here and be lectured by a man who calls himself king, yet, by his own admission, owns absolutely nothing."

Jakob looked up slowly and shot her a half-smile. "Nothing but thousands upon thousands of miles of vacant land."

She blinked a few times. She wasn't sure she had heard him right.

"Oballe is a frigid land. My people would never survive there."

"As far as I'm aware, sparse patches of good soil are a marked improvement over miles of desert. The frost peak is nearing its end as well, which will open up far more farming options. The men outside would have done just fine if they hadn't been overworked and underfed. I'd like to believe you wouldn't subject them to either."

Another minute of silence passed. Jakob ate his food calmly, as though nothing of importance was happening around him. There was something about the Draekon that she couldn't deny that she liked, and she hated this. Only rarely did she find an intellectual equal in a man. She stared at him for another second or two before she was finally able to process and understand the sensation he was evoking in her.

She grabbed the paper off the table. "I'm going to head up for the night. We will speak again tomorrow before I send you home."

"You haven't put anything on your plate. I thought we were having dinner."

She didn't respond, simply storming up the stairs with her guards and servants in tow.

As she reached the door to her room, she gave orders to be left alone, but allowed Kalara, who was already inside, to remain. Marijah sighed deeply and went over to the balcony, which was now illuminated by only the faint white moonlight. She pulled out the paper that she had taken with her from the table and looked it over.

After a few minutes, she glanced up to admire the lights of the city and how they illuminated and spread over the artificial lake in its center. The sliding door of the balcony opened behind her. "Kalara, I'm oka—"

Her words stopped in her throat. Two gray-skinned, red-haired men brandishing knives shut the door behind them, immediately moving towards her. She gasped slightly as one grabbed her and held his blade to her throat.

"Quiet."

Quexians. They were Quexians. She remembered seeing their kind before, but the name had escaped her initially.

One thug held her firmly around the neck from behind while the other stood in front of her.

"No reason we can't have some fun before we get it done, eh?"

"Shut the fuck up, Felgin. We ain't got the time."

The first man sighed. "Fine then. Time to go, Princess."

Marijah started struggling as the Quexian she was facing began to reach out toward her. He recoiled away from her attempts to kick him in the face, though she managed to land one. She reached a hand back and grabbed one of the metal spikes on the railing of the balcony. It wiggled slightly, piercing her skin, but the pain was nothing in the face of her adrenaline.

"I'm a fucking queen." she growled.

"Ooh, yeah. I *love* me a girl with some fire."

She fiddled with the metal some more. The spikes were meant to be decorative and had been put in place by her mother. She could only hope that maybe . . .

The man to her front stood only an inch away from her. His gray pupils stared down at her hungrily as she finally felt it come loose. She used the momentum from breaking the spike off to jab it into the neck of the assailant behind her, who fell to the ground. The

Quexian groaned, and thick purple blood dripped down onto her as she scrambled off to the side.

She stood and held the spike out in front of her as she backed up slowly. The shocked man in front of her stared wide-eyed at his dying companion, as though thoroughly unable to believe what he was seeing. The Quexian who had been behind her was now slumped against the railing, still grabbing at his neck. A second or two later, he fell limply to the ground.

The remaining assailant locked onto her with a look of ferocity she had never seen before. He charged at her immediately and she stabbed forward wildly, desperately trying to fend him off. Where were her guards? Where was Kalara?

He grabbed at the spike, slashing his hand open. Despite that, he managed to get enough of a grip on the metal to pull it out of her grasp and throw it from the balcony. She kicked his stomach as hard as she could and he stumbled backward, coughing as he pressed a hand to his gut. Taking advantage of the opportunity, she moved over so that her back was against the railing.

The man coughed and chuckled. "I wonder how much a queen's organs go for, especially the fun bits."

With that, he charged again. Marijah braced herself as a bright flash of neon light blinded her. A second later, she heard a loud thud, followed by her attacker's screams. Her face already felt wet, but it wasn't from her tears. The skies had opened, and it had started to rain heavily, a rare occurrence in this city. She focused in on the scene in front of her to the best of her ability.

A man with arms and a torso that were coated entirely in a strange, bright-purple light was standing over the Quexian, who lay flat on the ground. He lifted a lethal-looking arm into the air and brought it down heavily into the assailant's chest. The purple man turned to face Marijah. She almost screamed when she saw Jakob's face. He approached her slowly. She wanted to run, but her legs wouldn't comply. The light from his body forced her to squint harder the closer he got to her. The raindrops sizzled and evaporated almost instantly upon touching his purple energy as he knelt next to her.

"Are you okay? Those were Quexian assassins."

There were too many questions on her mind to even attempt to organize them. "Yes, I am. And I know what they were. Thank you very much. What I don't know is what the fuck *you* are!"

His glowing, pupil-free purple eyes, which had been blue only a short while ago when she had seen him earlier, gazed deeply into hers.

"There will be time to explain, I promise you. You need to believe me when I tell you that you aren't safe here. If Olivio has placed a target on your head, you need to step up your protection exponentially. Infiltration and assassination are the Quexians' specialties. They rarely fail to kill their quarry."

"That won't happen again."

"Can you be sure of that?"

Marijah turned to take another look at Quexian's body. His mouth was forever frozen in an endless, silent scream. She just shook her head and looked out over the balcony. Police vehicles were beginning to make their way through the palace gates as Jakob came over to stand next to her. The bright purple light faded from her peripheral vision, taking the heat with it. She turned to see the same Draekon whom she had seen sitting across from her in the dining hall.

"Why did they want me dead? I've never even contacted their kind."

Jakob shook his head. "It doesn't matter. Their entire society works for Olivio now. He must have known I was headed here. Killing you would have been catastrophic to my plans."

She tightened her grip on the railing as she turned to look back out over the city. "How long have the Alavites been in control of the Dom'Rai and Quexians? I rarely, if ever, hear news about their movements."

"Olivio founded the Chosen Army the very same year he was promoted to Hand. He stoked the flames of his people's resentment and filled their heads with the idea that the entire galaxy was owed to them. He began his conquest with the two nations that were least prepared for an invasion, which was brilliant on his part. By the time the Chosen Army got to us, it was way too large for a single army to stop. No one, including your mother, came to our aid, fearing that they would be the next target."

Marijah turned to look at him. "I don't understand. They conscripted the other two races. Why not the Draekons?"

To her shock, Jakob let out a small chuckle. "The only thing Olivio desperately needs more than total power is to know that he has wiped us from existence. The Alavites have hated my kind for a very long time, and the feeling is mutual."

She exhaled and turned her head slowly back toward the lights of the city as she attempted to process that mountain of information.

* * *

They looked out over the capital for what felt like an hour. Multiple guards made their way into the room behind them and began searching it furiously for any more signs of any Quexian presence. A few tried to get her to come inside, but she refused. Something about this mysterious and evidently supernatural man made her feel much more secure than an entire unit of her own guards. Perhaps he would be good for something after all.

She tapped her fingernails on the railing and turned back to him. "How did you get here so quickly?"

"I caught a glimpse of them in the halls and assumed the worst. I climbed up."

"Climbed?"

She looked down at the side of the palace. Several blackened spots along its side created what looked to be a small path leading from a balcony a few stories down from her own. Several cracks of varying sizes had also formed in the triple-reinforced glass.

"I assume you'll be paying for the damage to my walls."

"I thought I was King of Nothing," he quipped.

For a second, his static face appeared to show the slightest hint of a smile. He seemed to have some semblance of a soul after all.

She sighed. She needed to sign his treaty and she knew it. She turned slowly toward Jakob to deliver the news he had been waiting for, but he spoke first.

"There is one more thing I must ask of you, Marijah."

She felt her heart skip a beat as he dropped down onto a knee. No. He wasn't doing this. There was no possible way.

He ignited his entire upper body, turning it back into its neon-purple state in the span of what felt like half of a second. The heat from being this close to him was already causing her to sweat. He lifted one of his sharp purple arms into the air and stabbed it harshly into the floor at her feet, sending small chips of tile into the air.

He lifted his head slowly to look up at her with those eyes that she could now see as nothing but utterly and wholly beautiful.

But she couldn't do this. Not with a foreigner. Her mother would roll over in her grave.

"Marijah Jhael, Queen of the Seven Springs and leader of Pariso and the Joxun people, will you marry me?"

Yet, in that moment, as she looked down at him willingly submitting himself to her for the first time, nothing else mattered.

"Yes."

She could hardly believe the words that came out of her mouth. For a second, the world was silent. She had been proposed to over a thousand times by some of the most accomplished fighters in the system. But this . . . this was different. If Jakob could accomplish what he was after, it would make her one of the most powerful and respected women in the galaxy. All this being said, she felt an undeniable pull toward him as well. He wasn't remotely hard on the eyes and had proven to be far more worthy of being considered her intellectual equal than any man she had met thus far.

She reached down and slowly cupped his face in her hands. "I will sign your treaty, Jakob. Securing the future of my people is a dire necessity right now, and I could not call myself a queen if I didn't do everything in my power to do that. Though I am not responsible for my mother's actions, I will do whatever possible to make things right. We will expand into the new frontier that is Oballe, put our might toward crushing Olivio, and secure the prosperity of our new second home. You have my word not only as the Queen of the Seven Springs, but also as your promised one."

He was about to respond when the door to the balcony slammed open.

"My Queen, the handmaiden was with the assassins. She allowed them in and deactivated the palace alarms. We have arrested-"

She turned quickly to see two guards who had just stepped out onto the balcony. Their hands raced down to their weapons at the sight of Jakob. She held up a hand to them and nodded slightly to indicate that she was okay.

They remained completely still and seemed to be speechless. Annoyed, she waved them off, and they disappeared sheepishly through the doorway.

She turned back as Jakob stood slowly from his kneeling position. He still had a few inches on her, despite being shorter than any Joxun she had ever seen. He exhaled deeply and his arms and eyes returned to normal once more. She reached out hesitantly and touched his bare chest. It was incredibly warm, but in a bizarrely inviting and comforting way. He looked down at her and furrowed his brow as though he were expecting her to say something else. She reached back up for his face and pulled his lips to her own.

He didn't really do too much, but this was fine. She liked being in control.

XXVI

ZHADEN KARUK
CHAMBER OF THE PILLARS, OLERA CITY
CHA-LEH

"This is beyond unacceptable. What you propose is glorified treason, Karuk."

Garrond slid the yellow paper toward Zhaden, who planted his hand on it to stop it from falling off the opposite edge of the glossy marble table. He sighed and looked to his left at Kamro, who shrugged his massive shoulders. Zhaden turned back to face the Pillars, who all sat in their custom-made chairs in the spacious room. A school of glittery yellow fish swam by the large window behind the chairman, who sat at the head of the table.

Garrond placed both webbed hands down and sighed.

"Please do not be mistaken. The actions you took for our people and the job you did in representing what it means to truly be an Udul are both greatly appreciated and admired, and rightfully so. But this . . . this is too much. We cannot and will not sacrifice more of our brothers and sisters for a fight we have no role in."

Zhaden smiled and leaned slightly forward over the table. "Your words reek of cowardice, chairman. Do you fear a loss of our identity? Remind me which other living race has skin blessed by the color of the Cha-leh seas or enjoys the Salt Maiden's kiss of breath? Who else can swim nearly at the speed of a small ship and lives beneath the living waves? We are and will always be Udul."

Garrond narrowed his eyes, but he did not respond.

Zhaden continued. "I am not asking us to disavow who we are and what we stand for, but the galaxy needs to stand as a united front now more than ever. We must meet the Chosen Army with force now, before doing so is no longer an option and we are forced to kneel like the Dom'Rai. I will not see such a fate befall my people. I refuse."

He sat back in his chair slowly. The sharpness of the chairman's stare could have pierced the glass behind him.

"I do not question your patriotism. The rest of the Pillars and I do, however, share some legitimate concerns regarding your relationship with the new Draekon king."

Zhaden raised an eyebrow as the chairman continued.

"If we are to assume that every one of the remaining free systems signs this—which is incredibly unlikely—he will become one of the most powerful men in the galaxy essentially overnight. You're a fool if you don't think he knows exactly what he's doing. He has no qualifications or experience of any kind and has a dubious claim at best to the only throne he holds."

Zhaden chuckled. "Jakob has suffered with those who have sworn themselves to him and understands their strife and hardships in a way none of their respective leaders back home could ever hope to do. That kind of connection means something, and it spreads. No, he didn't go through years of schooling nor lead an impressive military campaign to unseat his predecessor. But he is as true a king as I have ever met all the same."

Garrond sighed and removed his glasses. "Zhaden, my point is this: I need to hear from your own lips that, if torn between your loyalty to your friend and to your people, you will make the right choice. I make no further commitments, but I need to hear this from you before we can move on."

Zhaden glanced left and right at the other Pillars, all of whom were looking to him eagerly. "My loyalties will ultimately always lie here. This much I swear."

Garrond nodded and stood from his chair. "Very well. We will convene again next week and decide at that point when to bring Koss in for a visit so we can get a better picture of who he is. After that, we will return to you with a decision."

Zhaden shook his head and stood up. "We don't have time for that. We need to move forward with this now."

The chairman looked at him as though his head were on backward. "Are you out of your mind? Something with this level of significance is not going to be signed within a month, let alone on the same day."

Zhaden looked back at Kamro. "Is there anything that can be done?"

Kamro shook his head. "The chairman has the final authority and say on all significant diplomatic and international affairs."

Zhaden looked straight into Garrond's eyes. "Very well. Perhaps I will use my newfound free time to hold some press conferences. I think the public will be very interested in finding out exactly why I was sent to Oballe in the first place."

Garrond bit his dark-blue bottom lip slightly. "That was a renegade act by a single Pillar who is no longer here. His actions do not define the rest of us."

Zhaden shook his head. "I doubt that is how the people will see it, and you and I both know the Udul people have rioted for far, far less."

Garrond slammed a fist down on the table, and most of the other Pillars jumped in surprise. He breathed quietly for a second or two before returning to his original position. "The guards will see you out. If I see you on government property again, I'll have you arrested."

He turned to exit the room as the other Pillars rose from their chairs silently. Zhaden felt powerful arms pulling him away from the table. He struggled, but this was one of the very few places where the guards were even stronger than he was. Kamro was being taken as well, though he was being far more cooperative. Zhaden turned his gaze back to Garrond, who was feet away from exiting the room. He didn't want it to come to this, but it was the only remaining option.

"I invoke my right to The Trial!"

Garrond and the other Pillars stopped in their tracks. He slowly pulled his hand away from the door and turned around. "You're less than a week removed from internment and you want to run The Trial?"

The guards stopped moving and loosened their grip.

"Yes."

Zhaden shook himself free of their grasp.

"And what exactly are you laying claim to?"

Zhaden turned to the man he loved more than anything with a smile on his face.

"The position of chairman of the Pillars." Kamro said confidently, as he stared directly at Garrond.

The chairman looked as though he hadn't heard him correctly.

"He has no right to—"

"Do you know where I spent the last ten years, while Zhaden was in the camps?" A slight smile crept across Kamro's face.

"I don't understand how that's at all relevant."

"Law school. Tell me, great members of the Pillars . . . prior to his imprisonment, who served as chairman?"

Garrond took a deep breath.

"Marok Karuk," the Pillar with the long white beard answered. A smile came across his face, and Zhaden knew right then that he had at least one of them on his side.

"And do tell me, according to article sixty-three of the constitution, who takes over for a Pillar in the case of an impeachment, sudden death, or illness?"

"I can't be expected to-"

"Their eldest child, assuming they are of sound mind and appropriate age."

"And if they have no children?" Zhaden chimed in with a smirk.

"Why thank you for asking, love. It would then fall to their eldest sibling."

Kamro shot a half-smile at Garrond, whose face tightened.

"So, it would seem to me that Zhaden has a very valid claim to the seat."

"You cannot use The Trial to lay claim to the highest position in Udul government. That is insanity."

"Actually, I did the research, and there is nothing in either the modern constitution or the ancient trial texts that prohibits someone from challenging for a position in the Pillars. It only states that a prize cannot be the ousting of a current member. You would not be fired but, rather, simply demoted."

Garrond ran a hand along his chin. He was clearly fighting to keep his composure. "Okay. Let's say Zhaden has a legitimate claim. I was still voted in legally and approved by the other members. Perhaps he should, in fact, hold the position of chairman, but that is irrelevant. He was not here when it mattered."

"Interesting that you mention the importance of timing." Kamro turned to the man with the beard again. "Tell me: who decided to begin the impeachment process for Chairman Marok?"

"Garrond."

Kamro turned to face Garrond again. "You did not impeach and arrest Marok because you care about Zhaden. You did it because if you waited until he came back, you would likely lose the seat. The Pillars would have voted for a familiar name over an unknown outsider, and I think you knew that."

The Pillars turned to look at Garrond, who narrowed his eyes. Kamro's smirk had begun to grow into a full smile. "I repeat, Zhaden is completely within his rights to lay and fight for his claim to the seat through trial. When he wins, he will have the authority to sign the treaty in the name of Cha-leh and its people. We will be ruled by the spineless no longer."

The Udul worshiped tradition above all else, and Kamro was playing to that angle perfectly. The trial had been a cultural staple for thousands of years. No one—not even the chairman of the Pillars—would dare challenge its results, which were considered the will of the Salt Maiden herself.

Garrond's face had turned from light blue to a strange purple. "The survival rate for The Trial is twenty percent. For your sake, I hope they taught proper burial procedures at your fancy law school."

With that, he walked out of the room with the rest of the Pillars in tow. The bearded man exited last and gave Kamro a slight nod and wink as he did so.

* * *

Although Kamro had played his part well that afternoon, he wasn't overly enthused about it. He had originally proposed a much more diplomatic approach, but it had gone up in flames rather quickly. The Trial, which had been the absolute last resort, had now become their only hope.

Zhaden spent the night staring at the ceiling and watching the moving blue and green lines of the water outside reflecting off the ceiling. He and Kamro had spent the past several nights making love, but it had become clear that there was little chance of this happening again tonight.

For a split second, Zhaden felt a sudden weight at the foot of the bed. As the sensation disappeared, it was quickly followed by a thud on the ground. He felt it again, and then it vanished quickly, accompanied by another thud. He sat up. It took his eyes a second to adjust before he could make out the white coat of the cub as the animal was attempting for a third time to jump onto the bed. Its paws reached out desperately for anything to grab on to before it slid back down with yet another bump. Zhaden chuckled and looked over to his left. Kamro had somehow remained sound asleep. Zhaden leaned forward as the cub tried for a fourth time. He grabbed its paw, and with the help of a small tug, it finally got its hind legs onto the bed and quickly curled up around Zhaden's feet. It began to snore softly only a minute later. He shook his head as he ran a hand along the cub's soft fur. He had spent ten years being only a single wrong move away from death, but he had never felt as close to it as he did now. Tomorrow he'd need to do something that, as a child, he had watched dozens of people die attempting. He lay back in the bed as the images flashed through his brain one by one. By the time he noticed the light coming through the blinds, he was unsure whether or not he'd slept.

* * *

Kamro was shockingly stoic as they traveled in the shuttle to the stadium. He did, of course, have every right to be mad. Zhaden had no reason to throw himself back into the jaws of death only days after being released. Yet, here he was.

The second the doors of the shuttle opened, the two men were blasted with an incomprehensible mass of cheering and screaming. Trial runs were an iconic event, and Zhaden's newfound celebrity status had apparently made this one the talk of the city in a single night. The two men were escorted into the stadium and walked together in silence until they reached the point where the contestants could no longer be accompanied. Kamro stopped and sighed before turning to Zhaden and kissing him lightly on the forehead. Zhaden said nothing, simply nodding slightly.

Kamro put both of his hands behind Zhaden's neck and stared intently into his eyes. "You die, and I'm bringing you back to kill you a second time. Understood?"

Zhaden nodded.

Without another word, Kamro rushed up the steps, flanked by security. Zhaden was directed to the locker room in the opposite direction. While he was there, two men outfitted him in the traditional Udul attire, which was made up of large, colorful, and ornate rainbow-fish scales. Another man approached him and held out a long spear composed of a single piece of sculpted steel. Zhaden took it and nodded. The assistants scurried out of the room, leaving him alone to face the large metallic doors that led into the arena. The roar of the crowd outside was too muddled for him to hear clearly, but he could make out the raucous cheers. He chuckled as they gave way to a series of gasps and murmurs. They had likely just been told what he was fighting for.

A few minutes later, the red light over the door began to flash before the metallic pane slid open. Zhaden exhaled sharply and marched ahead. He stepped into the small glass chamber, and the door shut behind him. The entirety of the stadium was now visible to him through the glass, although it was distorted by the water.

He looked down as the cool liquid began pouring rapidly into the chamber. The water rose slowly and silently as he stared straight ahead. Within a minute, he was totally submerged. It felt good to open his gills again. A second or two later, the glass pane in front of him slid open, allowing him access to what was essentially a colossal fishbowl. He stepped inside, kicking up sand with each step he took, and looked up at the crowd surrounding the dome on all sides. The water dulled the noise, but the whistles and applause were quite audible. It must have been ear-splitting outside the tank. Attempts to locate Kamro in the horde of blue faces were predictably futile.

Zhaden fanned his gills out and stepped in front of the massive rock structure in the center of the dome. He couldn't see it from here, but by this point, he knew the volcano-like opening at its peak all too well. He closed his eyes and said a small prayer to the Salt Maiden before reopening them and slamming his spear down three times into the ground, causing more puffs of sand to rise with each low thud.

Within seconds, a large mass of black and dark-purple scales slithered out of the top of the rock which began to spin before finally centering itself over Zhaden. Two large yellow eyes the size of tires flicked open, and the narrow horizontal pupils within them focused on him.

The gargantuan Akar eel flashed its teeth briefly and then lunged at him with a speed and ferocity that he hadn't expected, biting down on his arm and lifting him up. Zhaden dropped his spear. His armor kept the eel's teeth from piercing his skin, but the pressure of its powerful jaws was still extremely painful.

The beast turned its head straight toward the ground and slammed him down forcefully, kicking up a cloud of sand in the process.

Zhaden groaned as he turned to look up at the Akar's massive body, which had now slithered entirely out of its dwelling. The blue fins at the tip of its tail briefly brought back haunting memories of his childhood. He turned back to its face as he struggled. Its eyes were closed, presumably to protect them from the sand.

He extended his right hand as far as he could, but he was still an inch or two short of the end of the spear.

The Akar began to shake its head violently to the left and right. The rapid back-and-forth movement combined with the cloud of sand disorientated Zhaden, who gave up his quest for the spear; it could have been anywhere now as far as he was concerned.

Using as much force as he could muster, he threw a punch at the eel's closed eye. The impact caused it to forcefully pull its mouth upward, ripping the armor plating off Zhaden's arm but also releasing him in the process.

He looked to his left as a slight glint of steel caught his eye. The sharp teeth once again clamped down on him the second he took a step forward; this time the eel had bitten his torso.

Instead of burying him in the sand again, the beast began to lift him. Before he could finish wondering what it was doing, it began slamming him violently into the side of the tank, causing cracks to form behind him. His vision began to spot as he took three massive consecutive blows to the body, the force of which would likely have killed someone of a smaller race.

As the crowd noise faded away, the eel suddenly turned its head back to the ground, taking Zhaden with it. The world slowed down and faded to gray as the shadow of the eel grew and grew on the sand, engulfing him. It was going to slam him at full speed, and he wouldn't survive it.

He knew what he had to do.

He reached up and hit the quick release on his breastplate, causing it to pop open into two halves. With the scaly armor separated from his torso, he was able to slip out of the eel's grasp a mere second before the deep and booming impact.

His vision began to clear as he swam madly toward the spear. He could hear the eel slithering through the water behind him. He dove at the steel weapon and turned over onto his back. With the Akar's teeth inches from his now exposed torso, he shoved the tip of the spear up into the roof of its open mouth and swam quickly to his left. The creature hit the ground again with a deep, low boom that echoed throughout the dome.

Outside, the sound of the crowd's cheers began to pick up once more.

The eel shook its head violently in the cloud of sand it had created, this time struggling with the large, sharp object that was currently entrenched in its mouth. Zhaden swam rapidly toward the beast, eventually grabbing hold of the back of its head. It quickly directed itself upward as it felt him grab it. He nearly slipped off, but he managed to maintain his grip on two of the animal's large scales. The blurred images of the audience zoomed by his peripheral vision. Over the course of a very dizzying minute, he slowly made his way up to the creature's head, where the scales were smaller, but where his grip was unlikely to be strong enough to withstand the animal's next sudden turn. It was a more vulnerable position; he needed to act—and quickly.

He reached down and forced the eel's eyelids shut. It shook its head violently, nearly throwing him off yet again. He tugged harshly at its eyelids, causing the eel to move its head and redirect itself. This was his chance, and he'd likely get only one. He aimed at his destination as best he could and smiled at his own reflection as it grew larger and larger.

Crash!

The eel smashed almost effortlessly through the weakened portion of the wall that it had slammed him against earlier, sending glass flying in every direction. Water from the tank sprayed out over the shrieking audience, who ran for their lives as water was dumped onto the stands. Emergency crew members rushed in as liquid began to rapidly fill the stadium. A sharp, high-pitched ringing noise filled Zhaden's ears as the eel wriggled feebly beneath him, taking its final breaths.

As the ringing faded, it was replaced by a different sound. Cheers. Applause. Whistles. Zhaden turned to face the portion of the audience who hadn't just seen their lives flash before their eyes. They were on their feet and were chanting his name. He finally released his grip on the Akar's eyes, which remained closed, and he stood up straight on top of its head. The noise of the crowd rose to the point where it began to rattle the foundations of the arena. Mere moments later, he was escorted back to the locker room by security.

He spent the next hour or so alone in the locker room winding down from the adrenaline and checking himself for signs of injury. He looked up as the door on the far side of the room opened. There was barely any time to focus on the blue blur rushing toward him before he felt the tight embrace. He leaned back to look at Kamro, whose eyes were red.

"You are incredible. Absolutely incredible."

They kissed for a few seconds before stopping suddenly at the sound of someone clearing his throat. Zhaden looked back to see the Pillars standing sheepishly near the door. He hadn't noticed them. Coincidentally enough, Garrond was missing. The bearded member from the day before stepped forward. In his hands, he held one of the necklaces they all wore.

"Zhaden Karuk, you have emerged victorious from the Salt Maiden's trial in one of the most spectacular fashions the arena has ever seen. As The Maiden so declares, your claim is now valid and legitimate. You are now Chairman of the Pillars, and I, for one, cannot think of anyone better suited for the position."

As he attempted to place the necklace on his neck, Zhaden stopped him. "I can. And as Chairman of the Pillars, I declare myself unfit for office."

The old man blinked, and the Pillars exchanged looks.

"I . . . I don't understand."

Zhaden smiled. "Garrond spoke of experience and the importance of being fit for duty. While I still believe that Jakob fulfills these requirements, I do not have the same confidence in myself. Instead, I exercise my right as chairman to hand-select my replacement. I choose a man with more understanding of Udul law and culture than I could ever hope to have. If you would accept, Kamro Ravull, I would name you my successor." Zhaden turned to the man whom he loved more than anything.

Kamro's mouth was agape. "Zhaden, I ca—"

"You will." He turned back to the Pillars, who exchanged glances for a bit before cautiously nodding in approval.

"What becomes of Garrond now?" Zhaden asked.

"He will continue to serve as one of us. We will need to add another seat to the table. He went home once The Trial ended, but he will come to accept the will of The Maiden, as we all have."

Zhaden nodded before turning back to Kamro. "Chairman, what do you think our next move should be?"

Kamro looked back at him, before flashing that damn smirk again.

"Pull Garrond out from whatever rock he's hiding under and prepare the international fleet."

XXVII

CORVUS-JORG (CJ) DROC
UNCHARTED RAINFOREST, EMERALD COVE
ERUB

The cool air of the tropical night enveloped CJ as his clawdadon sprinted its way through the brush. He looked over his shoulder to make sure the rest of the crew was maintaining formation. Each of his men wore small night-vision goggles to give them a chance of seeing anything in the pitch black of the jungle floor, but even with the technological boost, their vision still paled in comparison to those of the notoriously ferocious nocturnal hunters that served as their mounts. They resembled large lizards, with bodies far longer than they were wide. Sharp, dexterous claws could be found at the end of each of their four powerful legs. The narrow, scaly tails that trailed behind them were nearly the length of their entire body.

CJ reached down to his right ankle and quickly tightened the strap that was coming loose around it.

He checked his watch and pulled up the GPS on it. They were within a mile of their target.

Movement. He held up a closed fist. The entire formation behind him halted almost immediately. Layla's head shot up and began to move slowly from side to side, her muscles tensing up in preparation for combat. She knew what a sudden stop meant. Slowly and silently, he drew his machete from his sheath as he scanned the area in front of him. Layla's forked tongue repeatedly shot in and out of her mouth of knife-like teeth.

CJ pulled slightly on her reins, stopping her from pouncing as a small furry animal sprinted across their path and disappeared into the night. He lifted his hand again and motioned the group forward.

For the next few minutes, they continued mostly in silence until he had to force another stop. There was no doubt that they were close to the harbor now, and the massive iron fence blocking their path essentially confirmed it. Within its borders, scattered seemingly haphazardly on the ground, were what looked to be dozens upon dozens of stun mines.

"Shit." CJ muttered. The clawdadons' scaly coating gave them almost unparalleled resistance to fire but, unfortunately, the same did not go for electricity. Triggering one of those mines would likely result in a painful death for both the beast and its rider. He looked down at Layla and ran a hand over her beautiful dark-green scales before turning to Watts, who was directly behind him. "I thought you had this area marked as clear," he whispered.

Watts shrugged. "It was. They must have just put this up within the last two weeks."

CJ grunted before slowly returning his gaze to the gate, analyzing it for a long moment. They could try to go around, but that could take hours. He did have one idea, and it might have been just crazy enough to work.

He turned back to the group and signaled for them to follow his lead. He directed Layla to the gate and went vertical as she began to climb it with ease. As he reached the top, he pulled back to stop her from continuing down into the mine-ridden soil. Having completed the easy part, he now pulled at her reins again and directed her to the closest tree. With the aid of the sort of trust and understanding that only a decade of working together could bring, Layla flung herself at it and dug her claws deep into the bark. He then turned her and directed her toward the next tree. Without so much as a hint of reluctance, she jumped there as well and repeated the process. He looked back and saw that Watts and two other rebels had mounted the fence and begun to follow suit.

    The two dozen or so jumps began to weigh on CJ as he reached the shore, and he knew he would pay for it in the morning. With one jump to go, Layla leaped and grabbed onto the final tree, but this one's bark was thicker and flimsier than the others. The large reptile lost her grip briefly, only just managing to reclaim it inches before her long tail touched the ground. CJ breathed a sigh of relief before commanding her into the water. She hesitated now. Layla had hated the sea ever since she had accidentally fallen into it as an infant and nearly drowned. CJ, who himself was only ten years old at the time, had taken it upon himself to dive in and save her. He had gone on to name her Layla, after his late mother. The two had become inseparable since.

    He leaned toward her ear and ran a hand over her scaly head. "Come on, girl. It's only for a short time. I promise."

    He felt her take a deep breath before giving in and diving into the sea. The coolness of the water was jarring and forced the breath from his lungs. Luckily, Layla knew to surface quickly before her rider, who was strapped to her, could drown. He turned her to face the crew, who were slowly hitting the water behind them. A few had had trouble with the final tree as well, but none fell as far as he had.

    Once they were all accounted for, CJ turned back around to face the lights in the distance. There looked to be five steel cruisers docked at the harbor. They would need to take and control them with only ten men each. Hopefully, they wouldn't be very strongly protected.

As the swarm of clawdadons slithered through the water, he locked in on his vessel of choice. CJ signaled the men to split into the groups they had planned out far in advance. The reptilian horde continued to advance slowly and silently, keeping their limbs and tails under the water to avoid splashing. A few voices could be heard coming from up above on deck as he and his team approached the metal hull of his chosen ship, so the team waited in silence and listened for a bit. Due to the shape of the ship, they were shielded from view of those on the deck when pressed directly up to its side. CJ made out about six different male voices, all of which spoke in his native tongue.

They were slurring their words and laughing. After a few minutes, a small stream of water rained down behind the group. Evidently, the bathroom was too far away for these drunkards. CJ looked left and right. He could barely make out the men hiding beneath the hull of the two ships next to him and couldn't see the other two groups that were farther away. He looked back and nodded to Watts, who drew a flare from his jacket and ignited it. The clawdadons sprang into action, digging their claws into the metallic hull of the ship and scaling it quickly and with seemingly minimal effort. Layla showed every bit of desperation to get out of the water as she powered through the hull faster than the other animals. The small holes their claws created wouldn't seriously damage the ship, but they would certainly need to be fixed before the assault, assuming the group was successful.

Despite the extremely loud and obvious sounds of climbing, the stream of piss continued. Footsteps and shouting could be heard from the deck. CJ and Layla reached the top first and found themselves face to face with a pants-less, headphone-wearing Erub solider who looked to be barely conscious. His eyes widened as he came face to face with them, freezing up for a moment that would ultimately be his last.

Layla grabbed a good chunk of his upper body in her teeth, shook him around, and flung him into the water behind her. The Erub soldiers on deck scrambled to draw their weapons, but they stumbled around pitifully. Empty bottles of booze littered the vessel, and CJ shook his head at the sight. If this was the kind of discipline the Polero imbued in his men, Sheressa had an even stronger reason to win this war. If this continued, the Erub nation would be the laughingstock of the galaxy soon enough.

The other clawdadons scurried onto the deck shortly thereafter. The "battle," if it could be called that, was very short. While special electric spears designed specifically for fighting or training clawdadons did exist, no one apparently had the foresight to keep any on board. As a result, every single one of the two dozen or so members aboard the ship suffered a similar fate to Layla's first victim, if not the exact same. After giving the all-clear sign, CJ unstrapped himself and dismounted from the saddle. He sent a few men to untie the ship from the dock, and others to the engine room. He and Watts made their way to the bridge, where he flashed the ship's main floodlights on and off a few times. The other four ships followed suit.

CJ had just begun leaning back in the captain's chair to take in the victory, when the harbor's alarm went off, shattering the quiet of the evening. The docks became drenched in blinding white light.

He picked up the radio and channeled into the appropriate ship frequencies. "We need to leave. Disconnect from the docks! NOW!"

There was no verbal response to his command, only the humming of the engine as it fired into life. All nine of his men scrambled to the sides of the ship and began cutting the ropes that were keeping it tied to the dock. The sounds of engines approaching echoed throughout the harbor, and CJ knew they were running out of time. He pushed the controls forward, sending the ship into motion. The ropes grew increasingly taut as the limits of their length were tested. It took several seconds, but the men eventually managed to create cuts that were deep enough to allow the force of the ship to do the rest. They broke off unceremoniously from the sides and back of the vessel and dropped into the water. He sent the ship forward at maximum speed as he pulled away from the dock.

He flicked his gaze between the other ships, taking note of the problems they were facing. Some were still held in place by the ropes. Others had managed to free themselves, but still hadn't started their engines. He had tried to explain the controls to the other men beforehand, but none of them had any experience with naval vessels, and these ships were a different model from any of the ones they had previously stolen. He could only hope that they would figure it out. He continued forward but lowered the speed a bit.

"We shouldn't slow down! They'll catch up!" Watts yelled as he made his way into the captain's quarters.

CJ held up a hand to shut him up, but he kept his head turned and his eyes on the ships behind them. Still no movement. He wiped the sweat from his brow and felt his heart sink as a flock of flyers emerged from around the harbor and began to circle the cruisers. "I'm turning us around."

He began to move the wheel, but Watts grabbed his arm. "CJ, we can't risk losing this one."

CJ, in turn, grabbed Watts's hand and tossed it off him violently. "We're going back!"

Watts then remained silent, crossing his arms, while CJ turned the ship slowly and began to head back to the other vessels. He would get back on Layla and make his way aboard one of them. The flyers would likely start dropping men in at that point.

His racing thoughts came to a screeching halt as streams of flames shot out of the vessels and coated the decks of the ships. They were a few hundred yards away, but the screams of the men aboard were audible even from that distance. He watched multiple flame-engulfed figures leaping from the decks as the cruisers turned into massive, floating fireballs. Soldiers, wearing full firesuits and armed with the proper weaponry, now rappelled in from the flyers and began stabbing the panicked clawdadons that remained.

Watts reached for the controls, and CJ did nothing to stop him. The ship quickly turned, moving away at top speed. CJ stared out of the back window of the bridge for a while, watching as more flyers surrounded the doomed and flaming vessels.

He spent the next two hours in silence on the deck. The remaining eight members of the team and their clawdadons were moving around slowly. The large reptilians began to emit high-pitched wails as they cried out in the night, presumably mourning the loss of their brethren. He slammed a fist against the wall, denting it. This would not go well for him back at the base. Not at all.

The process of docking the ship in their own hidden harbor, mounting, and riding back to the mountain base as the sun began to rise felt like an eternity. When the main doors of the base slid open, Sheressa's expression told CJ that his prediction had been spot on. He climbed off of Layla and walked up to his sister, who was wearing a long dark-green dress.

"What happened?" She enunciated each word slowly, as if it were its own sentence. The look in her eyes was so intense that CJ briefly worried that he would burst into flames.

He grabbed her arm and tried to walk with her. "Come on and I'll tell you—"

"I don't fucking think so!"

She withdrew her arm forcefully. The vein on the side of her head was visible and pulsating. "You're going to talk, and you're going to do it now in front of all of us. I want to hear it from your lips."

He looked around at the rest of the resistance leaders, who were all staring at him. He sighed and ran a hand over his sweaty forehead. "They burned them alive. They torched the ships. We got away with one."

"And why did *you* manage to make it out?"

The question sounded harsh, but he knew what she meant. "We broke free and got the engine going. We were the only ones that did both."

"Exactly! Because they aren't fucking sailors, and they don't know the ships, which just so happened to be the main reason I didn't want to do this."

"I gave them a thorough explan—"

"I don't give a shit what you did, Corvus! It clearly wasn't enough!"

"I can't be everywhere at once! I got my ship out! I did my job!" He hadn't meant to yell. This wouldn't be good. Raising his voice at Sheressa rarely turned out positively for him.

She smiled in an extremely sarcastic way. "Good for you. We got one ship. It only cost us forty fucking men and forty highly trained clawdadons. But who cares, right? Those grow on trees, after all. So, congratulations on your victory. From now on, if I say no, it means no. Understood?"

He stared down at her and bit his lip before nodding and mumbling "Yes."

She turned away from him and began walking rapidly. She spoke to a few of the other leaders as she walked. "We can't wait on this strike any longer. I want every able-bodied man at the docks for the next four days. We train on the ships we've got from sunup to sundown. No more cutting corners. On the fifth day, we rest, and on the sixth, we attack Mortobal with everything we've got. This is our time. We can only hope we don't come up forty men short in the fight." With this final sentence, she glanced back at CJ.

They walked for a few minutes before Sheressa stopped suddenly by one of the many makeshift doorways and motioned for him to come to her. "Corvus, we had a foreign visitor while you were out. I was going to have him killed, but he said you sent him here, so I put him in the cells. He's the Black one."

CJ raised an eyebrow. Sheressa turned and kept walking with the rest of the leaders. He wanted nothing to do with this prisoner right now, but he figured it was probably better than what would be awaiting him upstairs. He sighed, turned to the doorway, and started making his way down the dark stairwell. At the bottom, he passed the guards, who saluted him.

It occurred to CJ that Sheressa could have simply said, "He's the only one," as the dark-skinned Zantavi man sat alone in the cell at the back of the room. CJ walked over to him and stood in front of the bars.

The man stood as he approached. "You are Droc?"

"The lesser version, apparently."

The man looked confused.

"Yes. I'm CJ."

The man smiled, exposing a mouth that was missing a few teeth. "I am Hawati. You send message to King Josso, yes?"

It had been several days since CJ had sent word to the Zantavi king about his son and the treaty. At this point, he had almost forgotten about the whole thing.

"Yeah. Why are you here, Howotti?"

"It is Hawati. Do not worry; many make same mistake. His Majesty, ruler of the sands, sends me here to collect treaty from you. I try to explain this to pretty greeter girl, but she order me in prison."

"We don't have a greeter girl."

"Then, who is girl in fancy dress? In Saraii, most beautiful women work as greeters. Is different on this planet?"

CJ figured that explained why the man was locked in here. Sheressa didn't tend to take well to people making unsolicited passes at her, let alone complete strangers who were also foreign.

"That would be my sister. She's the one who is actually in charge around here; something I'm reminded of very frequently." He mumbled the very last part of the sentence.

He sighed as he turned back to Hawati. "I'll get you out of here, bud. I'll have the treaty brought to you too." CJ looked down at his feet for a second. "How, uh . . . How did the king react to the news about his son?"

Hawati shook his head. "Our King is devastated and looks forward to forming rescue operation with rest of TCI army. He is on way to Draekon planet now. He signs. Zantavi will join treaty."

CJ blinked a few times. The Zantavi army and tech level were middling, but their mines were some of the richest in the galaxy. "There is no TCI army. Only you guys have committed, and the Draekons have no army, aside from Jakob himself."

Hawati chuckled. "Oh, have you not heard, my friend? Joxun Queen has agreed as well. Hawati hear rumor that fish men also going to Draekon planet. Even Ayr people voted yes."

CJ wiped sweat from his brow. "I, uh . . . I'm going to go get you the treaty. I'll have them let you out. Wait here."

"Hawati will like to spend night. Very tired."

"I'm afraid I'm going to have to ask you to leave. We don't really want outsiders here. It hasn't particularly led to good things for us thus far."

Hawati looked confused for a second but nodded. "This is shame. Saraii accepts and loves all."

"It's a safety issue. It's as simple as that. I just want to take care of my people."

"I confused. I thought you say female Droc the one in charge? Why say 'my people'?"

CJ turned and raced up the steps without responding. His mind raced as he made his way toward his chambers. He didn't have time to go back and forth with this guy. On another note, it seemed that it was officially time to take Jakob's little passion project seriously, be it as an ally or a threat.

ACT III

XXVIII

JAKOB KOSS
COMMAND MODULE, JOXUN FLAGSHIP
OBALLE

The temperature shifted from cool to uncomfortably warm as Jakob walked through the large steel doorway and into the command module of the ship. The fact that it was surrounded entirely by tinted one-way glass made him feel more like a small, pallid creature in a zoo exhibit than anything else.

Marijah stood at the very front of the chamber, where no desks or bright screens could hinder her view of the large gray orb that filled the glass before her.

It was an unexpectedly harrowing experience to gaze out over it from the perspective of a god rather than a man. Jakob shook his head and refocused his gaze on the queen. She had taken it upon herself to wear an elegant black jumpsuit that was accented with a dark blue necklace and bracelets; this was the Draekon color.

Jakob himself had been subjected to several visits from Marijah's tailors, who had made every effort to get him out of his dirty Zantavic robes and into something much cleaner and significantly more elegant. He had never liked ornate designs nor bright colors, and his stubbornness regarding the issue had eventually forced a transition to an all-black outfit made from one of the cheapest fabrics available, much to the chagrin of the tailors, who had clearly expected better from the future husband of their queen. For him, it had been the most comfortable, and he couldn't have cared less what people thought about what he wore.

Rather than being tied around the waist, the two sides of the open-faced robe he now wore were held together by a gold chain that rested just above his breast; it was one of the few "luxurious" elements that he had reluctantly agreed to. He wore no shirt underneath it, as it didn't seem to make sense to do so anymore, given the fact that he could not seem to stop anything from burning off him whenever he ignited himself. His lightweight fitted black pants fell to just around his ankles, leaving his feet completely free and unrestrained.

He stepped closer to the woman whom he would soon marry, if only for political purposes. Her brown pupils stared straight ahead.

She reminds me of my own.

Her dark curls bounced slightly as she turned her head slowly to return his gaze before coyly reaching a heavily manicured hand out in search of his. He moved ever so slightly to avoid her touch.

But, then again, I did actually love mine.

Jakob sighed and stared up at the ceiling angrily. Marijah put her hand back at her side nonchalantly.

"You can't hold out on me forever, Koss. You do know that, don't you? I always get what I want at some point."

She smiled cockily and returned her gaze to the window. She had caught him off guard with that kiss back at the palace. He had mumbled some excuse and made his way back downstairs, leaving her to her guards and handmaidens. They had spoken fairly frequently over the next few days, but the topics had been kept strictly to politics. He couldn't remember the last time a single sexual or romantic thought had crossed his mind. It simply wasn't something he ever ruminated about. He had not expected her to take a legitimate romantic interest in him, and this had severely complicated matters.

"So, this was your home?"

He sighed as Karvenkull's tall black spires began to loom larger and larger in the glass before him. "It wasn't before. It is now."

She nodded. "It's beautiful."

He did a small double take. The sincerity of her tone caught him by surprise. "I know."

"I have sent the settlement ships to the locations you specified. They should be landing within minutes of us. They'll begin the process of either constructing new housing or repairing what's already there, depending on what they find."

Jakob nodded. "How many did we end up bringing with us?"

"We stuck with a relatively small group of around forty thousand for the initial scouting process. The huntresses will lead small teams of their men and comb the area you mapped out for me."

There was silence between them for a few seconds. Out of the corner of his eye, he could see her turn to look at him.

"My people are hard workers, Jakob. It will take some time, but one day, this place will be what it once was. Given how many women we'll be placing in positions of power, it may well be even better."

He turned and walked out of the command module without giving a response as the ship slowly began to lower itself to the ground. By the time he made it to the nearest exit of the four-story behemoth of a ship, the soldiers aboard had already stepped out and aligned themselves in neat blocks, creating a clear path between them. He stood, looking out over them for a few seconds.

Snow had begun to fall, but this was obviously neither new nor noteworthy there. Three sets of footsteps approached from behind him. He turned to see Marijah flanked by two of the tallest and strongest-looking Joxun men he had ever seen, each of them holding an elaborately decorated halberd. She walked up to him and slid her left arm under his right.

She spoke barely above a whisper. "We're doing this whether you like it or not."

He reluctantly bent his elbow and walked forward, escorting her down into the snow. The Joxun men on either side of them dropped down to a knee as Jakob's feet contacted the powdery Oballian frost once more. Each line of soldiers kneeled in turn as Jakob and Marijah passed them on their way to the castle's black gates.

You have done well, Jakob. But do you trust your friends to have done the same?

Once they were halfway to the entrance, the castle doors swung open, and several Zantavi soldiers spilled out. Both armies drew their weapons and took aggressive stances. Marijah yelled something in her native tongue, and her soldiers loosened up almost instantly. Someone from across the divide also yelled, only in Zantavic. Jakob scanned the crowd to see who had given the order. A balding, middle-aged man dressed in elaborate light-brown robes pushed through multiple soldiers, who seemed to be insisting that he stay back. The Joxun soldiers around them seemed apprehensive.

"Jakob Koss. It's an honor to finally meet you. I am Rey Josso. My lady." He bowed politely at Marijah.

"Your Highness," she corrected him.

Jakob turned his head briefly to look at her before turning back to Josso. He may not have wanted the same things she did, but he respected how she carried herself.

"A pleasure to see you here, King of the Endless Sands. I'm afraid I wasn't given any notice of your arrival."

He sighed.

"The comms system in your castle needs serious upgrades. We were unable to reach out in any meaningful capacity."

Jakob nodded. "Considering they haven't been used in a decade, I'd say that's an understatement."

As he spoke, Jakob scanned the group of Zantavis behind their king again. "Where is your son? I had expected him to return with you."

The man's expression fell, and his complexion grew significantly redder as he ran a hand over his face. "He's been captured. Again. My hope was to go after him after meeting with you and signing my copy of the treaty."

Jakob shook his head.

Rey motioned to a Zantavi soldier to come over, which the man did with a smile. He was missing several teeth.

The soldier produced the treaty from the inner pocket of his robes.

Jakob turned to him. "Where did you get that?"

"The boy Droc give it to me. He keep it after our prince's kidnapping."

Jakob nodded again. How CJ had managed to avoid being taken himself was another issue entirely, but he would figure it out later.

Something isn't right about this. The younger Josso strikes me as too smart to allow himself to get captured twice. Keep your wits about you.

"Shall we move this conversation inside?"

The Zantavi king appeared to be shivering slightly. This was about as large a departure from the climate of his home world as one could fathom.

Before Jakob could answer, the loud hum of approaching engines drew everyone's gaze to the sky. Not one, but two distinct fleets seemed to be approaching and growing larger by the second. Taking up the portion of the sky to Jakob's left was a swarm of rounded silver ships with dark-blue windows. Their announcement vessel unfurled the massive teal-and-white flags of the Udul people as it approached. It seemed some of these vessels had naval ships attached beneath them. This was a bizarre decision, given that most large bodies of water on Oballe were frozen over at this time of the year.

To his right was a horde of dark-gray, carbon fiber-coated vessels led by Ayr's large maroon-and-yellow banners. Jakob squinted as they approached. In front of this group and seemingly leading it was the matte-black ship that Tom and Koomer had taken off in the last time he'd seen them. It began to corkscrew as it approached the large clearing.

That Ayr does enjoy showing off, doesn't he?

The empty field surrounding the palace was enormous, but fitting two entire fleets of ships within it proved to be no simple task. Once they had all finally settled in, soldiers from both armies began to filter out in chunks between the massive husks of steel. Jakob broke off from Marijah and walked briskly toward the newly formed metallic forest and the plethora of silent men and women who stood beneath it. The Udul soldiers bowed as the Pillars made their way down the ramp. Zhaden's massive frame followed closely behind, tailed by the white bear cub, who had grown a bit since Jakob had last seen it. His oldest friend smiled as they made eye contact. Joxun soldiers ran in front of Jakob, creating a wall between the two men.

"Leave me. I know him."

The soldiers nodded and stepped aside. As the two met, Zhaden lifted Jakob in the air with a massive hug.

"The Udul people are with you, Jakob!"

Jakob chuckled slightly and patted him on the back, signaling that he wanted to be let down. "How hard was it to convince them?"

Zhaden looked back at the Pillars, who were taking their time walking over to them. "Oh, it was a fairly simple process. They agreed quite strongly with the treaty and its message. It only took a day."

The Pillars moved around Zhaden. There was one more than he had seen before. It took him a second to recognize him as Zhaden's lover, or significant other, or . . . whatever they went by. He extended a hand to him.

"Kamro Ravull. Chairman of the Pillars."

Zhaden had quite a few questions, but he decided that they were better saved for later. He reached over and shook the man's webbed hand.

"So, I guess we're just fucking garbage, eh?"

Jakob turned to his right toward the familiar voice. Tom stood with his arms crossed as Koomer approached from his left. He could see his own reflection clearly in their orange virixes. To Tom's right stood an extremely overweight, albeit extravagantly dressed, man whom he assumed was the High Skylord. Behind them, as with the Uduls, stood a large array of soldiers standing in a disciplined formation. In turning his head toward Tom, Jakob noticed that Marijah had made her way over to him again and now stood only just behind him to his right.

Tom opened his arms as though asking for a hug. "Nothing? Alright . . . well, fuck you too." He chuckled before bowing dramatically in Marijah's direction. "I heard the Joxun queen was a beauty. They weren't wrong. Damn."

Jakob stared down at the top of Tom's head.

"Yes. We—"

"Jakob offered his hand to me in marriage, and I accepted."

Tom shot straight back up so quickly that he nearly fell over. "Holy shit! I don't know what the opposite of getting cold feet is, but you've got that on lock."

Marijah rolled her eyes. "This one's Tom, I take it?"

"Yes." Jakob sighed, as if it explained everything.

"Ezekiel, if you would allow me a chance to speak, I'd much appreciate it." Tom sighed as the large Ayr behind him shuffled forward slightly toward Jakob. He extended an unexpectedly calloused hand toward him as he approached.

"Melvin Sprock, High Skylord of Ayr-Groh and her people. I have heard much about you, Neon King, and I look forward to learning how much of it is actually true."

Jakob took his hand and shook it. "Absolutely. We appreciate you coming on board. The galaxy needs every last man it can round up against Olivio."

"It is good to see you two again, my friends!" Zhaden moved over to Tom and Koomer and patted them on the back. The three began to speak among themselves for a bit before Tom suddenly threw off the small backpack he was carrying and pulled out the treaty, which he handed to Jakob.

"Wait. That was supposed to be in my office on the ship," said Sprock, his rising anger evident in his voice.

Tom shrugged. "Yeah, and I was supposed to have a loving household, an education, and a nontraumatic childhood. Such is life, my dude."

Jakob made eye contact with Koomer. "Everything go well?"

He nodded and looked down at his feet. It was odd to finally see him with a virix on.

"Ah, yes. Here is ours as well. Garrond?"

A particularly unhappy-looking member of the Pillars stepped forward and presented the treaty to Jakob halfheartedly before returning to his original position.

Evidently feeling left out, the Zantavi king eventually made his way into the circle as well. He introduced himself to the rest of the crowd before turning to Jakob. "We had some downtime while we waited, and I thought it would be best to put our seamstresses to good use. Gaze upon her."

Jakob raised an eyebrow as Rey motioned for him to turn around. Up at the top of Karvenkull, in the spot where the haunting white and gold banner had flown uninhibited for over a decade, an enormous black flag was being raised. Within a few seconds, it began to flap triumphantly in the wind. In its center was the Draekon symbol in its traditional dark-blue hue. Surrounding it were five beautiful bronze pendants forming the shape of a pentagon. It was the symbol that he had marked each copy of the treaty with and the very one he had first scrawled onto the wall of the barracks so many years ago.

As the banner rises, so do we all.

For the first time in as long as he could remember, a surge of joy rushed through him. This was real, and it was happening. He had dreamt about it and planned it out for so long that it would almost certainly take some time for it to truly sink in. Unfortunately, this was time he didn't have.

The Zantavi king had begun passing something out to the others, most of whom were still staring at the flag. He offered one to Jakob as well. It was a badge of some sort, and it was shaped in the exact same design as the flag, only with bright steel beams connecting each bronze pendant to the next, forming a metallic pentagon around the Draekon insignia. Jakob turned his gaze back to Rey Josso, who had placed the small badge over his own left breast. Jakob looked around the circle. The other members were all finding places to pin the metal pendant onto themselves. Zhaden stuck it directly near the collar of his sleeveless shirt, and Tom pinned it to the left breast of his jacket.

Jakob felt a tap on his shoulder and turned to Marijah.

"How do I look?" She had placed the pin in such a way that Jakob was forced to look at her particularly pronounced cleavage in order to see it. He quickly glanced away as she began to chuckle. Though it wasn't especially interesting to him, she was particularly well endowed in that area and appeared to enjoy making sure he knew it.

"The Zantavic steel addition was my idea," Rey Josso proclaimed with a sense of pride in his voice as Jakob turned back to face him. For some reason, Tom chuckled and shared a look with Koomer.

"So, I like the outdoors as much as anyone, but can we head inside and get warm? I'm freezing my fucking nuts off."

Jakob looked at Tom and shook his head. "No. Not yet. We're taking a small trip . . . all of us. Bring your most trusted guards with you, if you so wish. We'll travel in Tom's ship."

Tom made a noise that sounded like a cough. "We will? Alright then . . . Where to?"

Jakob said nothing, and simply shot a glance at Zhaden.

The short flight was mostly spent in silence before they touched down. When Tom opened the door, they all shuffled out slowly and silently. The abandoned camp was deathly silent, with an occasional blast of wind being the only break from the monotonous, all-encompassing nothingness. The small hills of bodies from the fight were in varying states of rot. Sprock began to retch almost as soon as the doors opened.

Jakob turned and faced the group once everyone was out, and simply nodded once.

The group spread out in silence. Jakob followed along with Zhaden first as he led the Pillars into the barracks where the two of them and Koomer had spent so many nights. The group came to a halt in front of the wooden platform that had served as his bed. It was several inches too short, even for a normal-sized Udul, and his feet had stuck out uncomfortably every night.

Kamro said something to Zhaden in their language as he wrapped an arm around him and pulled him in tightly. Jakob left the Udul group and walked past his own cot—the one he had occupied every night for over ten years. The crude drawings and writings from several sleepless nights were still visible in the cracked, aged wood. He ran a hand over them before quietly making his way out into the snow.

He found Marijah looking over the infamous clearing in which he had stood not too long ago. The floor was permanently stained with the blood of thousands, if not millions, of pale, nameless souls. With how utterly and unnervingly still she remained, she could have been easily mistaken for a statue, even as the wind whipped her hair and the black fabric of her jumpsuit in every direction. He went over and stood next to her in silence. Her face was flushed, but stoic.

They stayed there together in silence for several minutes, staring out over the emptiness. He remembered all the times he had stood in a spot that was not at all dissimilar to the one he was in now while being forced to watch the horrific and inhumane process that he wished he could erase from his mind.

Do not wish to forget it. If you forget, you may be inclined to forgive.

"I didn't believe you, Jakob. I really didn't. I deserve to stand in this spot and to feel the way I feel. I have to live the rest of my life knowing I allowed this to happen."

"Do you know what took place here?"

"I don't need to. I find that the dead can at times speak for themselves. I need to be alone."

He nodded and stepped away. It took him a bit longer to track down the three Ayrs in one of the multiple shipping-container buildings. They were standing over the rotting body of a Dom'Rai.

"I mean, if you sorta squint a bit, it kinda looks like he's smiling."

Tom seemed to always have such a way with words.

Sprock had produced a handkerchief, which he was now holding over his nose and mouth. Koomer had ignored the corpse entirely and was walking around the container while running his hand along its wall. He had probably spent more time in these buildings than most. Jakob turned back to the corpse. It took a second for him to recognize it as M'og.

The animal of a man had no worth in this world. Do not give him the luxury of your thoughts.

"Zhaden took care of him. Buried his horn right in the fucker's forehead."

A slight involuntary smile crossed Jakob's lips as Tom finished speaking. Perhaps some justice still existed after all.

Jakob nodded at the Ayrs before leaving them and making the trek to the Western Block, where he found Rey Josso sitting in front of an open cell.

"He's a good kid. He has always been such a good kid, and I have never been able to be there for him. He was in a cage then, and he probably is now again, all the while probably wondering where his father is."

Jakob placed a hand on the dark-skinned man's shoulder. "If Olivio has him, we will get him back."

"Jakob, I was a failure to Robert long before he was kidnapped. As a boy, things happened to him under my watch that I will never forgive myself for. I trusted another to do my parenting job for me, and they betrayed that confidence in the vilest of methods."

Jakob bit his lip slightly and nodded. He had never been a stranger himself to abuse, but, based on the sounds of it, this had gone further than mere beatings.

"Why do you think the Alavites want him so badly?" He asked, trying to change the subject.

"I don't know. I would trade myself for Robert in a heartbeat. That's the worst part. I've sent messages out and asked for their ransom price, but I've heard nothing back. I don't even have the option of negotiating with the terrorists. They just want to torture me, and I don't know why." He turned his head slowly to look up at Jakob. "I want them dead. All of them. I want them to suffer."

Jakob nodded and left the kneeling man to his thoughts. His footsteps echoed through the empty Western Block as he moved toward the door.

Everyone aside from Rey Josso was back at Tom's ship by the time Jakob arrived. Within half an hour, the Zantavi king joined the group.

No one seemed to be in the mood to speak.

"Alright, Tom. Let's head back." Jakob said as he began to turn towards the ship.

To his surprise, the Ayr hesitated. "I . . . um . . . I think you should see something."

"Tom, no."

Zhaden stared the Ayr down with a level of seriousness and intensity that Jakob hadn't seen in years.

"He needs to—"

"Tom, he doesn't." Koomer interjected in an equally serious tone.

"Take me to it. Now." Jakob insisted.

"Jakob—"

He shrugged off Zhaden's attempt to hold him back.

"Now! This is my planet and my home. If I want to see something, I will."

The Pillars, Marijah, Sprock, and Rey Josso exchanged confused glances. Koomer and Zhaden looked at each other with decidedly unenthusiastic expressions.

You already know what you will see. You've always known, haven't you?

Jakob gave no response to the voice in his head as the group marched toward the decrepit comms building. They needed to move quickly, as the sunset had crept up on them. Oballe's sun was dropping just below the rim of the horizon as they made their way to the top of the tower. Sprock needed assistance from both Tom and Koomer to make his way up the steps.

"Sky Tower's food must be fucking spectacular," Tom muttered as they approached the last few steps.

"Shut it, Ezekiel," he shot back.

The sky was now been drowned in a dim orange light. It was too dark to see it without assistance.

"Do it, Koom." Tom mumbled sheepishly and with a level of shame that Jakob had not thought possible from the Ayr, who was usually so aloof and sarcastic.

The one-eyed man extended his hand slowly toward a lever on the console. He shot a quick glance at Zhaden, who seemed to nod his approval begrudgingly. The spotlights activated with a loud click.

Even when we know, it's never quite the same as when you see it.

All at once, in a single and horrific moment, it came into view. Jakob turned to gaze out of the window as a variety of groans and gasps floated around behind him. He felt Zhaden's large hands on his shoulders. The yellow light had an interesting effect upon hitting the Draekons' pale skin. It almost made them look like Alavites, ironically enough. The trenches were bigger, and likely deeper, than he had imagined. It took him several seconds to be able to make out the first face in the disorganized heap of limbs, torsos, and genitals. The young man, staring lifelessly back at him, must have been around his age. His neck had been cut in the exact same place as everyone else's.

We must gain strength from this, Jakob.

This horrid, tangled mass of decay spread out in an alarmingly clean and organized spiral that stretched out farther than he could see. He scanned the never-ending mound of death for several minutes, attempting to find a single non-Draekon. That was all he needed: a single indication that this inhumane humiliation was meant for someone other than the Draekon people. For the first time since the liberation of the camps, Jakob failed objectively and undeniably.

Do not let Olivio ignite that fire in you. If you get reckless and overly aggressive, it will put TCI as a whole at risk. He wants you angry. He wants you vulnerable.

Loud retching echoed through the small radio tower control room as Sprock doubled over, and Jakob turned back around slowly. Tom had turned his back to the window and was staring down at the floor. Sprock, now on his knees, could have passed for a Draekon, given how much color his skin had lost. A few of the Pillars shielded their eyes, while others, including Kamro, looked ahead intently. Rey Josso walked up slowly to the very front of the room, kneeled, closed his eyes, and began speaking quickly in Zantavic. It seemed to be in the rhythm of a prayer. Jakob turned his head to the left to look at Marijah, who had moved in closer to the glass and placed her right hand on it. Her gaze was as intense as Jakob had ever seen it.

After about a minute, she turned her face slowly to him. Her voice was heavy. "Jakob . . . I . . . I'm so . . ." Her voice trailed off. He didn't blame her.

He looked away, back out over the motionless pale mass of what remained of the Draekon people. The temperature had not risen enough for the bodies to decompose, and it was impossible to know how long they had been accumulating for. The frost peak had begun eighteen months ago.

Do not leave them there. Not like this.

Jakob began to nod and stopped himself. The voice was so real he had begun to treat it like another person in the room. He turned back to Zhaden, who had tears running down his cheeks. Jakob gave the Udul a slight push to indicate that he wanted to be let go. Zhaden nodded and retreated slightly. He turned back to the glass as he reached a hand up to the chain that held his robe together. With a single, quick tug, it came undone and dropped slowly and silently behind him, leaving his shirtless torso exposed.

He closed his eyes and ignited himself, as he had done multiple times before. It had become second nature by this point. He thought he heard a gasp or whisper from behind him, but his focus was on what was in front of him. He swung a neon-purple arm at the glass, which shattered loudly in the night, allowing the frigid outside air to rush in. He moved forward and stepped onto the now-empty window frame. The soles of his feet were more than likely being stabbed violently by shards of glass, but he didn't care. He couldn't feel them.

"Uh, what the fuck are y—?"

Tom's voice faded quite quickly, only to be replaced by the rushing of wind as Jakob leaped forward from the three-story tower and over the main fence of the camp. He landed in a roll and immediately rose into a full sprint toward the edge of the trench. He slid to a stop as he reached it. The scene was somehow even more horrifying up close.

There is no need to look at this anymore. We will no longer be the pitied. Let us be predator, and not prey.

Jakob took a deep breath and jumped directly into the center of the mangled pile of corpses. It was impossible to get any sort of traction while stepping on bodies that must have piled at least ten to fifteen layers deep. He stumbled forward to the young man whom he had been staring at from the tower. He could now look him directly in his unfocused, dark-blue eyes.

He fell to one knee and slowly touched the tip of his arm to the middle of the man's forehead. The spot of contact remained illuminated in bright purple and exploded over his entire face before spreading rapidly to the adjacent corpse, and then the next, and then the next. Jakob stood slowly and made his way over to edge of the pile. Using his arms as climbing aids, he scaled the wall of the trench quickly and pulled himself back up and out of it before turning and looking back out over the uncovered mass grave. Bright lines of neon purple had spread out in every direction like the roots of an old tree beneath the soil. They connected all the corpses to one another.

One by one, in rapid succession, the bodies began to turn from pale to bright neon purple in the span of less than a second. Within two minutes, the combined light of all the bodies began to overpower the yellow industrial spotlights beaming down from the radio tower. This was very different from what had happened to Yozak and Marielle back at the palace. Perhaps the sheer volume of bodies affected how this process worked.

They're grateful. More than you'll likely ever know.

Before he could process a single thought, an ear-splitting boom rang through the night, and his eyes became flooded in purple. He tried to force them open, but the brightness was overwhelming. The small snippets he managed to process seemed to paint the picture of what looked to be a massive waterfall of purple light traveling upward into the sky. It reminded him of the death lights that he had become so used to seeing over the ten years at Izrok, only these were much wider and brighter.

Through his closed eyelids, he sensed the light fade. When he opened his eyes cautiously, he saw that all traces of neon purple, apart from those on his own body, were gone. He took a few slow steps toward the edge of the trench . . . or, at least, he would have, if it had still existed. The snowy ground now simply proceeded uninhibited as though nothing had ever taken place there. The carts and wheelbarrows that had lined the edges of the pit had been flipped onto their sides and now sat several feet from their original positions.

He took a deep breath and allowed himself to return to his normal form before slowly turning around and looking up at the broken window of the radio tower. Every single person he had traveled from Karvenkull with was staring down at him. It was too far to tell for sure, but several of their expressions seemed to indicate a mixture of shock and . . .

Birds fly away in a panic and rodents scurry into their holes at the sight of an approaching man. It is the nature of all living beings to fear what they do not and cannot understand.

XXIX

ZHADEN KARUK
TOM'S SHIP, KARVENKULL COURTYARD
OBALLE

The trip back to the ebony castle was drowned in about as much morose and pensive silence as Zhaden had expected. Of course, he had seen many purges over the years, and each had been more difficult to stomach than the last. But something about seeing all those bodies in that trench at once changed a man. It was his hope that any doubt the system leaders would have carried into Oballe regarding the importance of the treaty would now be crushed beyond all recognition.

The practice of taking and keeping prisoners of war for labor was hardly anything Olivio had invented, and it had been fairly commonplace historically across many different societies. But the Chosen Army had demonstrated that it would commit atrocities that superseded anything anyone could have possibly imagined.

Tom's ship shook slightly as they touched down in Karvenkull's rear open-air courtyard. They hadn't been left with much choice, given that the Udul and Ayr fleets had taken up essentially all the available space in front of and around the exterior of the castle. Jakob rose with a start, along with the others, as Tom began to open the rear entrance. He exited first along with the soon-to-be Draekon queen, or perhaps Jakob was to become the Joxun king? Zhaden wasn't quite sure how interracial royal arrangements were supposed to work. The Zantavi king, Tom, Koomer, and all the Pillars, minus Kamro, followed.

"Ugh. I can't believe they left me. If it isn't too much trouble, can you gentlemen lend me a hand? Sharp inclines don't agree with my knees very well."

The overweight Ayr leader looked at Kamro, who shot a quick glance at Zhaden and shrugged. He had hoped to stay behind to speak to his partner in private, but it seemed they would have to wait until a later time.

"No problem. Grab on." Kamro approached Sprock and offered him a veiny, muscular azure arm.

Had the circumstances been different, Zhaden might have swooned a bit. If there was anyone more attractive on Cha-leh, he had never seen him. He quickly snapped back to reality and situated himself on the opposite side of the large Ayr. They moved slowly down the ramp of the ship.

"Huh? You two are awfully dry. Are you alright?"

"I do not understand what you mean." Zhaden eyed the man questioningly.

"Aren't you people supposed to be slimy?"

He didn't even have to look. He could feel Kamro rolling his eyes. That Udul stereotype was as old as it was widespread.

Kamro sighed. "We're just dehydrated."

It was perhaps best to save the large man the embarrassment. The Ayr began to move by himself ahead of them once they hit the bottom of the ramp. Small sections of the Zantavi, Udul, Ayr, and Joxun armies were all represented in the large, organized blocks that had formed on either side of them, filling the courtyard. The Udul unit crossed their right arms over their chests as the two of them passed by.

Kamro turned to Zhaden and spoke quietly in Garyl. "That was . . . horrifying."

He nodded as the two continued to head toward the castle's back entrance.

"That is putting it mildly, yes. The bodies were beyond what even I would have expected, and I likely watched most of them die."

"Yes. I was also equally disturbed by the flaming man who made them disappear in the blink of an eye."

Zhaden turned his head to Kamro but said nothing.

"I don't doubt the importance of TCI. Not anymore."

Zhaden knew this tone. There was a "but" coming.

"But what this doesn't change is the concern the Pillars and I have about who is rapidly becoming this union's de facto leader, if not in title then in practice. Koss is not of this natural world, Zhaden."

"Jakob is as mortal a man as you or I. I've known him for years. He always had some control over the Shaz energy, but never like this. He assures me he is still new to this whole ordeal as well. He cannot explain how or why it happened."

"Shouldn't that be a major red flag? We don't even know if he's fully sane or in control of himself when he's like that. Besides, how long he has been this way or how comfortable he feels is irrelevant. Most free societies left in this galaxy are ruled by kings. We, the Uduls, are a rare exception to that rule."

Zhaden furrowed his brow. He didn't see where this was supposed to be going.

"Tell me, who is the one person who Uduls will listen to and whose authority they will respect over mine, the Chairman of the Pillars?"

"The Salt Maiden. But I don't see—"

"The authority of a king ends only where that of a god's begins. Tell me, which of those two do you think Jakob is really trying to be?"

Zhaden directed his gaze forward in time to glimpse the back of the Draekon's head as he turned the corner in front of them.

The remaining leaders walked further ahead, each speaking to a few of their respective soldiers.

"I know he is your friend and that you trust him. This doesn't affect my decision to sign the treaty, but we will be monitoring him very closely. We find his motivations questionable, even if his end goals do align with our own."

Zhaden squeezed his hands into fists. "The reason I am where I am, and you stand where you stand now is because of Jakob. He is like a brother to me. Unless I'm in need of an eye exam, I believe we both saw the same thing. He is adamant and forceful in his methods at times, yes, but I can hardly blame him. He is not this tyrant in hibernation that you seem so desperate to make him out to be. He is what we all are at times: a man with a clear goal in mind. He was beaten, starved, and tortured for years, so I will forgive him for being a bit adamant and assertive in his efforts to ensure it doesn't happen to anyone else."

Kamro opened his mouth to respond but stopped himself as a hand patted Zhaden's back.

"How you holdin' up, big guy? I'd ask you what the fuck it was that he did to the bodies, but I'm guessing you're as lost as me."

The Uduls exchanged glances. Tom had apparently maneuvered his way back toward them through the crowd.

"Anyway, thanks for helping that fat fuck off the ship. I'd say I forgot, but I try not to lie to friends as a rule."

Zhaden was not in the mood for lighthearted banter right now. He was let off the hook when the Ayr suddenly grabbed at both sides of his orange goggles.

"Huh? Hello?"

For a second, Zhaden thought the man might have gone insane. The cackling of a radio that soon followed alleviated this fear.

"Hey, I can't really hear you. Let me try to get better reception. Hold on."

Even from such a short distance, it was hard to tell who was on the other end. Tom ran off before he could get a good enough listen.

Zhaden looked back to Kamro, assuming they would be continuing their conversation from earlier. Instead, he looked past him and motioned for Zhaden to stop and look in that direction as well. He turned around to see the wide-open doors of the throne room. The crowd that had been ahead of them had vanished, and the soldiers had made their way to the seats of the enormous chamber. All the system leaders, apart from Kamro and Jakob, sat in the black stone seats up on the stage.

"We can discuss this later. It's time to get this done."

On that much they could agree.

They walked briskly into the enormous circular room, resisting the instinct to flinch at the sudden drop in temperature. A strange sense of anxiety and apprehension hung heavily in the air as the soldiers rose to their feet. Zhaden turned left into the front row of seats along with the rest of the Pillars, while Kamro continued upward onto the main stage. Zhaden ended up seated next to Garrond by pure chance. This was the first time that the two of them had been this close since their confrontation back on Cha-leh.

"Congratulations, Karuk. Let's hope this little dream of yours pans out."

The room stood in a state of awkward silence for a minute or two before mutters began to trickle in here and there. Where was Jakob?

Zhaden was seconds away from standing up and going to search for his small friend, when the room dramatically fell silent.

Everyone stood as one. With the advantage of his height, he was able to keep an eye on the new Draekon king as he walked quickly and unceremoniously to the stage. The open-faced black robe over a shirtless chest was an interesting decision, to say the least.

He slowed his pace as he arrived and made his way over to the black throne, a step above the rest of the system leaders. He turned just in front of it to face the crowd. Every eye in the room focused on him.

"There is not much I can say to you at this moment that you haven't already either heard from me or someone else. It's time for the galaxy to experience a new and long-overdue age of unity. We will accomplish together what we could never dream of doing alone. Tonight, we restore hope to people who have long forgotten what it even feels like."

Several soldiers in the front rows performed the Draekon salute that Jakob had done back at the top of the castle. He mirrored it back to them, and a large percentage of the room followed suit. The looks on the leaders' faces ranged from confusion to mild concern. Kamro shot a glance at Jakob and then toward the Udul soldiers, but his expression gave nothing away.

Jakob fell back slowly into the large black throne as he extended his arms onto their respective rests and pressed a button with his right index finger. The stone seats in which the leaders sat turned slowly, rearranging themselves to face each other. Black stone platforms rose from the ground between each pair of seats, eventually creating a massive pentagonal table that connected each leader to the others. According to Jakob, this functionality had been built into the castle to allow the old Draekon kings to convene publicly with their five Karums, or regional overseers.

"Gentlemen . . . Lady . . . Shall we begin?"

Each system leader summoned a soldier up with his copy of the treaty.

Lacking a Draekon representative, Jakob had Koomer deliver his copy to him.

"Leaders of the free systems, are you ready?"

It seemed that microphones had been built into the seats or were at least somewhere nearby that Zhaden was unable to see. Each leader stood from his seat and turned to face Jakob.

"We are with you, Jakob Koss!" the Zantavi king replied firmly and confidently before leaning over and signing his treaty.

The Joxun Queen rose slowly and elegantly. "You already know you have my gratitude, as well as that of the Joxun people. We stand by your side. Don't make us regret it." She winked at Jakob before ordering the soldier who brought her the treaty to stand in front of her so that she could use his back as a platform to sign on. Zhaden was unsure why she didn't simply use the table.

The portly Ayr leader stood slowly and with some effort. "The Ayr people have expressed overwhelming support for your cause. As it stands, I'm simply their messenger." He looked visibly exhausted, as he had likely done more physical activity today than he had in years. In lieu of a pen, he produced a seal from his pocket and stamped the paper forcefully.

Kamro exchanged a look with Zhaden before taking a deep breath and standing.

"On behalf of The Maiden's Great Pillars, we accept your offer and will join you in your fight."

He looked especially handsome under this lighting. There was something very attractive about seeing him in such a formal position of power. He sat back down in his chair, placed his hand into a small pan of ink provided by a nearby Udul soldier, and branded the treaty with his print.

Jakob nodded as Kamro finished and slowly lowered himself back into his seat.

"Very well then. My turn."

He raised his right hand to the sky, and within seconds, his index finger began to glow brightly. He lowered it slowly onto the page and touched it. A faint sizzle ran through the silent room. Jakob looked down for a second or two before grabbing his treaty, turning it, and showing it off to the crowd. It was a bit difficult to see at a distance, but it looked as though he had burned his fingerprint over the signature area on the page. Applause ran through the hall. Even the new TCI leaders joined in this time.

Jakob placed the page back down onto the table, and the same soldiers who had delivered the treaties now absconded with them.

"Very well. The first official meeting of the Treaty of Cosmic Imperials is now officially in session. We ask for silence during this historic moment, as we address—"

Jakob stopped abruptly and stared down at the entrance to the room. Zhaden followed suit, with a large portion of the audience also whipping their heads around out of curiosity. Tom walked quickly toward the stage. Something was off about him. He chuckled nervously and waved sheepishly at the crowd as he walked right up to the group. Several soldiers from each race near the stage began to move in, but Jakob waved them off.

Sprock stood from his chair. His face grew significantly redder in what was more than likely a mixture of anger and embarrassment.

"Good Lord! I apologize, Jakob. This is *exactly* the kind of thing I expect out of him."

Ignoring him completely, Tom climbed the steps and went directly over to Jakob before leaning in and whispering. He went on for a solid minute or two, during which time murmurs began to run through the audience.

"Yes. Go. I'll handle it."

Tom nodded in response and quickly made his way back down the steps before running back in the same direction from which he had arrived. Jakob leaned forward and placed both hands on the table in front of him before taking a deep breath. The audience quieted down in anticipation.

"Jakob, I will personally ensure that Ezekiel is properly—"

He held up a hand to quiet Sprock. "It seems as though we're going to have to postpone this introductory meeting for the time being."

The TCI leaders exchanged confused looks. Murmurs once again arose from the crowd.

Zhaden's thoughts went into overdrive. Jakob's next question did little to quell the brewing curiosity.

"How large of a military force can we realistically raise?"

The leaders answered his question with blank stares. Kamro stared at Jakob as though he were a ghost.

Marijah cleared her throat before speaking up. "Well, realistically, within the next few weeks, we could probably get a few million troops mobilized between all of us."

Jakob looked down at the table and shook his head. "No. Sooner than that."

The murmurs erupted into a cacophony of chatter.

Kamro leaned in toward him. "I'm sorry . . . How quickly are we talking about here?"

Jakob turned his head to the Udul.

"Tonight."

XXX

DARYN PERIC
NAVIGATION BRIDGE, NAMIRA'S SHIP
DEEP SPACE

Daryn tried to keep his vision focused on one of the thousands of white, blue, red, and orange specks long enough to discern any significant details, but each simply flew by the glass too quickly. Their fleeting, colorful nature reminded him of the vocay fish in the tank back at the Altar, and he let out a small sigh as he realized that he'd probably never see them again. He turned around in his chair and sat up to stretch.

He walked into the circular chamber that acted as the vessel's common room. Namira and her grandfather were sitting on the small sofa that was bolted onto the metal floor of the ship. Yeuma was lying on her back on the floor, just a few feet away from the two Zantavis. Her hands were behind her head, and she simply stared at the ceiling quietly, as though in a trance. Oslo and Da'garo were nowhere to be found. They were likely still enjoying the warmth of the engine room.

Daryn hadn't told anyone about his run in with The Fist, nor did he plan to. The entire crew had been so busy scrambling to get out of the cave that they hadn't even noticed the Zantavi jerking around on the ground. He would have fully recovered by now and might even be back on his tail. This was not an enviable position to be in. The Fist had come into Olivio's service around a decade ago, and Daryn couldn't think of a single time that the man had objectively failed an assignment. The only hope now was to try to form some sort of alliance with the Draekon king and whatever army he had managed to amass. If he was going to go down, he would not do so without a fight.

The bravado of his own thoughts shocked him. Once, he would never have dared to even think of the possibility of fighting back against Olivio – and here he was now, determined to do exactly that. The familiar electric jolt of anxiety that he had been expecting never materialized.

He crouched over Yeuma, who lazily shifted her amber eyes to meet his.

"Can I help you?"

"Are you practicing being dead?"

She scowled. "No. I was enjoying one of my multiple scheduled blank stares at the ceiling before being so rudely interrupted."

"Do you want some company?"

She rolled her eyes and shifted over a bit. He lay down next to her and mimicked her pose. They lay there in silence for a few minutes before she turned her head to him suddenly.

"You're not an idiot, Daryn, as much as I may treat you like one at times."

He furrowed his brow. He wasn't sure whether he should feel complimented or insulted.

"The Fist was there to rescue you. We both know that. Somehow, despite having every opportunity to leave, you're still here with us. What made you change your mind?"

He said nothing for a few seconds and simply turned away from his sister's gaze as he continued looking upward at the stainless-steel ceiling.

"For as long as I can remember, Olivio adored me. He kept me by his side and always wanted to make sure I was content and healthy."

Through his peripheral vision, he could see Yeuma's eyebrow raise slightly.

"Something you told me back in the cave stuck with me. Over the days we spent in here freezing half to death, I kept thinking about it. I realized that you, for all the headache you've put me through, offer me something he never could."

She propped herself up onto her elbow. "And that would be what?"

He turned to face her. "I treated you horribly. I let Olivio strike you and then blamed you for it. I hated you for embarrassing me in front of him time and time again when you were just lashing out because of the way things were. Even through all of that, you still wanted me to come with you. Even when I turned you down, you still came back for me when I did nothing to deserve it. Olivio waited two weeks, and he didn't even come himself. He loves me for what I represent, what I know, and what I can do for him. But I want to be loved for who I *am*. That's all I've ever really looked for from him, and you've done it thanklessly day after day and year after year. I can honestly say that I don't know if I'd do the same if the roles were reversed, and the amount of guilt that brings me is . . . I don't know."

He sat up. To his shock, Yeuma's yellow face had become slightly red. He had never seen her cry before, but he imagined this was what the early stages looked like.

"I can't fix what I've done to you and put you through. I can only try to work on getting you to forgive me, even if it's a just a little bit at a time."

Yeuma said nothing but using a surprising amount of force, she pulled him in for an embrace. She was a softie on the inside, after all, and after startling initially, Daryn relaxed into it. It had been a long time since his sister had shown him such affection, and he savored it.

The ship jumped suddenly, and Daryn's anxiety spiked. There it was again. He and Yeuma stood up quickly as the engine began to rattle. They were close.

Namira bolted up from the sofa and walked briskly to the bridge to check the navigation computer.

She turned back to them. "Five minutes. Get those two idiots up here."

Yeuma nodded and took off toward the ladder that led down to the engine room. Daryn joined Namira on the bridge, which was essentially one of the many openings around the large central common area.

"Have you ever been to Oballe before?" he asked softly.

Namira shook her head. "No. But I've heard things . . . horrible things."

Daryn said nothing for a few seconds. It was easier not to think about it. "You might want to wear something heavier. It's cold."

She turned to him. "Have *you* been there before?"

Daryn nodded. "Once. I was little. It's a beautiful place . . . or at least, it was back when I visited."

Now was perhaps not the time to tell the full extent of the story.

He turned as three sets of footsteps approached. Yeuma, Da'garo, and Oslo made their way to the bridge as the ship lurched forward suddenly, quickly redirecting his attention to the main window. The wormhole had opened up, and they were rapidly approaching the exit. Everyone grabbed onto something to brace themselves as the ship shot straight through the portal. A second later, the light gray orb that was Oballe exploded into full view. They maintained the silence for a few extra moments to take in the haunting beauty of the now-infamous planet.

Namira looked back at the rest of the crew. "Alright, so the plan is to land near a city and send scouting missions out each day until we figure out exactly where the capital—"

"Karvenkull. It's a huge black castle. I know the coordinates. We can go straight there."

Everyone turned to look at him. He had admittedly been quite bored all those years ago and had simply kept his gaze glued to the navigation computer once they had entered the atmosphere during the initial invasion. The numbers had, for some reason, remained at the forefront of his memory. The night terrors he suffered that involved Oballe always began with them.

Namira nodded slowly and motioned toward the computer. He stepped up slowly and typed each number in an almost robotic fashion.

"Okay then . . . I suppose that means we're ahead of schedule. I'll get us down there. Someone go check on my grandfather."

Daryn volunteered silently and then made his way back to the common area. The man seemed completely unperturbed by what had transpired. He smiled at him as he approached.

"Your granddaughter would like to know if you are okay." Daryn spoke slowly in Neatspeak, making sure to enunciate clearly. He could only hope that the man spoke it at least somewhat fluently.

"I'm not surprised. I'm fine. Have we arrived?" he asked in Daryn's native tongue.

Daryn took a second to collect himself. "You speak Alavic?"

To be fair, he had never asked, and the man had spoken to only Namira throughout the time they had been together.

"Of course. I served with your people for quite some time. I had to."

Daryn's interest piqued immensely. He slid into a seat next to him on the sofa. "What did you do?"

The old man chuckled. "It's quite private, I'm afraid. I worked in the Altar."

"So did I. I was The Hand's attender."

The man's eyes widened, and he straightened himself slowly. "You served Olivio?"

Daryn nodded.

"I worked under Valentino. Olivio . . . well, he released me from my duties, I'm afraid."

"What was a Zantavi doing working in the Altar anyway?"

"My people seem to find themselves working within its walls more often than some would think."

He gave Daryn a strange look, though he wasn't sure what the old man was supposed to be referencing.

"Valentino brought me in to do data collection and surveillance. He was a very paranoid man and insisted that I place my own proprietary surveillance tech around the Altar. He wanted to ensure no one was plotting behind his back."

"Are the cameras still there?"

The man chuckled. "No, no. Olivio had me remove them after he came to power . . . with a sword to my back no less."

Daryn was beginning to strongly regret not approaching this man earlier. "I'm sorry. I haven't gotten your name."

The man extended a dark, shaky hand. "Elan Klein."

Daryn took it. "Daryn Peric."

The man's expression changed entirely. He looked almost alarmed. "Peric?"

Daryn nodded slowly, and the man's eyes began to dart around the room.

He brought a hand to his chin. "That name means something to me. I can't quite remember what . . ."

The ship suddenly came to halt and began to descend. They had arrived.

"We will continue this conversation later, then. Oh, and do not mention any of this to Namira. She still thinks I was an oil salesman."

Daryn nodded before scooting around the table and climbing off the couch.

The rest of the crew had funneled into the center room as the ship began to descend slowly, eventually touching down lightly on the ground. Daryn moved over next to Yeuma as the crew began to pull clothes out from the lockers attached to the wall, throwing on the extra layers haphazardly. The temperature inside the ship dropped drastically as the door began to slide open, the frigid Oballe winds penetrating the metallic chamber. Small snowflakes blew in sporadically as they waited for the ramp to finish extending.

The entire crew moved to the open doorframe and stopped dead in their tracks. A conglomeration of Joxun, Ayr, and Zantavi soldiers flooded the area around the bottom of the ramp. All had their weapons drawn and held aggressive stances.

They seemed to come to a silent agreement that Namira should exit first, given the circumstances. She opened her jacket and extended her hands before doing a small turn to demonstrate that she was unarmed. Not a single soldier below produced so much as a whisper. Summoning more courage than Daryn imagined that he himself would have possessed, Namira walked down the metallic ramp slowly. He looked out past her and around the area. They were in the courtyard again, exactly where he had landed with Olivio so many years ago. A Zantavi soldier held up a hand to her as soon as her foot touched Oballe soil. Two others rushed to her side and patted her down before taking a step back. The front-most soldier looked behind him and motioned for someone out of sight to approach. He stepped aside, revealing an Ayr behind him. This man was wearing a virix, but it covered only one eye. It took Daryn a few seconds to realize that the man was missing his other one entirely.

"Who are you, and why are you here?" he asked in Neatspeak. He was smaller and looked significantly less muscular than those around him. Daryn quickly guessed that he wasn't a soldier.

"My name is Namira. My associates and I are here to meet with the Neon King."

"Why? All the system leaders have already been accounted for."

"He did not directly summon us, but we have heard the message he has put out loud and clear. We are no friends of Olivio. We simply want a better future for ourselves, and we're willing to fight for it."

The soldiers looked to the one-eyed Ayr, who, in turn, looked behind him and called others forward. Multiple Uduls dressed in extravagant robes joined him. One with a long white beard stepped forward and stared up at the ship.

"Come down and reveal yourselves! Keep your hands up!"

They all exchanged looks but ultimately complied. A fight right now was not at all in their best interest. They moved down the ramp one at a time, eventually arranging themselves in a horizontal line next to Namira.

The Uduls shot particularly sour glances at Da'garo, who had little issue returning them.

"Spies. Have to be," one of the Uduls muttered to the Ayr, who looked to be deep in thought.

"We aren't spies. The Hand and his army ran us out of our homes."

Yeuma looked at all of them as she spoke.

The Ayr ran a hand under his chin.

"For the time being, we're going to disable your ship and have you guys stay in there. I figure you'd prefer that over a cell."

"No. Listen . . . we just want a chance to speak to Jakob Koss." Daryn could feel the weight of the hundreds of stares upon him as he finally spoke up.

The Ayr looked at the Uduls before turning back to him. "You can't."

"Listen. I know that my kind isn't the most well liked here, but I swear that if I can just speak to him for—"

"He isn't here."

XXXI

CORVUS-JORG (CJ) DROC
Z480 CRUISER, EMERALD SEA
ERUB

CJ sighed deeply and slowly lifted his gaze from the water until the full scope of the traitorous Erub army's fleet came into view before him. They sat motionless in the calm waters, forming an uneven metallic barrier between his men and the sea-facing side of the ancient palace he had once called home. The good news was that they looked to have only about three dozen ships, as far as he could see. They could contend with that—although just barely.

CJ turned his head back to look at the tiny blip on the horizon; it was the rebel leader's vessel. Sheressa had wanted nothing more than to be on the front lines with her brother, but she understood that it would be more of a liability than anything else. He swallowed hard as he felt for the machete at his hip. He would give everything he had today and then some, but victory was far from guaranteed.

He squinted as a small dark shape broke off and distanced itself from the rest of the federal fleet. It was a motorboat, and on either side of it, a large 'New Erub' flag with its Alavic symbols ruffled violently in the wind. Looking at it made him legitimately ill. He turned around to face the several dozen men aboard the deck; they had all been waiting just as patiently and silently as he had.

"Hoist our real colors!"

The soldiers nearly stepped over each other in their enthusiastic rush to the massive flagpole at the center of the ship. Within a few seconds, the historic green-and-silver banner was at full mast and flapping assertively. He stared up at it, falling briefly to one knee as he held a hand over his heart. Several of the rebels on deck followed suit. As he rose, he looked to the soldier who was closest to the entrance to the lower levels of the ship.

"Prepare the motorboat." The man nodded and rushed down the metal stairs. CJ then looked to Watts. "You're with me. Let's go."

CJ had lost track of how many hours he'd spent giving detailed hands-on tutorials on how to operate and maintain the different types of ships in the rebel fleet. He had worked around the clock, and he guessed that he had probably amassed ten hours of sleep over the entire week. The losses on the night of the failed ship heist had weighed heavily on him, and he was determined to do everything he could to prevent a similar situation today.

CJ and Watts made their way down to the lower levels of the lone Z480 cruiser they had managed to snag that fateful night. It held several small compartments in its lower levels, and when these were opened, they would allow small vessels, such as life rafts or motorboats, to enter and exit without the need for them to be physically lifted onto the deck.

The two men climbed into their small boat and pulled away from the cruiser relatively quickly. Polero's ship had already stopped and was waiting for them at the halfway point between the two fleets. Watts sat in the back, keeping a hand on the motor as the powerful propellers launched them forward. CJ stood as straight as he could in the front, locking eyes with Polero as the wind and salty spray of the sea blasted his face and body.

The pretender crossed his arms and chuckled as his two heavily armed companions tied the boats together quickly as they united. He was wearing all-white robes with an elegant gold trim. CJ's instincts were screaming at him to whip out his machete and eviscerate the idiot right there on the spot, but he resisted. Even if it weren't strongly frowned upon in Erub culture, killing the man outright during this prebattle meeting would have been impossible, not to mention suicidal. On his head, he wore the jagged emerald crown that CJ had never seen on anyone but his father. Polero had a ludicrous talent for finding new ways to insult the history and culture of his own people. Seeing him adorned in that historic artifact while he was covered in Alavite garbage was nauseating, but this type of behavior was hardly out of character for him.

"And once again, the better Droc avoids meeting with me face to face. Why am I not surprised?"

CJ clenched a fist for a second before relaxing it. "She wanted to. But I wasn't going to subject her to having to look at you from this close up. It's painful enough for me."

"Well . . . I will assume you speak on her behalf. On that note, I'd like to offer you terms of surrender."

"I'm not here to negotiate, Raymond."

He chuckled. "Corvus—"

"Don't call me that."

He smiled. "Look at your fleet, and then look at mine. You have to know how this is going to turn out. I mean, come on. Either you die in an anonymous, watery grave today or you bring me Sheressa and I ensure that you live a happy, long, and luxurious life under my rule. What do you say?"

"I can't wait."

He widened his eyes a bit. "So, you'll do—"

"To see how many Alavite cocks I find in your stomach when I cut it open and dump it into the fucking sea."

CJ kicked upward, removing the line that had kept the ships together. Watts quickly restarted the engine and turned them back to the cruiser. Polero shook his head and looked infuriatingly smug as he grew smaller and smaller in CJ's view.

"So, you think we can beat them?" Watts had to yell to be heard over the loud whirring.

"We fucking better!" CJ yelled back, without turning around.

CJ didn't even wait for the motorboat to be fully lifted out of the water before he jumped back onto the ship's main deck and raced back to its upper levels.

The rebels all stood motionlessly, staring at him as he pushed the heavy metallic door open and stepped out into the fresh, salty air. He turned to the spot where he had originally been standing and began to walk slowly toward it, all the while keeping his eyes glued to Polero's large flagship. Without so much as blinking, CJ pulled a flare from his belt, ignited it, and tossed it onto the side of the deck. Within seconds, several large, bright-red bolts of light shot into the air, each accompanied by a loud, high-pitched screech. Every crew member scrambled to their positions. A ship's alarm activated, followed by another, and then another, until the entire the rebel fleet was in an ear-splitting uproar.

CJ grabbed the rail in front of him as the cruiser lurched forward and began to work its way up to its maximum speed. He moved quickly back to the bow. Polero's ships had begun to push forward as well, albeit in a much more silent manner. Several men on deck began to draw their weapons as the horde of cruisers on each side plowed through the green water.

CJ turned and motioned several dozen rebel archers toward the bow. They moved into position quickly. The neon-green glow of the powerbows on their backs was impossible to ignore, even in broad daylight.

"DRAW!"

From their backs each rebel pulled his weapon, along with a large metallic arrow.

"NOCK!"

Each rebel moved his arrow into position. CJ took a moment to glance to his left and right. The other rebel ships' archers were in the exact same position, and it seemed that they were being instructed by their on-deck commanders as well. The entire fleet was operating as a cohesive unit, and he breathed a sigh of relief. He turned back to the front with his hands behind his back. The shiny metallic hulls of the charging enemy fleet reflected a fair amount of light into his eyes, forcing him to squint.

"LOOSE!"

A flurry of deep *thunks* rang through the air as hundreds of arrows filled the sky, their flight paths highlighted by trailing streaks of light green. There was no time to track the damage they caused, as a comparable array of white-tailed arrows were now heading right for them.

CJ reached for the metallic handle on his belt and unhooked it before quickly raising it at a forty-five-degree angle and pressing the button on its side. In the blink of an eye, a large neon green digi-shield opened with a slight zapping noise, jolting so violently upon doing so that it nearly flew out of his hand. Many of the men aboard deck followed suit. CJ tensed up, bracing himself as the powerful and heavy storm of death rained down upon him. Several digi-shields were impacted so forcefully that they fizzled out temporarily, leaving some men to be hit by an arrow directly following the previous one. Groans and screams filled the deck.

CJ lowered his shield again once the downpour was over, and he turned to face the men on deck. The sirens had cut out, leaving only the soft splashing of the ocean and the rumbling of engines to form the soundscape of the battle. The flurry of arrows seemed to have taken out about a dozen or so of his men. He could only hope that their own strike had been just as effective.

The men around him looked hesitant and even slightly scared; he could see it in their eyes. He reached down and picked up one of the arrows that had struck near him, making his way on top of a small crate that had turned over onto its side.

The men looked up at him curiously as he held the arrow above his head. "They painted them in Alavite colors. They aren't even pretending anymore! Do you want the future of our planet to be dictated by a genocidal dinosaur sitting in his hot bath on Alavonia?"

"NO!" came the unified response.

"Fuck Olivio! And fuck Polero! NOW FUCKING DRAW!"

CJ reached up and broke the arrow in half, cheers erupting around him on board. He surprised himself, as he rarely swore that many times in a single sentence. Perhaps he had spent too much time around Tom.

The remaining archers responded with an unexpected level of enthusiasm as they ran back to their positions. The men, who had for a minute appeared conflicted, seemed to have strengthened their resolve.

The ships were growing closer by the second, and this would likely be the last volley before contact. Other archers ran over to take the places of the fallen soldiers. CJ scanned the frontmost enemy ship as best he could, searching for any signs of Polero's white Alavite robes, but he found none. The coward was probably hiding below deck.

"LOOSE!"

A horde of neon-green trails shot into the sky like a flock of angry birds. They met the white ones midway as the two dense packs crossed each other. Several arrows made direct contact, creating loud and vibrant explosions in the air. CJ and his crew raised their shields again. This time, he took an arrow directly, and deflecting it caused his shield to fizzle out for a few seconds.

Although he had learned about powerbows and arrows over a decade ago during his training, he was still shocked at how much force they could deliver, even at seemingly low speeds. The impact of the arrow, shot from hundreds of feet away, had been so powerful that it had forced him several steps back. He had never been hit directly by one before, but it was said to be one of the most excruciatingly painful experiences one could endure. It was perhaps merciful that the survival rate of a shot to the body was well below twenty-five percent.

He shook his shield until it came back to life before he quickly scanned the area around him again. They had lost more men than the previous time. He looked up suddenly as a shadow cast itself over the deck of the ship. The federal fleet had slowed to almost a halt around fifty yards away.

After a tense few seconds of confusion, a familiar sound emerged, causing CJ's heart to sink. A flock of flyers rose slowly into the air over the enemy ships, having evidently lifted off from the rear section of the decks. It took only a second to notice that they were the same kind that had burned his men to a crisp back at the harbor. He turned quickly and shouted to no one in particular.

"GET THE HARPOONS!"

Seconds later, two men appeared, each with one of metallic cannons in hand. CJ counted twenty flyers as they approached. Two seemed to be headed straight for his ship, and the nozzles beneath their chassis were already beginning to glow red.

One of the rebels fired at the closest flyer but missed, passing slightly to the right. The next man took an extra second or two but made contact. The vehicle stuttered and came to a grinding halt before nose-diving into the water. CJ left the bow and ran down the deck to check in on the other ships. The one to his portside had hit the flyer that had locked on to them, but a second had begun to rain down upon them before quickly being taken out as well.

A rapidly expanding trail of fire began to fill the right half of the deck, and the crew began to scramble to extinguish it. CJ turned and ran to the starboard side. He felt his heart skip a beat. The rebel ship here had either missed its shot or had been caught unprepared. Its deck was totally engulfed in flames that were growing stronger by the second.

He grabbed the railing and cursed under his breath. He hated the helpless feeling these types of situations brought upon him. The rebels from the ship now totally concealed in thick black smoke began to jump overboard. The vessel stopped moving completely; that was one down already.

He heard another clink of a bolt making contact with metal. It had come from . . . above? He shot a gaze upward just in time to see a flyer directly above him; he hadn't even noticed it before. Its nozzle was glowing red but quickly faded to black as its power gave out. CJ desperately dove out of the way as the flyer crashed down hard between the railing and the deck, eventually tipping over into the emerald sea. He looked over to his left to see Watts with an empty harpoon over his shoulder. He shrugged as if to say "My bad" before turning and disappearing into the crowd on the deck.

CJ was about to stand up when dozens of loud clunks caused by metal hitting metal filled his ears. Arrows rained down around him as he activated his shield and curled himself up into tight ball beneath it.

When he was sure that the volley had ended, he reached back to the now-damaged railing to pick himself up. He looked forward instinctively. The enemy fleet had gone back into motion and had covered a significant portion of the remaining gap while he had been distracted. They were now mere feet away.

"BRACE!"

The bows of the two ships impacted and scraped past each other, both rattling violently for a few seconds before they pulled apart. Several federal soldiers leaped onto their deck as both ships ground to a halt, and his crew rushed the invaders. CJ, who had been waiting for this moment for some time, flipped on his shield with one hand and unsheathed his machete with the other. Archers from both sides now fired of their own volition, mostly focusing their ranged counterparts on the opposite deck.

CJ took a deep breath as an enemy soldier rushed at him and blocked the first strike with his shield. It was quickly followed up by a second, which he was ready for as well. He made sure to put more force into the second block, forcing his attacker to recoil and giving himself the opportunity to strike the man's lower leg.

When the man fell onto one knee in pain, CJ followed up with a clean cut across the neck. Blood squirted forcefully from the new opening, covering CJ's fatigues and dirtying them much quicker than he'd intended. He turned around in a full circle. He could no longer see off any side of the ship due to the sheer number of people who were now on board.

He turned directly around as he made out footsteps coming toward him and clanged his machete against his shield as another soldier approached. The invaders had apparently been oriented on who to target. He found himself double- and even triple-teamed multiple times during the next several fights.

The deck of his ship was absolutely flooded with noise, whether from shouting men, metal against metal, or arrows whizzing by. He imagined that the rest of the fleet was experiencing very similar circumstances.

CJ fought alongside Watts for over an hour. The tropical heat was asphyxiating, and before long his shirt was clinging to his skin uncomfortably. Sweat poured down his face, infiltrating his eyes on multiple occasions.

He turned and stabbed the back of a soldier who was inches away from striking Watts, who wasn't even looking in the man's direction. He turned and backed up into him as more soldiers began to surround them both.

"Just a lovely afternoon workout." CJ shook his head slightly almost as soon as he had said the words. Joking during a serious moment? He really was turning into Tom.

Watts said nothing, merely chuckling in response.

CJ was in the midst of scanning for another target when a loud crash made him jump. He turned around to see the bow of a second enemy ship plowing directly into the side of his own. The entire deck rocked violently, almost everyone aboard stumbling and falling. The ramming cruiser, which seemed to have some sort of incredibly reinforced steel at the tip of its hull, began to turn sharply, slicing up the side of CJ's vessel in the process. As the deck began to dip slightly toward that end, the reality of the situation seemed to become obvious to everyone at once.

They were sinking.

Within seconds, every man on the deck raced for that of the nearby stationary enemy ship. The cruiser that had rammed them had already sped away, likely on its way to cause some more damage. Being fairly close to the starboard railing, CJ was among the first to make the jump. He sheathed his machete just before leaping across.

Despite being mostly immobile, the ships had drifted apart a bit as time had passed, causing a small gap to form between them. CJ had to dive for the railing and only barely got a hand on it. He slid his shield onto the deck to free up his other hand. Sounds of heavy splashing by those who missed the deck or fell overboard came from below. CJ summoned all of his strength to pull himself up onto the safety of solid ground.

"Shit," he muttered as he rose to his feet and found himself staring down two powerbow archers with their arrows nocked. His shield lay a few feet away on the deck in front of him. He remained immobile for a second or two, frozen still, before making a desperate break for it, diving across the deck for it.

He activated the shield the second his hands touched it and he immediately felt the impact of two arrows, which felt as though they could have ripped his arms clean off. These shields were barely designed to hold off one arrow, let alone two. But somehow, it had held. The archers began to scramble to reload, and CJ took the opportunity to charge them at full speed.

He sliced clean through the stomach of the archer on the left but did so with such force that his machete became stuck. He turned to his right as he heard a bow being drawn. He abandoned the blade as the first archer doubled over. Before the second archer could finish pulling back, CJ charged at him with the digi-shield, pushing it up against the man, who began to scream as the hot electrical plasma decimated his skin. Within a few seconds, he had pushed his attacker up against the rails, at which point it took only the slightest of nudges to send him toppling over into the water.

CJ turned and ran back for the machete as more and more men from his original ship flooded onto the new deck. It took him a second to locate where the hell his weapon was, until he realized that the man who had been doubled over a few seconds ago had now fallen to the deck—dead. He rolled him over and stepped on his chest as he pulled the bloody blade out forcefully.

He was able to get a much better view of the carnage from this ship, as it faced the direction of the battle. Fires were breaking out on multiple other doomed vessels, sending towering pillars of black smoke into the air. He stopped for a moment to take in the scope of the fight. This was the type of environment that his father had prepared him for all his life. This was what he had been born for, and he had never hated that fact more than he did right now.

A strange boom rang he didn't recognize rang through the air. He scanned the sea around him as well as the skies but saw nothing.

He blocked the strike of an approaching enemy soldier as he was suddenly forced back to reality. He deflected again, dodged to the left, and sliced the attacker's hand off at the wrist. The man fell to his knees screaming and grabbing at his stump, blood spewing everywhere. CJ brought the machete around with a single smooth motion and sent the man's head tumbling onto the deck. He hated killing, but he loved watching traitors die. It was a complicated trade-off.

He stood again and caught his breath, scanning around him for any sign of Watts. He moved quickly when he was not being attacked, and he eventually managed to locate him. Watts was standing toward the back of the ship, away from the fighting, and staring off toward Mortobal. A soldier began to move toward him from behind.

Something was wrong.

CJ ran toward them and jammed his machete through the attacker's back before throwing him forcefully onto the deck. He breathed heavily and looked up at Watts as he rose to his feet. The man still hadn't so much as twitched. He must have been having some sort of breakdown.

"Watts! Stay with me, man! You alright?"

Watts turned his head slowly toward CJ. His blood-soaked face was unreadable and expressionless. He dropped his cutlass onto the deck, causing a harsh clang. "I can't do it. I won't."

CJ took a step toward him. "What are you talking about?"

Another thundering boom nearly caused CJ to look up.

His blood ran cold as Watts reached for his collar and pulled it down, revealing a tight metallic band around his neck. On it, a timer was counting down with only fifteen seconds remaining.

"What—?"

"They put it on me during a scouting run while you were away." He put a hand on CJ's shoulder. "I was supposed to kill you, but I won't. Put that fucking crown on your sister. That's worth way more than I am."

It was down to six seconds now.

"Watts—"

"It's been an honor."

"Watts!"

The Erub groaned as several sharp blades infiltrated his neck when the timer hit zero, causing him to spew blood in a fountain-like way as he fell limply onto the deck.

CJ wasn't sure what noise he made. It was animalistic and nonsensical. He fell onto a knee, grabbed Watt's body, and held his head up. His lifelong friend spoke slowly and breathlessly. "They're . . . coming."

Watts' eyes rolled back into his head almost as soon as the last syllable left his lips. CJ's heart pounded as he tried to make sense of everything that was happening, but it was almost impossible. He thought he would be crying over his fallen brother, but he felt nothing. It wasn't real. It couldn't be.

"HOLY SHIT!"

He glanced up as several men aboard the ship began to cry out in shock. It wasn't until CJ put Watts down and rose to his feet that he understood why.

What looked to be at least thirty pristine white-and-gold naval ships had emerged from Mortobal's hangar and were now rapidly approaching them. The rebels already needed a small miracle to win the battle as it was. If a section of the proper Alavite navy was here, they had no chance.

Time slowed down. He looked around his ship. The rebels had mostly cleared the deck, and many had now joined him in staring at the approaching fleet. Death moved in on them by the second.

The rebels rushed to CJ's side to try to beat the Alavites back as the deck of their front-most ship slowed and contacted their own. CJ looked to his left and right. Other ships had begun sealing them in and preparing to board on both the starboard and port sides.

CJ looked back ahead of him as the first pairs of white-and-gold boots began rushing toward the rebel-controlled deck. He backed up.

"Get off the rails. Get to me!" he yelled.

Most of the remaining rebels did as he said. Some stayed on the rails and attempted to form a makeshift wall.

They did manage to push a few of the Alavites back, but the dark green of their uniforms was quickly surrounded and overwhelmed in an enormous tidal wave of white. Those who fell back to CJ formed a small circle, keeping their eyes and blades in every direction as more Alavites than CJ had ever seen flooded the deck.

He sighed and tossed his shield aside. There was no need for it anymore. He wasn't surviving this, but he'd be damned if he was going to waste energy deflecting blows when he could be using it to kill Alavites. He twirled his machete in his hand slowly as the horde moved in.

He jumped slightly as the full, ear-splitting blast of the loudest space-grade ship engines he had ever heard ripped across the sky, overpowering every other noise around. For a brief, panicked moment, he thought it might have been the rest of the Chosen Army, but this fear was put to rest with a single look at the confused faces of the Alavite soldiers in front of him. They stared up at the ship with widened eyes. CJ's curiosity forced him to follow suit.

It took a few seconds for him to comprehend what he was seeing. What looked to be at least one hundred ships of varying sizes and models had dipped through the clouds. The announcement vessel that led the pack unfurled an enormous black flag that he didn't recognize. It waved triumphantly in the wind as the mismatched horde followed it directly.

Multiple ships shot directly down onto the battlefield. Some began to deposit naval vessels directly into the emerald waters before taking off back into the air.

His confusion faded quickly, replaced by the extreme adrenaline rush that permeated his entire body. Rather than waiting for contact, CJ jumped at the closest distracted Alavite, and shortly thereafter, the entire deck was flung into chaos.

He hacked, slashed, dodged, and blocked blow after blow. His small team had been compressed into an increasingly smaller circle as more of them fell. He lost feeling in his arms, which he began to fear would give out at any second.

As they grew more exhausted, his precision and attention to detail faltered, and his machete was knocked out of his hand by the fifth or sixth Alavite soldier whom he faced. He breathed deeply and fell to his knees as they gave out.

The man in front of him raised his sword in the air before suddenly being lifted off the ground by his neck and tossed violently to the side. The figure turned quickly and lifted what looked like a large metallic spear into the air before bringing it down harshly on its victim. Within seconds, a blue webbed hand was being offered to him.

His vision had become blurry due to his exhaustion, but the voice was unmistakable.

"Do not die on me yet, my friend. We have only just begun!"

CJ smiled and grabbed hold of Zhaden as he was lifted to his feet. He blinked a few times and noticed that three Udul ships had pulled up next to his and had begun filling the deck. The Alavite soldiers had turned away from the rebel group to face the invaders, who were laying a fairly decisive beating on them. Within minutes, the remaining soldiers in white began a desperate retreat to their ship. The Uduls were ready for this too. From what he could tell, not a single Alavite soldier managed to set foot back on their polished, off-white decks.

"What . . .? Who . . .? How did . . .?" He couldn't form a coherent sentence to save his life right now.

"Holy fuck, dude. You look like shit."

He turned to his right to see Tom standing at the entrance of his own ship, which was hovering just off the portside railing. He was holding a bloody machete in his hands.

"More than you usually do, I mean. Anyway, I think you dropped this. Get your ass in here. We're off to see your sis."

As CJ stumbled forward, he felt two hands steady him. "I can't. Have to fight. Men dying." CJ's words seemed to have followed his body's unsteady lead.

Zhaden laughed at his comment. "My friend, the Uduls have hit the water. This battle is over." CJ turned and looked behind him to see that, incredibly, Zhaden was right. Udul soldiers had boarded every other ship and seemed to either control it completely or be fairly close to doing so. The stories of their proficiency at naval battles did not seem to be unfounded after all.

"You chose your location well, friend. The Alavites are far more organized and experienced on land."

"Well, thank you regardless. That goes to all the Uduls."

Zhaden shook his head. "No thank you is necessary for friends. But if you did indeed want to, you should thank TCI."

CJ said nothing and looked back up at the large black flag of the announcement vessel, which was traveling slowly over the battlefield.

Had it been possible?

"Where's Jakob?"

"He went to a different ship, I believe. I am sure you will see him soon."

He nodded and turned his head again. A movement in CJ's peripheral vision caught his attention. There was only one Alavite ship that was still in motion, and it was much smaller than the rest. It had apparently managed to break off from the pack and was now halfway to Sheressa's cruiser. It seemed to be powering forward at full speed.

Polero.

The mental and physical exhaustion of the day were suddenly discarded. Adrenaline filled CJ's veins.

"Tom, we need to—"

"Yeah, yeah, I see it. Help them in Zhaebae."

His head was turned in its direction. His tone was more serious than before, despite the nickname he suspected Zhaden had only just received.

He moved over to the hovering ship and had Zhaden help lift him into it. The entire vehicle bounced slightly as the Udul jumped aboard after him. CJ took the machete from Tom's hand and made his way over to a seat.

"Pull us up to it, and we'll jump out!" he called out to Tom as he took a seat.

"Way ahead of you. Let's get this fuckstain," the Ayr replied as he quickly slid back into his seat and put the engines in full gear.

Within a minute, they were traveling in line with the small Alavite ship. There were only two soldiers aboard the deck. However, they were both wearing gold armor—the same as those that had been protecting Pertinax. Polero had to be here.

The back door slid open. CJ moved slowly over to it as he tightened his grip around his machete. The wind whipped across his face as Tom pulled in closer.

"Fuck him up, my dudes." Tom chuckled as he shot a glance back at them.

As they drew about as close as was safe, CJ and Zhaden jumped forward and landed in unison aboard the deck. Surprisingly, the two golden guards did not move at all. They crossed their arms as though to communicate that they were unimpressed.

CJ moved slowly, keeping his machete drawn. Zhaden seemed to be just as confused as he was but followed suit, drawing a large metallic spear from a sheath-like holder slung across his back.

A moment later, the only door on the vessel swung open. CJ turned toward it, prepared to face down Polero. Instead, a masked man dressed in strange, almost skin-tight black armor emerged. The Alavite logo was engraved in silver on his chest. White hair protruded from the top of the man's head, which his strange mask–helmet hybrid left exposed. He carried a bizarre staff-like weapon with a concave blade at its side.

The strange figure went after CJ immediately, while the golden guards drew their weapons and charged Zhaden. They exchanged several blows as CJ was continually forced backward. He gasped slightly at the feeling of the solid metal railing at his back.

As his mind began to race for a solution, the man in black kicked him in the upper chest, sending him tumbling over the side of the cruiser. He grabbed desperately, and only just managed to get a grip on one of the metal rods.

The man vanished, and CJ took advantage of this, dragging himself back on board. Zhaden had, quite impressively, managed to take down both golden guards and had now switched his focus to the strange man, who was blocking his blows rather fluidly as he moved in an almost rhythmic fashion. CJ was on his way to join in when the door swung open again. This time, Polero appeared.

The two men locked eyes for a second before the coward scrambled out and toward the rear of the ship, where the tiny escape rafts were usually kept. The emotion of the situation was overpowering, and CJ sprinted after him.

Polero was mere feet away from the lifeboat when CJ dove and came down hard on top of him, slamming the traitor's face into the deck. He lifted his head forcefully before turning him around to look him in the green pupils. Polero chuckled slightly as blood began to run down his broken nose.

"Our people are savages, Corvus. Look at our history. Look at you right now."

CJ glanced down briefly at his camouflage attire, which had become so soaked in blood that it was now black.

"I wanted something different. I wanted stability. I wanted a society whose history I could be proud of."

"You wanted to sell out your people and your home to foreigners."

"That was never what it was about. We were never going to survive Olivio. Look what happened to the Draekons. I thought if we jumped on it early and joined willingly, we could avoid the bloodshed that has ravaged our history."

Polero fell into a powerful coughing fit. His voice sounded increasingly strained as he continued to speak. "You'll need to take charge someday, Corvus. You can't keep living under your sister's shadow, lest you end up like Rob-"

He was cut off as a large, vertical blade stabbed him violently in the forehead. CJ shot to his feet and readied his machete as the black-clad man pulled his staff up and twirled it. It apparently housed a second blade that could conceal itself within its base.

"I was tired of being a babysitter. I think we can both agree that this is a significant improvement."

That voice. It was slightly distorted, but CJ knew it from somewhere.

It didn't matter now.

He shot a glance back at the deck and saw Zhaden's crumpled body. Despair came over him for a split second until he noticed the stun prick entrenched in his neck. He turned back to the man in black and screamed as he rushed at him with his machete. They exchanged blows back and forth. CJ turned the anger he now felt pulsing through his body into fuel, using it to force the man back to the main area of the deck. He went for a killing blow, but the assassin rolled acrobatically out of the way. CJ had swung with so much force and intensity that his machete pierced the deck, where it remained stuck. He had time to give it a single pull before he was kicked backward and left exposed and unarmed.

Both men stopped to look straight up at the sky as Tom's ship zoomed right over them and continued straight past. He turned his head slightly to see where their cruiser was headed. His vision was becoming blurred due to his exhaustion and dehydration. They were nearly at the rebel leaders' ship. He turned back find himself face to face with the hidden blade from the man's staff.

A bright purple light flooded CJ's eyes. It seemed to be coming from behind his attacker, who turned to investigate the source as well.

Jakob looked at them for a second before launching himself forward, forcing the black-clad man to quickly readjust his staff to block. CJ tried to stand, but his legs had completely given out. He turned onto his stomach and crawled for his machete as the two went back and forth, sending harsh and powerful strikes each other's way. Tiny purple specks broke off of Jakob's arms with each blow and went floating off into the air.

CJ rose to his knees and pulled at the machete once he reached it. It still would not budge.

The man swung hard, aiming at Jakob's left arm with the blade at the end of his staff. The impact forced Jakob to turn slightly. He adjusted relatively quickly, but not fast enough to stop his opponent's side blade from slashing his bare back, creating a massive and nasty-looking cut.

Jakob groaned and stumbled backward. The man seemed about ready to add another body to his record when a series of arrows swept across the deck, which he managed to avoid by diving to his right. CJ turned his head around. The archers on the deck of Sheressa's ship began to prepare a second volley. The man in black pressed a button on his wrist and sprinted to the portside of the small vessel before jumping over the railing.

A second later, he reemerged over the edge, riding on the rooftop of a tiny triangular-shaped escape pod, which quickly turned and flew away into the sky faster than CJ had expected. He appeared to slip inside the coffin-sized ship as he moved farther and farther from the sea, ascending into the sky. CJ turned and gave the machete another tug and it finally came free.

He looked back at Jakob, who was kneeling over Zhaden.

A loud clunk drew CJ's gaze over to the other side of the ship. A disabling bolt. The engine died, and the ship came to a halt mere yards from the flagship. CJ hobbled over to the bow with what remained of his strength.

The cruiser extended its ramp onto the deck. Once it was locked in place, he ascended it slowly. Sheressa wrapped her arms around him before he even had both feet firmly on deck. He was sweaty, bloody, and dirty beyond recognition. This was going to ruin her dress, but she didn't seem to care.

"We did it, Corvus. The planet is ours again."

He nodded and looked up quickly at the TCI fleet in the sky.

"Jakob is here."

"I know. I called him."

He narrowed his eyes and opened his mouth to respond but was interrupted.

"C'mon, man. If anyone is going to fuck you up in a fight it'll be me, not the Alavites. It gave us a good chance to put the army to the test too, not to mention the world's best excuse to get out of a boring-as-fuck meeting."

Tom emerged from the crowd aboard the ship with his hands in his jacket pockets.

Sheressa continued staring at the ever-sarcastic Ayr as though expecting him to say something else. CJ had to wait an extra second or two for her to look back at him.

"I'm uneasy about holding a throne that we didn't rightfully win ourselves. It's not our way."

She narrowed her eyes. "Turn around, Corvus."

He did, albeit slowly. The combination of rebel and captured Alavite ships was beginning to move in toward them. The Uduls and rebel Erubs aboard them began to clap and cheer as they approached. Traditional Erub flags began to rise over the fleet, replacing Polero's disgusting variations.

"I don't think any of them care how it happened. We won. Polero and his idiot followers are dead."

He nodded and stared down at the ground. "So is Watts."

He felt a hand on his shoulder. "I'm so sorry, Corvus. He died for Erub and for our future. It won't be in vain. We need to make sure of that."

"We need to find the rest of Polero's men and—"

"Corvus, you need to calm the fuck down. You look like you're about to collapse. It can wait. Their leader is dead, and The Fist is gone. We're safe."

He lifted his head. "The Fist?"

She raised an eyebrow. "Yes. The man in black that you were fighting. He's one of the deadliest and most well-trained fighters in the galaxy. How do you not know that?"

He nodded slowly. Maybe he wasn't becoming as washed-up as he feared.

Sheressa rolled her eyes. "As I was saying, Polero loyalists are still our kind and have always been. We'll need to win them back."

"Throw them in prison until they stop being idiots, then."

"Then we're no better than him. That's not how I'm going to run my Erub, Corvus."

Sheressa walked past him and placed her hands on the railing as the ships began to form a circle around them. She signaled for one of the other leaders to bring her a microphone that was synched to the ship's speakers.

"True children of Erub, today is our day. Let us turn our vessels back to Mortobal and lay claim to what rightfully belongs to all of us. As your new queen, I will work toward restoring the traditions and values that the traitor Polero destroyed. You are all my children now, and I will protect you. All of you."

Cheers rang through the air as the sun began to set. CJ turned around and moved aside as Jakob made his way up the ramp and onto the deck. His eyes darted back to the small ship. Zhaden was being transported onto a stretcher while a small Udul vessel hovered nearby in wait, presumably to transport him.

Sheressa bowed politely to Jakob. "The true sons and daughters of Erub thank you for your aid, Jakob Koss."

What happened next left CJ speechless. Jakob Koss, king of the Draekons, leader of TCI, and now surely one of the most famous and powerful people in the galaxy, fell onto a knee on front of Sheressa. For a single, terrifying second, CJ thought the man might propose.

"It's an honor to meet you in person, Queen Sheressa. Anywhere the Chosen Army hides, we will rip them out root and stem. It's always an honor to help wherever we can."

CJ crossed his arms and narrowed his eyes as he attempted to figure out exactly what Jakob was playing at here.

"The same to you, Neon King."

He rose slowly. "Will you do us the honor of spending the night in the castle with us as our honored guests?"

Jakob turned to look at Tom, who shrugged.

"I suppose we will. We have more than a few men who could use the rest. I'll likely be taking off first thing in the morning; I have matters to attend to back home that need my immediate attention."

Sheressa bowed slightly. "Very well. It would be my honor to have you all. Erub owes you a tremendous debt."

All of this was making CJ very uncomfortable. He gripped the railing next to him tightly.

"I received word that Olivio has ordered an exodus of Feralla as it burns to the ground. It seems they've finally secured the surrender they've been after for so many years. We need every minute of every hour to prepare for whatever comes next. The army we put together haphazardly for today won't cut it. Not remotely."

Sheressa's expression grew more serious. "I know I am not in your union, and I have no right to ask anything of you, but please, for everyone's sake, crush Olivio and everything he has built. Once it's crushed, crush it a second time. Demolish the Chosen Army. In this, you have our support. Given the volatile political situation we will be facing in the foreseeable future, I cannot offer anything more."

"That is perfectly fine. CJ's efforts in the Oballe uprising have ensured the Erub people will always have a positive standing in TCI."

"So, probably a bad time for this, but a shit ton of our ships are really low on fuel. Definitely not just mentioning this because mine is on that list."

Jakob glared at Tom for a second or two before sighing.

"He's not wrong. We didn't exactly have time to top up, seeing as we essentially left at a moment's notice."

"Well, I can offer you what we can spare. It's the least we can do."

Jakob bowed politely.

The ships rearranged themselves and made the trip back to the Mortobal hangar in a blissfully uneventful fashion. CJ felt as though he'd lived an entire lifetime in the past several hours.

But one thing still bothered him. He should have been overjoyed and exuberant. After all, this was what they had been working toward for years. But something weighed on him as he looked at the cut on Jakob's bare back. He couldn't quite put a finger on it, but something about the infamous 'Neon King' made him deeply uneasy. He had said and done all the right things, and had it been anyone else, CJ would have bought him a round of drinks.

CJ walked over and stood next to him. Jakob seemed to always have the same, neutral facial expression regardless of what was happening. "Look. I appreciate what you did here today. But we're still not signing your treaty, Jakob. We just finished pulling ourselves out from under someone else's boot. We won't kneel to anyone else ever again."

Jakob turned slowly and looked him in the eyes. "I didn't expect you to. I would only like to ask something of you personally."

Here it came—the catch.

"What would that be?"

"As I told your sister, we're in for a long series of dark days. Olivio has never lost a war, and the Chosen Fleet will be here sooner than we all would like. The war that's coming is likely to be the biggest and most encompassing the galaxy has ever seen."

CJ looked away from Jakob and out over the ocean. The wreckage and debris from multiple ships lay strewn seemingly everywhere. Several dark-red clouds had formed above the surface of the water.

"What does that have to do with me?"

"You're a great fighter, CJ. Down the line, I may need you. All I ask is that you do for me what I did for you. Come to my aid when I need you. One time. I will need as many men as I can get when the Chosen Army comes knocking, and it's far from beneath me to ask for the help."

He glanced over his shoulder at the cuts on his back. CJ remained quiet for several seconds, trying to figure out what kind of game Jakob was playing. The Draekon looked back at him. It was hard to tell, but it did seem as though he was being sincere. Honestly, the deal seemed more than fair. He wouldn't be alive now if it weren't for TCI, as little as he may have liked to admit it.

"Okay. One time."

CJ offered a hand to Jakob, who reached out and grabbed it. It was incredibly warm.

XXXII

MARIJAH JHAEL
ROYAL BANQUET HALL, MORTOBAL
ERUB

Marijah lowered the silver goblet from her lips and set it down on the table. The wine here was surprisingly better than its Pariso equivalent, but those words would, obviously, never escape her lips. She glanced around the banquet hall, which was completely illuminated by green-flamed torches that had been described to her as "traditional." While that was nice, she would have preferred the brighter and far less eerie lighting of modern bulbs.

She sighed and leaned back in the comfortable plush chair she had been provided with. Perhaps she could learn to love this environment, at least for a night. The black tufts of Jakob's hair filled her view as she turned to her left. He, too, sat staring out over the enormous room and the hundreds of tables arranged in neat lines within it. Unlike her, however, he hadn't so much as touched his food nor his wine. TCI and rebel Erub bodies filled every seat in the hall, which itself was the size of a small hangar. Not to be outdone, Marijah had ordered one of her men to write down a reminder for her to authorize an expansion of The Jewel's own guest entertainment area when she got back.

Laughter, music, and occasionally drunken singing filled the air. She suppressed a smile as it occurred to her that Jakob must have been miserable in a place so completely full of mirth and cheer. It was impossible to tell, of course, as his expression hardly ever changed. She didn't know why, but there was something incredibly attractive about his bizarre apathetic and uncaring demeanor. Perhaps the years of seeing men crying and begging at her feet had finally taken their toll.

She stood from her chair slowly. Jakob turned to look at her as she rose. "Everything okay?"

She nodded. "Just going to stretch my legs a bit, love."

He responded by looking away, and she smiled. If he was going to hold out on her, she was at least going to have some fun with it.

She scanned the room for people whom she thought might make for some actual decent conversation, and spotted a table full of Uduls who were apparently engaged in some sort of drinking competition. They downed large ornate bottles of unlabeled alcohol within seconds and would shout something in Garyl after each one. At another table, the very large Ayr leader, whose name she didn't really care to remember, was ignoring the alcohol entirely and gorging himself on the food. It was rather unpleasant to look at. She turned her gaze away quickly as a slight tinge of nausea came over her. The Erub queen's brother, who she had been told was the hero of the battle, sat among several Erub rebels as he chatted with them. The new queen had asked him to sit at the main table with her, but he had ignored her request, choosing instead to be with his men. Whatever it was that they were talking about, it seemed to be serious in nature. She thought it best not to intrude.

Marijah's search came to a halt as she spotted Tom at the rightmost table in the room. He had his feet kicked up, and he was tipping his chair backwards, resting it against the wall. He seemed to be sitting on the outskirts of several conversations rather than participating in any of them. She moved gracefully over to him.

The Ayr looked up at her as she approached. She looked at her reflection in his orange virix.

"Queen Jhael . . . To what do I owe the pleasure?"

He was slurring his words slightly. These goblets held a lot of liquid, and there were at least four strewn around him.

"Just taking a walk around. You looked lonely."

"It's all good. Been chatting with the queen, mostly. I mean, the other queen. Ugh. Why couldn't one of you have been an empress or a duchess or something to make this less confusing?"

She smiled slightly to herself. Watching men being idiots just never got old.

She was about to turn, walk away, and find somewhere else to go to, when the Erub queen approached Tom from his side.

This was Marijah's first time seeing Sheressa Droc up close. The rumors of her beauty were, somewhat annoyingly, not unfounded. At least she would have someone to relate to. The current TCI leadership pool was a sea of testosterone.

"Having fun?" Sheressa asked as she touched Tom lightly on the shoulder.

He chuckled and smiled in a curiously attractive way as he looked up at her. "Of course. A bit less since you left though."

Marijah raised an eyebrow and alternated her gaze between the two of them. She knew those looks. If something had not already gone on between these two, then it wouldn't be long now.

"Queen of the Spring. I apologize for not greeting you earlier." Sheressa turned to Marijah and spoke in perfect Joxun.

"It isn't a problem. You clearly have a lot on your plate today. I didn't know you spoke the language of my people."

"I speak seven, actually."

It seemed that the Erub people's new leader was a bit of a showoff.

Tom alternated his gaze between the two women. It was hard to tell through his virix, but he seemed confused. It would seem he did not share in the queens' refined education.

"Will you come to the deck with me? I'd like to speak with you properly." Sheressa motioned to her left.

"Of course."

Marijah followed her as she led the way out of the hall and through a set of large arched doorways, eventually making it out onto a large stone deck overlooking the ocean. In the sky, Erub's large turquoise moon sat proudly in the black abyss. She couldn't help but stare at it.

"They say it used to be green millennia ago and that the sea itself changed to emulate it." Sheressa moved closer to her as she spoke.

"It's . . . amazing."

It truly was. She couldn't remember the last thing she had witnessed that had taken her breath in such a way, aside from when she had first seen The Jewel back home. The sound of the waves lapping against the shore was oddly calming, and the moon itself acted at the only light source. It was beautiful.

"Do you trust him?"

The question caught Marijah by surprise. For a second, she considered asking who Sheressa was referring to, but it seemed the implication was obvious.

"He's given me no reason not to thus far. Given that we're going to be wed soon, I'd certainly hope I do."

"You aren't alone then. It seems all the Neon King gets is adulation wherever he goes. I want nothing more than to distrust him the way my brother does, but he's done nothing but good for Erub so far." She turned to face Marijah. "Corvus does bring up a good point, however. Why do all of this? Why risk your own life and expend your time and incredible effort for people who did nothing for you in your own time of need?"

Marijah rested her hands on the cool railing overlooking the sea. "He's complicated. They say he who dares, wins, and Jakob seems to do little else but dare."

Sheressa nodded slowly.

"It took me until I saw the camps myself to understand that he's also broken. He seems to be doing what he can to ensure that no one else ever goes through what he and the Draekons did. That's the point of TCI."

Small, rhythmic chirping noises from the brush around them began to integrate themselves into the soundscape. They weren't random, as one might have expected, but rather seemed to alternate in a song-like fashion. Marijah raised an eyebrow.

"Chi-koree. Those little frogs have lived here longer than any Erub. They outnumber us ten to one. It's truly more their planet than ours." Sheressa smiled slightly as she spoke, but the grin quickly faded.

"I am new to all of this. Leading teams and planning operations is one thing, but ruling outright is another. My brother was groomed to be my father's successor, not me. I may well look to you for advice. We're bound to understand each other better than most would think."

Marijah chuckled. "Contact me whenever you'd like. I imagine I'll enjoy speaking to you more than most of the idiots I deal with on a daily basis."

Sheressa smiled again. Her dress ruffled lightly in the wind.

"Your father made the wrong choice. You've done well in correcting it."

"Corvus is a great man and an even better leader. I give him hell daily, and he puts up with me. I don't think I'll ever be able to repay him for what he did for the planet over the past few years. He doesn't even enjoy fighting. He's just good at it. I sent him out there, and he almost died today."

Marijah shut her eyes as the flashbacks of what she was about to say ripped through her mind. "My brother abused me for years and barely spoke to me until he wanted to use me. Savor your good relationship with your sibling. The two of you will be okay."

Sheressa seemed to be trying to find the right combination of words to say in response, but she was failing.

"You shared with me, so I shared with you."

Marijah's throat suddenly felt warm. She shook her head slightly to collect herself.

"What happened to him?" Sheressa asked as she moved a stray lock of hair out of her eyes.

"I was a coward. I never told anyone. I just couldn't, and I don't know why. One of the palace guards caught him in the act and ran off before I could stop him. Rienn was arrested and castrated the next day. Last I heard, he was in solitary confinement in a maximum-security prison somewhere on Norann."

Sheressa's eyes widened a bit. "They gave the prince a trial that quickly?"

"Sexual offenses don't require one. The witness was female. Our word carries much more weight than theirs—especially on matters like these."

"No execution?"

"It's been outlawed for centuries. We pride ourselves on trying to be a more civilized people. I can't say I never wished him dead, though."

Sheressa looked back out at the sea. The waves lapped quietly against the shore, and the chirping continued.

"I'm sorry."

"Don't be."

Several more seconds of silence seemed to confirm the end of this topic.

"When is your coronation?"

"I'm not sure. We'll think about that once I get more organized. We have a lot of work to do to fix the mess Polero created."

Marijah nodded. Her mind now returned to Tom as she looked back at Sheressa. She smiled deviously. "You know what one of my favorite parts of this is?"

She reached up, gently removed her crown, and showed it to Sheressa, who raised an eyebrow.

"I get to fuck whoever I want pretty much whenever I want them. It's a criminally underrated part of being queen. After years of never having a choice, now I have all of them. It's a fun perk and one that you shouldn't underestimate."

She looked left and right and leaned in slightly to Sheressa's ear. "You just won a civil war. The last thing you should be hesitating for is this."

Sheressa's face seemed to redden dramatically.

"I mean. . . I-"

Marijah smiled in an almost cocky way. "You're the authority now. You have the power. Get what you want when you want it. You said it yourself, you've got long and stressful days ahead. If any opportunity for a bit of fun comes along, grab it by the throat."

She pulled back and placed the crown back on her head.

Sheressa nodded and smiled slightly. "I think I may invite you over more often. Let's head back in."

"Sounds good to me." Marjah replied with a smile of her own.

It was getting late, and the size of the crowd in the room had decreased significantly by the time they walked back in. Some people had simply fallen asleep right in their chairs. Others lay sprawled out on the tables. Sheressa made a beeline toward Tom and grabbed his arm without breaking stride.

"What-?" Tom began to ask.

"Come on, Ezekiel." Sheressa muttered as the two began to move quickly, eventually disappearing through the massive double doors at the other end of the room.

The girl had good taste. The snarky Ayr didn't have Jakob's mind nor mystical qualities, but he was handsome and charming enough to make up for it. If she hadn't been a committed woman, she would likely have taken a shot at a relatively easy lay, as Tom didn't particularly strike her as the type to be choosy. It was not uncommon for women in Pariso to bed two men at a time. She would not have minded having Jakob and Tom at the same time in the slightest, as unrealistic as that might have been.

She noticed that she was biting her lip slightly as she approached her tired-looking husband-to-be. He wouldn't admit any weakness; this much she had learned so far. She figured she'd do the work for him.

"I'm heading up to the room. You can come if you want."

He looked at her, nodded, and stood. They made their way silently up to the suite that the male Droc had shown them earlier in the evening; it was one of several luxurious guest bedrooms in the castle. A large bed with dark-green sheets was next to the rightmost wall. Extravagant carpets, paintings, and random artistic ornaments gave the room a lovely decor that Marijah was all but certain Jakob wouldn't care about in the least. On the leftmost side of the room sat a large silver bathtub. As soon as they entered, Jakob walked over to it and began to run the water. She sat at the foot of the bed in silence as she watched him strip down while facing away from her. This was her first time seeing his full naked body. Her eyes widened as she noticed the massive cut lined in dark purple marks across his back. The wound looked to have been cauterized, albeit very crudely.

He climbed into the water slowly as steam began to fill the room. He groaned slightly as he adjusted himself, eventually resting his arms over the edges of the steel tub. Marijah removed her heels, which probably cost more than half the objects in this room, and she walked slowly across the cool tiled floor. He turned his head to look at her as she approached.

She dropped down to her knees next to the tub and reached for the sponge on the small wooden table next to it. Jakob raised an eyebrow.

"What ar—?"

"Shut up and lean forward, Koss."

She rolled up the sleeves on her dress. Jakob didn't move. He stared off in a random direction away from her.

"Jakob, look at me."

He returned his gaze to her, albeit slowly.

"Now."

She moved her hand to the back of his pale neck and pushed down gently. He sighed and bent forward, exposing his back. She dipped the sponge into the water and began running it over his cuts slowly. He recoiled slightly upon first contact, and a faint groan escaped his lips. She continued this process slowly and in silence for the next several minutes before suddenly stopping and dropping the sponge into the water.

"Fuck it."

She stood up straight, quickly stripped off her jumpsuit, and kicked it across the floor before moving to free her breasts from their restraints. The relief was indescribable after an entire day of having them bound. Jakob stared at her eyes and then briefly at her chest with a blank expression. She bent over as she slipped her thumbs between her skin and lacy underwear and slid them down to the ground. She stood there for a few seconds, exposing herself fully to his view. There were many uncertainties in this weird galaxy, but one thing she did know for damn sure was that she had a great body.

Jakob's expression didn't change. He scanned her up and down with a straight face as though examining an unimpressive piece of art in a museum. He raised an eyebrow as he resumed eye contact. She crossed her arms. Now, she was aggravated.

"You don't like men, do you?"

"I don't like most people."

"That's not what I meant. Do you have nothing to say?" She gestured at her naked body with her hands.

"You look healthy."

"Healthy? What the fuck is that supposed to mean?"

"I'm not really sure what you were looking for."

"Just move aside, Koss."

He hesitated for a few seconds but eventually pulled himself slightly to the front of the tub, leaving more than enough space behind him for Marijah to climb in.

She pulled him in toward her as she settled into the pleasantly warm water. She ran her hands over his surprisingly muscular shoulders and back for a few seconds. For once, he wasn't pulling away from her. The contrast of her olive hands against his alarmingly pale back was pleasing to look at, even in the dim light. Once she was satisfied with her tactile quest, she reached down and picked up the sponge to continue where she had left off. After several more minutes of silent work, Jakob turned his head around, locking eyes with her. She stopped abruptly and met his gaze. For a few seconds, they were paralyzed, staring each other down. She had never looked so intently into a Draekon's eyes for this long. His were as strange as they were gorgeous.

"Thank you, Marijah," Jakob said abruptly, and somewhat quietly.

She smiled, but not because of what he had said; after all, he damn well should have thanked her. No. It was something in his look. It wasn't the blank, apathetic gaze she had grown used to. Rather, it was one that seemed genuinely grateful, vulnerable, and, dare she think it, possibly even loving. This was her chance.

She let the sponge fall into the water and slowly wrapped her arms around him, pulling him all the way in until her breasts touched his bare back. She lowered her head slowly on to his shoulder. He didn't pull away nor even try to do so. One of his arms emerged from the water and grabbed hers. She had thought that he meant to pull himself free, but instead, it stayed put and even lightly caressed her own.

With an unexpected surge of courage, she slowly leaned in toward his neck and began to kiss it lightly.

XXXIII

DARYN PERIC
CREW BUNKS, NAMIRA'S SHIP
OBALLE

Daryn shivered as he pulled the brown scratchy blanket up a few inches and curled his legs up beneath it. If the nights on Saraii had been bad, the ones on Oballe were almost unbearable. The ship had been electronically disabled, leaving him and the rest of the Others stranded in the Oballe courtyard for the past two nights. His eyes tracked his breath as it puffed out into a small cloud before spreading out and dispersing into the air.

    He had experienced just about enough of this. He sighed and sat up slowly in the small metallic bunk built into the wall of the ship that he'd claimed for his own. Thankfully, the sheets it was lined with provided a desperately needed layer between his skin and the freezing cold metal. He wrapped the blanket around him and looked around at the other crew members. They had all somehow managed to fall asleep. Yeuma lay on the bunk right across from him with her head turned toward the wall. Namira's long white dreadlocks draped over the edge of her bunk and dangled over Yeuma's section. Da'garo's deep snores echoed through the room from the bunk directly above his own. Oslo, who had volunteered to give up his bed, slept on the sofa outside.

Daryn wasn't sure where Elan slept. The old man seemed to always be waiting in the common area of the ship regardless of the hour. Perhaps he would speak to him tonight. It wasn't as if there was anything else to do.

He was in the process of climbing down from his bunk when the small door to the room slid open. Elan entered the room and quickly turned to shut the door behind him manually.

The old man hobbled over to Daryn with surprising speed and whispered to him in Alavic. "You must come with me immediately."

Daryn raised an eyebrow. "What's going on?"

"There is something you need to see."

His interest was certainly piqued. He slipped his shoes on quickly before following the elderly Zantavi out into the center of the ship, keeping his blanket wrapped around him the entire time.

They walked quietly past Oslo, who lay sprawled out across the couch snoring. As soon as Elan stepped inside the ship's control sector, he turned and pulled the formerly automatic door shut behind them.

"Okay. So, what is so important then?"

The old Zantavi ignored him and instead opened a rusty, worn-looking container in the corner of the room. He pulled a large steel suitcase from it and placed it on top of the ship's dashboard before reaching into a small pouch that was resting at his side and withdrawing a small square chip. He opened the suitcase slowly. The back of it glimmered slightly in his eyes. It took Daryn a second to realize that he was looking at a screen. Elan pressed a button, and a small tray emerged from the right side with a loud click. He placed the chip into it slowly and jammed it back into the case. The screen flashed to life, flooding the room with blinding white light. Daryn was forced to squint for several seconds until his eyes adjusted.

"How did you get that on? We've got no power."

"Batteries. Don't know how much juice it has left. I need you to watch this. Listen to everything."

Elan's tone differed now from when they had spoken days before. He sounded scared . . . or perhaps excited? It was hard to tell. Regardless, Daryn nodded at him and leaned into the screen. On it, several Alavites in elaborate white robes sat in a circle. Priests. He could tell from the collars. Based on the angle and style of the footage, he guessed it must have come from a security camera. He slowly lowered himself into the captain's seat without taking his eyes off the screen. He knew this room. The Sepulcher. He had seen it in person only once, despite living at the Altar for most of his life. It was rumored to be the exact location where Alavon Acivorai's body was kept, and as such, within the faith, it was considered the most sacred site in the galaxy.

He squinted to try to get a better view of the man in The Hand's chair on the screen. He had seen pictures of Valentino IX before, but actual footage of the man was rare. Daryn wondered what exactly the holdup was, as all the seats in the room were filled. Everyone seemed to be waiting on someone or something.

He looked them over as carefully as the quality of the footage would allow. He didn't recognize a single priest, aside from a much younger Olivio. For the first time, he wondered what the current Hand's surname had been before his promotion, when it became 'The Tenth' (though most foreigners still incorrectly pronounced "X" as the letter, and this annoyed him greatly). His hair was still blond and completely present. It was odd seeing him this way. In Daryn's head, Olivio had simply always been old and wrinkled. He looked back at Valentino. He was taller, darker-skinned, and more muscular than anyone else in the room. He had no beard and kept his wispy white hair cropped short. He was tapping the exposed fingers of his gloved hand on the arm of the chair.

After another minute or so, the main door leading into the room opened, and a man in black-and-gold armor entered quickly, carrying a white bundle in his arms.

"I see everything went well. Be blessed on this day, Maximillian."

The man wore no helmet, but his role was clear, based on his armor. Valentino's Fist. Olivio shot up from his seat.

"My Hand! This cannot be permitted! This sanctuary is a sacred place!"

Valentino held his gloved hand up. "Silence, Olivio! I will decide what is and is not allowed. Sit down. Now."

Olivio complied slowly, but his eyes revealed that he was fit to burst with rage. The Fist, evidently named Maximilian, held the item up to Valentino, who leaned forward in his chair to examine it more closely.

"I ask that His Hand would bless him so he may live a righteous life."

He ran his hand over it, moving the cloth that was shielding it from the camera's view. It was a baby. It moved around slightly in its small white blanket. It couldn't have been more than a few hours old. It actually wasn't crying, but rather looking around as though taking everything in.

"What is his name?"

"Alexander."

"His mother?"

Maximilian shook his head. "She . . . didn't make it." His voice suddenly sounded pained.

Valentino nodded and held out his gloved hand to the infant as he recited the traditional blessing. When he was finished, Maximilian bowed his head and began to move away with the child.

"Do you mind if I hold him?"

Maximilian appeared shocked but nodded. "Of course not, my Hand."

Valentino smiled and ran his gloved hand over the baby's head. Maximilian took his post behind the two of them. The Hand spoke to the group but kept his eyes glued to the infant.

"As you all know, our sun has risen over my sixth decade in this post. As per tradition, I will be naming my successor in the event of my death or inability to perform my duties. As the Ninth Hand of Alavon, I declare that it is time to announce who will act as the tenth."

The priests all either straightened up or leaned forward in their chairs.

"As per the law of our Lord, once my selection is made, the candidate can only be stripped of their duties when Alavon Himself calls him to His kingdom. My word is His, and His word is law."

"His word is law," they all echoed.

"I have taken each of your histories into account, as well as your backgrounds, families, and service records. When everything came together, there was only one choice that could be made. It took me until mere minutes ago to settle on my choice. I looked into his eyes and saw something I'm not sure I've ever seen before. I saw wonder. I saw potential. I saw fire and passion. Most of all, I saw the light of our very Lord within his soul, just as Balthasar XIII, honored may he be, saw within me."

Valentino pointed the index finger of his gloved hand at his target. "It will be you, and none other."

To Daryn's shock, not only was Valentino not pointing at Olivio, but he also wasn't even facing in his general direction. His finger was aimed directly downward at the baby in his lap.

The other priests sat up in their chairs and stared at the wide-eyed newborn.

"He will lead us to a new golden age. Alavon has spoken it to me."

Olivio shot to his feet. The other priests exchanged confused and even concerned looks.

"This is insanity! You cannot select a newborn over men who have served you diligently for years! We will not be led by a child!"

"You are out of line, Olivio! You have the audacity to question the will of our Lord?! Perhaps you would have had strong words for Alfonso IV. If you took any interest in your studies, you would know that he took over the seat at only five and ended up leading our people into unprecedented levels of prosperity and peace by bringing an end to Alastair II's reckless and bloody war."

Daryn looked back at Maximilian. The Fist looked stunned and appeared to be trying to form words.

"This cannot be accepted. He is not even of holy blood! The Fist is not one of us, nor will he ever be! Besides, the child will only be in his early teens by the time you'll likely pass. He will know nothing, and we will be doomed."

"If you would take a second to think of me as something other than an idiot, Olivio, you would know I have considered that. I will have him serve as my attendant and teach him everything he needs to know until Alavon calls me to his side. I will also remind you that my predecessor was not of holy blood either. It is by no means a requirement to be Hand, nor has it ever been."

Golden guards began to move in silently from the outside the circle. Daryn's heart began to race. Olivio seemed close to being thrown out.

"Our empire will collapse if we are led for another few decades under your policies. We haven't even struck at the Draekons in a significant manner during your reign. That is unacceptable. They killed the very Lord we all serve, and yet, we sit here like fools while they frolic around in the snow and procreate."

"An entire race of people does not bear the blame for the actions of an individual. You of all people should appreciate that. The galaxy would think us sadistic and ignorant if you were to act as our representative. The fact that the Draekon people were ever forced off this planet in the first place is a blight on our history. Those wounds have been slow to repair and will continue to be."

"Our people are weak and exposed. We can't go on like this!"

"I have had about enough of your insubordination. I will see you in my chambers tomorrow for a disciplinary hearing. Get out of my sight."

Olivio smiled. Somehow, even across space and time, Daryn's heart sank. "No."

Valentino rose to his feet. "Excuse me?"

Olivio took a step toward The Hand. "I said no. You are incompetent, weak, and an insult to the position you hold. I am through listening to you, and so is everyone else. I will send word to your family."

"Word? Word about wha—?"

Daryn gasped as a golden guard behind Valentino ran his sword through his back. The Hand fell forward but rolled to his side, leaving the child safely on the ground. Maximillian reached for his sword but was struck through the neck from behind. He emitted a few strange gurgling sounds before falling limp. Other guards, who were now standing behind every other priest, reached forward and slit their throats. They each collapsed face first to the ground, and pools of blood formed beneath them. The baby rolled around carelessly in its blanket as he stared at both Valentino and its fallen father with wide amber eyes.

Valentino struggled up to his knees and grabbed at the blade of the sword that was protruding from his chest. He spoke breathlessly. "You strike at your own Hand, and for what? To take my place? You are not Alavon's choice. You will never speak in His name."

He looked Olivio right in the eye as the traitor approached him slowly. "Do you really think you're just going to get away with this? That the people won't reject you when they find out what you've done? Your day of judgement will come, and when it does, you better believe I will be by Alavon's side to see you take your sentence."

A jolt of adrenaline rocketed through Daryn's body as Olivio slowly crouched down and drew very close to Valentino's face. "Look around you, old man. I have all the support I need. In me, Alavon has not only a proper Hand but a champion of his original cause. I fear no judgement. I deliver it."

Before the injured Hand could respond, a golden guard to his left swung his sword down with great force over his left arm, lopping it off at the elbow. The sound of the gold gauntlet clanking loudly as it crashed against the tiled floor melded with Valentino's deep groans. Olivio knelt and picked up the glove as Valentino dropped lifelessly into the pool of his own blood.

Olivio shook the amputated hand out of it, and it plopped against the floor before he slid the glove onto his own hand. He turned his head slowly to look up at the guards. "Bring them in."

Several other gold-clad men came into the frame, and each carried a small, pale body. Draekons. They began to position them around the area. They placed the swords and knives used in the murders into the corpses' hands.

Another Alavite appeared. He was wearing the light-gray robes of an echo, the rank directly below a priest. His odd smile was familiar. When he spoke, his voice left no question as to who he was.

"A new day has dawned, Olivio. I am beyond giddy!"

"As the sole survivor of the unfortunate assassinations of everyone in here today, I am now Hand of Alavon by default. It is a burden I will gladly bear if it means securing the kind of future our Lord envisioned for us. You will address me as 'my Hand.'"

"Of course." The man bowed to him.

"As promised, you will be the first of my five, Pertinax."

The new priest nodded and smiled. "I assume it is safe to be in here around them? Forgive me for being cautious." Pertinax shot a glance at the Draekon corpses.

"We've been over this far too many times. They are safe. All of them are. Now, we will set down the path toward making sure it never happens again."

Pertinax still looked unsure but nodded. Daryn had no idea what they were referring to. How could corpses possibly be dangerous? The new Hand and his priest looked to the side as a golden guard approached carrying Maximilian's child in hand. The boy stared into Olivio's eyes in an oddly challenging manner.

"Shall we have them thrown in the sea? I'm not particularly fond of slicing up infants."

Olivio shook his head. "No. I want him here. Alive. Valentino was a senile and stupid man. Our Lord will forgive me for purging the world of the cowardice that he and his supporters brought to our empire. I doubt he will offer that same compassion if I slay the child. I will oversee his development and ensure he does not duplicate the mistakes of his father."

"My Hand?"

A second guard approached from behind. To Daryn's surprise, the man was carrying a second infant. In sharp contrast to the first, this one was bloody and screaming.

Olivio turned, and his eyes widened at the sight before him.

"It was thought that this one had perished along with the mother, but it struggled and practically pulled itself from the womb. It's a girl."

Olivio ran a hand through his blond hair. "I suppose she will stay here as well. I will have her sent to the preservers when the time comes."

Pertinax turned to Olivio. "My Hand, many will question why the assassins would kill Maximilian but leave his child—or I suppose children—alive."

"I don't know what you're talking about. Our fallen brother's children were brutally murdered by the Draekons, and we will make sure everyone knows it. These infants before you are Daryn and Yeuma Peric—two orphans left on the steps of the Altar. No one has seen the child's face, and very few know of the existence of the twin. I did not spend fifteen years studying politics and media relations without learning how to sell a story."

"Peric? That seems a bit too common of a surname."

"That's the point. Perhaps I have much to teach you as well. Make sure they are taken to my new chambers."

Pertinax and the guards who were holding the infants bowed and walked off screen. Olivio turned and seemed to notice the camera. He moved quickly up to it, staring directly into the lens as he approached.

"Bring me that damn Zantavi!" he called back to a few guards who seemed to be waiting for orders. They shuffled into motion.

Daryn and the young Olivio stared into each other's eyes for a few seconds. A rage the likes of which he had never known himself capable of experiencing overcame him, and he felt immense pressure.

He slammed the suitcase shut and bolted to his feet. The small cloud-like puff of one breath was only halfway toward being dispersed before another took its place. He breathed heavily for a few seconds as he stared straight ahead at nothing in particular. Silence enveloped him. He blinked a few times and turned around slowly.

Elan's face was unreadable. He spoke slowly and confidently. "Olivio is a fraud. The Draekon genocide; the invasions of the Dom'Rai, Quexian, and Carine systems; the very existence of the Chosen Army itself . . . everything the man has built and achieved has been based on lies."

Daryn shook his head. Things were happening too quickly for him to process.

Elan continued, "When I first started working at the Altar, I swore an oath to always serve The Hand, whoever he may be. The time has finally come for me to continue that."

Daryn nodded politely, unsure of what else to do. To his shock, the old man slowly fell to one knee.

"You are the lost heir of the Klell people and the rightful Hand of Alavon. I would call you the tenth, but I believe Olivio has more than soured that surname. I pledge myself to you in any way I can."

Daryn's heart began to race. He turned to look out the cracked window. "I . . . I can't . . ."

"It isn't your choice. You're only excused from the duty upon death. I know this has been thrust upon you, but you can't imagine the number of people who have been waiting for the change you could bring—myself included. As Hand, you have the ability to forge a better Alavonia and put an end to the inhumane war machine that Olivio has created, as well as the horrific reputation he has given your people."

It happened automatically and without thought. His hand shot out in front of him, balled in a fit of anger and resentment. He didn't even process the pain that resulted from hitting and fracturing the glass. His breaths came slowly and heavily, creating small clouds in the freezing temperature of the cockpit. He looked down at his hand, which now had small shards of glass embedded in it and had begun to bleed.

Elan continued, unfazed. "Alavonia bathes in corruption and deceit under Olivio's rule. But the people's loyalty is to Alavon himself—not to any one Hand. They will rise for their true leader. I have only been around you for a short time, but I can already see so much of your father in you. You are kind and just. You carry the moral compass and conscience that Olivio discarded eons ago. But perhaps most importantly, you spent over two decades at his side and still managed to remain true to yourself instead of becoming the clone of him that he wanted you to be. You are the last true chance for not only the Alavite people but also the galaxy as a whole. The Chosen Army won't slow down anytime soon, and people will continue to die needlessly. They need you. We all do."

They both turned suddenly as the door to the bridge swung open. Yeuma walked in with her scythe drawn. She lowered it upon seeing their faces. "The fuck is going on in here?"

He looked his sister in the eyes. In that moment, the entire convoluted mess became clear. If not for her own indomitable desire to live free, she would still be rotting in a cell. She had been right about the old man all along, and all Daryn had done was tell her how much of a disgrace she was. Daryn clenched his fists as the image of Olivio striking Yeuma with his gauntlet flashed through his mind. There was no anxiety now, only an incalculable level of anger and shame.

"Daryn?"

He moved quickly and decisively toward Yeuma and enveloped her in a tight embrace. She dropped her scythe on the ground and held him close as tears began to form in his eyes.

It was in that moment, in the small, freezing cockpit on a frozen planet millions of lightyears from his home, that Daryn Peric perished, and Alexander XI rose from the dead.

EPILOGUE

JAKOB KOSS
????, ????
????

Jakob.

He rolled around on the hard ground, trying desperately to open his eyes.

Awaken, Jakob.

He shivered heavily as his eyelids finally opened and he stumbled to his feet. It had been so long since he had last truly felt cold. The Shaz energy had taken over the regulation of his temperature a long time ago. He blinked a few times as he scanned the room. He wasn't with Marijah in his suite in Mortobal anymore. In fact, he wasn't quite sure where he was. Everything was tinted in black and white, as though it were a scene in an ancient film. As his vision cleared even further, he realized that he was in some sort of library. In front of him, white light filtered in through an enormous stained-glass panel. Etched onto it was the large silhouette of a man in an extravagant suit of armor.

Jakob turned his head around and took a few silent steps. He felt oddly light, as though he were floating.

"Where—?"

My home. Not as it is today, but as I remember it.

"So, you've taken me into the past, then."

Essentially. Yes and no.

"Why am I here?"

You haven't moved, Jakob. You're still sound asleep. I've simply taken your mind on a small excursion. I'm ready, and so are you.

This was annoying. He didn't have time for this. "Ready for what?"

For you to know the truth. I needed to see if you were who I thought you could be, and you've exceeded every expectation that I've set for you thus far.

Jakob spun around slowly, taking the opportunity to scan his surroundings as well as he could. "The truth?"

About me. About you. About what you are and why I am with you.

He walked over to the stained glass and tried to make out the race of the masked man on it, but the image wasn't nearly detailed enough for him to do so.

"You're a Draekon."

No. But my life would have been far easier if I had been.

Jakob looked through the glass now rather than directly at it. Flyers flew silently around the skyscrapers. He tried to see whether he could spot any specific individual in order to get an idea what planet he was on. But it was impossible from this high up. He began to walk to the other end of the library.

Through you, I will fulfill the unfinished promises I made in life. That prospect terrifies the Alavites. That's why they've been trying so hard to find me.

"You don't exist . . . at least, not in a tangible form. How exactly would they find you?"

I live within you, Jakob. As my host, you and I are one.

"So, the purges—"

Were designed to find me. Yes.

It was hard to tell whether the end of his questions were just that predictable or if the voice was actively reading his mind.

"So, what did you do to them?"

It is what they did to me that is far more significant.

He moved over to the massive tank at the end of the hall; apparently, it also acted as a fountain. A flurry of fish swam around within it. There didn't seem to be any two that were the exact same shade of gray, indicating that they were likely quite colorful in reality.

"What exactly is your end goal here? What are these so-called promises you need to keep?"

My objectives are quite simple and are fairly in line with your own: the eradication of the Chosen Army and a restoration of peace to the galaxy.

He reached out to touch the glass of the fountain but withdrew his hand quickly as he realized that it was entirely purple and had no skin or bones of any kind. He stared down at his body, which seemed to be composed entirely of Shaz energy. He took a deep breath before asking a question to which he wasn't sure he wanted the answer.

"Are you a god?"

This guessing game was getting tiring.

I wouldn't call myself that, though many would and do. I'm not all-knowing, all-powerful, nor universally omnipresent.

"Then, why us? Why care so much about the Draekons of all races?"

I made it my mission before my death to ensure the survival of your people. I loved them in life, Jakob, more than I think you'll ever know. The powers you and your people have had imbued within you were once my own.

"So, you had the Shaz before any of us did?"

Yes, though I rarely utilized it or made its presence known in the way you have. It was only in life-or-death situations that I allowed myself to unleash the energy and tear my foes limb by limb. They are after me, and they will be until the day you die.

"And when that happens . . .?"

I am released.

"Meaning what?"

That . . . is a more complicated matter. It is something Olivio and every Hand before him has sought. They think it's what they want. They're wrong.

Jakob was about to ask a follow-up question, when the entrance to the library suddenly swung open, and a woman rushed inside. She slammed the door behind her and moved quickly to barricade it with a small stack of boxes to her left. Her dress appeared to be ripped in multiple places, and the unkempt state of her dark hair suggested that it had recently been grabbed or pulled. She retreated into the library and toward Jakob as the door burst open loudly and with ease. Two guards with handheld rams entered first, followed by four more with swords drawn. A bald Alavite with a scarred face entered last and began to walk slowly before freezing in place.

Jakob looked around. The entire room had come to a standstill. It was as though time itself had frozen.

It has. At least for now.

He went over to the terrified-looking woman and got a good glimpse of her face for the first time. She was a Draekon like him. A strange and cold sensation overcame him as he tried to think of the last time he had seen a woman of his own kind in person. As he drew closer to her, he could feel his eyes widen involuntarily. He knew her face, but he couldn't remember from where. She looked to be in pain and had a few cuts across her face, but she was still just as breathtaking to look at regardless.

"Who is she?"

I'm shocked that you don't already know.

Time began to tick again. In the blink of an eye, the woman rushed past him before tripping and falling to her knees. The bald man and his companions walked toward her nonchalantly as she turned to look at them.

"Why?!"

Her voice was almost hoarse. She seemed on the brink of tears.

"The Klell people live by a set of rules, and we die by them just the same."

The bald man smirked in an oddly uncomfortable way as he stepped closer. The men behind him had now stopped, leaving him as the sole figure approaching the Draekon woman.

"Klell?" Jakob asked under his breath.

It was what the Alavites were known as prior to the Religious Revolution.

Jakob nodded slowly as he kept his eyes fixed on the scene before him. As the man reached the Draekon woman, he stood menacingly over her.

"I'm afraid treason will not be tolerated under any circumstances, Your Highness."

"Havak."

Jakob spoke the words as they shot into his mind.

Well done.

He had heard tales about the ancient Draekon queen's beauty. It would seem those had not been at all unfounded. He struggled with himself as he watched the scene before him. Every fiber of his being screamed at him to step in and help.

You cannot. This happened long before your time, and there is no changing the past; one can only learn from it.

"So, this is when they came after her? For killing Alavon?" Jakob noticed he was subconsciously lowering his voice, even though there was no chance of anyone else hearing him.

The voice in his head chuckled. *Is that what they told you?*

Jakob shot a glance to his side as a purple spectral figure appeared next to him.

"He was your King!" screamed the Draekon queen at the man looming over her.

"No true king of the Klell would lie with Draekon filth. He was a traitor, and he suffered a traitor's fate." he shot back.

The gears in Jakob's head began to turn rapidly. If what the man had just said was true, then that meant. . .

"History has the unfortunate habit of being propped up by the falsehoods of survivors."

Jakob looked back to his right, shocked to hear the voice coming from somewhere other than inside his own skull. The featureless man next to him had no defined mouth, but it still managed to speak without issue.

"Alavon was assaulted in his own bedroom in the early morning hours next to the woman he loved more than anything on all the planets of our galaxy."

As the figure spoke, the black and white world came to a total standstill, as though time itself had frozen. A series of purple Shaz silhouettes appeared in front of Jakob, playing out the scene that was being described. Alavon's was easy enough to pinpoint, as it was a bit taller and significantly more muscular than those around it.

"The Klell king fought despite being unclothed and unarmed. His skill and instincts were such that he was able to hold off a few men and allow the Draekon queen time to escape."

It was difficult to tell for sure, but it seemed as though the smallest of the figures had climbed out of a window before vanishing completely from of the scene. Alavon, for his part, was throwing the other men around like ragdolls. His arms appeared to have a bit of an aura around them, much like Jakob's own. Perhaps, he thought, it was just his imagination.

"But he could only hold out for so long."

Multiple men surrounded the king's silhouette, and until he became physically unable to handle all of them at once. One of the attackers, positioned directly behind him, produced what looked to be a small knife before stabbing it violently into the king's back.

"The other soldiers took turns stabbing and cutting Alavon's dying body, if only to be able to boast about having played a role in his death."

Jakob watched on as the featureless shadows pounced on the dying king like a pack of starving wild dogs. More blades penetrated Alavon's skin than he could count. Several of the figures, including the man who had first stabbed the king, moved out of the scene in a hurry, presumably in pursuit of Havak.

"And that brings us here." The figure to Jakob's left seemed to turn and look down at him. He returned the gaze and noticed the man was now wearing what seemed to be a long robe made from the same Shaz energy the rest of his body was composed of. The man motioned for Jakob to look ahead. When he did, the purple figures had vanished. Jakob refocused his gaze on 'real' variations of Havak and the bald man. Time appeared to have resumed, as the attacker was slowly removing a bloody dagger from his belt.

Jakob took a deep breath. He had seen so many deaths in Izrok at this point that he had thought himself immune to it, but this was different. He felt overcome by a strange combination of anger, frustration, and helplessness.

"Please . . ." She stared up at the man as he lifted his blade into the air with both hands.

"Farewell, Your Highness."

He brought it down forcefully on her neck. The impact made no sound, or, if it did, Jakob didn't hear it. She writhed on the ground for a few seconds before coming to a sudden and unceremonious halt. The man withdrew his blade and leaned in to look at her eyes.

"Now, we repair what you've broken."

He began to rise to his feet when he stopped suddenly.

"What . . .?"

Jakob took a few steps closer to the body and quickly realized what the man was reacting to. Havak's eyes had begun to glow a bright neon purple, providing a sharp contrast to the black and white of the rest of the scene.

After a second or two, her body slowly lifted itself into the air, as though attached to a rope that was pulling her. The glow of her eyes began to spread to the rest of the corpse as she grew brighter and brighter.

"You too?" the bald man said under his breath.

He approached her slowly and with clear trepidation. Jakob turned his head toward the door for a second. The other Alavites had fled. He reached out his hand to her. "Share this power with me."

As the tip of the man's finger was mere inches from her body, her hand reached out and violently grabbed his. He began to scream almost instantly as the fiery Shaz energy burned through his skin.

"If you insist," came the raspy, high-pitched response from the corpse.

Jakob initially wasn't sure what happened next. A large blast of Shaz energy shot both outwards in a massive tidal wave and directly upwards in a familiar spire in less than a second. A violent, booming eruption ripped through his ears, leaving him drowned in blinding light. He wandered for a few minutes without being able to see anything but white in every direction. By the time the features of the library began to take shape around him once more, he realized that there was hardly anything left. Rubble and debris completely enveloped every inch of the once beautiful tiles around him. The walls had caved in, and the large stained-glass window had been shattered into oblivion. Sirens began to blare from seemingly every direction as he approached an exposed opening in the wall. He could see smoke, purple burn marks, and clear signs of massive structural damage for several blocks.

"Havak was the first of your kind to wield the Shaz, but I made a mistake in giving her too much of it too quickly. To avoid a similar catastrophe to this one, I distributed the energy equally among every single living Draekon, as well as every one of them who would ever be born. I believed they would direly need it in the dark days that were soon to follow. This also ensured that future deaths would be followed only by an increasingly harmless visual spectacle instead of a violent and catastrophic explosion."

Jakob turned back to face the purple figure, who was now directly behind him.

"What happens when *I* die?"

The figure shook its head. "The blast you just witnessed was a release of less than a quarter of the total Shaz energy, which is what Havak possessed. You have all of it. Your death will bring about the greatest single destructive force the galaxy has ever seen."

Jakob glanced down at his hands. That was a lot to take in.

"I'm sure you are familiar with what happened next?"

Jakob sighed. "They came at my people with their weapons drawn and forced them to abandon their lives and homes."

The figure nodded. "Correct. The galaxy saw just over a thousand years of peace following the exile. It was not until the Klell people underwent their infamous religious revolution and renamed themselves 'Alavites' that the horrible machine we see today was put into motion. That was the origin of The Hand, his priests, the Fist. . . all of it."

Jakob turned back to the man. "I don't understand. They killed Alavon. Why would they suddenly turn around and worship him?"

"The men who carried out the brutal murder swore an oath of secrecy and took the truth of the situation to their graves. Every Hand, from the very founder of the religion all the way to Olivio, has been raised to believe that Havak was responsible for Alavon's death, which, over the years, has become the single greatest lie ever told."

The man took a few steps toward the edge of the ruined library and looked out over the charred street. Jakob followed behind slowly.

The figure sighed and turned back to him. "I think we've spoken enough with me in this state. It is time for you to know me, Jakob Koss. No more secrecy. I trust you, and more than that, I need you." Jakob's eyes widened a bit as more features began to slowly appear on the man's face, making him more and more recognizable as a distinct individual.

A beard, yellow eyes, and a strong jaw . . . the face was unmistakable. He had seen it too many times on everything from billboards to graffiti drawings.

Jakob began to shake his head slowly. "No. . ."

"Now more than ever, the galaxy needs someone that can bring peace and safety to every person on every planet. I believe that someone is you. I always have." The man reached out toward him. "Will you work with me?"

A flood of thoughts broke through the dam of Jakob's mind. He hesitated for several seconds while keeping his eyes locked on those of his newfound mentor. This didn't make any sense, yet it was the only possible answer.

He took a deep breath before reaching out and grabbing the surprisingly warm hand of Alavon Acivorai.

The TCI Series Continues in

TCI: ABSOLUTION

PREVIEW

ZEKE
TOM'S HIDEOUT, TRAX TOWN
AYR-GROH

Zeke's mind flickered like a broken light bulb, going from consciousness back to the darkness of sleep over and over again. He had spent too long adrift in his own mind, endlessly floating from thought to thought and dream to never-ending dream. Finally, there was a spark of life, a way out. He tried his best to force his eyes open to no avail. Slowly but surely, the beautiful sensation of being alive filled him to his core as a bright light shone through his closed eyelids once more.

    He could feel his breath and the warmth of the water that surrounded his skin on all sides. He was awake, at least somewhat. His hearing returned via a loud and screeching ring before eventually focusing itself in on the only stimulus it could: low, muffled voices, both male. It was impossible to discern what they were saying. The bright light invaded his eyelids again. He needed to know what was happening. He tried to force his eyes open again, and briefly succeeded before water rushed into them and made him force them shut. He exhaled strongly through the respirator attached to his mouth and nose out of frustration.

    "Oh shit." Came the muffled male voice from outside.

    A slow, high pitched beep began to ring directly in Zeke's ears, completely drowning out anything outside his glass tube. Within seconds his head began to feel cold, then his face. His shoulders and chest followed. It took him a while to realize the water was draining, exposing his skin to air for the first time in years. A high-pitched beep sounded repeatedly, echoing painfully inside the tank.

"Stop it! Reverse this shit!" yelled the same voice from earlier.

"I'm trying!" came the equally desperate response of a second male voice.

Zeke knew this could only mean one thing.

He forced his eyes as wide open as he could possibly muster. They ached horridly, having been used to the dark for so long. He didn't care. Burning tears dropped down his face as he forced his scalding pupils to focus in on the large, splotchy blobs in front of him. The room was dark, but the figures seemed to be aiming a flashlight of some sort directly in his face. With the water now almost entirely out of the tank and the beeping coming to a halt, he could now hear the outside world perfectly.

"EXTRACTION PHASE ONE COMPLETED." Declared the female robotic voice in his ears.

"You said he left! What the fuck?" The man on the left sounded panicked and began to back up slowly.

"He… he did. It's not possible. He can't be here. He left with the High Skylord over a week ago!"

"Okay, then who the fuck is this, then?"

Zeke turned his rapidly focusing gaze towards the second man.

"Oh fuck, he's awake."

They began to approach the tank slowly.

"You think it's his long-lost twin?"

"Not exactly long lost if he's been kept in a tube."

Zeke found that to be an astute observation.

"Why would Ezekiel do that?"

"Who cares. No way the guy is as successful as he is without being into some weird shit. Did you grab the money?"

Zeke turned his gaze to the shorter and pudgier of the two.

"Uh... Yeah. He took most of it, but I grabbed some loose bills. At least we'll get out of here with something." The second man responded.

They drew even closer now. Were it not for the glass, Zeke would have been able to smell their breath.

"This is fucking weird, dude. We should get the hell out of here before the cops show up."

"I'm not exactly terrified of them without Sprock around to-"

Crash.

Zeke's arm shot through the glass and grabbed at the man's neck. He could feel the wonderfully orgasmic sensation of pain as the shards scraped against his skin. Before either of the men could react, Zeke pulled his first victim's head towards him forcefully, smashing even more of the tank's glass and leaving his face practically sliced open.

Both men screamed. The second one backed up and tripped over his own two feet. Zeke punched again at the now extremely unstable glass with his free left hand, causing it to shatter entirely.

He was free again. Oh, and how good it was. He used his left hand to remove the respirator from his face and toss it behind him.

"Hey man, just take it easy. . ." The fear in the second man's voice was palpable as he slowly retreated.

Zeke smiled, exposing his array of jagged and sharp teeth. In a single motion he turned the head of the barely conscious man to his side and chomped down with all his might at the victim's neck. He pulled back forcefully, ripping out a series of tendons and arteries with ease.

The second man shrieked and fell to the floor after tripping over himself.

Zeke chuckled before biting down again, sending blood spraying across his entire face. He released the limp body, wiped his mouth with the back of his hand, and walked towards the second man who now scrambled to the opposite end of the room and was desperately waiting for the ladder to lower.

Zeke grabbed a small, black battle hammer off the nearby workstation and pressed the button on its handle, causing the weapon to extend to its full length. He walked slowly and confidently toward his next victim. It was unfortunate there was no wind down here. He loved feeling the pain of his naked body freezing.

The panicked man turned around to face him and thrust a knife into Zeke's chest before he had any time to react. Zeke stared down at it and then back at the man's eyes. He broke into a laughing fit as he withdrew the blade and tossed it aside. Not so much as a drip of blood spilled from the wound.

The man stared at him wide eyed and fell to his knees.

"Look, just please-"

"You've got too many teeth."

Thump.

The hammer swung with such force that the man fell unconscious almost upon impact and splayed out on ground right in the path of the lowering ladder. Loud cracking began to echo through the room as it attempted to force its way through the unexpected obstacle that was the limp body on the floor. It took around five or so minutes for it to finally power down and give up, but not before nearly going straight through the back of his head and torso.

He sighed and looked around the room. Tommy was not going to be happy about all this mess. He shrugged and moved over to the wardrobe. It was probably best to not go around naked. People would think he was a lunatic or something. He moved quickly over to the sink and washed himself off before staring into his reflection in the mirror and smiling at it with a mouth full of jagged canine teeth.

He wiped off the hammer and pressed the button on its handle again, causing it to contract back down into a much more manageable size. As he placed the weapon in its sheath, Zeke realized had no idea what day or even year it was. How long had he been in that tube? He turned to look at it and the body lying in the ocean of blood nearby. He supposed it didn't matter. It seemed Tommy wasn't going to be coming to play any time soon, not if he was on Erub.

He walked over to the ladder, stepping over the mangled corpse in the process, and made his way out of his prison. As he stepped into the Ayr-Groh sun for the first time again his lips widened into a huge smile. Two police flyers had landed just outside the alleyway and seemed to have sent two officers down into it.

"Excuse me! Stay right where you are sir!" yelled one.

He kept moving. The office reached for his blade.

"Sir I said... Wait. Ezekiel?"

The second officer had now caught up with the first.

Zeke smiled widely and began to cackle as he reached for the hammer at his hip. The faces on both cops suddenly became extremely serious, as though they had just witnessed their wife drown their newborn in a sink.

The one on the left spoke to the other in a voice that was barely audible and reeked of poorly disguised fear.

"Call for fucking backup.

Made in the USA
Middletown, DE
10 August 2019